HONOUR ABOVE ALL

HONOUR ABOVE ALL

Yvette Ward MacDonald

OC Publishing

Honour Above All
Copyright © 2024 Yvette Ward MacDonald

All rights reserved under international copyright conventions. No part of this publication may be reproduced, stored in or introduced into a retrieval system, or transmitted in any form, or by any means, without the prior written permission of the author.

First published in 2024 by

Halifax, NS, Canada
www.ocpublishing.ca

Cover and interior book design by David W. Edelstein.
Cover background photo by Alexander Jawfox on Unsplash;
Lady Justice photo by simpson33 on iStock.

ISBN 978-1-989833-43-8 (Paperback edition)
ISBN 978-1-989833-44-5 (eBook edition)

*To Kevin, my husband and lifelong companion,
whose love has been my greatest inspiration.*

True honour is not in the absence of wrongdoing but in the unwavering commitment to uphold one's integrity, maintain one's dignity, and earn the trust that is placed in us.

As Mary Clark drove along the deserted path leading to the grand home of Robert Kerr on the outskirts of Ottawa, she was imbued with nostalgia, having travelled up this beautiful lane numerous times in her youth. The estate was a prominent landmark at the threshold of the city. Safely nestled among tall, mature trees on top of a hill, Mr. Kerr's house overlooked the Ottawa River, which flowed serenely under the clear evening sky.

She stopped in front of the house and stepped out. The grounds had changed. She was disheartened to see that the flowerbeds, once manicured and neatly maintained, were now overgrown with weeds. She shifted her gaze to the lone structure. The house had fortunately remained frozen in time, a massive three-storey brick building well placed on ten acres of land. The most beautiful home in the area, it projected an air of limitless wealth and power while exuding a warm, relaxed ambiance. Mary's mind swam with memories as she admired the house. Her fondest were from when she spent her weekends away from school here with her friend, Courtney Kerr.

Her first visit had been exactly one month after September 8, 1954. Like most Canadians of that era, Mary would always remember that date. It was the day sixteen-year-old Marilyn Bell became the first person to swim across Lake Ontario, inspiring the young students at Elmwood, the private girls' school Mary attended. For weeks the girls—fifteen-year-old Mary among them—spoke of nothing else, marvelling at how one could swim such a distance.

Elmwood School was located in the stately residential neighbourhood of Rockcliffe Park—an independent village within the greater Ottawa area—and was well-known in the province for its high-quality education. It catered to the elite young women of Ottawa and area, as well as from countries around the world. Mary, who came from a modest background in Bathurst, New Brunswick, had been able to attend only because her maternal uncle had taken her under his wing and had offered her the opportunity. She owed much to his generosity.

It was at Elmwood that she met Courtney. Still vivid in her mind was the day she and her uncle stepped out of the airport taxi in front of the imposing façade of the school. The campus was a maze of crisp uniforms and unfamiliar faces, evoking a mix of excitement and anxiety. Though her uncle's commitment to her education was evident, the demands of his job as a probation officer could not be ignored. "Mary, I wish I could stay with you longer, help you settle in, but duty calls. You're going to do great here, and I'll visit whenever I can."

She assured him that she was perfectly fine with that, yet she felt a moment of hesitation at the door of her assigned room. A tap on her shoulder brought her attention to a pretty, confident-looking girl with long blond hair. "Hi there! You must be Mary," the stranger greeted with a welcoming smile. "I'm Courtney, and we're going to be roommates. Care to join me? I'll show you around."

Together they navigated the halls as Courtney, who had been a student at Elmwood the previous year, shared anecdotes about their classmates and the school's hidden gems, and Mary found herself laughing, the initial nervousness dissipating. From that moment, Elmwood appeared less formidable, and Mary's anxiety was replaced by a sense of reassurance.

Though Courtney was charming and engaging, Mary soon recognized that her roommate was self-centred. Yet her self-focus did not diminish her appealing and pleasant demeanour, making her enjoyable company. Craving friendship, Mary came to rely on Courtney, and in the days that followed, a meaningful connection developed between them, leading to a genuine friendship. Courtney invited Mary to the Kerrs' home for the Thanksgiving weekend of that year.

That visit, too, was indelibly etched in her mind—the sleek limousine pulling up in front of the school as Mary stood at the entrance, holding her suitcase; the chauffeur opening the back door; Courtney running boisterously toward her brother, Richard, who was waving to her through the glass; and the comfortable opulence of the positively joyful drive to the Kerrs' residence.

In the years that followed, there were countless invitations to Courtney's home. Unfailingly, Mr. Kerr and his wife, Eugenie, went out of their way to ensure Mary felt welcome. They greeted her with genuine warmth and friendliness whenever she visited. Mr. Kerr made conscious efforts to include her in conversations, asking about her interests, involving her in discussions, and inviting her to join various family activities. Through these consistent gestures, a strong sense of belonging was cultivated in Mary.

In those years this residence was full of activity, punctuated by great food and celebration. But tonight, twelve years after that first visit, Mary was here on a sombre mission. In her position as a junior lawyer with Woodbury & McLeod, the law firm that handled Mr. Kerr's affairs, she had been tasked with initiating the proceedings for the sale of the Kerr residence, a responsibility that came on the heels of her ongoing efforts to sell Mr. Kerr's import-export business.

I have a bad cancer, and my doctors tell me it's terminal. My primary objective now is to straighten out my financial affairs and see to it that my will is in order. Since Richard is not interested in pursuing a career in the company, it will have to be sold, and I want to make sure that it's carried out properly. As you know, my company name is well recognized, and I have a large, well-established clientele. In my papers is a list of potential buyers for you to pursue. Mr. Kerr had casually surrendered this to Mary during her initial hospital visit two weeks ago, treating it like any routine business deal.

Five months earlier, Robert Kerr was diagnosed with lung cancer; he was told he had less than one year to live. He sought help from top oncologists in Europe, then, having exhausted every treatment available, he had returned home and was now undergoing extensive chemo and radiation therapy at the Ottawa Civic Hospital. The cancer was in its final stage. Wanting to use these last moments to set things right, as he put it, Mr. Kerr had contacted the senior partner of Woodbury & McLeod to request a meeting with Mary to outline certain requirements. Although he was a long-standing client of Mr. McLeod, he had specifically requested Mary because she was a friend of the family.

Over the years, Mary had come to know Robert Kerr well. He had struggled from poverty to a lucrative business career, and she greatly admired him. So much so that when she decided to study law, she had sought his advice, and he had become her mentor. Her parents died in a car accident during her second year of law school, and in the aftermath, her relationship with Mr. Kerr took on an even greater role in her life. Following her graduation from law school, magna cum laude, it was he who had recommended her to the firm of Woodbury & McLeod.

She was also impressed by the fact that Mr. Kerr had served in the military and was a decorated war hero. Mary remembered him leading the parade on Remembrance Day, tall and proud in his army uniform decorated with medals. She had always known that November 11 represented more to him than just a time to recall the combats of war and the comrades lost in battle. In 1937 he had married his childhood sweetheart, Sandra Blake, who twelve months later bore him twins, Courtney and Richard. Upon Major Kerr's return from the battlefield, however, it had been his in-laws who greeted him at the train station. His wife, their only daughter, had succumbed to tuberculosis.

Mary had never met Sandra. She had only known Eugenie, Robert's second wife. She recalled the first time she met her.

OCTOBER 1954

Mary was awed by the idea of spending a weekend with Courtney's family. She had suspected that her new friend came from an affluent background, but nothing had prepared her for the magnitude and sheer beauty of the Kerrs' place, the house like no other she had ever seen.

Courtney had informed her that Eugenie was not her real mother. Apparently, she had immigrated to Canada from France and had married their father shortly after his return home from the war. From the way Courtney spoke about her stepmother, it was abundantly clear that she and her brother cared little for their father's wife. That was confirmed when Eugenie stepped outside to greet them upon their arrival.

"*Bonjour, les enfants. Bienvenue à la maison,*" she said, smiling, and then offered to assist them with their luggage. She was somewhat younger than Mary had envisaged and had a kind face and gentle demeanour.

"We can manage," Courtney replied, not even bothering to look up at her. Richard ignored her.

A flicker of embarrassment shot across Eugenie's countenance.

Discomfited, Mary introduced herself and said, "It's extremely generous of you to have me in your home."

"*Avec plaisir,*" Eugenie replied, still smiling. "*Je vous souhaite un joyeux séjour.*"

Mary, who, like Courtney and Richard, understood French, was touched by Eugenie's gracious words of welcome. She subsequently saw little of Mr. Kerr's young wife during that visit, except when Eugenie joined them to share the simple but excellent meals she had prepared for the family. The rest of the time she kept busy inside the house, the radio softly playing classical music in the background.

Mr. Kerr, who had been absent the entire weekend, joined them to share their last meal at the house. He was civil to Eugenie, but it was evident to Mary that husband and wife had little in common and that Eugenie was a foreigner in her own home. She continued to smile yet seldom spoke.

In subsequent visits, Mary felt sorry for Eugenie. She wished for her a more suitable partner in marriage and could never witness Courtney and Richard's mistreatment of her without feeling helpless and ashamed. When she could stand it no longer, she expressed her concern to her friend, conveying both her feelings and the pain Eugenie must be enduring due to their actions.

Unfazed, Courtney continued, along with her brother, to harass Eugenie, falsely attributing every conceivable character flaw to her. They subjected her to discourtesies, meanness, and small yet palpable forms of disrespect—anything to make her presence wholly unwelcome—all of which were gradually eroding Mary's friendship with Courtney.

If their ill treatment affected her, Eugenie showed no sign of it. On countless occasions, Mary watched her return sympathy for offence and esteem for contempt. Mary came to acknowledge there was nothing Eugenie could do to alter Courtney and Richard's opinion of her. Their repudiation of her kindness was seated in their own prejudices and small-mindedness.

On one of their visits, Courtney grumbled, "I wish she would wear something decent instead of those thrift-shop finds of hers. For the life of me, I can't imagine what she does with the allowance my father gives her."

Mary did not share her friend's low opinion. Eugenie intrigued her. Her style of dress did not express position or status but a whole, undiminished, and comfortable person. She wore no makeup, embracing her natural beauty. Her hairdo was perhaps not the latest trend, but it possessed a unique charm that hinted at a more individualized style. Her beautiful blue eyes, too, had a delicate, moving quality. Tall and slim, her proud carriage asserted her beauty in a quiet, subtle way. To Mary's eyes, Eugenie's natural sense of style and elegance held a certain charm, which she doubted Courtney could ever hope to attain.

As Mary prepared to enter the house, a tingle of uneasiness went through her. Needing to steel herself for the task ahead, she thought back to her conversation with Mr. Kerr at the hospital. She could still hear his words. *I've spoken to the children over the telephone, and neither of them wants the house. They've already taken out what they intend to keep, so I want you to sell it with whatever contents remain. I've instructed Richard to assist you with the sale. If you have any problems, bring them up with him.*

Mary had spent three hours with Mr. Kerr at the hospital that afternoon, attentively addressing each business item on his list while he methodically checked them off, one by one. He had been uncharacteristically sombre, and just as she was leaving, he said, "Since my diagnosis I've had plenty of time to reflect on my life and have come to the sorrowful realization that I haven't been much of a father to my children—or husband to Eugenie, for that matter. If I had my life to live over again, things would be different."

That was all he said, but his revelation had shocked and saddened her. She wanted to say something consoling, but words escaped her. She had mumbled something about having to visit the house after their meeting and that she would be back to visit him the next day. She left the hospital feeling disappointed with herself and had driven directly to his residence.

As she unlocked the door, a sound coming from the nearby trees startled her—only the wind. Relieved, she made her way inside.

Her heart skipped a beat. The house had been stripped of all its valuable furnishings, yet the interior retained some of the magic she remembered from her youth. Like the exterior, it exuded quality and prestige.

Again, Mary felt slightly uneasy. She had been here before but as a guest. Tonight, gearing herself to inspect the house before it went on the market, she felt like an intruder. But she reminded herself of the purpose of her visit and dismissed the thought. Mr. Kerr had given her a job to do, and she would do it with the professionalism and efficiency that was expected of her.

She walked with purpose across the tiled floor of the atrium, the sharp sound of her footsteps echoing through the vacant room. She proceeded to the living room, then the dining room, library, and kitchen that occupied the main floor. A wide, beautiful glass staircase led from the expansive kitchen down to the family room, media room, and service rooms on the lower level. It took her two hours to tour the house, even with the elevator. After she finished inspecting the six large bedrooms with adjoining baths on the second floor, Mary came to a short passageway with a door at the end. It presented a flight of stairs that led up to another closed door. *Undoubtedly the attic*, she thought.

She was tired and was tempted to disregard it. Surely, like

the rest of the house, everything of note had been removed. Nevertheless, she decided to do a quick check, just in case. She turned on the light and mounted the stairs. She hurried through the door and was met by a puff of stale air, the smell of a room too long shut away from the remainder of the building. A perfunctory survey disclosed an empty space. *As I thought.*

Mary turned to leave but from the corner of her eye caught sight of an object pushed against the wall at the far end of the room. Curious, she walked over to inspect it. It was a trunk with Eugenie's name written on the lid. Eugenie had passed away several years earlier, following a car accident. Obviously, her stepchildren had not considered her trunk valuable enough to take with them and had left it behind for some stranger to dispose of. For some reason, this made Mary want to cry.

Quelling her emotions, Mary opened the lid. At first sight, there was nothing of significance inside: an old violin, a delicate looking music box, and books by various authors. Upon probing more thoroughly, deep in the chest Mary discovered a package of letters tied together with a pink ribbon. She wasn't sure what to do with them. They were in all probability of a personal nature.

As a lawyer, Mary was routinely required to read private documents. In this case, however, she debated whether it was necessary to encroach on Eugenie's privacy. Yet there was something compelling about the letters, and she eventually gave in to her curiosity. The top letter in the bundle dated back to 1945. It was a brief message from Eugenie to her sisters in France, written in French.

My dear sisters,

Since I have not heard from you for several years, my most earnest desire is that this letter will find you safe and in good health. I am mailing it to our old address in the country, because all my other letters to you in Rennes have gone unanswered. I fervently hope somebody there will have some knowledge of your whereabouts.

I hear that these are harsh times in France, and I fear for your well-being. Please find enclosed a money order for you. I beg that you not find this too impersonal. I wish to help, and since it is not possible for me to assist you directly, I am doing so the only way I know how.

As for myself, I have wonderful news for you. I have recently married. His name is Robert Kerr. I met him in Montreal. I have only known him for a short while but am supremely happy.

He has twins, a boy and a girl from a previous marriage. They are somewhat unruly right now, but they lost their mother early in their childhood and have had no serious supervision since then. I do care for them and will endeavour to gain their affection. I can never replace their real mother, but since I too lost mine at an early age, I feel their pain.

Please write to me, for I miss you all and long for your news and assurance that you are all well.

Love,

Eugenie

P.S. Is our dear friend Mr. Obolensky still alive? If so, please extend my deepest affection to him.

Her sister Danielle had used the back of this letter to write her response:

Dearest Eugenie,

Oh, what joy to hear from you! It has been at least five years since your last letter, and we feared some dreadful misfortune had befallen you.

I apologize for the writing paper. We have survived the war, but times remain harsh, and even this little luxury is unaffordable. As the Germans retreated, they destroyed what they could and pillaged the food and livestock in the surrounding farms, leaving everyone destitute. We have had to sell most of our belongings to buy the little food that is available. We moved away from Rennes during the occupation, but our plans are to return to our old address next week. Françoise and Pauline are optimistic that things will be better for us there, but I remain skeptical, for the entire country is suffering.

We received your money order and thank you sincerely. It will be most helpful on our journey back to Rennes. The whole family is here and imploring me to express their love. Mr. Obolensky, too, is with us. Before leaving Rennes, we invited him to share our home because his injured arm had rendered him incapable of managing on his own. He has been with us ever since. He is delighted to hear you are well and asks that we convey to you his love and best wishes.

Regrettably, not all is well. Françoise's husband has been listed as missing. His division was forced to surrender at Saint-Valery-en-Caux at the beginning of the war. We learned later from a soldier who managed to escape that Jacques was sent to a camp in Germany as a prisoner of war. He has not been heard from since. Outrageous stories are reaching us about those camps, and whatever hope we had of seeing Jacques alive has been dashed.

Do you recall Claude Garneau, who lived in Chatres-de-Bretagne? He and Pauline were married since you and I were last in touch. He too disappeared during the occupation but was released from a German prison after the war ended. Claude had been working for the resistance and was taken prisoner by the Gestapo. While everybody assumed he had been executed, Pauline refused to believe he was dead. He did survive, but only just. He was so brutally tortured that we consider it a miracle he is still alive. The greater tragedy is that he will never be able to walk again.

Forgive me, Eugenie, for bringing all this grief to you, but war has bred such devastation in our lives that we sometimes wonder what there is left for us. We are thankful you are safe and well in Canada.

We were thrilled to hear about your marriage. We all know what a caring and nurturing person you are and are confident that yours will be a happy home.

Once again, thank you for your letter and the money order. Know that our lives have been made less tragic because of you.

Your loving sister,
Danielle

Mary sifted through more letters, all of them thanking Eugenie for her continual financial support. One post-marked from Rennes, France, and written December 15, 1947—two and a half years after the war ended—read:

Dearest Eugenie,

We received your letter a couple of weeks ago. Thank you for writing and thank you for the money. No words can serve to describe how grateful we are for everything you have done. We are so fortunate to have someone like you to help us. Our neighbours are all suffering, especially those who have no one to turn to. As much as we can, we try to come to their aid, as you have for us, but it is a never-ending battle merely to survive.

I have tragic news for you. Mr. Obolensky passed away last week. We had grown to love him dearly and will miss him but are happy that he is now reunited with his family. He reminisced about them near the end. This surprised us, for as you know he never mentioned his past. Yet we all knew how deeply grieved he was about his family. It turns out that his wife and two daughters were killed in the Russian Revolution.

Do you remember that beautiful music box of his that you so admired when you were a little girl? Well, it belonged to his wife, which explains why he clung to it so avidly. He spoke warmly of you before passing away, about your devotion to family and friends, and asked that we send you the music box with the instructions that you not hesitate to sell it, should you ever be short of money. He, himself, had refused to part with it because it

*was his lone link to his family. After his death, it would
no longer matter.*

*We, too, want to give you a special gift for Christmas
and thought you might like to have Papa's violin. It is the
one thing of value in the house, but never once were we
tempted to sell it, even when times became gruelling. As
you know, it has been in the family for four generations,
and we can't think of anyone who is more deserving of it
than you. Please be assured it comes to you with all our
love and appreciation.*

*By this time, you have most likely received Pauline's
letter and the photograph she enclosed. She found it
recently while going through the family album. It was
taken the day you departed for Canada. Since it's the
only picture of all of us together, she felt you should
have it.*

*Wishing you and your family the quiet beauty of a
peaceful and joyous holiday season.*

Your loving sister,
Danielle

Mary found the photograph in another envelope. The
four sisters were posed together on some foreign pier. In
the background was a ship. She immediately recognized
Eugenie, a beautiful young woman peering shyly from under
her wide-brimmed hat. The sisters had their arms around
each other's waist, showcasing the closeness of their loving
family. As Mary studied the image, she noted the striking
resemblance between Eugenie and one of her sisters.

Studying the photograph, Mary felt disheartened. At one

time Mr. Kerr had been the object of her admiration and Eugenie just marginally valued. How could she have been so naïve? Had she undervalued Eugenie because her life was devoid of power and acclaim? She had had no medals to display and had never been invited to lead parades or preside over high-ranking events like her husband. Yet here was a woman who had not only been able to endure the hardship of living in a new country with a different language and culture and much adversity but had flourished in it.

Mary remembered how incredibly kind Eugenie had been, in spite of the callous treatment she received from her stepchildren. Ignoring their insults about her French accent, dingy clothes, and lesser social status, she had focused on the more important things and had lived with dignity. She had spent most of her spare time doing volunteer work in the local hospital's "opportunity shop," where Mary herself shopped now and then. Even there, as Eugenie sorted clothing in the store's back room, Mr. Kerr's young wife had given everyone who came in contact with her a special gift—that of unconditional respect.

Mary carefully returned the old violin, the music box, the letters, and the books from where she had taken them, all the while reflecting on her years of friendship with Courtney and her friend's miserable treatment of her stepmother. Eugenie had deserved better. With a pang of guilt, Mary wondered how she might have been more supportive of her.

As Mary drove home that evening, she thought about how life had been most cruel to Eugenie, a tender, solitary soul with a heart-softening smile. On top of her stepchildren's rejection and her husband's indifference, Eugenie had been involved in a car accident, resulting in a severe concussion and two broken hips. After an extended stay in the Ottawa Hospital, she had been moved to a long-term care facility fifty miles west of the city. From then on, Mary had heard very little about her. She and Courtney had gone their separate ways after graduating from Elmwood—Mary staying in Ottawa, and Courtney moving to Toronto. Richard, too, had moved to Toronto. From Mary's minimal contact with Mr. Kerr in the past few years, she gathered that Courtney and Richard had each returned to live in Ottawa but had completely excluded Eugenie from their lives.

As much as she admired Mr. Kerr, his neglect of Eugenie had often left Mary disappointed, and she wondered what role it might have played in his children's behaviour toward his second wife. Like all children, Courtney and Richard learned from what they observed. And any guest in their home would have seen that Mr. Kerr had little time for the person rearing his children. It had been a marriage of convenience—more his than hers.

Seeing the house again, even without furniture, had brought back with astonishing clarity Mary's memory of that beautiful day when she had rented a car to visit Eugenie. It was one of her last memories of her.

AUGUST 1959

On a short break before resuming her law studies at Ottawa University, Mary had undertaken the long drive into the country to the nursing home. The midday sun streamed through the car window, and she closed her eyes for a brief moment and felt its warmth envelop her. A moment of pleasure in just being alive.

When she finally found the home, Mary was appalled. Considering Mr. Kerr's great wealth, she had envisaged a charming manor or villa secluded in the country at the end of a long driveway. In marked contrast, she found an old, red brick, two-storey structure that resembled a factory more than a nursing home. *This can't be it.* Then she noted the sign above the front door: Pleasant View Nursing Home. A rather ironic name, for the view was anything but pleasant. Mary found it hard to believe this institution had actually passed the provincial inspection code. She willed herself to the front entrance. The door was locked, but below the doorbell was a printed memo directing her to ring for admittance.

A receptionist ushered her to Eugenie's room, which was situated on the main floor in the rear of the building.

Mary hesitantly pushed open the door and was met by a repugnant scent of cleaning fluid and disinfectant soap. Stretched on the bed, asleep, was a broken person, no longer the tall, elegant woman who had walked with confidence. Mary's first instinct was to leave. She might have had Eugenie not awakened and smiled warmly at her.

"*Ah, Marie! Bonjour!*" Eugenie had always called her by the French version of her name.

"*Bonjour, Madame Kerr,*" Mary answered. She approached the bed and kissed her on both cheeks. Straightening, Mary glanced about the sparsely decorated room. Except for a night table with a few personal items, a wheelchair, and a vinyl-covered visitor's chair beside the orthopedic bed, it was void of any indulgence. The only other thing she noted was another door almost immediately beside the one she had opened, which she surmised must lead to the bathroom. The room was filled with a loneliness so palpable that Mary could think of nothing else to say. She pulled the chair up beside the bed and sat down.

Eugenie's soft blue eyes lit up. "*C'est gentille* of you to come and visit! Tell me, how did you find me?"

"Mr. Kerr told me where you were."

"*Oui*, of course. *Mon époux* did mention you might come to visit." Her eyes softened even more. "Have you seen Courtney and Richard *récemment?*" she asked. "How are they? Are they well?"

Mary felt a rush of affection for her. Here was a woman

who had passively suffered through years of Courtney and Richard's indifference and ridicule, and still she maintained a keen interest in their lives. "I've had little opportunity to see them lately," Mary replied. "But as far as I know, they're fine."

"I haven't seen them *depuis mon accident*," Eugenie announced forlornly. "*Mon époux m'a confié*—confided— that their *maman's* death at the Royal Ottawa Sanitarium has made them extremely vulnerable, creating in them an *aversion* to hospices of any kind."

Mary considered telling Eugenie that she just needed to give her stepchildren time, that once they surmounted their fear, they would eventually come to see her. But she knew Eugenie would see through the lie.

Eluding Eugenie's gaze, Mary once more scanned the desolate room. Sadness threatened to overwhelm her.

Eugenie must have sensed it. "I was never one to mind about where I lived. It is sometimes more *désirable* to be by yourself in a small empty room than to feel *seul*—alone—in a huge crowded one."

Mary could empathize. As a child, she had never been free of the profound emptiness weighing against her. Even now, a deep melancholy lay beneath her tranquil exterior. And at night, the terrifying dreams.

Eugenie continued. "It's *ironique* how fate plays an infinite part in one's life. I learned about this nursing home from *une amie*. She was a resident here and *une compatriote française* from France. After my accident, I chose this place for the garden and *le personnel*. They are most caring."

"Garden?" Mary repeated.

Sitting up in her bed—positioned to give her a view of the window—Eugenie pointed toward the outside.

Through the window Mary saw a courtyard dominated by a garden with a vibrant assortment of vegetables, herbs, and flowers. Geraniums and sunflowers were glorious in the afternoon sunlight. Vines of purple clematis clung to the wing of the building that ran perpendicular to where they were sitting, and rose bushes bloomed everywhere. And past the garden was a receding forest. There was a dreamlike quality to the scene. "How beautiful!" she exclaimed.

Eugenie beamed. "As I mentioned, *les membres du personnel* are most caring. They wheel me out into the garden, every day—well, whenever the weather permits. It's a community garden, and all of us get to work in it. Working with our hands, creating something beautiful, and feeling *la joie* of growing plants, all these things are intensely rewarding." She pointed to the left corner of the garden where raised beds, surrounded by a meandering path, created an eye-catching landscape design. "That *section là-bas* is mine. I call it my Acadian Garden."

Mary gave her a questioning look.

"Before moving to Canada, I lived in Brittany. Did you know that most of the Acadians in your country came from that area?"

"No, I didn't."

"Like me, they sailed from Saint-Malo."

"What brought you to Canada?" Mary asked.

"I had always wanted to visit this country, the birthplace of *mes ancêtres*. I never told anyone, but *mes ancêtres* were from Canada, Acadians who lived here a long time ago—going as far back as eleven *générations*."

"How interesting! I had no idea."

"*C'est vrai.* At the beginning of *le Grand dérangement* in the seventeen hundreds, *mes ancêtres*, on my father's side, lived in Port-Royal, now called Annapolis Royal, in Nova Scotia." Eugenie took a deep breath and released it slowly. "When they learned the English were deporting Acadians, they fled to Île Saint-Jean, now called Prince Edward Island. Soon after, the English caught up with them, and *mes ancêtres* once more fled—this time to Nouveau Brunswick. They ended up in a place they named Sainte-Anne-du-Bocage, not far from where you grew up. Didn't you say you were from Bathurst?"

"Yes," Mary replied. "What an excellent memory you have. But I'm curious. If your ancestors are from Canada, how did you come to live in France?"

"The English pursued *mes ancêtres* to their new *location* in Nouveau Brunswick and deported them to France." Eugenie's voice weakened. "It was *un passage tragique*. The husband lost his wife at sea, along with two of his children, aged nine and thirteen. His oldest daughter, Françoise, and her family also died during the deportation."

"What happened to them?"

"*Leur navire, Violet,* sank in the mid-Atlantic."

"Were they not on the same ship?"

"*Non.* Families were often *séparées*—sisters, brothers, even spouses."

Mary repressed a shudder. "And those people deported to France," she pressed, "what became of them?"

"*Malheureusement*, misfortune met them there, too. They had lived *trois générations* in what was then Acadie, so they had little in common with the old country and were never really accepted. All they could think about was returning to their place of birth. *Mes ancêtres* couldn't afford the voyage, yet they never ceased to hope that one day they would be able to return to their Acadie."

Eugenie glanced down and adjusted the blanket around her legs. When she looked up again, her soft blue eyes locked with Mary's. "With time, *mes ancêtres* came to recognize France as their country, but they never lost sight of their history. At night we would assemble around the stove, as *mes ancêtres* had done, and my *papa* would recount the old stories about Acadie, exactly as they had been passed on to him—the Mi'kmaw people helping them, the dykes, the farms. All this was so much part of my *éducation* that I needed to come and see this beloved country they had yearned to come back to for two centuries. I landed in Montreal and my intention was to eventually make my way to Nouveau Brunswick. I wanted to visit Sainte-Anne-du-Bocage, but I didn't have funds *suffisants* to finish my journey. It was the Depression and times were *impitoyables*. Fortunately, a rich family hired me as a maid. Shortly after, the war broke out, so I remained in Montreal. That is where I met Robert. He was a friend of the people I worked for and came for a visit at the *termination* of the war. For me, it was, um, how do you say in English, *un coup-de-foudre*?"

"Love at first sight?"

"*Oui*," Eugenie replied, nodding. "He looked *formidable* in his uniform...*et un héro, en outre*. But what impressed me *le plus* about him was the love he held for his children." Again, Eugenie paused for a moment, as though savouring the memory. "I must admit to a certain amount of *anxiété* when he asked me out. I couldn't imagine what he saw in me. He was fifteen years older than me and much more experienced. And we were *pratiquement* strangers. But I concluded that anyone who loved his children as much as he did had to be *un homme admirable*. He spoke about them a great deal. So, three weeks later, we were married, and I moved to Ottawa." Eugenie straightened out and smiled. "I seem to be pouring out *mon histoire de vie entière*—my whole life history."

Mary returned her smile. "Do you miss your home in France?"

Eugenie did not answer immediately. "*Non*," she answered, eventually. "*Mon papa*, like his *papa et les ancêtres* before him, had sought to return to Canada, to visit Acadie, so I felt I belonged here. That's why, after his death, I decided to take the trip he was never able to make. I needed to see for myself the land of Évangeline."

Mary was familiar with Henry Wadsworth Longfellow's poem, *Evangeline*. In it she had read how the Acadians were forcibly removed from their colonies, their homes burnt, and their land confiscated. In the poem, the Acadian heroine, Evangeline, separated from her betrothed, Gabriel, during the expulsion, spends her entire life seeking him only to find him as he lies dying as an old man.

As Mary reflected on the story, she thought it ironic that some two hundred years later Eugenie was faring no better than her ancestors, or perhaps only fractionally better. True, she had not been deported, but neither had she been fully accepted. Pondering the injustice of fate, Mary observed Eugenie, who merely smiled at her. Mary looked away, feeling embarrassingly inadequate. Her eyes were drawn to the garden outside. Perhaps because of the warmth and glow it brought into the room, the inside no longer appeared so clinical. Engrossed in this new revelation, she started at the sound of Eugenie's voice.

"There's a song my sisters and I use to sing, when we were young."

Mary turned to see Eugenie smiling mournfully at her. "It's called 'Évangeline.' It was our favourite song, and *maman et papa* would sing along with us. He had *un voix terrible*, but he would cry out the song with all his heart as he played his violin, his voice *resonant* above everyone in the room."

Mary had heard the beautiful, soul-wrenching folk song multiple times during her youth. The song, like the character Evangeline, encapsulates the history of the Acadians and had become a touchstone for Acadians everywhere, bringing them together. Although she was not Acadian, listening to its lyrics often brought tears to her eyes.

Mary stayed with Eugenie that afternoon much longer than she had intended. She even had tea with her in the main lounge and discovered that the atmosphere at Pleasant View Nursing Home was indeed amiable and comfortable. It amazed Mary the number of friends Eugenie had among the other residents, despite being decades younger than the majority of them. All were delighted that someone had come to visit her.

When the time came for Mary to leave, it was with a heavy heart and remorse that she had not been more supportive of Eugenie in the past. But the most disturbing sensation of all was the foreboding that she would never see her again.

And so it was. Four months later, on December 9, 1959, alone in her room and at the youthful age of thirty-eight, Eugenie passed away from complications stemming from her car accident injuries.

After spending most of the morning at the Canada Lands Survey Records Office on Catherine Street, Mary stepped out of the building into the brilliant sun almost directly overhead. She was meeting her friend Rachel Vogue for lunch as she did the first Monday of every month. Her watch indicated she had a little more than an hour to spare. If she hurried, she might have just enough time to drop off her papers at the office on Somerset and make it to Chez François, located across the river in Vanier.

As she entered Woodbury & McLeod, Caroline, the front desk receptionist, greeted her. "Coyle was just asking for you."

Coyle was the managing partner of Woodbury & McLeod, and all the employees referred to him by his last name. Though his position required him to deal with all the lawyers and staff in the firm, Mary could not imagine why he would ask to see her.

"Is he in?" As soon as she uttered the words, Mary remembered that Coyle seldom left his desk for lunch. A ferocious worker, he frequently worked through the hours not knowing what time of day it was—especially on days when he was not needed in the courtroom.

Caroline bowed her head with a knowing smile. "I'm sure he is."

Without saying anything further, Mary pivoted and walked toward Coyle's office, checking her appearance in the glass walls that lined the hall. She was wearing a suit that outlined her slight frame and was in keeping with her elegant look. With her honey-brown eyes and long, light-brown hair drawn back in a sophisticated roll, she appeared stylish and professional. One could hardly describe Mary as fashion conscious, but she always strived to look her best. As she approached Coyle's office, she saw him standing beside his secretary's desk, positioned outside his door. He and Kate Donovan were quietly discussing a file he was holding in his hand.

Everybody in the firm knew Coyle was fond of Kate. An attractive woman in her early fifties, she was wholly dedicated to her work, her entire person exuding an air of calm and efficiency. She must have been alerted to Mary's presence, for her large brown eyes shifted her way.

Coyle, too, looked up. "Good morning, Miss Clark," he said in his deep, mellifluous voice. "Please go in, I'll join you momentarily."

Mary nodded and stepped into his office.

She took the seat facing the desk, with her back to the door. She had been here on one other occasion to deliver a file, material she had researched for him, and had had little time to observe the surroundings. While she sat, she scanned his workplace. In spite of the large window on one wall, Mary found it somewhat confined, all the available space taken up with large bookcases, their shelves overloaded.

Coyle obviously doesn't believe in framed certificates, she acknowledged mutely. It was not because he lacked them. From the rest of the staff, she learned he had graduated with honours from McGill University and was a Rhodes scholar, a notable combination.

"My apologies for keeping you waiting," she heard from behind. His manner was like his speech—calm, reassuring, confident.

"I understand you were asking to see me?" she replied, turning to face him.

Coyle, tall with dark, receding hair, walked around his desk and seated himself. From what she knew, he had to be in his early forties, but he looked a decade younger. "Yes. Thank you for coming in," he answered.

Mary simply smiled at him.

"How are things coming along with Mr. Kerr's affairs?" he asked without preamble.

"So far, they have presented me with little difficulty."

"Excellent. I normally don't intervene in matters of wills and estate management, but Mr. McLeod suggested that perhaps I could be of service to you."

Those were not the words Mary had overheard booming out from behind the conference room door the morning she was given the assignment. Robert Kerr was one of the firm's most prestigious clients and a personal friend of Henry McLeod, who had reliably handled his affairs. When Mr. Kerr requested that Mary take over for his last will, McLeod was incensed that a junior lawyer with the firm—a dilettante and what's more, a woman—should be offered that task. His words had been more like: *I need someone to watch over that girl so she doesn't screw up the whole damn thing. Frankly, I think this is way beyond her depth. But for some reason, Robert insists on having it this way. Therefore, we have to take precautionary measures. The last thing we want is for those kids of his to file a lawsuit against the firm as a result of Clark's inexperience.*

Such declarations were typical of Mr. McLeod. He was intolerant and a chauvinist. Yet Mary could not help wondering how Coyle felt about having to supervise her. From a distance, she had observed that he was more open-minded than his employer and clearly had no tolerance for his prejudices regarding women lawyers, but Coyle's expertise was in great demand and, surely, he had to resent playing nursemaid to an "inexperienced" lawyer, as McLeod had so bluntly stated.

During the five years she had been with the firm, most of Mary's work consisted of research in the library, some clerical work, and assisting other lawyers. Only twice had she been assigned actual court cases. They were welfare situations, which Mr. McLeod occasionally took on to promote the firm's community image. Even when the chips were down, with no plausible defence, Mary had come out fighting, proving that when pushed, she had the tenacity to push back. It had surprised and pleased her when, in both cases, Coyle had come forward and complimented her on her perseverance and efficiency.

"Has Mr. Kerr's house been sold?" Coyle asked her now.

"No, but we do have several offers."

He handed her a file from his desk drawer. "This belongs to you." He must have noted her apprehension, for he added, "Nothing to be alarmed about. It's a Kerr file, which was overlooked when all the others were passed on to you. I think it unlikely this one has any information of enormous consequence. It's a good idea, however, to keep all the files together."

Mary gave him a grateful look. "Thank you."

He rose from his chair. "I'm confident of your competence to work on this estate on your own but will make myself available to you, should you require any assistance."

"I appreciate your offer to help. Undoubtedly, I'll require it before I'm through," she replied as she stood to leave.

"A word of caution before you go."

"Yes?"

"Mr. Kerr is a very powerful man who has amassed considerable wealth, as you know. He's liberal-minded but also unorthodox, meaning he frequently does the unexpected. So I suggest you carefully document everything you do to ensure there's no misinterpretation of your work—a complete record."

Concerned, she asked, "Are you aware of anything that might suggest a problem with Mr. Kerr's will?"

"No. Merely a precautionary measure."

Documenting her work was something she invariably did. But it was good to be reminded. Again, she thanked him and then departed.

She was now late for her rendezvous with Rachel. As she rushed to her car, she tried to make sense of her brief meeting with Coyle. He had offered her his assistance because Mr. McLeod had requested it, but even that failed to clarify why he, whose specialty was criminal law, would involve himself in Mr. Kerr's estate.

Despite the unconventional circumstance, she felt exhilarated by the prospect of working with Coyle. But she also realized that as a junior employee working on her first major assignment of enormous importance and complexity, she would have to pass the intense scrutiny of her employer, Mr. McLeod, who obviously expected her to fail. She could not afford to make any errors.

Fifteen minutes later, and half an hour late for her lunch date with Rachel, Mary arrived at the restaurant. Her mind was still focused on work as she pushed her way through the double doors. She spotted Rachel waving from across the room. It was a popular restaurant, and the place was packed.

Mary acknowledged her with a slight motion of her hand and made her way to the corner table at the back of the restaurant. "Hi! Sorry I'm late."

"No problem, I ordered some tea and was reviewing a file while I waited."

Rachel was five years older than Mary, petite, with piercing hazel eyes and a mop of untamable black hair. In her dark blue suit, she met a lawyer's recommended dress code for the courtroom, but that was about it. Everything else about her suggested an unsophisticated lack of attention to appearance—one of those lawyers whom people tend to underestimate, and whom Mary knew was positively brilliant. Female lawyers were a rare sight in Ottawa at the time, and the two had sought each other out, forging a strong bond based on their shared experience of breaking through gender barriers in the legal profession.

"Take a seat," Rachel invited, stuffing her file into a bulging black leather briefcase sitting on the floor beside her.

Mary hitched her shoulder bag onto the back of the

chair opposite her and, with an air of absolute abandonment, seated herself. When she looked up, Rachel was staring at her with an inquisitive look. "Something you want to share?" she asked.

Mary lifted an eyebrow. "Can you be a bit less obscure?"

"Well, I've never seen you so radiant. What or who brought that on?"

"I don't know what you're talking about."

Just then, the waitress arrived to take their orders. Both requested the special of the day: penne with pesto, red peppers, and mushrooms. They declined dessert, ordering another tea and coffee instead.

"Well?" Rachel urged.

"Well what?"

"Are you going to tell me what it is you're so jubilant about," Rachel prompted, "or do I have to drag it out of you?"

"Nothing, I tell you. The only incident that arose today that could remotely be considered pleasant is Coyle informing me that we'll be working together on this estate I'm managing. But I can't see how that would affect me in the way you're suggesting."

Rachel rolled her eyes. "You mean that handsome, inscrutable, sexy Coyle at McLeod & Woodbury?"

"He's not that sexy."

"Are you kidding?" Rachel exclaimed. "He's like a walking aphrodisiac. One whiff of him and just about every woman in the Ottawa legal system becomes weak at the knees." She took a deep breath and closed her eyes. After a moment she opened them and said, "I put very little trust in men, but I would allow him to manage my affairs, any time."

Mary smiled. Rachel was right. Women seemed to find Coyle irresistibly attractive. Admittedly, he was. But Mary had eyes for one person only, and that was her fiancé, Peter. That had not prevented her, however, from observing how most female employees in her office openly sought to ingratiate themselves with Coyle. She had watched him turn a blind eye to them. He was scrupulously polite but always maintained a professional distance. Rumours flying in the office were that he was engaged to be married, which would explain his behaviour.

"Why haven't you presented him to your friends?" Rachel asked.

"In case you haven't noticed, Rachel, I'm not part of his social circle. Outside of the office, I know nothing about him."

"That's because you're too caught up with that fiancé of yours." She paused and raised one eyebrow. "How is Peter, anyway?"

Mary smiled. "Fine."

Rachel glanced at Mary over the top of her teacup and frowned. "He's not my favourite choice for you, you know."

"Rachel, don't ever let anyone accuse you of subtlety." Mary never ceased to be astounded by her friend's directness.

"Well, there's nothing to be gained from beating around the bush, so I may as well tell you straight out."

"Yet you were the one who introduced him to me at that SPCA fundraiser."

"I couldn't help it. He practically coerced me into doing

it. Besides, I judged you too shrewd to fall for the likes of him."

There was another pause, where neither spoke. Then Mary asked, "What is it about Peter you find objectionable?"

"Peter is amiable enough, but he's a mama's boy, with no sense of responsibility or reliability—qualities you, Mary, ostensibly value in people, especially one you intend to spend your life with."

Peter was certainly devoted to his mother. In fact, it was this very trait that appealed to Mary. A man who cherished his mother would most likely cherish his wife. "Is being devoted to one's mother so wrong?" she asked.

"No. Not when she's a woman of great strength of character, which is definitely not the case with Mrs. Burbidge."

Mary had only met Peter's mother once, in spite of the fact that she and Peter had been together for over a year. The Burbidges spent long periods of time in warmer climes.

"How do you happen to know so much about her anyway?"

"Over the years, I've met her at several social functions that I was duty bound to attend on behalf of the firm. She's an unscrupulous woman who loves power. I could barely stand her. To be cloistered with Peter's mother for any length of time would be enough to make you want to commit murder. I'm astounded she's survived as long as she has."

"I don't see how that should affect Peter."

"Peter is pretentious and thinks the world revolves around him. Sentiments which, I assume, were instilled by his mother, who is shallow and egotistic. People like that tend to function solely for themselves. Not someone you can rely on." Rachel stared at Mary across the table, seemingly analyzing the effect of her words. Her voice softened. "Believe me, Mary, he will hurt you in the end. I know you. I know what you value in a relationship, and Peter will never be able to give it to you."

Mary sighed softly before responding, "Rachel, I appreciate your honesty, and I understand that you have your reservations about Peter. I value your opinion, but I also believe in giving people a chance to prove themselves. While your experiences with Peter and his mother may not have been positive, I've seen different sides of him that make me hopeful for our future together. I hope you can trust my judgment and support me in this decision. After all, love has a way of revealing the best in people."

"Mary, I know I'm overstepping boundaries, but I'm worried for you. Everyone at the office sees you and Peter as the ideal couple. But they don't know you as well as I do. You and Peter are like night and day." Rachel raised her shoulders and shook her head helplessly. "What puzzles me is that you are such a rational individual in every other respect. It's hard for me to comprehend why you would be so taken by him."

As Rachel spoke, Mary thought about how Peter called her after every storm to make sure she was safe and sound, how he prepared a meal or picked up a boxed dinner from a local restaurant whenever she was too tired to cook, and how he continually left notes in her briefcase and coat pocket, reminding her how much he loved her. And then there was the time he made a huge donation to the Ottawa SPCA—substantial enough to be acknowledged in the local paper. When she asked him what had motivated him to give so much money to the animal shelter, he'd said, "Because few people ever think of helping them, and they need it the most."

Rachel was still talking. "From my past record, I suppose I should be the last one to tell you that." Leaning over the table, she added, "Mary, if I'm being a nuisance, it's because I feel you are too trusting and frequently don't see people for what they are. This early in your relationship, it's easy to be mesmerized by Peter's good looks and easy charm. He's the type that you like instantly when you meet him. But the more you get to know Peter, the more you realize how little there is to him. It's like chipping away at a beautiful object and finding it hollow inside."

"Rachel, I should be offended, but I'm not, because you're sincere and you care for me. But you're mistaken about him. If only you knew him as I do. You may work with him, but you've never seen him at his most tender moments. He's tender and so very loving."

"I know Peter far too well not to be aware of his charm," Rachel replied. "I can appreciate the romantic and sexual excitement that marks the beginning of any relationship. Those sensations, however, are not what life is all about. There has to be more to an individual beyond the capability to delight or beguile. What disturbs me about Peter at work is that he operates on an alternative moral code. He continually picks the easiest route to everything—any means, sometimes devious, as long as it helps achieve his goals. He's the only person I know who views rules as optional."

"Are you implying Peter is dishonest?"

"No. What I'm saying is I have a particular abhorrence of some of the things he does. One doesn't become disingenuous overnight. It takes time. As I observe Peter, this is where I feel he's headed, and I'm afraid for you. I fear that one day you'll find out he's not the sympathetic person you believe him to be, and you'll be wounded by it." Rachel sighed. "I suspect that my negative intuition about your fiancé boils down to the fact that I've gone through a marriage breakup, and I wouldn't wish it on you…even on my worst enemy, for that matter."

Their tête-à-tête was interrupted when the waitress came with their food. They were both silent until she left and, for a while, focused on their food.

Rachel's words had given Mary pause. Their conversation had ended prematurely, without resolution, but she didn't want to maintain it. She looked at her friend's plate, which had hardly been touched. "Are you not feeling well, Rachel?"

Rachel pushed her plate to the side. "I'm frustrated, outraged, and depressed. Otherwise, I'm fine."

"Things not going well with you at work?"

"It's nothing like that." Rachelle paused, then said, "I was just thinking about Angela, my new neighbour."

"The one with the thalidomide child?"

"Yes."

"Do you care to talk about it?"

"What can I say? Except that when I think about it, it makes me want to scream."

Rachel didn't have to justify her anger. At their last lunch date, she discussed the young mother's situation with Mary, who knew about the drug, thalidomide. Its tragic outcome on the one hundred women who had taken it had been well documented. "How is she?"

"Well, how would you feel if you were the mother of a child whose birth defects were caused by a presumably safe medication you took to fight morning sickness during your pregnancy?"

"I'm sure she must be experiencing extreme guilt."

"Exactly. Yesterday I went over to her apartment for a quick visit. When I inquired about her husband, she told me he was having a hard time coping with the child, that they were in the process of separating. Can you believe that bastard?"

Mary shook her head. "The death of a child often leads a previously devoted couple to separate or divorce. For some, the effects of thalidomide are a comparable tragedy."

"What enrages me, Mary, is that too many of these mothers have been deserted by their husbands and have been left to care for these children on their own."

Mary grimaced, acknowledging her words. "How old is the child now?"

She recalled Rachel's description: *The cutest little fellow you ever saw—a perfect little boy with big blue eyes and curly blond hair.* Rachel had stopped abruptly to move bits of food on her plate with her fork, then whispered in a low, dispirited voice, *Except that he's armless.*

"Jesse turned five last Christmas," Rachel answered. A strained chuckle escaped from deep inside her as she added, "He was to be their Christmas gift."

Both remained quiet. The silence magnified the awful irony.

It was Mary who broke the silence. "Let's hope the father doesn't abandon them completely."

"Personally, I'd like to bring the clown to court and take him for every penny he has."

"Have you suggested it to her?"

"No. From what I can observe, she's still in love with that spineless, pathetic sap and would be ill disposed to allow it."

"Well, if she feels that way about her estranged husband, there must be goodness in him," Mary replied. "And with time, once he has had a chance to grieve, he may come around."

"It's already been five years, for heaven's sake! How much more time does he need?"

"Well, for some people, there's no end to grief."

"Yeah." Rachel's tone was sarcastic. "And would you like to know what really pisses me off?" she blurted a bit too loudly. The couple at the adjacent table turned to stare at them, and she lowered her voice to a fierce whisper. "This whole damn disaster could have been averted if we had had more responsible people in the federal health department. Not only did they not recognize the danger of that drug, but they sanctioned it until March 1962, three months after European countries had banned it, despite explicit warnings that the drug was the cause of severe birth defects."

The idea that anyone would permit such a tragedy made Mary mute.

"What we needed in that sector was a woman, another Frances Kelsey," Rachel continued, with the same insistence she used whenever she was frustrated with the male-dominated system of government.

Mary nodded as she recalled the newspaper articles about Frances Kelsey, the pharmacologist who stood against the approval of thalidomide in the United States. Just as she said, "We could use more like her today," she became aware that the couple from the next table was leaving. She glanced at her watch: 1:30. "Dear me, I didn't realize it was this late. I know how much you care for this young mother and her child, and I hate to interrupt our conversation, but I must go. Would you mind terribly?"

"No, of course not. Thanks for listening." Then with an expression of both discomfort and affection, Rachel added, "About Peter, I'm sorry for mouthing off the way I did. I can be a real pain in the butt at times."

"No, Rachel. What you are is a concerned friend, who has persistently been honest with me. I wouldn't have you any other way." Mary glanced at her watch again. "I really must go. Don't forget dinner at my place tomorrow night."

"I'll be there."

Mary took out her wallet.

"My treat," insisted Rachel.

"Thanks!" Then looking directly at her companion, Mary said good-naturedly, "And Rachel, I appreciate how trying it can be for you to be pleasant around Peter, but you might try feigning it for my sake."

"I promise I'll be on my best behaviour."

"I want you to do better than that."

"Get out of here before I make a scene and embarrass you before all these people," Rachel threatened, throwing her hands in the air.

"See you tomorrow," Mary called back to her as she hurried toward the exit.

Mary returned to her workspace, an undersized cubicle tucked away in a corner of the firm's library. She sat at her desk and opened the file Coyle had handed her. She tried to concentrate on its contents, but her eyes trailed across the documents. Her elbow on the desk, she leaned her head against her hand and stared unseeing at the bare wall. She was recalling her conversation with Rachel, her opinion of Peter now marred by it. She attempted to chase away her friend's warning, but it kept cropping up, giving her misgivings. She respected Rachel's judgment in most things but could not comprehend her contempt for Peter. Was it possible Rachel knew him better than she did? They did work for the same law firm. *No. She has to be mistaken. Peter is nothing like what she described.* Rachel's impression of him had to be influenced by her own tragic life with her ex-husband, Daryl.

Mary tried to recall what Rachel had revealed about Daryl. They had met in Toronto, while Rachel was visiting relatives—the standard tale of two people meeting on a holiday, falling in love, and getting married. According to Rachel, she had been astounded at her good fortune. Coming from a broken home, she had never envisaged she would be able to find someone who could love her. Yet she had met and married a man who had sworn everlasting commitment and love to her. That had lasted no more than five years. Mary could not recall what had prompted the breakdown of their marriage—Rachel's account had been elusive. She had simply confided that she had gone through horrible times after their estrangement. For a long while she had doubted that she would ever recover.

Although Rachel was a myriad of things, victim was not a word one would use to describe her. Among the other confidences Rachel had shared, Mary learned that when her friend had had her fill of passing affairs, she had set out on a quest to rebuild herself. This she had done by focusing on her strengths and discovering new paths to success and fulfillment—obtaining her law degree, becoming involved in the community, and volunteering her time to needy causes, especially the SPCA. Her new profession and working with abandoned and abused animals had delivered her from the emptiness she had felt since the breakup of her marriage. It had also given her the freedom to explore new ideas.

Mary had once asked her, "Did you know your marriage was failing before Daryl announced he was leaving? Or was it a shock?"

Rachel looked restrained and was quiet for some time. Finally, she said, "When a man tells you he loves you and all the evidence points to the contrary, it's ludicrous to continue deceiving yourself."

Rachel was not what you would call a pious person, but she had firm values and adhered to them, which might explain why she never remarried. Her Roman Catholic background held a greater influence than she would admit even to herself. Or it could be she had arrived at the point in her life where she was content to live alone. To Mary, it was obvious Rachel was a survivor—but at what cost, nobody would ever know.

Mary's thoughts reverted to her friend's cruel words against Peter. She knew Rachel would never have voiced them unless she had been truly convinced that Mary's future was at risk. This weighed heavily on her. For the first time she wondered if Peter was completely honest with her. Was it possible that he was not the person she believed him to be? What is it that made some people more trustworthy than others?

She shook her head, refusing to doubt her fiancé. For doubt could only demolish what they shared together. And more than anything, she wanted—no, she needed—a relationship based on love and trust.

M r. Kerr's health was fast deteriorating, and Mary found herself spending more time with him at the hospital. In the beginning it was all business, but over the past two weeks they had grown closer.

His eyesight was failing, and she read to him—his business documents and the newspapers. Despite the fact he was dying, he remained prodigiously interested in what was happening, not only around him but in the world at large. Mary noted that everything seemed to touch him more acutely than ever.

Frequently, after their business session was over, she would wheel him to the sunroom or activity room. There was a piano there, and she would entertain him. He loved the songs that had been popular during the war, and she had made a point of procuring the music so she could play his favourite melodies.

One afternoon, almost as soon as she had seated herself at the piano, he demanded to be wheeled back to his room. Once he was comfortably settled in bed, she asked, "Why didn't you want me to play for you?"

"I wasn't in the mood."

When she did not say anything, he added, "Courtney and Richard had promised to come and see me today. Both called to say they couldn't make it."

Mary felt for him. She fell into another sad silence.

"Forgive me, Mary, if I appear not to appreciate your beautiful music," he said. "I can't tell you how much your visits mean to me."

Mary studied her hands, almost afraid to look at him—afraid he would see her contempt for his children in her eyes. Finally, she looked up and said, "Is there anything I can do for you, Mr. Kerr, before I leave?"

"No. When you get to the point I'm at, there's not much one really needs." He sunk his chin to his chest and closed his eyes like a man experiencing profound grief. Then he murmured, "It doesn't matter much in the scheme of things. See you tomorrow, Mary."

Mary was dismayed. This wavering, indecisive person wasn't anything like the fastidious businessman she remembered. "What is it, Mr. Kerr?" she asked.

He barely looked at her. "What is what?"

"You're troubled. I can see it."

A glimmer of vulnerability flitted across his face. Then his expression hardened. "All my life, my entire focus has been on my business, not only for me but for what I could give my children. Now that I'm dying, it doesn't seem all that meaningful. Tell me, what have I accomplished other than to augment the wealth of shareholders who most likely don't need it?" He looked around at his stark hospital room, his bed, the night table beside it, the door leading to the bathroom, as if seeking an explanation. Finally, his gaze rested on her. "At the end, it's all so banal. Worse still, I've prevented my children from having the opportunity of making it through life on their own merits." He paused and turned to look out the window.

Mary said nothing. Lately, he had been doing a lot of verbal brooding, and it was debatable whether he was addressing those words to her or merely thinking aloud.

While she stood there, powerless to leave, he once more turned to face her. Mary had deemed Mr. Kerr too spirited, too strong-willed to ever break down, and yet there was a mist of tears in his eyes. Speechless, she could only watch—wholly unprepared for the following disclosure. "You know, I deeply regret not visiting that friend of yours who was a patient in Élisabeth Bruyère Hospital." With this he looked away, gazing expressionless into space, indicating their meeting was over.

Mary was inured to his curt behaviour and never felt slighted by it. She knew he was hurting, and her heart ached with compassion. Fearing any consoling word from her would be viewed as pity, she picked up her briefcase, bid him goodbye, and discreetly departed.

His words, however, had not been lost on her. He was referring to Dr. Cowen, and memories of their friendship flooded back as she left the hospital.

She had met Dr. Cowen at the start of her second year of law school. Her university friend Francis MacDonald, newly employed as director of the Élisabeth Bruyère Hospital Foundation, had begged her to play piano for a fundraiser he was organizing, an afternoon tea party on the lawn of the hospital. Initially Mary had declined, explaining that she seldom performed in front of an audience. But Francis had persisted, and Mary had relented. She would forever remember that day.

SEPTEMBER 1959

Self-conscious and uncertain, Mary arrived at the hospital and made her way to the site where the festivities were to take place. While sitting at the piano sorting her sheet music, a kindly looking, white-haired man was wheeled beside her. The nurse introduced him as Dr. Marshall Cowen.

"I'm pleased to meet you," Mary said, extending her hand in reply to his smile.

Mary was struck by the strength in his grip as he took her hand in his. "I see you're going to play the piano for us. How delightful!" He had a warm voice, and Mary was immediately comfortable with him. "Have you chosen your music yet?" he asked.

"No, not yet. I'm afraid I don't play much popular music. I'm trying to decide what pieces in my repertoire the audience might enjoy."

"Any music would be very much appreciated."

Spurred by his words, Mary began to play the famous barcarole from *The Tales of Hoffmann* by Jacques Offenbach. It was a romantic piece, and she played it with poignant sensitivity. When she finished, she turned to Dr. Cowen and could see that he had enjoyed it immensely. Heartened by his reaction, she resumed playing, switching to her favourite composer, Frédéric Chopin. As she played, people ceased what they were doing in order to listen.

At one point, she glanced at Dr. Cowen and saw tears flowing freely down his cheeks. Alarmed, she ceased playing. "Dr. Cowen, is my music distressful to you?"

"Please forgive this show of emotion," he said, shaking his head. "I don't normally carry on this way. But music has always been a big part of my life, and hearing you play that particular piece brought back tender memories."

"Should I continue playing, if it's so painful?"

"Please do. I'll try not to trouble you with my emotional outbursts." His watery blue eyes saddened even more. "Like you, my wife was an accomplished pianist. She loved Chopin's music and frequently played that particular piece for me. She passed away several years ago."

"I…I'm so sorry, truly." Having said it, Mary sensed how inadequate the words were.

"No need to be. We had a wonderful life together, and hopefully I'll be joining her soon." Then, with a half-hearted glance at himself, he murmured, "It's tough being disabled like this."

Mary's heart went out to him.

Later, as she was leaving, Dr. Cowen asked with a smile, "Will we have the pleasure of hearing you play again?"

Despite the smile, she noted a wistful look in his gaze. "I'm afraid not. I was solely invited to play for this one special occasion."

"I'm awfully glad you came. You played charmingly—a definite boost from our standard routine."

Despite his gallant words, it struck her how lonely he must be. She thought of her deceased grandfather, who had been a central figure in the early years of her life—at least as much as he could be while living in a distant city. He, too, had loved music and had lived in a nursing home for six months before passing away. Though she had been unable to visit him, she would like to think that there had been someone like her to play the piano for him. "I'll try to come next Tuesday, if that suits you. I'm a law student at Ottawa University, but I have no classes in the afternoon."

Dr. Cowen beamed. "How generous of you! I will count the days until then."

In subsequent visits, Mary learned that Dr. Cowen had been taken to the hospital with a broken hip. Unfortunately, due to his age, the severity of the break, and underlying health conditions, a hip replacement was not deemed a viable option, and he was unable to regain mobility. Consequently, he had been transferred to the geriatric ward and, more recently, to the extended care unit.

As weeks went by, she could see he was lonely, perpetually struggling to maintain an appearance of calm and cheerfulness. She made more time to be with him. During their initial visits, the conversation was cordial, cautious, conventional. They chatted primarily about things happening around them, current events, natural history, and, of course, music. But as her visits became more frequent, he spoke freely to her, and she recognized he was remarkable man—well-read, intelligent, and sensitive to issues of the time.

He was a surgeon and had served in the war, operating in tents with the battles raging a short distance away. Before his retirement, he had been head surgeon of a major hospital in Toronto. On one occasion, he read to her a touching letter he had recently received from a former patient, thanking him for having saved his life.

He had a daughter, whom he spoke about frequently. She was away in Paris, studying historical archaeology at the Sorbonne. That explained why she never came to visit, but Mary regularly saw envelopes on his dresser with her return address written on them. "She's an amazing person, exceptionally intelligent," he said one day, his voice full of pride.

Mary knew he missed his daughter profoundly and endeavoured to cheer him up as much as she could. Relegated to sitting in a wheelchair, Dr. Cowen's physical health deteriorated; his mind, however, proved inviolable. He never complained, but Mary recognized his solitude and pondered on how life could be so merciless. Here was a man who had enjoyed the status conferred by power and had done immeasurable good in the world. Yet at the end—except for his daughter and that one patient—he remained abandoned by those he had once served.

One day during this time, she was walking on Sparks Street and happened to meet Mr. Kerr. He was glad to see her, as always. In their brief conversation, he informed her of Courtney and Richard's present whereabouts and suggested that she should try to get in touch with them. Shortly after that meeting Mary conceived the notion of bringing Mr. Kerr and Dr. Cowen together. They had so much in common. They were the same age, had both served in the war, and had each experienced personal loss. Mary cherished her time with Dr. Cowen, but she felt he needed male companionship.

When she proposed this to Mr. Kerr at their next

encounter, however, he fixed his eyes on her, unmoved. "Does this Dr. Cowen not have a family of his own to visit him?"

Mary fought to contain her shock. Had he misunderstood her? Surely, her request had not been unreasonable, yet he was transparently uninterested.

In the brief silence that followed, she was suddenly reminded of her moral obligation to Dr. Cowen and questioned whether she had compromised the privacy of her friend by going to Mr. Kerr without his permission. Regretting her action, she muttered, "Oh! Of course he does. I considered bringing you together only because you have so much in common, with both of you having served in the war."

Mr. Kerr never visited Dr. Cowen. While his neglect of Eugenie had always been a source of sadness for Mary, she had expected more compassion from him toward a fellow veteran. His decision not to visit Dr. Cowen left her bitterly disappointed. Despite Mr. Kerr's genial and social nature, she came to realize he was nothing more than a polished businessman, a brutal but clear realization that was slow coming to her.

In the months that followed, Mary continued to drop in on her physician friend. Her time with him became the richest and most rewarding of her day-to-day life. Every so often, they would just sit and chat. On most occasions, he would ask her to play the piano. He unfailingly cried when she did, and she would refrain from looking in his direction.

Then one day he informed her he had been diagnosed with an inoperable liver cancer. He died two months later, shortly after her parents' death. His last words to her were, "Thank you."

MAY 1966

Thinking now about Mr. Kerr, Mary found it odd that her suggestion that he visit Dr. Cowen should be what he would remember after all this time, especially when there were innumerable business details left to consider. Was it because he had learned through his own illness the affliction of being alone and abandoned? It is not unusual to reflect on past actions when facing imminent death, and it is possible that in self-examination the bleak reality of his mortality sensitized him to Dr. Cowen's own suffering. Like him, Dr. Cowen had been a patient in a hospital. A patient in need of companionship. And when asked to visit him, Mr. Kerr had shrugged him off—a decision that now left him feeling shame and guilt.

I t was early the next morning, and Mary was staring out the window of Mr. Kerr's hospital room. It was open, and she could hear people laughing outside, a stark contrast with the atmosphere in the room. Then came the sudden blast of car horn. She turned to Mr. Kerr and was relieved to see he was still asleep. These days he unfailingly dozed during her visits, but she did not mind. It meant he was no longer in pain. This particular morning, they had already had a brief meeting, and Mary was waiting for him to wake up because she knew there was more they needed to discuss.

Her gaze drifted back to the view outside the window, this time to the heavy traffic on Carling Avenue, commuters going to work. Feeling the warm spring breeze through the tiny opening in the glass, she allowed her mind to wander to the meeting when he had asked her to be the executrix of his will.

Surprised, she had responded, "Shouldn't it be Richard? I'm sure he would expect it."

"It has to be you," he'd answered. "I know it's asking a lot. Serving as an executrix of an estate can be a challenging responsibility. It requires significant time and effort to understand the duties and how to fulfill them. I need a professional to do it, someone I can trust." He had paused, and then emphasized his next words. "With you as my executrix, I can be assured that my wishes will be upheld."

She had wanted to know more about his reason for choosing her but had detected the note of finality in his voice. So she replied, "If it's that important to you, I will do it willingly."

Mary was still pondering his decision when the door to the room swung wide and a kind-looking woman walked in. Her name tag identified her as Doris Martin, Certified Nursing Assistant. "Oh, I didn't realize you were here," she said apologetically. "I'll come later to make up Mr. Kerr's bed."

Before Mary could react, the nursing assistant exited and gently closed the door.

Her voice must have wakened Mr. Kerr. He opened his eyes, and his face brightened to a smile upon seeing Mary. "You still here?" he asked.

"You can't get rid of me that easily," she replied.

Once again, he smiled. "In that case, why don't you make yourself useful and fetch my briefcase from the closet?"

She handed it to him and watched as he reached into it and pulled out a large brown envelope. "I wanted you to have these personal papers," he announced. "Nobody else will want them."

Mary accepted the envelope and proceeded to open it. Inside were several documents, which she studied briefly. Among them were Eugenie's marriage certificate, her Canadian citizenship papers, her will, and a handwritten envelope, with a European postmark, addressed to Eugenie. Mary pointed to the marriage certificate. "When I visited Eugenie at the nursing home, she mentioned you were married in Montreal."

"Yes, at Saint-Marc Roman Catholic Church. It was a small wedding, just a few of my close friends." He hesitated a moment. "Eugenie wished it so. She was extremely reserved."

Mindful of an emotional tremor in his voice, Mary moved to the next document. "I see Eugenie had a will."

"Yes, when I rewrote mine shortly after our marriage, I suggested she write one too." He paused for a while. When he spoke again, there was a hint of a smile on his lips. "I remember her pointing out how outlandish that was. She had so little—just the trunk she had brought with her from France. But when I insisted, she said, '*Mon très cher époux, everything I have is yours.*' Unfortunately, I never learned to speak French fluently, but I remember that particular phrase of hers." He shook his head sadly and then fell silent. Lately, Mr. Kerr's reminiscences tended to bring about long periods of silence. At first Mary had not been sure how to react. Over time, however, she had grown familiar with his quiet reminiscing and no longer felt excluded by it. She simply waited for him to resume the conversation. This time, his silence seemed to last forever.

Mary reached down among the papers and picked up the handwritten envelope. She noted it was sealed and that the return address was Rennes, France. The postmark on it was December 1959.

"That letter arrived shortly after Eugenie passed away. It's from her sister Danielle. They corresponded regularly in French. I didn't bother to open it. I'd already sent the family a telegram informing them of Eugenie's death and didn't think it necessary. I would have had to have it translated."

Mary thought but did not say, *I could have done that for you.*

"I know you speak French," he added. "Feel free to read it if you wish."

"I will. I suspect it's personal, family news…but just in case."

She was about to place the letter in her briefcase when Mr. Kerr retrieved it from her hand and examined it pensively. "How beautiful my Eugenie was. So much love in her." A wretchedness seemed to creep over him. "How could I have allowed myself to neglect her so?" he murmured.

Mary knew this was a rhetorical question, more a stream-of-consciousness outpouring than anything else. She found it puzzling how people take for granted the very things that merit their gratitude the most. Even the most rational and open-minded people sometimes fail to recognize and appreciate the true value of someone until it is too late. Eugenie had been loving and caring to Mr. Kerr and his children, yet her kindness had gone unappreciated by them.

Mr. Kerr stroked the envelope. "Strange what I remember about her—her unaffected ways and her total disregard of social status. A woman for whom ambition and wealth meant nothing. Those were the things that ultimately drove us apart. Thinking about it now, I realize those were the same qualities that had impressed me the most about her at the beginning of our courtship." He said this with a heavy sigh, like someone admitting they had failed.

"Mr. Kerr?"

His head snapped up, his eyes alight. "What?"

"About the letter…I could translate it into English for you, if you wish."

"No…too late," he replied, handing it back to her.

It was hard for Mary to comprehend what he was saying. Reflecting aloud had become a habit with him these days, and he often spoke in fragmented, disjointed sentences, more to himself than to her.

She placed the letter and the other documents into her briefcase. "In that case, I'll keep it amongst your papers." When he did not respond, she asked, "Did you ever meet Eugenie's family?"

"When I went to Europe to be assessed for my health, I went to Rennes. I had this address for Danielle and found myself in front of the family home. Eugenie had frequently spoken about it. I had no intention of going in or making my presence known. I only wanted to see where she had grown up. It was a hot day, and I suddenly felt weak. Almost immediately, a woman came out of the house and asked whether I was ill. For a moment, I mistook her for Eugenie. You could have sworn they were twins." Mr. Kerr turned to gaze out the window again. When he turned back to Mary, he had an incredulous look in his eyes. "She was dis-tressed over my well-being, and despite my insistence that I was fine, she pleaded with me to go into the house, out of the sun. Inside, she offered me a drink of lemonade. I couldn't get over how kind-hearted and sensitive she was. Like my Eugenie, she exuded a warmth and innocence, almost childlike."

"Was she Danielle?" Mary asked.

"Yes."

"Did she speak English?"

"Not fluently but enough to introduce herself and convey her concern for my well-being."

"Did you tell her who you were?"

"No."

"Why not?"

"I honestly can't say…maybe because I was dogged by memories that refused to be forgotten."

Mary was keen to hear more about his meeting with Danielle but decided not to question him further; she had never seen him so desolate. Instead, she asked, "Did Richard or Courtney ever meet Eugenie's family?"

"No, I'm afraid they were not interested in connecting with them. As you know, my children disliked their stepmother. I could never understand why. She was incredibly generous and loving to them." There was another pause, and Mary saw bewilderment and a shadow of ambivalence in his eyes. When he spoke again, his words were ones of resignation. "Unfortunately, Eugenie entered their world at an immensely challenging stage. Already, there had been too much upheaval in their lives. I…I wonder if things might have been different if I had spent more time with them. Mary, I'm curious; in your mind, what is the role of a father?"

The query not only startled her but also awoke painful memories. She looked at him with a dreadful uncertainty. "Ideally, I presume, the same as a mother—to assist, to encourage, to teach." She had to resist the impulse to add, *to be there for you without fail.*

"To teach," he repeated feebly, as he lay back against his pillow and dozed off again.

That same day, after a quick café lunch, Mary guided her car toward Mr. Kerr's residence. She had invited Courtney and Richard to do a general inspection of the house before concluding the sale. They were meeting her there today.

Mary wanted to inspect the grounds before their arrival. She parked the car at the gate and stood there for a few moments, breathing in the fresh air, then walked unhurriedly up the path. It was a splendid day. The light breeze was warm, soothing, and it whispered through the trees. At the end of the long lane, after several bends in the path, the huge, formidable house came into view.

As she neared the building, she saw a red sports car parked in the driveway. The front door of the house was open, and she could hear voices coming from inside. Obviously, Courtney and Richard had already arrived. She glanced at her watch to confirm she was not late. Their rendezvous had been set for two o'clock, and she was relieved to find that it was only five minutes past one. Adjusting the strap of her briefcase securely over her shoulder, she picked up her pace and arrived at the main entrance just as Courtney and Richard stepped outside.

"Hi!" Courtney called out and moved closer to kiss Mary on the cheek, engulfing her with the scent of her expensive perfume. Dressed in a perfectly cut, champagne-coloured suit with matching high-heeled shoes—her blond hair and makeup flawless—Courtney gave the overall impression of affluence. But it was a look that lacked conviviality and openness.

"Hello, Courtney. It's been a while," Mary said by way of a greeting.

Courtney nodded, her response less than enthusiastic.

Mary turned to Richard. His face was tanned, and he wore a business suit that made him look cultured and sophisticated. He was tall like his father and had inherited Mr. Kerr's intimidating blue eyes.

He held out his hand. "Good afternoon, Mary."

"I'm glad you were both able to make it," she replied, accepting his cool, deferential reception.

When Mr. Kerr's doctor, a personal friend of the family, had called to notify Richard of his father's failing health, Richard, an advertising executive, had explained that he was in the middle of a complicated business negotiation and that timing was crucial; events in the next week or so could either make or break the deal. He had concluded by saying that his father, being a businessman, would appreciate why it was impossible for him to visit just then. Similarly, Courtney—both her beauty and her modelling career in decline—had told the doctor that she was in the middle of a shoot but would try to visit her father at the earliest date. That had been five weeks ago.

Remembering how disappointed Mr. Kerr had been, Mary asked, "Have you been in to see your father lately?"

Courtney answered. "No, we plan to visit Dad later."

"We felt this matter was more urgent," Richard elaborated. "Any further development on the sale of the house?"

Mary was disappointed by their lack of empathy.

Admittedly they were not close to their father, yet Mr. Kerr had never been uncaring or unsupportive. Though he had shared little quality time with them, all his efforts had been directed toward providing for them financially, even in their chosen careers. But Mary also recalled that Courtney and Richard had been part of a household where life was seen as a business, focused on profit and competition. So it was not surprising that their father's imminent death should cast little shadow over their lives.

Careful to keep the sourness out of her voice, she replied, "Yes, there are several offers. The best to date is slightly over one million dollars, way below its worth. We could no doubt get more if we were to hold out a trifle longer."

"No, you may as well go ahead with the sale. Courtney and I have no use for the house, and we want the matter settled as promptly as possible. It will be one thing less to fret about after Dad's gone."

Mary was struck by the apathy with which he spoke.

"Yes," affirmed Courtney, turning to check her reflection in the glass door in front of her. "I have a new contract coming up, and my agent has notified me of numerous appearances I will be making, so I doubt I will have time for anything else."

"In that case, I'll go ahead and set up the papers," Mary said, then remembered Eugenie's trunk in the attic. "I see you and Courtney have removed most of the furniture. Are you aware of Eugenie's trunk in the attic?"

"Yes. We saw it and have no need for it."

"What would you like me to do with it?" she asked.

"It's worthless. Get rid of it," Richard replied with a dismissive wave of his hand.

It occurred to Mary that there was one other option. "Eugenie has a sister living in France with whom she'd been corresponding. If you're willing, I could ship it to her." Before he could reply, she added, "Of course, I would require a document releasing it from the property. I could draft a legal paper with the particulars for your father to sign, if you like."

"Throw it in the garbage, for all I care," Courtney snapped.

Emotions raging, Mary did not trust herself to respond. Instead, she feigned searching for a pen in her handbag. How heartless Courtney had become! When she first met Courtney, she had found her friend interesting and fun to be with, though rather self-centred. She now questioned whether there had ever been any real friendship. Mary sensed there was something very amiss, very inept about Courtney—as if a crucial part of her was missing.

"I'm not sure that shipping it to France is such a good idea," said Richard. "It would only add to our expenses."

"I'm certain some sort of financial agreement could be worked out with her sister," Mary offered.

"Why go through all that trouble?" he asked.

"Receiving it would probably mean a great deal to her family," Mary replied.

Richard turned to his sister, who shrugged.

Looking irritably at Mary, Richard said, almost to himself, "I suppose it's one way to get rid of the hideous thing. So you may as well draw up the papers for my father to sign." Then he swung around and started for the entrance, turning briefly to say, "Now, I'd like to attend to the more serious matter of selling this house, if you have no objection."

Together they inspected the main floor and lower level. After they had finished there, they took the elevator to the second floor and set out down the long corridor. Painstakingly they walked through every room, overlooking nothing as they went along.

They were preparing to leave when Mary pointed in the direction of the attic. "While we're here, would you like to inspect the contents of Eugenie's trunk before I ship it to her relatives? There's a beautiful music box, which you might wish to keep as a memento."

Richard grimaced and Courtney arched her eyebrows. "God forbid!" she said.

Mary was so incensed by their arrogance that she had to look away. She silently accompanied them to the foyer then out the door. When they reached the car, she managed to say, "Thank you for taking the time to inspect the house."

Courtney kissed her briefly on the cheek. "Let's do lunch soon."

Mary smiled slightly but doubted it would happen.

Richard offered his hand. "Well, goodbye. I expect I'll be hearing from you shortly."

"Goodbye, Richard. I will call you the minute I hear from the realtor."

Mary watched as he and Courtney drove away. She was vastly relieved to see them go but felt forlorn, for she and Courtney had once been close. Now, however, she doubted they could ever be again.

That thought followed her as she re-entered the house. In the foyer, she debated what to do next. She was tired and was tempted to leave but decided to revisit the attic. She needed to act on the matter of the trunk before Richard and Courtney changed their minds. For the next hour she methodically went through Eugenie's trunk and itemized its contents. As she was doing so, she remembered the letter from Danielle, which Mr. Kerr had never read. She pulled it from her briefcase and opened it.

December 7, 1959
Dearest Eugenie,

Astonishing news! Mr. Orlov, an old Russian nobleman, came to visit us yesterday. He was a close acquaintance of Mr. Obolensky and was shaken to hear of his demise. Apparently, they had served in the same cavalry regiment of the Russian Imperial Army during the First World War. While here, Mr. Orlov revealed the most extraordinary things about our mutual friend. He told us that Mr. Obolensky had received the injury to his arm on the battlefield. As a result, he had been forced to relinquish his commission as captain in the Hussars. Upon his return home, however, he learned that his wife and their two daughters had been killed while trying to escape from the advancing Red Army. According to Mr. Orlov, Mr. Obolensky came from a distinguished family in Russia. He was a distant relative of the Tsar. And that beautiful music box, which you now have, was a gift to Mr. Obolensky's wife, Helena, from her godmother, Czarina Alexandra, before the Russian Revolution. Apparently, it's worth millions of dollars. It's interesting that Mr. Obolensky refused to sell it, even during the war when he was literally starving.

So much is clear and understandable to us now—the elaborate military uniform and magnificent sword we found among his possessions after he passed away, his lame arm, and especially his reluctance to speak about his wife, children, or his past. It must have been too painful for him.

Unfortunately, nothing in the world can alter what has happened to our dear friend. It is consoling, however, for us to know you will never be destitute. We are overwhelmed with happiness for you, Eugenie. We recognize you were never one to value material posses-sions; nonetheless, we sincerely feel you deserve this good fortune and much more.

Love,
Danielle

That evening, in her home office, Mary sat down to draft a letter to Danielle to send along with the trunk as soon as she could arrange for shipping. But Danielle's last letter had created an ethical dilemma for her.

Richard and Courtney had given her permission to dispose of the trunk, and she debated the necessity to tell them about the value of the music box. She now under-stood that the decorative jewels enclosing it, which she had assumed were imitations, were likely real. She recognized that although Courtney and Richard had shown no desire for the trunk, they had not been privy to the newly discov-ered information.

Fighting fatigue, she pondered the known facts, which only led to more questions. As Mr. Kerr's estate lawyer, she was bound by the standard legal and ethical obligation to act in her client's best interest. How could she presume to act in Mr. Kerr's best interest and withhold such knowledge from him? And since she had been ordered by the senior partner to work with Coyle, did she therefore have a professional responsibility to confer with him, for guidance and direction?

Grappling with emotions that continued to cloud her judgment, she placed a sheet of paper in her typewriter and wrote:

May 20, 1966
Danielle LeBreton
1041, rue DesRosiers
15005 Rennes
Dear Madam,

    My client, Mr. Robert D. Kerr, has invited me to contact you.

    We are in the process of selling his home, and it is the family's wish that Eugenie's trunk and its contents be forwarded to her sisters. I trust it has arrived safely.

    Mr. Kerr has requested that I convey to you his regrets for not writing to you personally. Unfortunately, he is ill and incapable of handling this matter himself.

    Should you require further information, please do not hesitate to contact me.

    Yours respectfully,
Mary Clark, B.A., LL.B.
Woodbury & McLeod
Barristers & Solicitors

Two months had passed since Mary started working on Mr. Kerr's estate, and she was at work early. She had a full day ahead, and she wanted to get a head start. So much had occurred lately that she was at a loss as to where to begin. A week ago, Mr. Kerr had signed his will. It had been a long process, but she felt satisfied with her work so far. The house had been sold, and the closing date was fast approaching. Still, there was a great deal of tidying up to do. She was opening a file when the phone rang. It was Mr. McLeod's secretary.

"We've just received a call from Richard Kerr. His father passed away during the evening."

Mary clasped the side of her chair as a crushing numbness spread through her. "Was there anyone with him when it happened?" she asked.

"Apparently not."

"Thank you," Mary uttered, her voice barely audible. She heard the click as Miss Williams hung up. Mary leaned across her desk and set down the receiver, her face blank. She sat there, numb, fully removed from the room.

"Miss Clark?"

She turned toward the voice. She was vaguely aware of a presence and heard, "Are you all right?"

She shook her head to clear it. Facing her was Coyle with a look both questioning and sympathetic.

"Mr. Kerr is dead," she intoned.

"I was just informed," he said. "I understand you were very close to him. Please accept my sincere condolences."

Yes, they had been close. He had needed her in these last weeks, and she had found contentment in helping him and being there for him.

Dazed and hovering on the verge of tears, she whispered, "He was all alone."

"So I was told."

She tried to say something else, but the words lodged in her throat.

"Courtney and Richard will need some time to grieve," Coyle added, his voice compassionate yet commanding. "It's advisable, however, that you get in touch with them shortly after you have the will probated to set up a meeting. Knowing Richard, he'll want to be brought up to date with the present state of his father's estate."

Mary remained silent, did not even know what to think. She was struggling to breathe normally again. Mr. Kerr's last directions with regard to his will dictated it should be read only after his funeral. At the time she had been filled with a mixture of shock, curiosity, disbelief, and apprehension. Now all she could feel was fear.

Robert Kerr had been a prominent and esteemed member of the community, and close to three hundred people came to pay their respects at his funeral. Mary wondered how many of them had been genuine friends.

Upon hearing about Mr. Kerr's death, Peter, who had been in England for an extended business transaction on behalf of his firm, had proposed that he accompany her to the funeral. Grateful for his offer of support, Mary had accepted. Edged against him in the crowded, penultimate pew, her hand gently grasped by his, she desperately tried to dispel the despondency that pressed heavily on her. She could never attend a funeral without evoking her parents' death, all the pain and misery coming back to her. Over time she'd been able to put aside the feelings of guilt and abandonment, but now, with the death of her friend and mentor, she felt more vulnerable than ever.

She watched Courtney and Richard follow the casket as it was being wheeled to the front of the church. In a beautifully tailored black suit and a short veil that concealed most of her face, Courtney leaned on her brother's arm, her head bowed, crying silently. Richard, dry-eyed, seemed to accept his father's death with just a modicum of emotion.

The funeral centred on prayers for Mr. Kerr's soul. The mention of his name brought tears to Mary's eyes, and she fumbled in her bag for a handkerchief only to discover she had forgotten to bring one. Peter, sensing her distress, offered her his. Throughout the service she went through the motions but at the end could hardly remember anything about it. Everything blurred as her mind alternated between Mr. Kerr, Eugenie, Courtney, and Richard—remembering the good times they had shared together. Imbued with an increasing sense of loss, she sat back in her pew, tears coursing unchecked down her cheeks.

Finally, the service was over, and Mary stood trembling

as the casket was rolled toward the entrance of the church, the pallbearers walking alongside. She wanted to reach out and touch it as it passed by. But Richard's glacial stare—and what she read in his mind—stopped her cold.

Mr. Kerr had stated to Mary and his children that he wished to be buried next to Eugenie. Yet when planning the funeral, Richard and Courtney had insisted on burying him in their mother's family plot. As executrix of his estate, Mary had felt it her duty to carry out the wishes of the deceased and had told them that she could not allow them to contravene their father's wishes, that she personally, as his lawyer and executrix, had an obligation to see that he be buried where he chose.

Another matter of contention was the reading of the will, which they had insisted be done immediately after their father's death. There, too, Mary had had to oppose them, given that Mr. Kerr had dictated in his will that it be read after his funeral. These two disagreements had created an even greater rift between her and his children.

There was no visitation, no graveyard service. Instead, a few relatives, business associates, and close friends of the family were invited to a special reception room at the funeral home for a cold buffet. Courtney and Richard were there to greet everyone. When Mary approached them and offered her condolences, they nodded but remained silent. Remembering the harsh words that had passed between them, Mary decided it was just as well. Their friendship had long been lost, and there was nothing left to say.

It being Saturday, neither Peter nor Mary was expected at work, so Peter drove Mary directly to her apartment following the reception. After he had turned off the ignition, she turned to him, her eyes pleading. "You'll forgive me, Peter, if I don't invite you in, but I'm worn out and need to lie down."

He looked at her, concern written all over his features. "I'm not comfortable with the idea of you being alone, not in the state you're in."

"There's nothing wrong with me."

"Mary, though you're putting on a brave front, I know you're hurting. Mr. Kerr meant too much to you not to care. And the last thing you need right now is to be alone." When she failed to reply, he added, "I didn't see you eat anything at the reception. When was the last time you ate?"

"I had breakfast."

"That was this morning, and it's three o'clock in the afternoon."

Again, she remained silent.

"At least let me pick up some food at Chez François, and I'll bring it over to you," he persisted. "I promise to leave as soon as you've eaten."

"I couldn't possibly eat anything."

"You have to eat."

"Really, Peter, I just want to go in and lie down."

He reluctantly acquiesced. The resistance seemed to have gone out of him, leaving him leaden and resigned.

Touched by his concern, Mary reached for his hand and held it tenderly against her cheek. "Don't worry, my love. I'll be fine."

Without a word, he took her in his arms and cradled her. "Promise to call me, if you need anything."

"I promise."

He released her and summoned a small smile, but the worry in his eyes indicated so much more.

"Love you," she said, as she opened the door of the car and stepped out.

"Love you, too," he replied, again with a smile.

He waited while Mary walked up to the entrance and let herself into the foyer. She gave him a brief wave and watched his car drive away. Despite her anguish, she could not help feeling fortunate to have such a caring person in her life. A shadow of guilt darkened her thoughts as she recalled Peter's disappointment at not being invited in. She knew he was genuinely concerned about her well-being, but there was nothing he could do for her. Preying on her mind was the reading of Mr. Kerr's will and how Courtney and Richard would react to it, a subject she could never broach with Peter. It was too confidential—too unbelievable.

Mary stepped into the Somerset Tower elevator and was whisked to the fifth floor. She hastily made her way to the Woodbury & McLeod boardroom, feeling apprehensive. She was late. She had allowed herself plenty of time for the meeting but had been delayed by a last-minute telephone call relating to Mr. Kerr's will. Any type of tardiness in her office was unacceptable and could earn a stern rebuke. The door was ajar, and she slipped in.

Seated at the large oval oak table with the calm assurance of a lawyer waiting to plead a case he had every confidence of winning was Coyle, looking modish in his Harry Rosen suit. Mary had asked him to be present for the reading of Mr. Kerr's will because she feared Courtney and Richard would not only be disappointed, but angered by it, and she was disinclined to face them alone.

"Sorry I'm late; it couldn't be helped," she offered as apology. She took her seat at the head of the table, noting that Courtney and Richard were not present. She anxiously glanced at her watch.

"Courtney and Richard are seldom on time," Coyle assured her.

Mary wondered how he knew that, then figured that people at the same echelon would have common knowledge of one another.

Patiently, they waited. Since they had already fully

discussed Mr. Kerr's will, their conversation drifted toward small talk, during which Mary struggled to suppress her anxiety.

After a full twenty minutes, Courtney arrived, wearing a striking cerise linen suit. Richard, impassive and detached, followed behind her. Mary and Coyle rose and went to greet them.

"Once again, I wish to offer my condolences," Coyle said. "Your father's death is a tremendous loss to the community. He will be greatly missed."

"Thank you," they both replied.

As Mary approached Courtney, she briefly scrutinized her former friend. What she saw disappointed her. Courtney had always been preoccupied with social status and wealth. Now, however, her expensive clothes, stylish hairdo, impeccable makeup, and beautifully manicured nails gave the impression of one who depended too much on her beauty. Everything about her was artificial. Mary suddenly felt sorry for her. Regarding her with heartfelt sympathy, she smiled consolingly. "I regret having to meet in these circumstances."

Courtney merely nodded in reply. Expecting no more from her, Mary turned and offered her hand to Richard, which he accepted with a curt smile.

Coyle was standing behind his chair, waiting for them.

Indicating the two empty chairs facing him, Mary invited Courtney and Richard to be seated. Without saying a word, Courtney settled in one chair, and Richard sat in the one beside her.

The boardroom was beautifully furnished, designed to provide a comfortable ambiance and impress the firm's clients, but today there was a stiff, eerie, almost ominous silence in the air.

Resuming her seat next to Coyle, Mary took a deep breath and let it out before addressing Courtney and Richard in a calming but determined voice. "Before he died, your father examined his life's accomplishments at length. In writing his will, he wanted to do what was best for you. Although his will remained a concern for him, it was his most fervent desire that you would understand. He insisted that I remind you of the immense love he held for you both."

Courtney and Richard exchanged glances, a blank look passing between them.

Mary opened a file and started to read:

"This is the last Will and Testament of me, Robert David Kerr, of the City of Ottawa in the County of Carleton, and Province of Ontario.

"I hereby revoke all Wills and Testamentary dispositions of every nature or kind whatsoever by me heretofore made.

"I nominated Mary Anne Clark as the sole executrix of my—"

"I suggest you skip the lawyer jargon and just say what he left us," said Richard, interrupting her.

Mary eyed him then read on, omitting nothing. She did this not to be spiteful. She did it because this is what Mr. Kerr had instructed her to do.

Throughout the reading, Courtney sighed and Richard, too, exhibited signs of boredom. Even when Mary read the part about the special trust fund their father had specifically set up for them, they evinced no reaction. It was already common knowledge, and their sole interest now was what else he had bequeathed to them.

When Mary arrived at that crucial area of the will, she paused and looked at Courtney and Richard. Her hesitation was deliberate, for she suspected the next sentence would test their devotion to their father's memory. Mary's grip tightened on her document. She was annoyed that her hands trembled as she did so. Struggling to maintain a business voice, she read on:

"Because my children are over the age of majority and are self-supporting, and because I have already made generous provisions for them, I am not leaving them anything other than the revenue created from the sale of my primary residence on Ridge Road and the special trust fund mentioned above.

"I direct my executrix to establish another trust fund to be known as the Robert Kerr Palliative Care Trust and to transfer the residue of my estate to such trust for its use totally, which residue includes all my stocks, bank accounts, and savings plan and the business that I own. My executrix is empowered to liquidate my estate or any parts thereof and provide the proceeds to the trust. I also direct my executrix to appoint one or more trustees to operate the trust and to establish its operating procedures, which will be for the benefit of residents of palliative care facilities in the Ottawa area."

The silence was so absolute that Mary thought Courtney and Richard had not comprehended her words. She was about to say something when, almost together, they stood. Courtney was the first to speak. "This is outrageous. Why on earth would my father do a thing like that?" She was not asking, she was merely brooding, looking past Mary. Already, her face had turned two shades redder than her heavy makeup. "He had to be out of his mind," she spluttered.

"At no time did my father indicate to me his intention of leaving anything to this trust…whatever you call it," Richard exclaimed, addressing Mary angrily. "He incessantly stated we were his sole beneficiaries."

"That might have been so before his illness. But when confronted with death, it seems your father saw things differently. Yet it was imperative to him that you know this was not an act against you and Courtney but a—"

"I'm not interested in your explanation. It's evident he couldn't have been in his right mind when he wrote this will. I plan to contest it. I will never—"

Coyle cut in firmly. "That is your prerogative, but his directives are all very legal."

Courtney and Richard resumed their protestation, both speaking at once.

"I've no knowledge of what you discussed with your father before he died," Mary interjected. "This will, however, does convey his last wishes."

"Not as far as I'm concerned. And I will fight it in court, if I have to." Richard's tone had become calmer, but the threat in his voice was indisputable.

Mary judged that further argument was pointless. She did not bother to reply.

This provoked an unexpected reaction from Richard. He eyed Coyle with an expression of unambiguous contempt and blurted, "How can you be part of this… this scam?"

If Coyle was disconcerted by Richard's allegation, he concealed it admirably. "I'm sorry, Richard. You state being informed by your father that you and your sister were the sole beneficiaries of his will. I've no idea what altered your father's mind. All I know is this is how your father directed Miss Clark to draw up his last will. As the firm working on behalf of your father, it's not our position to question his decision on how he chose to dispose of his assets. Notwithstanding, this will does represent his dying wishes."

Despite Coyle's words, Mary sensed what he must be thinking—that though it was not the firm's position to question their father's decision on how he chose to dispose of his assets, it had been Mary's professional responsibility, as his legal adviser, to advise Mr. Kerr on the potential problems that could arise regarding his decisions, how best to safeguard that the will be carried out, and how to avoid having it challenged successfully.

Indeed, Mary had brought up those precautionary measures with her client. She had even recommended he put conditions in the will that in the event the will was contested, the bequests to his children be conditional on their acceptance. Failing that, all his assets would then be donated to the trust fund or a named charity. She had stressed to Mr. Kerr that this might not prevent his children from challenging his will, but it would up the ante if they did. But for reasons of his own, he had declined to act on her advice. Possibly because—as much evidence as there was to the contrary—he wanted to believe his children would not challenge his will.

By that time, Mary had realized his will was taking a dangerous route and had insisted that Coyle be brought into the picture. But Mr. Kerr had been adamant. "I beg you not to do that. This has to be between you and me." And once more, she had allowed her deference to him to override her better judgment.

Richard bristled. "Well, we'll see about that." His eyes smoldering, he stormed out of the room, the sound of Courtney's heels echoing as she followed behind him.

Coyle remained seated, and Mary allowed a long silence to stretch out. "Regardless of my misgivings, I had hoped for a different scenario," she admitted at last.

"It was inevitable," he replied.

"What do you think will happen now?"

"Legally, Courtney and Richard have a first claim on the estate, as children of the deceased. They will undoubtedly contest the will."

"What are their chances of winning, if they do?"

"With these cases, one can never tell. They will almost certainly attack it on the ground of mental capacity. If so, it's up to you to uphold its validity by proving beyond a shadow of a doubt that Mr. Kerr was mentally capable. I wouldn't worry too much about it. I've read the will. Thanks to your efficiency it's solid, and I'm confident it will stand up to challenges in court. I must caution you, however, that with a good lawyer any will can be shot to pieces."

Mary frowned. "How reassuring."

"One more thing," he said. "While Mr. Kerr was in the hospital, did you ever have him mentally assessed?"

"No. I didn't. Should I have?"

"Considering the people you were dealing with, it might have been advisable."

"I didn't have him assessed because I was firmly convinced he was mentally competent and acting according to his own wishes. His own physician, Dr. Hereford, and Elaine Travis, head of the recovery room unit at the hospital, acted as witnesses to his will."

Mary intuited that Coyle had hoped for a different answer. His response confirmed it. "In order to get the will declared by the court to be legitimate, Dr. Hereford and Elaine Travis would have to swear under oath in an affidavit of execution that they were witnesses to Mr. Kerr's will and that Mr. Kerr and the witnesses were all present and all watched each other sign. But that doesn't necessarily indicate that Mr. Kerr was rational and perfectly sound when he wrote it. I appreciate it is not common practice for a lawyer to have someone mentally assessed by a medical doctor prior to making out a will. The norm is to presume the person is competent unless there are signs to the contrary. But in this case, where Mr. Kerr was sick and not in the best frame of mind—perhaps because of the drugs he was on—you might have taken the precaution of asking a medical doctor or an independent party to speak with Mr. Kerr to satisfy yourself he was competent and lucid and therefore capable of making out his will."

Before Coyle was finished speaking, Mary realized she had committed a grave error. A crafty lawyer, privy to the family dynamics and anticipating the will to be contested, would have requested the testator be assessed. Flushed, she said, "I deeply regret that oversight. I should have foreseen this."

"Hindsight is a wonderful perception, Miss Clark," Coyle said soothingly. "I've reverted to it myself. Let's see what happens. As I stated earlier, the will is solid, so that should prove to your advantage."

Mary nodded hopefully, but inside she knew better. She murmured a vague reply and rose to leave.

Gently closing the door behind her, she reflected on Coyle's question. A chill raced over her skin. She had made a grievous error in judgment in not having Mr. Kerr mentally accessed or, at least, having an impartial party speak to him. Coyle may well have berated her for overlooking that logistical detail, but he had not. Actually, he had been more forgiving than she deserved, and that bothered her. Yet there was nothing he could have stated that she was not now tormenting herself with. Why had she not considered requesting a mental assessment for Mr. Kerr? Could it be that, subconsciously, she had feared affronting him? Clearly, she lacked the hard-heartedness her work sometimes demanded. And in her profession, that was a liability.

Mary was filled with trepidation throughout the week that followed. She was certain that Courtney and Richard were going to challenge their father's will, and she dreaded the confrontation that would ensue. She worried about everything, especially the lawyer they would have representing them. And for the first time since taking on the management of Mr. Kerr's estate, she recognized, with foreboding, her own inexperience and vulnerability. When she arrived home from work on Friday, her head was buzzing.

The phone rang. She was tempted not to answer, but she picked up the receiver just as she thought the call would ring out.

"Mary?"

"Peter!" she exclaimed, warmed by the sound of his voice.

"Mary, where have you been? I've been calling for the last hour. Have you forgotten Mother's reception this evening?"

"Oh Peter, I had such a wretched day at work, it completely slipped my mind."

"Well, we can't miss it. Mother has been planning it for weeks."

"Of course not! I'll be ready when you get here."

"Fine. I'll be there in half an hour."

Mary rushed to her bedroom. She could not believe she

had let Mrs. Burbidge's reception slip her mind. *What will she think of me?*

Shortly after Peter had revealed their engagement to his parents back in January, he had reserved a table at Wilfrid's Restaurant in Ottawa's premier hotel, the Château Laurier, deeming it a fitting place to introduce them to her. It was there that Mrs. Burbidge had proposed a formal reception to celebrate their engagement sometime in late June when her garden would be in full bloom. "It'll be another opportunity for us to get better acquainted, my dear," she had said. "We won't likely see you before then. We will be in Europe until the spring. Peter just caught us before our departure."

Peter had told Mary that ever since his parents' honeymoon in Lisbon, Portugal, they had developed a tradition of jetting off to Europe every year to escape the harsh winters in Ottawa.

So, Mary had graciously replied to Mrs. Burbidge that she looked forward to the event but was taken aback when Peter's mother added, "And would you mind terribly keeping the engagement strictly hush-hush, so it can be announced properly at the reception?"

Peter had often talked about his mother's formal garden, and Mary could understand why Mrs. Burbidge would want to delay the reception until it was at its best. But she couldn't understand why they should keep their engagement a secret. She had looked at Peter, expecting him to object, but all he did was nod and smile, while his mother continued, "Such a lovely ring my son has chosen for you, but it would be best if you didn't wear it until the night of the reception." Mary could barely disguise her shock as she once again looked to Peter for an objection, only to be disappointed.

She had been surprised by Peter's subservient nature toward his mother and had expressed this to Rachel, to whom she decided to confide, despite Mrs. Burbidge's request for secrecy. According to her friend's assessment, Mrs. Burbidge was so domineering that Mary should not be at all surprised by Peter's behaviour.

This was not something Mary wanted to dwell on, so she quickly discarded the thought and rushed to get ready. There was no time for a shower, so she freshened up and slipped into the first suitable outfit she found, a simple black cocktail dress, which she decorated with a single strand of pearls.

Half an hour after his telephone call, Peter drove up to the entrance of Mary's apartment building. She was waiting for him in the lobby and hurried to the car as it pulled up against the curb. "Sorry, Peter," she said, sliding into the passenger seat beside him.

"No need to worry." He smiled down at her and added, "Have I mentioned lately how beautiful you are?"

"Every day." She smiled back at him. He, too, was strikingly good-looking, six feet tall with light blond hair and captivating blue eyes.

Peter headed northeast. As she thought about the evening ahead, Mary realized with a start that in the rush, she had forgotten to put on her engagement ring. It had been so long since she had worn it that it had completely slipped her mind. Hoping Peter would not notice, she remained silent, directing her attention to the road.

They had just passed the prime minister's residence at 24 Sussex Drive and the massive gate marking the entrance to Rideau Hall, the Governor General's residence, when he asked, "How are things going with Mr. Kerr's last will?"

"Honestly, I'd rather not talk about it." Peter knew that Mary never discussed the details of her work, but they would typically share with one another how things were going, in general.

"It's just that Courtney and Richard Kerr were in our office this week to see Mr. Beasley. I found that rather strange."

Mary stared at him as the terrible reality of his words hit her. They were contesting the will. Panic swept over her, a temporary paralyzing fear for herself and the threat such a suit would mean for Mr. Kerr's wishes.

After she failed to respond, Peter asked, "Are you all right?"

She gathered herself and tried to sound reassuring. "Of course. Why do you ask?"

"You've become very quiet all of a sudden."

"It's been a long day, and I just needed a few moments of calm before the reception."

By then they had reached the opulent borough of Rockcliffe Park, the exclusive neighbourhood where the upper crust and the well-heeled business tycoons of Ottawa lived and the location of the school Mary had attended with Courtney. An address many would like to have but few could afford. The motto on its coat of arms is *Inter Arboribus Floremus*—amidst the trees we flourish. Characterized by its parklike setting with mature trees, generous lots and gardens, and houses set within a rich green landscape, it was a place people would visit just to admire.

They came to two high, ornamental iron gates, both open, and Peter made his way through the wide entryway and proceeded along a broad tarmac drive with luxury cars lined up along the lane. And, suddenly, the house was in front of them. The alarm in her mind was dispelled as Mary stared in pure astonishment at the building. Peter seldom spoke about his father, other than to say that he worked in real estate, but through her co-workers she learned that Mr. Burbidge had made a fortune. Mary had imagined that the Burbidges would have an imposing home, but the palatial house amidst its well-tended garden and neat surrounding lawns exceeded her expectations. Evidently, Mr. Burbidge's success as a real estate developer was substantial. As they drove up to the front entrance, Mary glanced at the mirror on her side of the car to guarantee her hair was in place.

"Nervous?" Peter asked, grinning.

"A little."

"Don't worry. You'll knock everyone off their feet."

Mary looked at him with a renewed surge of love and wonderment as he manoeuvred the car around the other vehicles. How caring and sensitive he was. When she was with him, she felt unique and beautiful and cherished. And at moments like these, she was reminded again of her good fortune for being selected over all the other women in his circle of friends. Many had sought his attention, yet he had chosen her.

Peter parked in the reserved area in the forecourt of the building and stepped out of the car. In his customary courteous style, he went to her side and opened the door for her. And together, her arm tucked gently into his, they walked toward the magnificent front door.

The house was already crowded with guests. All were in formal attire, the ladies radiant in clothing from the pages of a fashion magazine. For a brief second, Mary wished she had taken more time dressing for the occasion. But it was too late to do anything about it, and she dismissed the thought as Peter escorted her nimbly through the crowd, introducing her as he went along.

A young woman in a black dress and white apron came to meet them. "Good evening, Mr. Burbidge."

"Good evening, Maria. Are Mother and Father around?"

"You're most likely to find them in the south parlour, Mr. Burbidge."

"Thank you, Maria." Without speaking another word, Peter continued to lead Mary through the crowd to the southern end of the house. As they entered the parlour, he waved to his mother, who was surrounded by guests. "There she is. And Dad is with her. Super!"

Peter's mother acknowledged his signal and unhurriedly made her way over to where they were standing, her husband following behind. Mrs. Burbidge was a handsome woman, not what one would call beautiful, but she radiated poise and self-assurance—a woman entirely comfortable in her milieu. She had dark grey hair with a touch of white in the front. Considerably taller than her husband, she presented an imposing figure.

"Welcome, my dear!" she said to Mary. "You will forgive me for not being at the door to receive you into our home properly, but you and Peter are late arriving, and I had guests to attend to." Mrs. Burbidge was smiling broadly, but the words *late arriving* were grudging and her air reproving.

"Unfortunately, Mother, it was unavoidable."

Mrs. Burbidge's face gave a twitch of impatience. Then, giving Mary a listless look, she turned to her son. "Peter, dear, I have a delightful surprise for you."

"Oh?" he said, blank-faced.

"Guess who arrived in the city this week, back from Paris?" Without waiting for an answer, Mrs. Burbidge called out to a young lady engaged in conversation with several other guests. "Daphne, do come over, please."

Mary glanced at Peter and noticed him go tense. She followed his gaze and saw coming their way a tall, attractive woman in a flowing gold and blue gown and lighter coloured shoes that complemented it beautifully. Around her neck was a string of pearls, and her earrings were pearl, too. Mary had seldom seen an ensemble so elegant and so sensual at the same time. The woman moved gracefully through the room, ignoring everyone except Peter, whom she embraced. "Peter, darling, I could hardly wait to see you again."

Peter gave an odd little laugh that Mary found surprising and misplaced. "It's nice to see you too, Daphne. It's been a long time. Are you here for a visit?"

"No, I've had my fill of travelling. I've decided to come home to stay."

Ignoring Mary, as if she were an insignificant guest, Daphne went on, "And how have you been, Peter?"

It made Mary slightly self-conscious. She also felt an instinctive antipathy toward Daphne, which surprised her. Nobody had ever provoked in her such an instantaneous negative reaction.

Peter turned to her. "Mary, allow me to introduce Daphne, a childhood friend," he said with heightened colour.

Daphne cast a disparaging glance over Mary, then offered her hand. "I've been looking forward to meeting you all evening." The words were uttered softly, but there was a definite aloofness in her voice.

Before Mary could reply, however, Daphne was once more facing Peter. "Oh, it's so good to be back!"

Peter appeared both hapless and disconcerted, seeming not to know where to direct his eyes.

With a proprietorial gesture, Daphne interlocked her arm into his. "Peter, darling, there's someone I'm dying for you to meet." Redirecting her attention to Mary, she asked, "Do you mind if I take him away from you?"

Mary knew Peter had no choice but to go along, but she could not help wondering if there was perhaps a double meaning to Daphne's last comment.

"They were always so very close," Mrs. Burbidge said as she watched them walk away.

Mary's eyes lingered on them, and she did not respond.

All this time, Mr. Burbidge had remained silent, but when Mary turned his way he smiled, a kind smile, full of sincerity. Mary marvelled at the resemblance between father and son. At sixty Mr. Burbidge still had a trace of blond hair among the white. His blue eyes gave her the impression he was uncomfortable with his present situation, but he was discernibly content to let his wife have her way.

As the evening pressed on, nothing about it turned out as Mary had anticipated or hoped for. By the time she had met most of the guests, she was drained and was fighting a migraine. The conversation about money and power—who had it and who did not—was suffocating, and she was impatient to leave. During her limited time with Peter's mother that evening, Mrs. Burbidge's non-verbal communication made it clear that she regarded her son's involvement with her, a woman from the middle class, to be incompatible with their social position. This explained the coldness Mary had detected at their first meeting.

Most of the evening, except for that brief episode with Daphne, Peter had stayed faithfully at Mary's side, introducing her to people he knew, but when the guests began to leave, she suddenly became aware that he was no longer in sight. She went looking for him in the south parlour and in the main reception room, but he was nowhere to be found. She accepted another glass of champagne from one of the servers and then worked her way around the drawing room, hoping to find him, but to no avail. With no place else to go, she joined three sophisticated looking ladies who were chatting amiably on the opposite side of the room. They greeted her then prattled away as if she were not present.

"I was absolutely furious," exclaimed the one with the stern face.

"So, what did you do?" inquired her companion.

"Well, what could I do? In no uncertain terms, I told

this lowly nitwit that she had had no business talking to me disrespectfully and that I would report her to her superiors."

"Good for you," replied the other. "That's exactly what I would've done. Imagine the impertinence of that sales clerk. It's a shame how some people are not taught better manners."

"What else can you expect from people like that?" acknowledged the third.

Feeling both awkward and mildly amused by their self-importance and ignorance, Mary excused herself, put her glass down on a side table, and moved away. Not long after, she sighted Peter coming out of the library.

Upon seeing her, he smiled. "Oh, there you are, Mary! I was just coming out to get you."

Behind him was a tall, lean man dressed elegantly in a dark suit and blue tie whom Mary recognized as the senior partner of Beasley, Grant & Skelhorn, the law firm Peter worked for. Peter had introduced her to him at office parties held at the Rideau Club. Despite his flawless smile and charming demeanour, her dislike of him had been immediate. In her opinion, he was an ambitious man who, despite outward appearances, had never learned to discipline his prejudices against women lawyers.

"I believe you have already met Mr. Beasley," Peter said.

A benevolent smile extended across Mr. Beasley's face as he extended his hand. "It's indeed a repeated pleasure, Miss Clark."

Mary accepted his hand. "How do you do, Mr. Beasley?"

To forestall any further conversation, she turned to Peter. "I came to get you so we can say good night to your parents before leaving."

"Of course, Mary." He then addressed his employer. "Will you excuse us, Mr. Beasley?"

"By all means," he replied. With what Mary interpreted as feigned regret, he excused himself and departed.

When they found his parents, Mrs. Burbidge exclaimed, "Oh, surely you're not leaving? Mary, my dear, you've just arrived and haven't seen my garden yet. Why don't you let me show it to you while Peter gets his father a drink?"

Mary stared at Peter, imploring him to decline. But he didn't. "Mother does have a beautiful garden. You'll be quite impressed by it," he mumbled sheepishly.

When she gave him a chiding look, he checked his watch. "It's ten o'clock. Another half-hour won't make much difference."

Mrs. Burbidge took Mary by the arm and led her away, saying, "Come along, my dear." Her tone was distinctively polite, but Mary could hear how specious it sounded. Obviously, Peter's mother had something else reserved for her. As they walked into the garden, she was filled with foreboding that her silent fears about Mrs. Burbidge were about to be realized. She was right. Once outside the hearing range of her son and husband, Mrs. Burbidge swung round to face Mary, her exuberance gone. Her eyes were cold and unwavering. "You may as well know that my husband and I highly disapprove of your engagement to our son." Her words came out hard and unfeeling, leaving no possibility of misinterpretation. "We have high hopes for Peter's future and have never given up on the idea that he and Daphne will marry someday. They grew up together and are kindred. Being a lawyer, you have to recognize how partnerships are attained in big law firms. Daphne comes from a prestigious family, and a person with her background can help promote his career. You, Mary, are an insubstantial person with no social status whatsoever and can only hinder it."

Despite her presentiment, Mary was shaken. How does one react to such blatant rudeness and inflated impression of self-importance? It was natural for a mother to have reservations about a future daughter-in-law, and Mary had anticipated concern, dislike, jealousy even—but not this.

"Mary!"

Numb with disbelief, it took a moment for her to register Peter's voice. "Dad wasn't all that keen about a drink, so we decided to join you."

Grateful for the interruption, Mary fought to regain her sang-froid. She mustered a smile, not wanting Peter or his father to suspect something was amiss. "In that case, we better leave," she replied almost in a whisper. "It's late, and I have an early commitment tomorrow that requires preparation."

"But we've yet to make the formal announcement of your engagement," Peter's father interjected, his voice filled with disappointment.

Mrs. Burbidge's voice rose sweetly, "How unfortunate that you have to go, just when we were finally getting acquainted. It has been such a pleasure having you here with us this evening, my dear."

Mary resisted the temptation to expose the hateful hypocrisy of this woman and instead responded with false amiability, "Thank you. It's an equal pleasure to be with people who have the enormous capacity to make others feel welcome."

Mrs. Burbidge glared at her in hostile silence.

Had Mary been more prudent, she would have recognized that making an enemy of Peter's mother could mean family suicide. Right then, however, her annoyance overrode anything else she felt, and she was beyond caring.

eter and Mary were both silent on their way to the car. Once inside, Mary settled back in her seat, closed her eyes, and mulled over her altercation with Peter's mother. She felt that the new life she was stepping into was hostile, insecure—not the happy family she had envisaged. *That woman is utterly ruthless.*

It had taken everything in her power not to let her irritation burst out during her confrontation with Mrs. Burbidge. Now the immensity of her anger over his mother's arrogance overwhelmed her. Anger that, for the present, had no outlet. She would speak to Peter about the mishap, but not yet. It would have to wait for her to regain a measure of calm.

Instead, she said, "Tell me about Daphne and her family."

Peter appeared taken aback by her inquiry but answered, "Her father is a senator and a friend of Prime Minister Pearson. Her mother is retired now but was a concert pianist; she toured extensively throughout North America, Asia, and Europe, performing in places like Carnegie Hall and the Lincoln Center."

"What about Daphne?"

"She's a childhood friend, nothing more."

From Mary's perspective, Daphne's comportment hinted at intimacy more than friendship. Since Peter was clearly disinclined to offer more enlightenment, she became quiet and peered outside the car window as he made his way through the city. Her face stayed passive, but inside she was fighting growing pangs of frustration, and all she could think about was getting home.

Peter must have sensed she was not in her normal state. "What is it, Mary? Have I offended you in any way?"

It was more what he had not related. But with no appropriate response, she remained silent.

"Did Mother say anything to upset you?"

"I'm just a little weary," she replied. "It's been a long day."

Peter was apparently disinclined to let the subject drop. "I know Mother can be demanding at times. And as for this evening, I had no previous knowledge that Daphne would be there. That was Mother's idea. She's always trying to get us together." He again glanced at her, his expression sincere. "You have nothing to worry about there. It's you I love, you I wish to spend my life with."

Mary remained silent, and a few minutes later, Peter pulled up to her apartment. He stopped the car but made no move to switch off the ignition.

"Would you like to come up for a drink?" she asked. Despite her conflicted feelings, she was unwilling to let him go just yet. There were too many unanswered questions.

"What about that urgent work-related matter you mentioned at the house?" he asked, unaware that Mary had made up the excuse in order to leave.

"Just a quick one, if you don't mind," she replied.

"Not at all," he answered, and she opened the car door to let herself out. "I'll be up as soon as I park."

"See you shortly then," she replied. She headed inside, and minutes later Peter entered her flat. Mary could hear him from the kitchen and called out, "I'm just getting some ice. Please make yourself comfortable."

There was a long silence before he answered, "Fine. I will." His voice sounded less animated than usual.

"Is something wrong?" she asked.

Again, there was a long silence, and she thought maybe he hadn't heard her. Then he said, "Mary, I hate to do this, but would you mind if I took a rain check on that drink? I didn't realize how tired I was."

Mary had hoped to take advantage of their time together to bring up her brief skirmish with his mother but decided it could wait for another time. She left the kitchen and walked up to him.

Gathering her into his arms, he kissed her—a long sensual kiss. He gently released her and murmured, "I love you so much. No man can love a woman as much as I love you." He caressed her hair lightly, sweeping it from her eyes, and she buried her face into his shoulder. Her heart swelled as his lips brushed her forehead. It was a moment of supreme happiness, and she did not wish it to end.

Her heart sank when he whispered gently into her hair, "Forgive me, Mary, but I really should be going."

Pulling away from him, she tried to inject lightness in her voice. "Good night then. See you tomorrow at La Roma?" They had a standing weekly lunch date at the family-owned and operated restaurant on Preston Street in Ottawa's Little Italy, their favourite meeting place.

"Sure thing," he said as he brushed past her to collect his trench coat, which was draped on the sofa. He tucked it securely under his arm then kissed her lightly on the cheek before heading out the door.

Leaning back against her pillow that night, Mary reviewed the events at the reception. She could not dismiss Mrs. Burbidge's words to her, about Daphne's "prestigious" family and her own complete lack of "social status." Mary had been hurt by them. Perhaps because they were undeniably true.

She was aware of the workings of large, prestigious firms and understood that partnerships were primarily given to male lawyers—those who could bring in clients. Some lawyers, who were prodigiously talented, could build a substantial client base through their professional success. Coyle was one of these. He had established a reputation for his expertise in criminal law and had yet to lose a case. But more frequently, clients were attained through social contacts. It was a matter of whom you knew. Consequently, a young lawyer from a rich and high-ranking family would be given preference and be hired by a firm because of the clients he might attract. Peter was obsessed with becoming partner in his firm. Mary loved him dearly but recognized he could never make partner on merit alone.

Her mind dwelled on Peter's disappearance at the reception, during which time he had been in the library with Mr. Beasley. Before finally falling asleep, she was plagued by questions: *Did their meeting in the library have anything to do with Courtney and Richard's presence in their office? Why involve Peter? What could he possibly do for Courtney and Richard?*

It was well past mid-morning when Mary left her apartment for work the following Monday. She was troubled, for she had spent the last hour searching for her briefcase with no result. Already late, she hurried to the parking lot, hoping perhaps it was in her car, though she seriously doubted it. Upon a quick inspection, however, there was no sign of it. Frustrated, she sat herself behind the steering wheel and hurriedly drove to work, hoping to find it there.

Once in her cubicle, she combed the entire space, but her briefcase was nowhere to be found. She collapsed into her seat and tried to convince herself that it had merely been misplaced, then tried desperately to remember all the feasible places it could be. Definitely not in Peter's car, because she had made it home on Friday before joining him. It had to be in her apartment. She would search more closely that evening. With that thought, she turned her gaze to her desk. Today's mail had already arrived, and she decided to sort through her correspondence. One, especially, caught her eye.

Five minutes later, she was standing at the entrance of Coyle's office.

"Mr. Coyle, I find myself in need of your assistance."

"Oh, how may I be of service to you?"

She withdrew several documents from her folder and handed them to him. "It appears that Courtney and Richard have already commenced legal action against the estate."

Before she could say anything else, he hit the intercom button.

"Yes?" came Kate's voice from the other end.

"Miss Donovan, please hold my calls for the time being, will you?"

"As you wish, Mr. Coyle."

He motioned to Mary to be seated and then briefly examined the papers.

"As you can see, I've already been served," Mary said.

"I expected as much," he replied. "They haven't wasted any time, have they?" There was a moment of silence while he glanced through the documents from Courtney and Richard's lawyer, contesting their father's will.

"They've come forward with allegations of testamentary incapacity and accuse me of exerting undue influence to benefit from the estate," Mary said. "It's not true, of course. Not even remotely."

"Their reaction is standard," Coyle replied. "To void the will, they're accusing you, but it's our firm they will be attacking."

Mary immediately understood the message Coyle was sending. Courtney and Richard would argue she, as the adviser for Woodbury & McLeod, had lured Mr. Kerr to create the trust fund, allowing the firm to profit from managing the charity after he died. She remembered Mr. McLeod's words booming out from behind the conference room's door and recognized the harm such allegations would have on the firm. She was well aware of her employer's negative attitude toward her as Mr. Kerr's estate lawyer, and she knew this Notice of Objection would undoubtedly further his low opinion of her competence. She felt compelled to say, "Their allegations are entirely false."

"They're desperate and are willing to say anything that will favour themselves in the eyes of justice," Coyle said. "Similar claims in the past have proven effective in court."

"So, you believe they have a case here?"

"It's achievable, yes. Any good lawyer can make one."

He placed the documents on his desk and pointed to the date on the accompanying letter. "They're acting swiftly on this matter and are utilizing their top guns, Beasley, Grant & Skelhorn. It's my belief they hope to catch you unprepared or will try to intimidate you—conceivably both."

Mary thought that on the latter, especially, they had succeeded extremely well. A nervous laugh escaped her lips. "I've studied these issues and am familiar with the procedure. Only now, with those words directed at me, they take on a more threatening meaning."

"In general, executors are not liable, personally, for the debts of the estate," stated Coyle, sympathetically. "But if the children can prove you misused assets or acted in an improper manner, you could be held responsible."

"I recognize that," Mary answered quickly. "I guess I feel more disillusioned than anything. It's disheartening for me to think they would willingly dishonour their father's memory like this over money. Mr. Kerr was rational and completely sound. And they know it."

"I appreciate that fact should be important," Coyle acknowledged, "but it isn't. Unfortunately, in litigation, even the truest intentions can be defeated by a court decision."

"Have you any recommendations for me?" Mary asked.

"As I mentioned to you at our last meeting, Mr. Kerr's will is solid. But when dealing with family contesting a will, it's not always that cut and dried. I see several noteworthy possibilities here. If this ever gets to court, I'm afraid you may be in for a long, expensive litigation. Even though the will is perspicuously defined, it's possible that Courtney and Richard will get something out of it in suing. Therefore, you may wish to compromise and subscribe to a fair settlement, now, before it ever comes to that." He stopped to ponder his words and then gazed at her gravely. "Another reason you want to avoid a trial is that these cases tend to carry a lot of bad publicity with them. And Mr. McLeod will most certainly be averse to that."

"I admit mediation is at times advisable," she replied, "but Mr. Kerr was adamant that his will stand as written. He hoped differently but anticipated that his children would contest it. For that reason, he specifically put in conditions that his estate defend the will. It entitles me to fees from the estate in my exercise to do so."

"A definite deterrent to the beneficiaries litigating," Coyle commented. Without saying another word, he rose from his chair and walked to his bookshelves. He studied the covers of several volumes before he pulled out one. Mary recognized it: *The Canadian Law of Wills: Probate*, by Thomas G. Feeney. Coyle sifted through it until he found what he was searching for. Turning, he read: "To quote the Supreme Court of Canada, where evidence [of insanity] has been given, even though not conclusive or not preponderant, a jury, if there is one, must be directed that if their minds are left in doubt they must find against the validity of the will."

Coyle looked at Mary. "If Courtney and Richard cast doubt on their father's sanity, it is up to you to extract that doubt. In your testimony, you, as executrix, must produce evidence to show that Mr. Kerr was mentally competent. On the allegation of undue influence, however, they must prove the will was a result of undue influence and does not reflect their father's wishes. This would mean Mr. Kerr's mind was besieged by pressure exerted by you. In that case, it's insufficient to show mere persuasion. Courtney and Richard's lawyer would have to prove your undue influence amounted to coercion. I needn't define that word for you."

"No," Mary replied. That word resonated deep within her. She had heard the definition innumerable times in law school and could almost hear her professor instructing them: *Coercion has been defined to mean that the testator has been put under such condition of mind that if he could speak his wishes to the last he would say, "this is not my wish but I must do it."* Mary exhaled a long breath, then went on, "But the burden of proof of undue influence is on Courtney and Richard. They would have to prove that. And this is a difficult allegation to prove."

"Precisely." Coyle returned the book to the shelf, walked over to his desk, and picked up the papers. He silently scrutinized them for a moment and added, "With Beasley, Grant & Skelhorn representing them, that would be a minor thing. They're not to be taken lightly."

"I'm of the same opinion."

"All you can do right now is start preparing your defence against their actions," advised Coyle. "Get all of your evidence in order and develop your approach. I also propose that you brush up on the Ontario Probate Law and Procedure."

"Consider it a *fait accompli*."

Once more he examined the document, then said, "After you've had a chance to work on the file, I will want to revisit it in detail with you. Let's meet here…let's see, today is Monday…say, Wednesday morning at ten o'clock."

Mary nodded her gratitude.

As she was leaving, he signalled for her attention. "One other thing, it would be advisable for you to get in touch with the witnesses to the will. Who are they?"

"Elaine Travis, she's head of the recovery room unit at the hospital, and Dr. Hereford, Mr. Kerr's personal physician."

"Oh yes, I remember now. Well, you would be well advised to reach these people and inform them that they may be required to speak on Mr. Kerr's behalf."

"I will attend to it today."

"Do you have any further questions for me?" he asked, handing over her documents. "Is there anything else I should know?"

She could think of several things but could not bring herself to voice them. Instead, she shook her head. "No, I believe we've addressed all we can for the moment." Afraid he might notice the tension that had been steadily building up inside her, she quickly vacated the room.

Wednesday morning Mary was at her desk, preparing for her appointment with Coyle. Her concern over her missing briefcase had become alarm, then panic. After having searched for it in every conceivable spot—at home, in her car and office—she had to concede it was lost. But another more distressing possibility was that it had been stolen, along with the papers she had placed in it—papers she had intended to secure in the safety deposit box she had purchased. She closed her eyes. Even as she struggled to reject that thought, she knew that she would not see her briefcase again. This alarmed her beyond any presentiment she had ever known, for the papers inside were never meant for public scrutiny and could be disastrous if the wrong people were to access them.

The phone rang. Pushing her trepidations aside, she picked up the receiver.

It was Mr. McLeod's secretary. "You're wanted in Mr. McLeod's office immediately."

Mary's pulse quickened. "May I ask what for?"

"Just come," Miss Williams said, in her usual professional voice.

Fear swept through Mary as she hurried toward the executive suite. A summons to Mr. McLeod's office was not a good thing for a junior employee; it had to be nothing less than a crisis, carrying unfavourable implications for her.

A knot had formed in Mary's stomach by the time she reached the desk of Miss Williams, a stately woman in her late forties with grey hair and a no-nonsense demeanour. The secretary inclined her head toward the door of the connecting room. "You may go in, Miss Clark. They're expecting you."

They? questioned Mary silently. She paused nervously outside the huge oak door. Then, taking a deep breath, she threw back her shoulders, gave a perfunctory knock, and walked inside.

Mr. McLeod's spacious office was unlike any other on the floor. The large windows had a street view, and the walls were covered with framed certificates and photos of McLeod posing smarmily with local dignities and politicians.

Mary was surprised to see Coyle, who rose from his chair to greet her. There was something troubling about his smile that she could not place, and that sent a jolt of disquiet through her. Acknowledging his greeting, she made her way to the chair in front of Mr. McLeod's desk and sat down to prevent her legs from buckling under her.

Projecting authority across the desk was the Beast—the nickname bestowed upon Mr. McLeod by junior employees. With his dark eyes pinned on her like a raging bull, she could sense the hackles rise on the back of his neck.

"Good morning, Mr. McLeod," she greeted him.

He did not answer. He simply shifted in his chair and grunted, his huge-knuckled hands clasped on his desk.

She was frightened but, determined not to show it, she took time to glance around the room. Mr. Woodbury, the senior partner, was seated at a comfortable distance. He was an amenable man in his sixties, who steadily showed courtesy to his employees and spoke to them as responsible adults—he was not scornful and condescending like Mr. McLeod. Forever formal, Mr. Woodbury stood briefly to acknowledge her. "Good morning, Miss Clark. It's always a pleasure meeting you."

"And you, too, Mr. Woodbury," she replied mechanically, with a warm tone to her voice that was out of character with how she felt. Anticipating the worst, she sat erect, her gaze resolutely forward.

Mr. McLeod's glacial, combative eyes remained fixed on her. Then he opened a file lying in front of him and extracted what appeared to be a letter. "What in the hell is this all about?" he demanded, throwing it across the desk.

Mary picked up the paper and scanned it with growing apprehension. Her entire body stiffened as she read the letter of intent from Beasley, Grant & Skelhorn, accusing her of fraud in dealing with the Kerr estate.

"Their allegations are totally unfounded," she exclaimed.

Staring one more time at the document, another disheartening thought occurred to her. *Is Peter aware of this?*

"I'm confident that you can clarify everything," Mr. Woodbury intervened softly.

"She damn well better," snorted McLeod.

Mary felt under attack and glanced at Coyle to see his reaction.

"Mary," he said, calling her by her Christian name for the first time, "there's apparently an issue over a music box. At a recent meeting with Mr. McLeod, Ralph Beasley, Courtney and Richard's lawyer, claimed that his clients knew nothing about it when they consented to return Mrs. Kerr's trunk to her family—that you manipulated them into believing the contents inside were nugatory."

"That's an absolute falsehood," she protested. "I specifically remember suggesting they keep Eugenie's music box as a memento. It was they who deemed it worthless."

"It appears they have evidence that would indicate otherwise," Coyle said with characteristic openness.

McLeod took out another document from the same folder and slid it toward her. "Can you explain to me why this information was never revealed to us or to Courtney and Richard Kerr?"

Once more, Mary picked up the document offered to her. It was an appraisal sheet for a music box of Russian origin valued at three million dollars, a copy of the document she had elicited from an appraisal company prior to Mr. Kerr's death. Her mind started to race. *How did they get hold of this? Certainly not from the appraisal company.* Panic spread through Mary's body as she remembered her missing briefcase. She opened her mouth to speak, but nothing came out.

"Were you aware this music box was worth three million dollars?" demanded McLeod.

"Yes."

"Yet you told no one about it?"

"Mr. Kerr wanted it that way. He insisted it be returned to Eugenie's family along with the trunk."

"And where is this music box now?"

"In a safety deposit box in my apartment." Recognizing the gravity of her situation, she attempted to explain. "I only learned about the value of the music box after meeting with Courtney and Richard. I did inform Mr. Kerr. I assure you, I—"

"Surely you don't expect us to believe that, do you?" McLeod broke in. "Robert was too much of a businessman to do something so irrational. Why would he release it if he knew it was worth three million dollars? His children have already pointed out to Beasley there was no great love between their father and their stepmother."

"I can't explain the motivation behind his decision. We never got into that. But with the approach of death, one loses the taste for material things."

McLeod looked at her, wide-eyed. It was plain to see that her explanation held little relevance to the matter in question.

She tried to elaborate. "It could equally be an atonement toward his late wife, Eugenie, a form of penance for his and her stepchildren's ill treatment of her. Mr. Kerr did speak of a few regrets near the end. All I know is that when he did decide to release the trunk to Eugenie's family, he insisted that I not inform his children about the value of the music box. He also instructed me to excise all evidence of the music box from his file."

"Why all this secrecy?"

"He stated that any knowledge of it would only add to their displeasure. By removing it from the file, it would alleviate the risk of them finding out about it."

McLeod leaned forward. "His children have an alternate explanation. They claim you purposely withheld evidence of the music box principally because you planned to keep it for yourself."

Mary could not disguise her shock. She shook her head in disbelief. She turned to Coyle and said, "Surely you don't believe that?"

"Mary, what I believe is immaterial. What is essential here is what proof you have to support what you're saying."

A wave of anxiety swept over her. "None, I'm afraid. The only proof I have is in some legal documents, which have disappeared with my briefcase."

"Most unfortunate," McLeod grumbled.

Mary was too numb to speak. She listened as Coyle challenged her employer. "With all due respect, Henry, I wonder at the wisdom of rushing prematurely to a verdict. Miss Clark has been an employee here long enough for you to recognize her integrity."

"Whether I believe her guilty or not is beside the point. The fact is Robert's children can sue her and our firm for wrongly administering the affairs of their deceased father's estate. We're talking fraud here, and this can be a prolonged and costly exercise. Fortunately, Courtney and Richard have offered to settle these discrepancies quietly and are willing to avert court proceedings if we turn over the music box and consent not to fight them when they contest the will." McLeod paused briefly before addressing Mary directly. "I think we can appreciate the corrosive publicity this would bring our firm if this issue of the music box ever came out in court. Therefore, I've already informed their lawyer that we accept their offer."

That they had acted on this matter as if she were of no consequence aroused in Mary an indignation so intense that she had to struggle to maintain a respectful voice. "You mean that you and they have decided this without consulting me?"

"Young lady, this is not your decision to make. It's mine," McLeod snapped, flicking his hand out. He glared at her. "You've already undermined our firm, and I'm not going to let an upstart junior employee drag our name through the local papers or let us be publicly embarrassed because of your incompetence and possible unethical conduct. Do I make myself clear?"

Before Mary could even consider the impact of her words, she blurted, "Yes, I hear you but can't believe you're doing this. I've been loyal to this office, but your concern over image rather than the rights of the client makes me question that loyalty. For your information, my primary duty as a lawyer has always been to serve the best interest of my client." Mary's voice became stronger as she spoke. "Let me tell you something else, Mr. McLeod. Mr. Kerr was not only my client, but a dear friend. And if Courtney and Richard think I'm going to step back and let them contest their father's last wishes unchallenged as you suggest, they are gravely mistaken."

Mr. McLeod sat back as if Mary had struck him physically. He inhaled and was about to bark at her when Mr. Woodbury interrupted quietly, his face expressing respectful, awe-struck curiosity. "If Mr. Kerr was a friend of yours, as you say, wouldn't it be preferable to put an end to it now, in lieu of dragging his name through the court?"

Mary knew that she had to remain calm. "I gave him my word that his will would stand as written."

Woodbury's expression softened slightly, but he didn't reply.

Mary returned her attention to Coyle. His eyes urged circumspection. He did, however, try to come to her rescue. "What Miss Clark is endeavouring to say is that she was hired by Mr. Kerr because he trusted her. Accordingly, she feels it's her duty to act out his wishes as he conveyed them. I find that highly commendable."

"We can't have this firm associated with fraud," McLeod shouted in his piercing voice, his stare cold and demanding.

Mary was trembling. She glanced around the room and felt utterly defenceless against such force. She recalled Mr. Kerr's words at her last meeting with him: *They will most definitely fight you on this. Will you be able to face them?* She had replied, *You needn't worry, Mr. Kerr. Your instructions will be carried out to the letter.* It was that memory that gave her the courage to speak out. "Mr. Kerr was my client. I, more than anyone, was privy to his wishes." Without realizing it, she was on her feet facing Mr. McLeod. "Please tell Courtney and Richard that if they persist with their plans to challenge their father's will, I intend to fight them every inch of the way."

"Miss Clark, if there should be a trial, it could be damaging to your career, my dear," remarked Mr. Woodbury, ever the diplomat.

"I'm compelled to agree with you, Mr. Woodbury, but what you propose here is far more repugnant, not only to me but to the memory of Mr. Kerr. I would rather endure the consequences than accept this humiliating offer." With a nod to the other men Mary said, "Good day, gentlemen," and moved toward the door.

"You come back here," Mr. McLeod yelled after her. "I'm not finished with you."

By this time, Mary was so lost in a haze of emotions that she was not thinking rationally, or the following words would not have been voiced. "But, sir, I'm finished with you." It had been an involuntary retort, which she regretted immediately, but it was too late to snatch it back.

Mr. McLeod went red, speechless. Then outrage quickly surfaced. His eyes like lasers, he focused on Coyle and bellowed, "You better shake some sense into that foolish, misguided girl."

"Why should I, when I share her view entirely?"

"What?" demanded McLeod.

"I'm saying, Henry, that I'm averse to the way you're handling this matter. As the senior partner, you're capable, and you're a genius when it comes to legal matters. Presently, however, you're moving in a direction I am completely uncomfortable with."

McLeod shot him a disapproving glare. "Had you been more vigilant in your supervision, we wouldn't be in this mess."

Mary listened in total fascination as Coyle said, "Miss Clark's record and previous performances leave no doubt in my mind that she is perfectly capable of handling Mr. Kerr's estate. Irrespective of all that, as the matter stands now, I support her position and have no intention of changing her mind. As a matter of fact, I propose to defend her in court, should it come to that."

"I'll see you dismissed from the firm before that happens."

"In that case, I believe there's nothing else to say," Coyle replied, rising from his chair.

"I want her out of here, out of the premises. Do you hear me?" Mr. McLeod's apoplectic roar receded as Coyle followed Mary out of the room.

Mary returned to her cubicle, her brain feverishly reviewing the meeting with McLeod, Woodbury, and Coyle. Her clash with Mr. McLeod was very troubling, but it was nothing compared to her alarm over the disappearance of her briefcase. The appraisal document produced by him in his office had been an identical copy of the one among her private papers. How was it possible? The likeliest explanation was that her briefcase had been stolen. Why? By whom? It had to be someone working on behalf of Courtney and Richard. With this realization came a thought even more distressing. There were other documents in her briefcase, papers relating to the music box and Mr. Kerr's will, which she had extricated from his file to avoid the possibility of them being discovered by anyone who might misinterpret them. She felt numb, entirely disconnected from the room in which she sat. How could she have been so imprudent? Why had she not destroyed those papers? In retrospect, it was easy to recognize what actions she should have taken. But it was too late to do anything about it. Defeated, she started to pack, Mr. McLeod's last words—ordering her dismissal—ringing in her ears. She would pre-empt him.

She had barely finished clearing her desk when Eleanor Reid walked in with her sparkling brown eyes and customary effervescence. "Mary, I just heard about the confrontation in Mr. McLeod's office. I can't believe it. What a terrible thing to happen. Is there anything I can do for you?" Eleanor was a junior employee in the accounting department and was liked by everybody. As such, she was a reliable source of office news, which she was always eager to share.

"Thank you, Eleanor. No."

"Everyone in the office is appalled that McLeod would do this to an employee. Especially you, who has been wholly dedicated to the firm." When Mary did not reply, Eleanor continued, "And I heard Coyle stood up for you."

It never ceased to amaze Mary how quickly news travelled in their workplace. Before she could say anything, Eleanor forged on. "Lucky you. I would commit murder if I thought Coyle would act on my behalf."

They heard a discreet cough and looked up.

Coyle was standing in the doorway, seeming mildly amused.

Eleanor's face became beet red. Awkwardly, she excused herself and immediately vacated the room.

Mary met his gaze with defiance. "Are you here to see me out of the building?"

"I've come to see if I can be of service. I'm not sure that I can be of any help, but I would be happy to serve as counsel."

"You asserted as much in Mr. McLeod's office, yet I can't help wondering why you would want to do this, to help me. You and I scarcely know each other."

"Well, it could be that I'm highly susceptible to a lady in distress, or perhaps it's because I hold a dim view of people who abandon their own when things get challenging. Then again, perhaps it was seeing you stand up to someone like McLeod." Coyle gave a short laugh. "That was some performance."

In Mr. McLeod's office, Mary had been driven by Mr. Kerr's last wishes and had dared to speak her mind. But she now was overcome with doubt. "The charges against me are grievous, with no foreseeable defence. One could almost call it a lost cause."

"The start is not propitious, but then cases rarely are at first," he replied.

They shared an uneasy glance, then she murmured, "I doubt that I can afford your services should it go to trial."

"That need not be a concern. If you accept, I will be doing it pro bono. I should stress, however, that you are not entirely on your own, despite my offer. Since you were acting on behalf of Woodbury & McLeod, the firm remains responsible for any legal fallout. Your dismissal does not negate that."

"I'm...I'm lost for words."

"If you decide to fight Courtney and Richard on this, however, you need to recognize the full extent of your predicament."

"I've no choice. I made a promise to Mr. Kerr."

"Clearly, being charged for fraud instead of giving in to McLeod's demands is not something you want. But then, difficult choices made are not always what people hope for. I respect you for that."

"What will happen to me?" Mary knew the answer but needed to hear it from him, someone more objective than herself.

"It comes down to this," he answered in a steady voice. "Before this new evidence, you would merely be facing a loss of your job and potentially disbarment proceedings for violating the lawyer's code. Unfortunately, they now plan to sue you for fraud. That's more critical. They can initiate a criminal or a civil action against you. A criminal case is a very detailed and unpredictable process. There are no guarantees. And if found guilty in a criminal court, you would most likely be ousted from further practice in Ontario and could face a jail sentence."

"Oh, is that all? I feared I might have to confront McLeod again," she replied, a spark of mischief in her eyes.

This elicited a smile from Coyle. In a more sober tone, he said, "As you are aware, criminal action is undertaken by the government Crown attorney and is intended to find the guilt or innocence of the accused. It would not result in any monetary award to Richard or Courtney. An ensuing civil action, however, could follow, and a finding of guilt could result in a monetary award for them."

Mary reflected on Coyle's words, her mind racing with the possibilities. She was quick to discern the outcome. "It would be unusual for a dispute over the terms of a will to be a criminal case. They are most often civil cases. However, Richard and Courtney might try this route because a finding of guilt in a criminal case would be very compelling evidence in a subsequent civil action and would inexorably lead to a settlement out of court."

Coyle took his time before responding. "For the Crown attorney to take on a criminal case against you, however,

Courtney and Richard would have to convince him that there is sufficient evidence to convict. A criminal case needs proof beyond a reasonable doubt, whereas a civil case need only find proof on the balance of probabilities."

"For that reason, allegations of fraud are not made lightly," Mary admitted, picking up his line of reasoning. "For if they fail to establish it, Courtney and Richard may well be ordered to pay the costs. I suspect that is why they sought a settlement before anything else."

"Precisely."

"As I said, my case doesn't appear promising."

"Well, I've seen worse."

"Nobody believes me."

"I believe you."

"Why?"

"You were offered a way out, yet you stood your ground. Had you been guilty, you would have welcomed their offer. I applaud your courage."

"Standing my ground was easy. It was more in rebuttal to what McLeod implied. As for the courage, I don't know. I may live to regret my actions one day and may not show such audacity ever again."

"Yes, you would. Loyalty and courage are not things you think about. They are so innate, they simply come about." Coyle paused then added, "Courtney, Richard, Beasley, and McLeod, for that matter, obviously failed to recognize your integrity when they attempted to manipulate you into giving in to their demands."

"My honour is all I have," Mary replied. "Accepting Courtney and Richard's offer would've labelled me a criminal, in addition to forcing me to go back on a promise made to their father."

"I have every confidence your honour will remain intact," said Coyle. "Right now, however, there's not much we can do until we hear from Beasley, or the prosecution serves us with actual charges. I need to warn you that opposing someone like Ralph Beasley is not going to be easy. We have an arduous task ahead."

Mary knew that Coyle's assessment of Beasley could not have been more accurate. Beasley might not qualify for a personality award, but he fully understood the law and used it to his benefit. "I don't savour the prospect of opposing him," she admitted.

Coyle studied Mary closely. He must have perceived the alarm in her eyes, for he asked, "Is there something else troubling you?"

After a slight hesitation, she replied uneasily, "My briefcase is missing. I had important papers in it regarding Mr. Kerr's estate. In the wrong hands, they could be damaging."

"To whom?"

"To me and to this case if it should ever go to trial. But there were also papers that would exonerate me."

"In that case, you must find it. A briefcase doesn't magically disappear."

"That's my unfortunate dilemma. I've searched everywhere and can't find it. I'm now convinced it was stolen. That appraisal document presented by Mr. McLeod in his office could only have come from my briefcase."

"It's conceivable that Richard and Courtney's lawyer came by it legitimately."

"I doubt it," she replied.

"What other papers were in your briefcase, other than the appraisal sheet?"

"Most of them had to do with the trunk and music box: a letter to Eugenie Kerr from her sister Danielle, informing her of its true value; my letter to Danielle notifying her of Mr. Kerr's wish that the trunk be sent to her; and a document signed by Mr. Kerr authorizing it."

"Why didn't you keep those documents in Mr. Kerr's file? What you've done is highly irregular."

"It may be against every rule of our office procedures, but Mr. Kerr wanted it that way. When he made up his mind to return the trunk and its contents to Eugenie's family—after I had informed him about the value of the music box—he was adamant that I keep that specific information private. And as the executrix of his will, I felt obligated to respect his wishes."

As Mary uttered those words, she recognized that she had acted irresponsibly. With any other client, she would have consulted with Coyle before following such directions. Taking Coyle into her confidence, or better yet putting it in writing to him in a dated letter following a discussion with him on the matter, would have provided documentation and allowed Coyle to be a witness. But Mr. Kerr had been so insistent that it be done his way that she had allowed her esteem for him to override her professional obligation to Coyle and the firm. It was obvious to her now that she had not been thinking like a lawyer. She should never have consented to take on the responsibility of managing Mr. Kerr's estate. She was too emotionally involved.

"Did he tell you why he wanted it done that way?" Coyle asked.

"When I asked him, he said it was enough that he was leaving his entire estate to the Robert Kerr Palliative Care Trust. He didn't want his children to learn they were being deprived of an additional three million dollars."

"Mr. Kerr put you in a most vulnerable situation. Presumably, you took steps to protect yourself?"

"Yes, I itemized everything in the trunk, including the music box with its appropriate value, and wrote out his instructions to me in a memo, which he signed."

"And you still have that memo?"

"It was in my briefcase along with all the other documents."

Coyle was silent for a time. Then he said, "I recommend we wait and see what happens. In the meantime, we should try to reconcile with Mr. McLeod. Would you be willing to walk to his office with me, Miss Clark, to revisit the issue? Now that he has had time to calm down, he may have reached a different conclusion."

Mary somehow summoned a smile. "I sincerely hope so." She had taken on a tone of assurance, but it was faked. She did not want Coyle to detect how concerned she was.

⁓

"Were you finally able to reason with that woman?" Mr. McLeod shouted as Coyle and Mary stepped into his office.

Knowing very well McLeod was referring to her, Mary replied, "I'm afraid my view regarding Mr. Kerr's estate remains unchanged."

"Then you're fired," he barked. "I won't have a junior lawyer, especially a woman, dictating to me."

"Listen, Henry, you may wish to think this matter through before making any precipitous decision." Coyle was calm, yet an intimation of disapproval had come into his voice.

"What is there to think about? A three-million-dollar music box, which nobody knew about, goes missing, and she has it in her apartment. It's hard to look at these facts and not doubt her innocence."

"You haven't heard the full story from her side. As you well know, in every case, there are extenuating circumstances, and I urge you to reconsider. I trust Miss Clark. I've observed her in the performance of her duties in the office, and she comes across as an honest person with high professional standards. What you propose is alien to her character and behaviour."

"Yes, but I doubt she was ever tempted like this before. The opportunity of getting your hands on three million dollars can easily make people do things they normally wouldn't do."

"Henry, you're making—"

McLeod raised his hand, cutting him off. "Nothing will convince me she didn't want that music box for herself. So, I'm going to instruct the personnel office to get rid of her before Beasley destroys her and this office with it."

A grim expression settled on Coyle's face. "In that case, I advise you to arrange for my pink slip, as well. If this is how you treat your employees, I have no desire to be part of this firm."

"Are you, too, going against me on this?"

"I have no alternative. She has been a faithful employee, and we should back her up."

Evidently, being challenged twice in one morning by members of his own staff was more than McLeod could tolerate. Pressing the intercom button, he ordered, "Miss Williams, I want you to accept Mr. Coyle's and Miss Clark's keys to this building and see to it that they are escorted from our offices. Immediately! Do you hear?"

When they walked out of the office, all Miss Williams could do was gape at Coyle, pleading for some sort of understanding. Being escorted out could only mean one thing, and her features showed she could not reconcile herself to the idea of him being fired. He was far too valuable an employee.

"No need to disturb yourself, Miss Williams," he assured her, giving her his usual disarming smile. "I know the way."

Once she had vacated her office and turned in her keys, Mary retired to her apartment. No sooner had she arrived than the telephone rang. She picked up the receiver. "Hello?"

"Mary!"

"Peter!" she exclaimed, warmed by the sound of his voice.

"Mary, I just heard."

Again, Mary was amazed how fast news travelled in their business world. Before she could reply, he added, "Of course I don't believe a word of what they're saying. There has to be an explanation."

"Well, I've been fired. You can believe that, at least."

"Oh, Mary. Tell me what happened. What can I do to help?"

Briefly, she related her version of what had transpired and then finished by saying, "Right now, there's nothing you can do. I have to see this through and hope for the best."

"I have a meeting with a client in half an hour, but I'll come over as soon as I've finished," he said, his voice rueful and compassionate.

"Isn't today your night out with the boys?" she asked.

"I can always cancel."

"No, Peter. I want you to go out and enjoy yourself. Besides, I'm afraid I would hardly be good company tonight."

"I couldn't possibly leave you alone at a time like this."

"Really, Peter, I'll be fine. How about we meet for a quiet dinner tomorrow night at La Roma? It will be more relaxed, and we'll be able to talk."

She heard a long sigh and could almost see him at his desk debating what he needed to do, or perhaps what he should do. "Are you sure?" he asked.

"Entirely."

There was an uncomfortable silence. "I should be with you," Peter said.

"I'll be fine," she repeated.

Again, there was an uncomfortable silence—so long that she could almost believe he had terminated the call. "Very well. If that's what you wish."

"Yes. I'll see you tomorrow."

"And, Mary." There was a note of concern and empathy in his voice.

"Yes, Peter?"

"I don't want you to worry. We'll get through this."

He spoke those assuring words with such confidence and tenderness that it made her want to cry. Biting back her emotions, she managed to say, "Thank you, Peter. I'm so glad you called."

"Until tomorrow then, my dearest," he replied and then ended the call.

Slowly, Mary put down the phone. She felt emboldened. All was well—at least for now. And she felt relief. Perhaps she had been waiting for someone to share her burden. She knew she should call Rachel, but she felt too tired to have to recount her situation in the detailed way her friend would expect. Then she remembered that Rachel was pleading a case in court today, which was probably just as well. She would call her later that evening.

Once more, the phone rang, and she picked it up, wishing even as she did so that she had left it to the answering machine.

"Mary, I just got back to the office. Peter told me you were fired," came Rachel's voice across the line. "I had no idea."

If it were anyone else on the phone, Mary would have found a way to end the call right then, but Rachel had been her friend too long for her to do that to her. Instead, she heard herself say, "It all happened so quickly, I didn't realize what was happening myself."

"Peter also told me you were accused of theft," came Rachel's voice, slightly rising. "Of course, I don't believe any of this for a single moment. You're far too honest."

"Well, their accusations may be false, yet they are indeed accusing me."

"McLeod can be a real nightmare, but he's smart. I would have thought he was too smart to believe you would even consider doing such a thing. How does he expect to get away with firing you on such a ridiculous charge?"

"Unfortunately, there is a lot of circumstantial evidence against me, Rachel."

"And can he prove it?"

"He's accused me, so obviously, he feels he can."

"Is there anything I can do to help?"

"No, thank you, Rachel. But knowing that you care is consoling."

"Oh, Mary! I feel so helpless."

"Don't. Coyle has taken up my cause."

"You're kidding!"

"No."

"In that case, you've got nothing to worry about. He's never lost a case."

Mary wished she was as confident. "Well, this may very well be his first."

"Don't say that, Mary. Don't even think it."

"I'm sorry, Rachel. I'm feeling a little sorry for myself right now. But with a good night's rest, I'll get over it."

"Alright, Mary, I'll let you go." When Mary did not reply, she added, "I understand you have a lot on your plate right now. If there's anything I can do to help, whether it's running errands or just being with you, please let me know."

"Thank you, Rachel. Your offer means a lot to me, but I'm fine for now. Whatever happens, I will keep you in the loop."

"Whatever you say, Mary. You know I'll always be there for you."

"Yes, I do," Mary replied. Having exhausted the conversation, she bid her friend farewell and ended the call.

With her favourite Mozart concerto playing in the background, Mary poured herself a glass of wine and sat on her comfortable sofa to reflect more thoroughly on the day's events and consider her options. Now that she was committed to following through with Mr. Kerr's will, she was compelled to acknowledge the consequences of her actions and felt it full force. She was without employment, and charges against her were pending. They could even lead to imprisonment. How could this have happened to her, who had aspired her whole life to be a lawyer serving with dignity and honour?

When she graduated with a law degree from Ottawa University, she had been ecstatic. And ever since then, her greatest ambition had been to prepare herself for that big moment where she could prove herself competent and trustworthy. To that end, she had overcome the boredom of her work by devouring law manuals and spending hours in the courtroom observing the more able and distinguished lawyers defend their clients, thus acquainting herself with the rules of law and the expertise required to wield them. Doing this had served to assuage her frustration at not being more relevant in a career that gave preference to male colleagues.

Among all the trials she had witnessed, one in particular had made an impression on her. It was when a woman had come into their office pleading for her husband, an accountant for a large corporation in Ottawa, who had been charged with appropriating funds belonging to the company. While relating her husband's story to Coyle, she swore he had been framed and bemoaned the fact that no one would take on the case because it seemed doomed to failure. Plus, she had no money. Someone in the legal system had directed her to Coyle, saying that if anyone could help her, it was he. Indeed, Coyle was known to be the best among the top lawyers in Ottawa, an opinion held by practically everyone, even his adversaries. He never bullied, nor was he lenient toward his opponents. And yet they all respected him.

After listening to her story, Coyle had put his trust in her and taken on the case pro bono. Furious, McLeod had railed against the futility of the case—not to mention the lost income that would ensue from it—contending their firm was not a welfare institution. Despite his fierce disapproval, Coyle had gone ahead with it, doing the necessary work on his own time.

His defence had been brilliant, showing the accused had indeed been framed. There was much publicity following the trial, and when the truth was exposed, it revealed the frame-up had been orchestrated by the top company executives to cover up a plot of corruption existing between them and an official employed by the City of Ottawa. Mary recalled that when the accolades came streaming in, it was McLeod who had stood up front claiming all the credit, saying he had been behind Coyle all along.

Now Coyle, in a similar manner, was fighting for her against the accusations of her once most trusted friend.

These thoughts brought other memories. One that would forever remain was the odious circumstance that had brought her to Elmwood School—that stage of her youth was written indelibly in her brain. For so long she had managed to forget it. She had even convinced herself she had conquered it, which gave her a sense of security. But Mr. Kerr's death and the chaos that followed had eroded that feeling of safety. Tonight, the grief of her youth persevered. Life, she discovered, remained tenuous.

She glanced around the room and shuddered. Whatever happened now, her personal background would soon be a matter of discussion. She had indeed been uncommunicative about her life, secretive even, and the idea of it being exposed to acute scrutiny daunted her. Suddenly, her resolve weakened. It now seemed that she had leaped into the abyss without thinking anything through, without any understanding of the full force opposing her. *It's still not too late to retract,* she reasoned. *Let Courtney and Richard have what they want. They'll end up having it their way anyhow. They always do.*

Those were the thoughts that challenged her as she sat in the fading light of dusk. They threatened to overwhelm her, and she was painfully reminded of Coyle. He who had gambled everything for her, someone he barely knew. Why? Especially when the evidence was so heavy against her. Though she had spoken her mind and projected a self-assured image in Mr. McLeod's office, she had felt vulnerable and helpless. Had Coyle perhaps sensed this in her? No, it had to be more complicated than that. When it came to human emotions and motivation, nothing was simple.

There was something else that intrigued her about Coyle, but she had too much to contemplate just then. As she replayed the events that had followed Mr. Kerr's death—Courtney and Richard contesting the will; her refusal to back down; her dismissal from the firm; and Coyle being there for her when all had seemed lost—she realized that arguing with herself was futile. She would go on with her decision to fight this. She had no other choice. This summation should have provided her with some relief. Instead, she felt depleted and alone. And yet, she knew better than most that there were worse fates than loneliness.

With the greatest effort, she rose from the couch. She had had no dinner, but the idea of food nauseated her. She made her way to her bedroom and fell onto the bed, too fatigued to undress, and lay there dazed until she at last succumbed to sleep.

Two weeks later, Mary and Coyle were seated at a plain wooden boardroom table in the Ottawa Courthouse. It was a small room, bleak and soulless with one high, narrow, uncurtained window.

Across from them was Hugh Baxter, from the Ottawa Crown Attorney's office. In his early forties, tall with lean features, Baxter could be described as mildly handsome, were it not for his hostile eyes and unsmiling face. In the past, Mary had had several opportunities to observe him in court, and intimidating hardly came close to describing him.

In Canadian courts, there is a noticeable absence of theatrics and browbeating. The questions asked by either prosecution or defence must be germane and fair, or the judge will not allow them. But in Baxter's case, he regularly pushed the limits and expended his power of office to coerce people. Worse, he appeared to enjoy it.

His severe deportment exhibited a ruthless "law of the jungle" attitude, which Mary found highly disturbing. She knew he was working against her, and she needed to construct in her mind an argument, a rebuttal, in anticipation of his charges. But she felt inadequate, her case predestined to failure. Turning her gaze to Coyle, she made a valiant attempt to smile, arming herself against the clash that was bound to come.

Without preamble, the Crown attorney opened his file and addressed them both. "Miss Clark has been charged under section 341 of the Criminal Code of Canada for fraudulent concealment. Given the gravity of these charges, it's unequivocally a criminal case. Unless we come to some resolution at this meeting, I will direct the Crown to go to court."

Coyle appeared unfazed, imperturbable, as if Baxter had declared nothing at all noteworthy. "What would you have in mind?"

"A guilty plea to a reduced charge," Baxter answered. "Otherwise, she would be liable to imprisonment for a term not exceeding two years, the maximum sentence under Criminal Code section 341."

"My client has already been offered a settlement and has rejected it. What makes you think she would accept one now?"

"That was before it became a breach-of-trust case." Baxter then turned his cold, piercing gaze to Mary. "You understand that if you decide to go to court and plead not guilty and are found to be, you risk a much greater sentence."

"What's the alternative?" Coyle asked.

"None, I'm afraid. You will need some pretty strong evidence to get a not-guilty verdict, and I don't see that happening."

Baxter's steel-cold eyes met and held Mary's. "You're a lawyer," he said. "You recognize that if this goes to trial, you will be found guilty. According to Mr. Kerr's children, there have been various inconsistencies in your behaviour regarding their father's estate. They accuse you of a litany of things: that you were incompetent in dealing with his estate; that you used undue influence, clearly favouring one beneficiary over another; that you put your interest ahead of those of the estate; and that you actually stole from it. On all these points, they are willing to testify."

"Nothing they say is true," she replied, her gaze straying to Coyle who was leaning back against his chair, assessing the situation.

Baxter reached into his portfolio, pulled out two papers, and handed them to Mary. "I would like you to read these."

She accepted them and started to read with frantic concentration, willing herself to finish both letters.

Coyle must have noticed her discomfort. "What is it, Mary?"

She continued to stare at the correspondence in front of her. *These could only have come from my briefcase.* "How did you get these?" she asked.

"They were sent to me anonymously."

Coyle reached out and took the letters from her rigid hands. The room was uncomfortably silent while he read them, his features grave and impassive.

A moment ago Mary had felt anxiety at the unknown. Now she felt a cold dread come over her as she observed Coyle read the letters. One was the missive to Eugenie from her sister Danielle, informing her of the true value of the music box. The other was the letter Mary had typed, following the discovery, expounding Mr. Kerr's wishes that the trunk be sent to Eugenie's family.

"Both those letters will be brought in as proof of guilt," Baxter warned, directing his attention to Mary. "As you can see, nowhere in your memo to Eugenie's sister do you mention a music box. As well, all inquiries are directed back to you. Having elected to keep the box, that control would inexorably facilitate things for you." He paused and gave her a sardonic smile. "Rather calculating, I'd say. But despite the preponderance of evidence against you, I am prepared to plea bargain."

Coyle remained solemn and offered no response.

Mary, who had worked hard at learning how to mask her emotions, merely straightened herself in her chair.

"I need your answer," Baxter demanded.

"No," she said, emphatically. "I will not plea bargain."

A look of incredulity crossed his features. "Surely you must know what will ensue if you fail to comply?"

"I've no other option. For me, there's only one thing worse than being falsely accused of something, and that's pleading guilty to something I didn't do."

The Crown attorney threw his hands up in the air. "In that event, we've exhausted our discussion here." He then addressed Coyle. "You're a formidable lawyer, the best in the profession, but she doesn't have a hope in hell of not being found guilty, and you know it."

Coyle met Baxter's stare with his firm, unwavering look. "That may be your opinion, but it isn't mine. I've the greatest admiration for Miss Clark and am perfectly confident that she will be justified and exonerated."

With an irritated sigh, Baxter stood. "In that case, we'll see you in court." Bluntly he added, "I'm aware that you've ceded a partnership with your former employer to prove Miss Clark's innocence. A pity it will all be for nothing."

Baxter then glanced accusingly at Mary. "It will be my duty to find you guilty. And you will be. I promise you."

When she remained silent, he collected his papers, returned them to his portfolio, and said, his tone verging on annoyance, "Miss Clark, you will be required to attend the Crown court at a date to be determined." He walked out, his words resonating in her ears.

Mary sat, near paralyzed. For the first time since her dismissal from Woodbury & McLeod, she saw with horrible clarity that Coyle could never get her out of this, no matter how proficient he was. She leaned heavily on the table "Oh God! I can't believe this is happening."

"You'll get through this," Coyle assured her.

"Actually, it's you I'm concerned about."

"Me?"

"You've given up so much, and as Baxter stated, it will all be for nothing."

"Have you so little faith in me?"

"In you, I trust," she replied simply.

"Then why this sudden dejection?"

"I'm afraid you may come to regret your decision to help me."

"Not at all. My work with Woodbury & McLeod had become less gratifying in the last while, and it was inevitable that I would one day leave them."

"As far as I could see, you pretty well had free range to do whatever you wanted," she replied.

"How would you know it was what I wanted?"

"Isn't it what every lawyer covets: a partnership, success, and admiration from his peers, even his adversaries?" Mary shook her head with bewilderment. "Why are you help-ing me?"

"Do I really owe you an explanation?"

"No, but you have too much to lose and nothing to gain."

"Isn't that for me to decide?"

"It is, yet I can't get past the idea that you sided with me because you felt sorry for a defenceless novice lawyer. Your actions were more a reaction to Mr. McLeod's ill treatment of me than a conviction of my innocence." This was some-thing that had loomed in the back of her mind all along. She knew it was essential it be voiced.

"Is that what you think?" he asked.

Embarrassed by her own words, Mary looked away. Coyle was easily the most self-controlled person she had ever known. It seemed he never did anything without con-sidering all the ramifications. But this is what mystified her. She could not figure out why he would sacrifice his career for her. He had to pity her. And that bothered her. She did not want anyone's pity, especially his.

Resolutely, she turned to face him again and ventured to say what else occupied her mind. "It's safe for me to assume that when I was first accused, nobody, even I, thought it would ever come to this. If you didn't see it then, recognize it now, while you still have an opportu-nity to reconsider, to change your mind. I'm certain Mr. McLeod would welcome you back with open arms, if you were to drop my case."

"Has it ever occurred to you I might be doing this for my own benefit? Intolerant, I may be, but a victim, I'm not. Be assured that regret is the least of my worries." He stared at her with his deep penetrating eyes. "Why can't you accept that?"

"Forgive me. I merely…" She hesitated, too astounded to continue.

Coyle's features softened. "I'm afraid you're stuck with me. Besides, I'm all you can afford."

Despite herself, Mary smiled. Without money in her budget, her alternative was to appear *in propria persona*, something highly frowned upon by judges. In the legal circle, an attorney representing themself was referred to as a lawyer having a fool for a client. Giving Coyle a wistful smile, she said, "In the present circumstances, having you as my lawyer is the best thing that could possibly befall me. I'm truly grateful."

Coyle proceeded to gather his papers. "Now that this matter is reconciled, let us move on to more pressing things. First thing on the agenda is to decide whether you want the trial by judge or jury. I suggest a jury."

"Why not by judge?"

"Well, most of the judges in the system are decent enough, but even the best of them can be swayed. Mr. Kerr was well-known and respected by all. It's impossible to predict what their feelings for Courtney and Richard will be. Both can be extraordinarily charming and persuasive. For those reasons, our best chance lies with a jury."

"The only hesitation I have about a jury is they are notoriously fickle," she said. "One can never tell which way they'll go."

"Yes, that's true. But I know how to work on them."

When Mary did not comment, he suggested, "Why don't we wait and see what happens before we decide."

Mary nodded. Still, she remained ambivalent, and she looked into Coyle's eyes probingly. During the entire meeting with Baxter, Coyle's face had been unreadable, presumably for Baxter's benefit. But now that the Crown attorney was gone, he appeared wary for the first time since she had known him.

"Mary, it's evident someone is feeding Beasley and Baxter information. Might it be anyone you know or even suspect?"

"No! Yet those papers could only have come from my briefcase and are being used against me. I can't imagine who is behind all this. Outside yourself, I've never discussed Mr. Kerr's case and saw no need to release his papers to anyone."

"Not even with your fiancé?"

Clearly, word of the engagement had spread, even without a formal announcement. The question was not offensive or unwarranted, yet she was disconcerted by it and answered vehemently, "Of course not. It's of no concern to him."

"I understand he is employed by Beasley, Grant & Skelhorn," Coyle said matter-of-factly.

"If you're suggesting he's the leak, which you can't possibly be, I would say it's inconceivable, because at no time did I breech confidentiality. In any event, Peter would never do anything like that."

"Can one ever use the word *never*?" Coyle asked.

Not wanting to pursue the conversation, she gave him a sharp glance.

"Mary, I'm not intimating anything. I'm simply conversing. Somebody is passing on crucial information to

Baxter, and it's imperative we find out who it is. Peter works for Beasley, who is colluding with Baxter in this case. Could some of that information have inadvertently come from him…from papers he might have come across in your home?"

"No! Definitively not."

"Who else but you had access to those letters Baxter produced?"

"No one, I tell you."

"Well, all I can say is that on every count, your opposition is one step ahead of you, anticipating all your moves and dependably enough to keep you off balance. Doesn't that strike you as against the odds? Conjecture is not unexpected in court cases, but in this particular one, all probabilities are beyond my comprehension."

"Like you, I'm deeply concerned, but I have to disagree with the idea of Peter being involved. We have nothing to reproach him with. He couldn't plausibly have anything to do with this."

"How can you be so sure of him?"

"I simply am; that's all."

"Well, that's not acceptable to me, Mary."

"What makes you think he's implicated?"

"Because I assume that he, more than anyone else, would have access to your home, including your briefcase. I mean no impertinence, but if I'm to defend you, I need to consider every possibility. I don't know how else to say it, but an overly ambitious man might see this as an opportunity to advance his position with his firm."

Mary studied Coyle's face; his expression could only

mean one thing. It was several moments before she could speak. "You're serious, aren't you?"

"Entirely."

Though it was the reply she had expected, she was still rocked by it. She breathed deeply and blurted, "It's unthinkable that Peter would do such a thing. It would utterly destroy what we share together, which is too heinous to contemplate. I refuse to even debate the likelihood of such an act on his part. As for the letters, they had to have come from my briefcase. I'm now positive it was stolen."

Coyle was silent for a moment and then said in a tone that could be interpreted as appeased, resigned, or both. "Your fiancé must be pretty special for you to be that defensive of his values and principles. Needless to say, I'm touched by the loyalty and trust you hold for him. For your sake, let's hope you're right."

The days that followed were among the worst Mary had ever experienced. She was officially charged with fraud and awaiting trial scheduled to be heard in front of a jury in the Ottawa Courthouse on November 21.

With the charges came horrific headlines in the two Ottawa papers: "Local Lawyer Accused of Fraud," followed by an account of what had happened or, at least, what they assumed to have happened. More affronted than outraged, Mary read the report of how she had been dismissed from her firm, both papers championing Courtney and Richard. The journalists had taken pains to paint Mary as the villain and the Kerr siblings as the victims. The articles were accompanied by photographs of Richard and Courtney that had been taken the day of their father's funeral, pictures that spoke a thousand words.

Sitting in her living room the day the papers first ran the story, Mary pulled in a deep breath. She closed her eyes for a moment to keep at bay the apprehension that threatened to grab her. She wondered how one could get away with writing an article that was so completely false. Yet it was not the inaccuracy of the articles that dismayed her but rather the foreboding presentiment that some force was working against her, and the worst was yet to come.

The phone rang.

Feeling tired and not in the mood to talk to anyone, she allowed it to go to her answering machine.

"Mary, it's me," came Francis's voice, with a trace of worry. "I heard about what's happening, and I wanted to reach out. I can't imagine how difficult this must be for you. Just know that I'm here for you if you feel like talking. I understand if you need some time alone, so feel free to call me whenever you're ready." There was a pause, after which he added, "I'll be checking in on you again, but don't hesitate to reach out if you need anything."

Mary moved to pick up the phone but was too late. The line was dead. She briefly contemplated calling back, then the phone rang again. Anticipating Francis on the other end, she swiftly grabbed the receiver and exclaimed, "Hello!"

"Mary, it's Peter."

Taken aback, she failed to answer.

"How are you?" he asked.

"I've been better."

"Forgive me, darling. That was a mindless question. Obviously, this is a trying time for you. But things will improve; you'll see." There was a pause. Then, "I just received a telephone call from Mother. Apparently, there's an important matter she needs to discuss with me tonight." Before Mary could reply, he went on, "I did mention to her that you and I had a dinner engagement, but she said that what she has to say is urgent and can't wait. She even suggested you come along."

A flicker of alarm ran across Mary's face, her senses warning her that there was something dubious about the invitation, especially given how Mrs. Burbidge felt about her, a nonentity. "Oh, Peter. This hasn't been a good week for me. Would you mind terribly if I didn't go?"

"Sorry, Mary, I already accepted on your behalf. I can't possibly cancel."

Mary wished he had consulted her before accepting his mother's invitation but understood she had little choice but to go. Still, she hesitated.

"Mother is probably concerned about you and wants to offer her support," he persisted. "She did say she was eager to see you again."

After our disastrous last meeting? Most improbable. With the accusations against her, published in the papers, and the impending trial, Mary was certain she was less desirable to Mrs. Burbidge as a daughter-in-law than ever before, and her expressed desire to see her sounded more like a challenge than an invitation. Mary speculated on what motives would move Mrs. Burbidge to suggest this meeting. *What conspiracy is she planning against me? Will there ever be a time when I stop fearing for my future?* Mary wished now that she had spoken to Peter about the confrontation between her and his mother. But there had been so much happening in her life recently that she had failed to bring it up.

Peter spoke again. "I promise you it will not be a late night."

"Very well then," she relented.

When Peter showed up at her apartment, he spotted the newspapers on the coffee table. He walked over to Mary and folded her into his arms. She leaned against him, too emotional to talk. "I wouldn't put too much emphasis on what they write if I were you. You know how the media work. They're all for you one day and rage against you the next. They'll come around to your side when they get the full story."

"Maybe so, but it doesn't make things any easier for me at present."

He drew her closer. "I regret imposing this family dinner on you tonight. I neglected to see how taxing this Kerr business is to you. If you genuinely prefer to stay home, I'll understand."

Mary was totally mystified. Then came disbelief. The last month had been pure torture for her. How could he possibly not have been aware of it?

Before she could think further, he said, "If you do decide to come, it won't be a late evening. That I can promise you."

Mary loathed the idea of being in Mrs. Burbidge's company but knew she had to go. She was engaged to Peter and needed to make some effort to reconcile with her future mother-in-law. "Very well then," she replied, trying to convey an enthusiasm she did not feel. "A little diversion is perhaps what I need at the moment."

"That's my girl," he whispered warmly.

They hurried to his car and drove to Rockcliffe Park. As they approached his parents' home, Peter murmured, "And, Mary…"

"What?"

"Don't let anything my mother may say bother you," he said, anxiety written all over his face.

Your mother doesn't bother me; I seem to bother her, she was tempted to comment, but she refrained and remained reticent.

They were hardly inside the door before it became apparent to Mary that she was in for a difficult time.

Peter's parents were there to receive them. "How nice to see you again, my dear!" said Mrs. Burbidge, giving Mary an extravagant smile. Then speaking over her shoulder to Peter, she called out, "Being late has become a habit with you lately, I dare say. This is not like you."

"Sorry, Mother, but the traffic was heavy tonight, and I was late getting off work," Peter replied, handing his coat to Maria, who then turned to Mary to accept hers.

Mrs. Burbidge let out a sigh—one of a mother whose patience was running out. "Come along then, I want you to greet our other guest." Taking her son by the elbow, Mrs. Burbidge ushered him away. Without even turning to see if Mary was following, she shot over her shoulder, "Mary, my dear, have you met Mr. Beasley?"

Mary was barely able to contain her shock at this revelation. Swinging around, she came face to face with Peter's employer as he entered the hallway from the living room.

He smiled at her warmly. "Miss Clark and I have had the pleasure of meeting through our mutual profession."

Mary felt a frisson of fear slide down her spine. She knew him too well not to recognize the smile and mildness in his voice as deceptive.

"Profession?" frowned Mrs. Burbidge. "Oh, yes. I momentarily forgot that Mary was once employed by the law firm of Woodbury & McLeod before this loathsome affair concerning Mr. Kerr's estate. Unfortunately for you, Mary, the local newspapers have been having a real field day with that story. You're receiving as much coverage as the plans for Expo 67, and I can't help but wonder where all this…" She paused, then continued with a smirk, "Well, we won't go there, will we?" Her tone was not only antagonistic, it was venomous.

Peter glanced at Mary, his expression a mix of concern and determination. Then he addressed his mother and said, "Mother, I think it's unfair to bring up that subject when Mary is here as a guest. Let's focus on the present and treat her with the respect she deserves."

Over the stillness that followed, his mother's expression became one of wounded naïveté. "Oh, have I affronted you? I assure you, it was unintentional."

It was indeed a callous remark with which to begin a visit, but Mary feigned not to have been affected by it. Instead, she acknowledged Mr. Burbidge's invitation to the living room and took the chair he offered her.

Peter's father gave the impression of one weary, downcast. "May I pour you a glass of white wine, Mary?" he asked.

"Thank you," she replied, appreciative that he remembered her preference.

"Even if you are convicted, Mary, I will stand by you, because it's incomprehensible that anyone would do such a thing," Mrs. Burbidge stated blatantly.

Mary was tempted to retort. It was obvious Mrs. Burbidge was incapable of saying anything to her without that stab, that repugnant air. But she decided to let it pass. She smiled as genuinely as she could and said, "It's unfortunate not everyone can have your good sense and judgment."

Mrs. Burbidge shifted in her chair, her dislike for Mary tightly controlled but evident all the same.

Mary switched her attention to Beasley. "It would seem you're a friend of the family."

He cleared his throat, but before he could reply, Mrs. Burbidge intervened. "Ralph is a long-time acquaintance."

By this time Mr. Burbidge was back with Mary's drink, a bewildered look etched in his features—one that implied his wife's declaration overstated. He opened his mouth, presumably to comment, but no words emerged. There was a long, inelegant silence until he raised his gaze at Mary, then smiled gently. "Peter tells me you're from New Brunswick. What part, exactly? We've been several times to Fredericton and found it to be a lovely city."

"Albert, make yourself useful, will you, and get me another drink?" commanded Mrs. Burbidge.

"Of course, my dear." He nodded and once more proceeded toward the liquor cabinet set against the wall.

No one spoke, and Mary began to feel uncomfortable. She turned to Mrs. Burbidge, who was sitting erect in her chair and staring straight at her. Mary shrivelled back at the malice in her eyes. She desperately wanted to leave this ominous gathering but knew that she had to stay, for Peter's sake.

Finally, Mr. Burbidge emerged with a drink in hand and offered it to his wife. "Here you are, my dear."

Though his presence broke the silence in the room, his genuine warmth served only to emphasize the general cheerlessness. It was so oppressive that Mary could almost hear the quiet sighs of relief when Maria came in to announce dinner was ready.

The evening meal commenced affably enough with

casual conversation but soon degenerated when Mrs. Burbidge turned to Mary and produced a grim smile. "Tell me, my dear, what are you doing, now that you're no longer employed?"

Mary heard the blatant sharpness in that *no longer*. To cover the uneasiness that fell upon the table, she replied, "I was rather looking forward to the supplementary time to make arrangements for the wedding."

Mrs. Burbidge fixed her cold, defiant gaze on Mary. "I must admit my astonishment when Peter first announced your engagement, given his close kinship with Daphne."

To no one in particular, Peter said, "Daphne and I were friends, nothing more."

Maintaining her glacial stare, Mrs. Burbidge pressed on. "Until the announcement of your engagement, Albert and I had anticipated Peter and Daphne would get married."

"Forgive me, Phyllis, but if that's what you thought, it was in your—"

"Albert, it's immaterial now," she cut in, her irritation plain.

They were saved from further conversation when Maria walked in to serve the dessert. Mary remained staring stonily at her plate. As for Peter, she was troubled to discover that he was much like his father, shrinking under his mother's oppressive dominance.

Another torturous silence followed. It was all of two minutes, but it seemed an eternity, extracting all the energy from the room.

Subtly, Mary observed Mr. Beasley, speculating why he

was there. Certainly not for socializing, for he was clearly not skilled at informal, across-the-table small talk.

After dinner was over, Mrs. Burbidge folded her napkin and placed it on the table. Standing up briskly, she announced, "I know that Albert has a matter to discuss with Ralph this evening, so this may be a good time for them to retreat to the library."

When Mr. Burbidge made no attempt to move, his wife glared at him, making it obvious that her suggestion had been more a command.

He bent his head over his dessert plate as dejectedly as if he had just been reprimanded. Then, folding his napkin, he addressed Beasley in a subdued voice. "Do you mind?"

Beasley did not reply but rose expediently from his chair to leave, as though the invitation had been expected.

Mr. Burbidge shot Mary a look of mute apology and then followed Beasley through the door.

The withdrawal of the two men gave Mary pretext for a deferential exit. She was about to speak when Mrs. Burbidge said, "Before you head off, Peter, I must insist you spare a few minutes with Mr. Beasley, your father, and me in the library. As I pointed out to you over the telephone, we have deep concerns about your future, which we need to share with you." With undisguised intolerance, she glanced at Mary. "As this is a family matter, I'm sure you won't object if you're not included."

"Mother, Mary is my fiancée. If there are concerns about my future, she should be present."

"Peter, this is a private matter between you, Mr. Beasley, your father, and me," snapped Mrs. Burbidge, acidly.

Peter stared at his mother, as if he might challenge her, but he turned his gaze back to Mary. "Would you mind terribly?" he asked.

She did. In her mind, his mother's request was offensive as well as a breach of good manners. But to avoid creating a scene, she replied, "Go ahead, Peter. I'll wait for you in the living room. I may even take a stroll in the garden."

"Very well, then. But don't stray far, for I won't be long," he conceded, his eyes imploring understanding.

As Peter and his mother were leaving, an unmistakably feigned smile curled at the corners of Mrs. Burbidge's lips. "Goodbye, my dear. Do make yourself comfortable." This was voiced so benevolently that it made Mary question whether she ever meant anything she said.

Mary retired to the living room and sat, waiting, pondering. *I should never have come here this evening. I was a fool to think I could endear myself to that insufferable woman.*

Half an hour passed, and she was still waiting for Peter.

Another ten minutes later, Maria came in to ask if she needed anything, a cup of tea, perhaps.

Mary declined politely and decided to wait outside. She stepped through the patio doors into the near darkness of the late evening. She proceeded languorously, almost surreptitiously along the path through the garden. As her vision became accustomed to the night, the evening flowers became more discernible in the shimmering moonlight. The evening air felt refreshingly cool for late July. Overhead there was a canvas of stars—something she rarely saw in the city because of the numerous lights. It took her breath away, and for that brief period, at least, she forgot about the foursome inside. Enjoying the moment, she strolled through the extensive grounds. When she neared the back of the house, the sound of raucous voices imposed upon the serenity of the evening. Curious, she moved toward the disturbance, her pulse quickening with each step. As she grew closer, she identified it coming from the library, and Mrs. Burbidge's words came out strong and brutal through the open window. "Her position has become a disgrace to our family. Leave her, before she destroys us."

A coldness, unlike any Mary had ever known, enveloped her. She closed her eyes, fighting vertigo. After several moments, she opened them again and waited for the waves of shock to dissipate.

"Your role in this disappoints me, Father. How could you ask me to do such a thing?" Peter's voice shook with passion and frustration.

Mr. Burbidge's reply was instant. "Peter, when did you start thinking I could ask for anything? Whether you believe it or not, I don't—"

Mrs. Burbidge interrupted. "Your father doesn't see things as clearly as I do."

"Mother, you flatter yourself," Peter replied.

Despite her torment, Mary felt a deepening affection for Peter. This, as far as she knew, was the closest he had ever come to challenging his mother.

"We all know she's guilty," cried Mrs. Burbidge.

"Mother, I beg you not to prejudge her. You don't know the full story…only what you've read in the papers. And they write without knowledge of the facts."

"Well, ask Mr. Beasley here. He'll tell you," she persisted.

"Peter, I empathize with your feelings toward your fiancée," Mr. Beasley said. "It must be very hard on you. But you must recognize that she's guilty." He spoke calmly enough but with an emphasis on "guilty." "You've been a great asset to us and have proven yourself trustworthy and dedicated to our cause. But you can't be for us and supportive of her at the same time. She's your fiancée, but if you're a smart lawyer, you'll heed your mother's concern. There's a promising future for you with our firm, but not if you go against us on this. You'll have to make a decision. Just don't delay too long. I'm running out of patience. The sole reason I haven't come down hard on you on this matter is because of my loyalty to your parents." He voiced this with such callousness that Mary silently questioned what loyalty he could possibly be referring to.

"Promise us you'll consider Mr. Beasley's offer," demanded his mother.

"I promise nothing." Peter's retort rang out.

Though Mary was unable to make out what decision Peter was required to make, the conversation seemed more ominous than ever, more threatening. She waited for it to resume, but in the heavy silence that followed, she heard a door close. Thinking the meeting must be over, she quickly retraced her steps to the house and entered the living room through the patio doors just as Peter emerged. He was unaccompanied, and she could see that he was distraught.

"Come. We're leaving, Mary," he announced, leading her to the front door.

As they started to drive toward the city, Peter frowned

and said, "I apologize for Mother's behaviour toward you this evening."

"You needn't worry about it," she replied, managing to control her voice. Then, unable to hold back, she added, "I'm not too sure why I was invited to your parents' home this evening. Your mother's reception, at least, made it plain that I was not welcome."

"Mary, I'm so sorry. I had no idea that was going to happen. It must have been awful for you. But you have to believe me, it has nothing to do with you personally. Mother is obsessed with the idea of my becoming a partner in Beasley's firm."

"If that's the case, my present situation cannot be considered beneficial to you."

"Becoming a partner is hardly my concern right now. It's you I'm concerned about and remain committed to."

His words were reassuring, yet Mary could not help wondering exactly why Peter's mother wanted her to attend a dinner with Beasley, whose firm was representing Courtney and Richard in their suit against her. Even more, she was struggling to comprehend what part Peter may have been asked to play on behalf of his employer.

By the time Peter pulled up at her building, clouds had overtaken the sky and a light drizzle had begun. He declined her invitation to come in yet turned off the ignition. Mary studied him, trying to discern what he was thinking. He had hardly spoken a word since leaving his parents' house. His eyes had been fixed on the road, and he appeared lost, deep in thought. It was apparent he was hurting, and the idea stabbed at her heart. *What demands were made upon him?* She wanted to query him but did not know how to frame the question.

After a long silence, he said, "We've had so little time together lately, Mary…I mean just you and me."

"It's been an arduous time for us both."

"But even when we are together, you never discuss your impending trial with me. I know that your professionalism prevents you from disclosing personal information about Mr. Kerr, and to that end you have been scrupulously discreet, but being kept in the dark like this is driving me crazy."

Mary detected the trepidation in his voice and felt nauseous with guilt. "If I haven't discussed my trial with you, it's because I don't wish to burden you with my problems."

"*Burden?* Oh, Mary, can't you see? It's so much more upsetting not knowing what is happening to you."

"It would have served no purpose, only made you worry over something you have no control over."

"It's about trust," Peter replied. "People committed to each other share everything, good or bad. But you only share with me the positive things in your life. Do you always have to be so heroic?"

"I don't feel heroic at this moment."

"Then let me help you," he pleaded.

"I know you have my interest at heart, but there is nothing you can do."

"Please allow me to be the judge of that. Can't you see that whatever affects you touches me as well?"

Mary was taken aback. She had not realized that in her efforts to protect him, she had actually caused him greater hardship. She confided, "I have to say that things are not going well with my case. Our position is tenuous. As a matter of fact, it's growing more precarious by the day."

"How can that be?"

"Coyle is convinced someone is feeding the other camp information."

"Does…does he know who it is?"

"No." She threw herself into his arms. "Oh, Peter! My whole case is crashing down. Coyle won't admit it, but I'm certain we've already lost it."

Peter drew her closer. "Mary, it wouldn't be the end of the world if you did."

"You forget that I could go to prison."

His demeanour instantly changed. "They assured me there was no chance of that."

"They?" she asked.

Gently, he released her. "It's only natural that I should be concerned about you. I made a few inquiries at the office.

Most employees are pretty tight-lipped, but I was able to extract some facts from one who is more vocal than the rest. It's his opinion Baxter does not have enough evidence to convict you of fraud. He doesn't think Beasley believes it, either."

"I'm not so certain," she replied.

"Well, I am," he countered. "Just by looking at you, anybody would see you're innocent."

"I'm grateful for your sentiments. But you know as well as I that the look of innocence has no bearing whatsoever in court. And from what I've observed this evening, my apparent virtuousness hasn't influenced your mother the least bit."

His eyes met hers with something like comprehension. "Please forgive me for placing you in such an awkward situation. It was extremely discourteous of my mother to invite Beasley, especially when she knew he was representing Courtney and Richard in their suit against you. I wasn't aware he was going to be there. It was a heinous affront to you. And excluding you from the meeting like that was so rude." There was a note of bitterness in his voice.

Mary wanted to bring up the conversation she had overheard outside the library, but it would reveal she had been eavesdropping. Seeking to put the unpleasantness away, she smiled gently. "She's worried about you, as a mother should be."

Peter stared at her, conflict twisting his face.

"What is it, Peter?"

When he didn't answer, she went on, "I can see that something is bothering you. Won't you tell me what it is?"

After several moments of silence, he said, "I love you very much. You know that, don't you?"

Able to feel the tension between them, Mary held her breath and waited for him to continue.

He turned his pleading eyes on her. "I can appreciate your commitment to Mr. Kerr and don't mean to sound unsympathetic, but aren't you pushing it too far?"

She was so shocked, she did not know how to respond.

"Even if they don't have sufficient evidence to convict you," he continued, "all this publicity can't be helping you."

She remained silent.

Slowly and deliberately, he took her hand into his. "Darling, I admire your loyalty to Mr. Kerr. But if he were the man you say he was, he wouldn't have wanted you to lose your job and reputation over this whole affair."

"Can't you see, Peter, that if I give in to their demands, my job and reputation are worthless?"

"But isn't this what is happening to you now? All those outrageous things they've written about you in the papers. I've seen how disturbed you are by them."

"Not as much as I would be if I gave in to their demands," she was quick to reply.

"Mary, what difference can it make? Mr. Kerr is dead and none of this will affect him."

"Nonetheless, I will not allow them to say he was senile. It would be an indignity and a betrayal to his memory. It would also be admitting culpability for something I didn't do." In the silence that followed Mary paused to reflect on her words. Then she said, "Can you imagine what such an admission would do to my career? Do you believe for one moment that another law firm would dare hire me after that?"

"Not a law firm perhaps. But with your education and intelligence, you have scores of options. Mary, it's time you recognize the enormous risk you're taking." His eyes became desperate. "Face it; you can't fight these people and expect to win. They're too powerful."

The entire evening had been too much for Mary—first Mrs. Burbidge and now Peter. Disillusioned by both, she felt disoriented. Her determination had weakened, but her resolve remained. "I will not stand by and let Mr. Kerr's memory be tarnished for his children's convenience," she insisted with all the force she could muster. "I just can't. You, more than anyone, should be able to understand that."

"I do, Mary. And I admire you for it. But one has to recognize when to let go. Can't you see that you're never going to win this case? Everybody is against you, even your own firm."

Mary cradled her face in her hands in an attempt to blank out the total desolation that gnawed at her. "Dear God! Do you think I don't know that?"

He put his arms around her and hugged her. "Please forgive me for upsetting you. If I appear troubled tonight, it's because I'm afraid for you."

She struggled to hold back her tears. But when he softly stroked her hair and whispered words of comfort and reassurance, she was unable to contain the sob that was choking her.

Drawing her closer, he whispered, "Don't cry, Mary. Please!"

"I'm grateful for your concern," she murmured, then tried to wipe the tears. "But whatever happens, I'm prepared to take the responsibility for the outcome."

"That's what troubles me," he replied, releasing her gently. "I don't believe you fully appreciate the potential danger that awaits you."

"Why do you say that?" Mary asked. "Is there something you know that escapes me?"

"No, except that I'm a realist, and you're not."

"You needn't concern yourself about me, Peter. Despite my worry over the outcome of this trial, I trust Coyle's capability. If anybody can bring this case around, it is he."

"Don't believe that, Mary. You may feel secure saying it. But it's a misplaced confidence. There are too many powerful people against you on this, people who will stop at nothing to get what they want. And already they have too much evidence against you."

"How do you know that?"

"Your case is never openly discussed, and certainly not with the staff, but it's difficult to work at the office without knowing what is happening." With that, he started the engine and smiled at her. "You know I will support you no matter what you decide. But I urge you to seriously consider the consequences before going ahead with this trial."

Mary stepped out of the car and watched him drive away, his words ringing through her head. In the calm and silence of her bedroom, she found herself increasingly troubled. Peter's voice had been more distressed than usual and his smile unconvincing. Mary suspected there was more to their conversation than what he had revealed, which compelled her to again question what pressures his parents and Mr. Beasley had placed on him in the library that evening.

It was Thursday morning, the last week of July, and the city of Ottawa brooded in the summer's heat as Mary parked her car behind the grey stone Parliament Buildings on Wellington Street. The high temperatures had come early this year, and it promised to be another sultry day. But Mary was too preoccupied to notice. She had a ten thirty appointment with Coyle and was going over in her mind what she would say to him.

She walked two blocks to the Chambers Building, a prominent and distinctive structure that featured a blend of historic architecture and modern construction. Closing the door behind her, Mary moved through a foyer richly pan-elled in mahogany and with antique light fixtures that cast a gentle glow across an empty space. She took the elevator to the third floor and headed down the corridor. She arrived at number 310, in the far left corner, and stepped tentatively into a waiting room.

Kate Donovan looked up at her, smiled, and inclined her head toward Coyle's office. "He's waiting for you." Mary was not surprised to see her; Kate had been too devoted to Coyle to work for anybody else.

Returning her smile, Mary nodded and opened the door.

"Good morning," Coyle said, looking up from his paperwork. "Any trouble finding my office?"

"Good morning, Mr. Coyle. No trouble at all. The

instructions you supplied were excellent," she replied. Briefly assessing the room, she added, "It's my first time in this building. I'm impressed."

"It's functional and, at the moment, it suits my requirements perfectly." He walked to a small table alongside his desk, sat down, and pointed to the chair beside him. "Make yourself comfortable."

Mary had observed that, whenever possible, Coyle avoided having people sit directly opposite him. She suspected it was his way of making people feel more relaxed and responsive. There were so many things she had come to admire about him—this sensitivity, his intelligence, his integrity.

Once she was seated, he smiled. "We're going to be spending many hours working together; therefore, I suggest you call me Patrick."

No one among the people she knew had ever called Coyle by his Christian name. She thought Patrick suited him. It was a strong name.

Coyle sorted through his papers and pulled out a fresh writing pad.

"This morning I would like to explore in more depth your affiliation with the Kerr family."

As much as her memory allowed, Mary detailed the events that had brought them together, how she and Courtney had become friends and her subsequent visits to the Kerrs' residence.

Coyle asked about the dynamics of the Kerr family, and Mary shared her observations. Coyle listened silently, solemnly, following every word. Now and then he regarded her with a fervent look but never interrupted. She sensed he was learning more about the situation by what she did not say. When she concluded her briefing, he asked, "How would you rate your friendship with Courtney? Would you say you were close?"

"In the beginning, yes. As I mentioned, she and I were roommates for three years, from grade ten to grade twelve, and we easily created a bond. We shared everything…our dreams, our aspirations. But it all ended after we graduated. We saw less of each other. Our interests changed, and our paths diverged." Mary paused, stirred by the memory. "We went our separate ways. Courtney moved to Toronto and then went on to live in New York, which seemed to be the best place for her to further her fledgling modelling career. I remained here to pursue my law degree. I continued to see Mr. Kerr and Eugenie but didn't see much of Courtney after that. And when we did get together, it became obvious we had very little in common. Presumably there had not been enough to keep us together, so we grew distant from one another. Years passed and I did not hear from her until Mr. Kerr appointed me to manage his estate. From what I've observed, time has solidified our later feelings for each other."

When Coyle didn't say anything, Mary carried on. "I was young when I first met Courtney and was easily impressed by her and her affluent lifestyle."

"And what about Richard? How well do you know him?"

"I saw him whenever I visited their home, on weekends and holidays. It's difficult to describe Richard. The only word that comes to mind is *tolerable*. We never got close. In reality, he's not the type one gets to know particularly well." Mary failed to tell Coyle that Richard had made an advance toward her on one of her early visits to their home. Even at that youthful age, she had been able to discern that he was an unabashed flirt who was more interested in the conquest than the affection of the woman he sought to impress. She had rebuked him openly. On no occasion had they talked about it, all a distant memory now; but an ill-disposed relationship had developed between them.

"Both Elmwood School and Ashbury College, which Richard attended, are well recognized for their values, as well as their high academic standards," Coyle said. "It's unfortunate neither Courtney nor Richard benefitted from them."

Mary nodded. "Courtney was an unhappy person and had no interest in what the school had to offer. I remember how she complained continuously, either about the school or the teachers. No matter what they did for her, it was seldom enough."

"What about yourself? How did you feel about the school?"

"I felt privileged to be a student there, a feeling, I might add, not shared by all the students. I attributed part of that to my not having grown up rich, not having the expectations often associated with status." Her words were greeted by a few seconds of silence, and Mary wondered if she might have offended him. It was possible that he had grown up rich. "It's not that I feel all rich people react that way," she explained, "but it was certainly the case with Richard and Courtney." She continued, "What I'm attempting to say is that I was only able to attend Elmwood through my uncle's generosity, which made me more appreciative of my good fortune than most students. My mother's brother had no family of his own and had taken me under his wing, so to speak."

"I'm inclined to agree with you," Coyle replied. "People who feel entitled are more prone to take things for granted." He paused, and Mary wondered if he had detected in her voice the quickly controlled quiver of emotion. "Tell me about your immediate family," he continued.

On principle, Mary avoided speaking about her mother and father. It unfailingly brought up memories of a childhood she would rather forget. "There's really nothing to tell," she started self-consciously. "I've no siblings and my mother and father were killed in a car accident during my second year of law school."

"Oh, Mary, I'm so sorry."

"You needn't apologize. You had no way of knowing."

As she had expected, the knowledge of her parents' tragic death seemed to dissuade him from pursuing that line of inquiry. He switched to another topic. "And about your uncle?"

"He was diagnosed with pancreatic cancer shortly after I moved to Elmwood. I was able to finish my studies there through a special fund he willed me. He was thoughtful that way. He was a fatherly and protective presence in my life. I'll never—" She stopped abruptly, unable to continue.

He nodded, acknowledging her decision to keep some things to herself. Again, he changed tack. Drawing his chair closer to hers, he said, "Now, about this music box, I need to hear your version of the story."

After Mary had finished telling him about the trunk, the letters, and her frequent visits to Mr. Kerr in the hospital, a silence stretched, as though he was collecting his thoughts. Then he said, "And about your briefcase; I gather you still haven't found it?"

"No. And I've no idea where it is."

"Then we'll have to assume it is in the hands of someone favouring Courtney and Richard."

"Without a doubt," she replied. "How else can we explain Beasley and Baxter coming up with my personal papers?"

"Mary, you're being accused of withholding vital information to which you were privy. I believe you, but proving it is a different matter. If only you had shared that information with me when Mr. Kerr was still living. I would have directed you to take greater precautions."

"Had I any knowledge it would come to this, I would have."

"The fact that your papers are missing is not going to help you." He paused, his eyes fastened on her. "Now about the trunk, Courtney and Richard argue they were notified about it but nothing about the music box. Otherwise, they would have kept it as a memento from their stepmother."

"They're lying. The afternoon that we inspected their home, I distinctly remember bringing it to their attention and suggesting just that. They smirked at the idea, discrediting it totally. Their derogatory comments at the time were so repugnant it took all my willpower not to retaliate with an insult."

"Can you prove that you brought it up?"

"No, but they know I did."

Again, there was a pensive silence. After a moment, Coyle eyed her with a solemn expression. "What you say to me is privileged. It will be between us two. But before I move ahead with this case, it's imperative I know the whole truth."

"I understand."

"At any time, did you consider keeping the music box?"

"No. Not for myself."

He inclined his head to one side. "What do you mean by 'not for myself'?"

"Well, when I found out about the value of the music box, I did contemplate sending it to Eugenie's family without informing Mr. Kerr of its true value. I even wrote a letter to that effect," she confessed, feeling rather embarrassed.

"What moved you to do that?"

"It's hard for me to explain, except that I felt they deserved it more than Courtney and Richard. But the morning after the discovery, I knew I had to tell Mr. Kerr. And I did. And at the end, it was his decision, not mine, that it be sent to Eugenie's family."

"And what did you do with this letter?"

"Unfortunately, it's among the papers in my briefcase."

Coyle looked at her with a mixture of surprise and concern. "Why didn't you rip it up after you decided to tell Mr. Kerr about the music box?"

"I wanted to be thorough and transparent in my communication with Mr. Kerr and felt it was essential to preserve any written evidence that might shed light on my thought process at the time."

"I see," said Coyle, his expression shifting from surprise

to comprehension. "Preserving the letter as a precautionary measure makes sense, especially in such a sensitive situation. Good thinking, Mary. Yet there's another question that requires an explanation."

Mary waited.

"In Mr. McLeod's office, you stated the music box was in your apartment. Once Mr. Kerr gave his agreement, why didn't you forward the trunk with the music box inside?"

"I intended to. But with Mr. Kerr's death, his funeral, and the responsibility of his estate, I was so overwhelmed with work that I didn't get a chance."

Coyle looked at her uncertainly again, and Mary sensed what he had to be thinking—that there was more to her story than what she was willing to reveal.

"Do you doubt my innocence now that I've admitted being tempted to withhold information from my client?" she asked.

"In life, we can't always control our thoughts. It's how we deal with them that defines us," he replied. "Mary, I trust you in all that you've reported to me. But without proof, nobody else will."

"I agree."

"It's most unfortunate, however, that you did not inform me or someone about the music box."

Since there was nothing she could say in her defence, Mary remained quiet.

Coyle pushed himself back from the table and took a couple of steps toward the window. He stood there gazing at the new National Arts Centre under construction in front of his building and, across the street from it, the National

War Memorial. Then he returned to the table, sat down, and stared deep into her eyes. "Inside the court, you will be attacked from all directions, meaning that your private life will surely be subject to critical scrutiny by Baxter. Is there anything about your past that I need to know?"

"No," she answered, uncomfortably aware that her voice lacked conviction. She watched him lean back in his chair and saw the resignation settle on his strong face. Despite having affirmed his belief in her, she recognized he must find it hard to accept all she had disclosed. It equally occurred to her with growing alarm that others would be sharing that view.

As the summer faded into fall, Mary could see that her upcoming trial had become a strain on Peter. He spoke unwaveringly about her trial with increasing and uncontrolled frustration. And no matter what she said, he found a way to use it against her. There were even times when his frustration would turn to anger, and he would verbally lash out at her. Mary fought to contain her growing impatience but was barely succeeding. Unfailingly the altercations ended the same way, with Peter walking out and slamming the door.

Tonight was no different. It was Thursday evening, the last week of September, and Mary had been looking forward—admittedly without much hope—to a quiet dinner with him in her apartment. With that heartening prospect in mind, she had prepared his favourite menu: coq au vin followed by a chocolate mousse cake. She had laid the table with her best linen and candlesticks. She had even bought flowers at the ByWard Market and had arranged several bouquets around the room. Yet throughout their meal, she felt that now familiar hostility between them and struggled to maintain some measure of stability. She was about to express her growing concern for the welfare of their relationship when, out of the blue, he blurted, "Why didn't you settle with Courtney and Richard when you were handed that option?"

Mary knew where he was leading and could not reckon what was driving him. Nevertheless, she allowed him to give vent to his anger.

"You were wrong and perhaps even misled to think you could fight them. Can't you see what this is doing to us?" When Mary remained unresponsive, he persisted. "When will you learn? One does not buck the establishment. It's pure suicide."

Mary could tolerate it no longer. "Peter, we've already discussed this. Must we quibble about it again, especially when it's too late to do anything about it? It's out of my hands. Coyle's in charge now."

"But it doesn't have to be too late. The charges can still be dropped. If only you were not so damn obstinate."

"There was more to it than that, and you know it."

"No. I don't. So why don't you enlighten me?"

"I've tried, but you don't appear to understand. How can I describe what you can't possibly perceive?"

"The trouble with you, Mary, is you're unwilling to compromise. You never bend. You constantly have to adhere to the established system. Can't you break the rules, just once?"

"You mean like you do all the time?" These words had come out involuntarily, and Mary immediately regretted her harshness. Yet the last months had proven them to be true.

Mary had become aware there was more merit to Rachel's assessment of Peter than she, personally, had been willing to admit. Since her affiliation with Coyle, and in light of Peter's extreme mood changes, she found herself unconsciously comparing him to Coyle and was greatly disturbed by it. How dissimilar they were. Both were lawyers but dealt with their careers differently.

While Coyle's approach to his profession was hard, methodical work and dedication toward his clients, Peter, equally intelligent, did not fight for his clients. He was complacent and lacked the drive that motivated Coyle. But then, maybe it was because all his life, things had been served up to him on a silver platter.

There were moments, when enmeshed in these sour reflections, she had questioned her compatibility with Peter. Then, when she least anticipated it, he would do something totally altruistic, fortifying her conviction that he could also be caring. It was this side of Peter that endeared him to her, the side of him that pushed aside any whisper of trepidation she may have held.

Mary did not miss the note of petulance in Peter's voice when he responded. "Yes, like me. And you'll see that I'll get ahead much faster than you. Ten years from now you'll still be doing research in the library, drafting motions and preparing files for junior lawyers in your office and be condescended to by the narrow-minded male establishment."

An icy chill raced over her skin. Peter knew this was a sensitive subject for her, and she was upset that he had brought it up this way. Despite her elation when she was hired by Woodbury & McLeod and her determination to prove herself by giving everything to her work— total dedication and far more hours than were required—she had soon discovered that being a lawyer and excelling in her field did not necessarily open the doors of opportunity extended to most male lawyers. Because of the discrimination that pervaded the entire legal profession, the most she could reasonably hope for was an attorney position with low pay and little chance for advancement. Resenting Peter's argument as well as the unfairness of the legal system, Mary answered, "More than likely, but I will at least have the satisfaction of knowing that I'm the best at what I do, which is more than what most can say. And one other thing, you may not rate me high in your books, but I grew up with the notion that no matter your position in life, everyone has something to give."

"Forgive me, Mary. I meant no offence."

"Before today, I might have accepted your apology, but not anymore. You speak great lines about my work being equal to yours, but I can see now that they are only hollow words."

"Mary, that's unfair."

"How would you explain then that you'd rather see me yield than fight for things that I believe in?"

"You don't understand."

"It's you who doesn't understand. A position is meaningless unless you've earned it."

"Unlike you, I want more out of life," Peter retorted. "And if that means breaking some absurd rules, so be it."

"It's unfortunate you feel that way, for it goes without saying that when one contravenes the rules as easily as you do, eventually, inevitably, the rules start to mean nothing."

"Mary, you're a dreamer. You go through life dreaming about things unlikely ever to materialize. When you're young, you can afford those fantasies. But what you don't realize is that things change as you get older."

"They only change because we allow it," she fired back. "Dreams may not be a major part of your life, but they are of mine. I need to believe there is something nobler out there than what we have." She looked at him wistfully. "There was a time when I could share my aspirations with you, and you would listen."

Peter's features softened. And for a moment, Mary thought that she had finally broken through to him, that he had seen how important going through with the trial was to her. This made her disappointment even greater when he said, "I can't seem to get through to you that you have everything to lose and nothing to gain by going through with this court case."

Mary recognized the futility of their argument. Frustrated and annoyed for having allowed herself to be drawn into it yet again, she started to pick up the dishes from the table. The telephone rang. "Would you mind answering for me, please?" she asked.

She watched Peter walk away and pick up the extension in the living room. "Hello, Peter here." There was a short pause. "Oh, hello, Linda."

Linda Belcher and her husband, Garry, were friends of Peter's who habitually called Mary's number when they failed to reach Peter at his apartment.

To provide him with privacy, Mary went to the kitchen to make tea. From there, she heard him say, "Great! See you tomorrow night then." When Peter appeared at the door, he was beaming with excitement. "Linda and Garry have two extra tickets to the ballet tomorrow night and have invited us to join them. I told them we would."

"Peter, I wish you had consulted with me before accepting. I would have reminded you that Coyle and I have scheduled a meeting for tomorrow evening, which I'm positive I mentioned to you."

The unconcealed anger she read in his face was unlike anything she had ever seen. "Ever since this trouble with the Kerrs' estate, we've hardly spent any time together," he roared. "You're seeing more of Coyle these days than me."

"For God's sake, Peter, he's my lawyer!"

He did not respond.

Alarm flickered in Mary's mind. Peter was being completely irrational and selfish, not the man she had consented to marry. Indeed, what she assumed they had in common was fast evaporating, and she was beginning to think she was clinging to a broken relationship. Struggling to put that treacherous thought out of her mind, she pleaded. "Peter, I don't enjoy this. But this trial was forced on me, and I have to see it through. Can't you accept that?" When he declined to answer, she took a deep breath and went on. "If you want the truth, I'm frightened about the way this case is developing."

"Why? You've done nothing wrong."

"Perhaps not, but Mr. Kerr's children and their supporters think differently. I know you don't approve of all the time I'm spending away from you, but I no longer have a choice in the matter."

"Why can't you arrange to rendezvous with Coyle some other time? It can't make that much difference."

"How can you suggest that after all he's done for me? He's been fired and has lost a partnership with the firm, all because he stood up for me. The least I can do is accommodate his schedule."

Peter stiffened.

She moved to the stove and tended the teapot. Despite the mounting uneasiness inside her, she pressed on. "This is a challenging time for us both. But what I'm most concerned about is our relationship, which is becoming more fragile every day. I recognize that your heavy workload and my indictment aren't facilitating things for you at the office, but I..." She turned to face him, but he had left the kitchen. Worn out and more disillusioned than ever, she followed him and reached the front entrance just in time to see him march out of her apartment, the slam of the door reverberating.

Sick at heart, Mary sat at the table. She reflected on the past five months, focusing primarily on Peter's behaviour. Because of her, his position within Beasley, Grant & Skelhorn was indubitably being threatened, and that troubled her. Yet she was angry. Angry with him for not understanding, and angry with herself for playing into his anger, unleashing sentiments she had difficulty reconciling. The golden shimmer that had surrounded their early days together was gone, vanished. Mary felt empty and cold and lonely.

She found herself going back to one of her conversations with Rachel and recalled word-by-word what her friend had said: *Peter is amiable enough, but he's a mama's boy, with no sense of responsibility or reliability—qualities you, Mary, ostensibly value in people, especially one you intend to spend your life with.*

Rachel had always been outspoken. And most times Mary marvelled at her far-sightedness, the way she perceived things that normally eluded most people. Yet Mary had summarily rejected her opinion. She had been so sure of herself then, but now her friend's words lingered, causing her to confront the stark truth about Peter, and, in turn, her own choices and values. The path ahead seemed uncertain, the emotional landscape altered, and Mary grappled with the weight of self-reflection in the face of a relationship transformed.

Twenty-four hours later, Mary was sitting in her living room waiting for Coyle to arrive. She looked anxiously around the room to assure herself that everything was in order. This was her sanctuary where she felt sheltered and protected, the only place she had ever considered home. More importantly, it suited her. Sizable and tastefully furnished with twin sofas, a coffee table, and a display cabinet featuring a phonograph and stereo set, it was painted in warm colours and decorated with an eclectic collection of prints. She looked out the window, which had a view of the Rideau Canal. She happened to see Coyle emerging from his car. It had now started raining, and she watched him quickly make his way to the panel on the wall of her building. The doorbell rang, and she heard him through the intercom. "Patrick here. I'm afraid I'm early. May I come up?"

Mary pushed the key to activate the door and heard the buzzer sound. A few moments later, she greeted him into her foyer.

"Miserable weather, isn't it?" he stated as he handed her his coat.

"Yes. And I'm afraid it's going to get worse."

She hung his coat and ushered him through the living room, the whisper of classical music in the background. They walked down a short passage to a smaller room and, at its entrance, Mary made a vague gesture and said, "I made the second bedroom into an office."

Coyle stepped inside and scanned the room: two chairs arranged in front of a large antique desk set against a wall, floor-to-ceiling bookshelves across from it, and the apartment-size upright piano that occupied the space between two small windows, radiating warmth and coziness in an otherwise professional setting. "A useful room," he acknowledged. He approached the piano and looked back at her. "You play?"

"For my own enjoyment," she replied. After a brief hesitation, she asked, "May I offer you a refreshment…coffee, tea, or an alcoholic beverage perhaps?" Until now they had held their meetings in his office, and she was unsure what approach to take. Should she treat him as a guest in her home, or should she keep it strictly business?

"Scotch would be nice, if it isn't a trouble," he answered appreciatively as he set his attaché case atop the desk. He then shook his head apologetically. "Forgive me; I ought to have asked what you had."

"Not a problem. It's Peter's favourite drink, and I have a fifteen-year-old single malt in my cupboard. Please excuse me while I fetch it."

When she re-entered the office, carrying a tray with a cup of tea, a bottle of whiskey, an empty cut glass tumbler, and a container of ice, he was standing in front of her bookshelves. At the sound of her footsteps, he turned and motioned around him. "Quite the collection. I see you like to read."

She smiled and then pointed to the container. "I didn't know whether you took ice with your Scotch."

"Yes, thank you."

She placed the tray on the desk. "You may wish to serve yourself."

Coyle poured his drink then set the tray aside and waited for Mary to sit down. He then pulled the other chair closer to hers and seated himself. He opened his attaché case and pulled out his files. One slipped from his grasp, and he quickly bent down to scoop up the papers that had spilled onto the floor.

As he did so, Mary noted the initials N.P.C. engraved below the lock of his attaché. It was a beautiful leather case, presumably given to him by someone special in his life.

The file restored, Coyle set his case on the floor then took a pipe from his pocket. "Oh, may I?" he asked.

"Yes, by all means. I never noticed you smoking before."

"An old habit I revert to occasionally. It helps me to think."

She handed him an ashtray. "Is there something else I can get for you?"

"No, that's fine."

She waited while he filled his pipe and lit up. He emitted several puffs of smoke, then leaned back in his chair, his gaze meeting hers. "We have a lot of work ahead of us, so we had better get started." Propping the pipe on the ashtray, he began to sort through his papers, his hands moving deliberately.

When Coyle arrived, Mary had felt chastened and exposed—a residue of last night's quarrel with Peter. Now, inspired by Coyle, she regained some of her confidence, and they spent the evening examining her file, down to the most miniscule detail. Coyle finally leaned back on his chair and said, "I believe we've accomplished enough for the time being." He closed the open file and again picked up his pipe, which he revived. He sat, smoking reflectively for several moments. He gazed in the direction of the living room and said with a smile, "You obviously enjoy that particular piece of music."

Mary was initially bemused then blushed. "Depending on the mood I'm in, I select a composition and program it to repeat. Not an unusual occurrence here, I'm afraid. I hope it hasn't been too distracting?" Mary had always found the first movement of Mozart's Piano Concerto No. 24 in C minor to be exceptionally soothing.

"No. I, too, enjoy Mozart. His music is alleged to have transformational powers over people's well-being," he remarked.

"I would agree. He's among my favourite composers."

Coyle nodded pensively, then glanced at his watch. He tapped out his pipe and stood up from the desk. "Forgive me, it's later than I realized. I really must go."

He placed the files in his briefcase, and Mary moved with him to the door. She retrieved his coat and turned to him. "Thank you for coming. I feel we accomplished a great deal tonight."

"Yes, we did. Yet there is much to do, and we should meet again soon. How about ten o'clock on Monday? In my office, if that suits you. We can order in if we run into the lunch hour."

Mary remembered her first-Monday-of-the-month standing lunch date with Rachel and realized she would have to cancel. Knowing her friend would understand, she replied, "Ten o'clock is fine."

He studied her for a moment, his gaze too penetrating for comfort. Then empathy surfaced in his eyes. "I know you're concerned about the outcome of the trial, but try not to worry. You'll do fine."

"I'll try," she said as she handed him his coat. He shrugged into it, then brushing past her opened the door and quietly closed it behind him.

Mary returned to the living room and collapsed into the sofa. Her back against the cushions, she curled her legs up under her and allowed her mind to turn to Peter. What had he done all day? He had not reached out to her, and she felt troubled. All his other emotional outbursts had invariably been followed by a telephone call, begging her forgiveness for his lack of understanding—his apologies sounding sincere and genuine. His anger yesterday, however, had been one she had never witnessed before. It had frightened her. Desperate to clear the air between them, she contemplated ringing his apartment to reassure him and herself that all was still well between them, despite their disagreement. But she suddenly felt the loss of her calm energy and reasoned it would be better to call him in the morning. She would take a long bath instead.

As she retreated from the semi-dark room, her eyes stopped on an object resting on the floor beside the other sofa. Peter's briefcase. He had departed in such a huff following their argument that he had obviously forgotten to take it with him.

She glanced at her watch. It was just a little before ten. If she left immediately, there would be sufficient time to drive to his apartment and catch him before he retired. Then she remembered the ballet performance at the NAC. Had he decided to attend without her? She did not think so. That would be totally out of character.

Feeling a burst of longing for him, she hurried outside to her car. It was still raining, and thunder rumbled in the distance. She was cold, and it was hard to imagine being more miserable, but she needed to be with him.

She headed for Bank Street and turned right on Somerset. The restaurants, brimming with late-night customers, exuded merriment. Mary sighed. She and Peter frequently had dinner with friends at these restaurants, walking distance from his apartment.

By the time she arrived at his building, it was ten thirty. Stepping into the rain, she locked the car and approached the front entrance. His apartment lay in the more residential part of Somerset Street—a modern structure surrounded by trim gardens and lush lawn. Drawing her coat more tightly around her, she hastened up the long path to the door. She glanced up at the third floor to see if there was light coming through his front window. Either he had chosen to join Linda and Garry at the ballet performance or he had gone to bed early. She hesitated for a moment, debating what to do next. She decided against calling him on the intercom. If he was already in bed, she didn't want to wake him. One option was to let herself in just long enough to deposit his briefcase and then leave. A couple was leaving the building, so she took advantage of the open door and entered the posh lobby.

When she reached his apartment, she produced her key and let herself in. All the lights were off, and the apartment was quiet. She placed the bag on the floor and was about to leave when she heard, very faintly, laughter emanating from Peter's study. Soundlessly, she made her way through the wide corridor toward the room, the spill of outdoor streetlights guiding her. At midpoint, she stood still, irresolute, listening, alert for anything that might indicate a presence. She was beginning to wonder whether her brain had played tricks on her when, once more, she heard laughter, this time followed by low murmurs. Her anxiety mounting, she moved closer, tensing at every creak her steps elicited. Unequivocally, now, she could hear Peter's voice and then that of a woman. The words *We're grateful to you for* and *Baxter is sure to get a conviction* resonated from the room, the woman's voice suddenly recognizable.

Mary's subconscious alerted her to the impending scene behind the door, and she cried out in muted pain. The urge to turn and flee gripped her, but something in her refused to believe and pulled her forward. *This isn't happening. This isn't happening,* she repeated to herself over and over again. But the mantra did not stop the cold dread from overtaking her as she furtively took the last step to the door and pushed it open.

Staring back at her from the softly lit room were Peter and Courtney. Wine glasses on the coffee table, they were seated on the couch, which Mary herself had helped select for Peter's home office. She blanched and raised her arm to stifle her cry of disbelief.

Courtney withdrew from Peter's embrace, her expression

merely showing resentment at the intrusion. "Has nobody ever taught you to knock before entering a room?" she sneered defiantly.

Mary gaped at Peter—the betrayal so prodigious, her pain so palpable, she could scarcely breathe. Her words came out a gasping whisper. "Oh no! Oh God! Oh no!"

Peter was standing now. If Mary had been able to focus, she would have seen the fear in his eyes, the reverberating fear that comes out of the realization that there is no redemption.

Mary spun and ran out of the apartment. In the background, she could hear Peter cry, "Mary, wait! Mary!"

Stupefied, Mary staggered back to the elevator. Inside, she leaned against the wall, struggling to regain control. She didn't press any buttons on the elevator's panel but felt it moving. When it halted, the door opened into a now crowded lobby. Blindly she ran forward, bumping into people—barely seeing the front entrance. As she stepped into the showery night, a gust of wind pelted her with rain. Somehow, she managed to drive home, though later she couldn't remember doing so. By the time she got to her building, the weather had deteriorated into a full-blown storm. The thunder rumbled and growled. She entered by the side door, adjoining the parking lot. Although she could hardly see for the tears in her eyes, she was relieved to find the back hall empty. She stumbled to the service elevator, everything spinning and lurching around her. Inside, she pressed the button to the second floor and again leaned against the wall. Coyle's observation, *Someone is feeding them information*, seeped into her befuddled brain and gnawed at her.

When this new reality hit her, a cold hand gripped her heart. How could Peter have deceived her so? When? How? Why? What did he have to gain? She searched her memory for plausible answers. But none came. Instead, she was overtaken by an immense anxiety, so intense that she could scarcely breathe. *Must get back to my apartment*, she told herself. She closed her eyes in the hope of blanking out the dizziness that was slowly overpowering her but could barely focus when she opened them again.

Finally, the elevator came to a standstill, and through blurred vision she saw the door move. She rushed through it, heading straight for her unit, only to realize that she was hardly advancing. Her steps tenuous and heavy, she lurched forward. She felt the doorknob in her hand, the pins and needles spreading up from her fingers. Filled with a blinding terror, she clutched at the handle for support. But the effort was futile. Her knees buckled under her, she collapsed, and her head snapped back onto the hardwood floor. A searing pain pierced through her, and then blackness.

When Mary regained consciousness, she was lying on the floor and someone was holding her close, depriving her of any voluntary movement. She made an effort to focus, but all she could see were faceless people moving above her.

She heard a distinctive voice. "Mary! Mary!"

Coyle?

"Mary, I need to get you inside. Where is your key?"

She tried to answer, but nothing came out. She opened her eyes and peered at the blurred crowd that had congregated.

"Please, step back. We need room for her to breathe." Coyle's voice came to her as though from a distance. Then in a softly modulated tone, he pleaded, "Mary, I need your key to get you inside."

She nodded lethargically and slurred, "In my pocket." She made a move to stand. "I…I…" she started but was unable to finish and settled back on the floor. She felt herself gently brought to her feet. With the little awareness she had remaining, she noted her keys in Coyle's hand. Supporting her, he unlocked the door, pushed it open, and guided her across the foyer toward the living room. As he lowered her tenderly on the sofa, she closed her eyes, overwhelmed with sleepiness. She felt something—a blanket perhaps—lowered to cover her.

When she became fully conscious again, Coyle was leaning over her. "What happened, Mary? How was it that you were outside?"

She could remember nothing. All she could think about was the throbbing pain in the back of her head.

"Mary, I'm going to call a doctor."

"No, no!" she cried. "I don't want you to call anyone. I don't need anyone. Just help me to my room. I...I'm so very tired."

Mary struggled to her feet, and it all came back to her, Peter with Courtney. A deep moan escaped her lips, one of grief and denial. Of despair. Once more, she could feel the space crumbling all around her, and she almost collapsed. Coyle scooped her up in his arms, carried her to her bedroom, and gently set her on the bed, where she curled up in a fetal position. All she wanted was to sleep.

When her eyes opened again, she found herself alone in her room, with no recollection of how she got there. The drapes were drawn, but she could see the light through them. In the distance, she heard voices. She strained to get up but found herself powerless to move. "Peter..." she whispered and slipped into a world of semi-consciousness.

Several times, she woke to the shrill ring of the telephone but lacked the energy to answer it or even care. Finally, she opened her eyes, looked up, and saw Coyle in the doorway. "Good morning, Mary," he said pleasantly.

"Good morning," she replied, attempting to smile but not succeeding. "What happened?"

"You had a bad fall." He walked across the room, sat down on the side of her bed, and handed her a glass of orange juice. "Here, take this. I found a full carton in your refrigerator."

She managed to sit up enough to be able to accept the offered glass. As she raised it to her mouth, her hands shook a little.

"Let me help you," he insisted, supporting her hands while she took a sip. After she had finished, he set the half-empty glass on the night table.

She looked down and saw that she had been stripped of her clothes and was presently wearing one of her nightgowns.

Coyle said, "You were drenched, and we were afraid you'd catch pneumonia if we didn't remove your wet clothing." When she remained silent, he continued, "I assure you, everything was proper."

"We?" she managed.

"I called a physician friend of mine, who lives not far from here. She came over to ensure that you were in no danger."

"Oh…" Mary brought her free hand to her head.

"How are you feeling?"

"A bit drowsy. I have this galling pain in my head."

"As I mentioned, you had a bad fall…a possible concussion. My friend suggested I stay with you, in case of complications. Any blurred vision?"

"No," she replied and then struggled to sit completely upright, draping herself with the sheet as she did so. Gradually her head began to clear, and images assaulted her. With the remembrance came pain, a scorching emotional pain that stabbed all parts of her being, leaving her powerless to speak. A wail emerged from her constricted throat.

She felt out of control and absurdly irrational, but she had been struggling with too many issues for too long, and there was no reserve left in her.

With the utmost care, Coyle took her into his arms. Helpless, she allowed him, the tears running down her cheeks. When she regained control, he forced her to look at him and said, "Mary, something happened after I left you last night. What was it?"

She saw it all again, her pulse thudding at the memory: the laughter followed by low murmurs; the panic she felt as she stumbled through the door; Peter's alarm and Courtney's cheap jibe. Thinking about it filled her with such despair that her voice was strangled by it. She tried to speak but was unsuccessful.

"Mary, your fiancé called last night and has been calling all morning, asking to speak to you. Should I dial him?"

"No!" she cried.

"Why not?"

"Just don't. Please."

"I'm not sure I understand." When she did not enlighten him, he repeated, "What happened last night?"

"It was Peter all along."

Her words were met with a blank stare.

"It was he all along who deceived us," she cried, as she collapsed against his chest and began to shake.

Coyle drew her closer. "Oh, Mary! I'm sorry…so terribly sorry."

He held her until she ceased shaking, then released her. "I have no wish to cause you additional distress, but you need to tell me about Peter."

Tears spilling from her eyes, she gave him a précis of what had transpired.

Coyle listened intently, his expression tempered by empathy.

Even after recounting the previous evening's events, she could hardly believe her words. She felt lost, dispossessed. And when she spoke again, her voice was barely audible. "I can't believe Peter would betray our relationship like that. We meant too much to each other. But, as unbelievable as it may be, I'm now convinced that it was he who stole my briefcase." She took a deep breath and tried to think clearly. "I'm confused. How did you happen to be here?"

"Sometime after reaching my apartment last night, I discovered the absence of an important document. I realized I must have missed it when I collected the papers off the floor of your office, so I hurried back. Luckily, I gained access to the building through a group of partygoers entering at that moment. Despite the late hour, I hoped to find you still awake. Instead, I found you unconscious on the floor in front of your apartment."

The telephone rang, harsh and insistent. Mary stiffened. When she made no attempt to answer, Coyle picked it up. "Hello?"

He tensed and covered the mouthpiece with his hand. "It's Peter."

"I don't..." She shook her head, not finishing.

"I'm afraid she's not available to take your call," Coyle spoke into the receiver.

After a brief moment, he turned to Mary. "He insists on speaking to you."

The grief hit her again, greater than she had ever felt

before. She dropped her head and doubled up in pain—too much pain even to cry.

Coyle's tone hardened as he addressed Peter once more. "You'll have to try again another time." Then came the sound of him hanging up the phone. Unable to meet his gaze, Mary waited for him to speak.

After a pause, he uttered her name. She raised her head but focused on the door behind him.

"Look at me, please," he pleaded.

Mustering her damaged pride, she met his gaze.

"Mary, I'm due elsewhere in half an hour. Is there someone I can call to be with you?"

"No, thank you. I've burdened you long enough."

"No burden, trust me." He paused. Then, intense concern in his eyes, he said, "I am loath to leave you alone like this."

"Please don't worry about me. I'll be fine." As she uttered this, it suddenly occurred to her that it was a ludicrous response. How could she ever be fine again?

"Allow me at least to get you breakfast before I go."

"I couldn't possibly eat."

Coyle gently placed his hand on her arm. "The best thing for you to do then is get some sleep. I'll call around one o'clock to check on you."

"There's no need for you to call."

"Maybe not, but I will."

Mary somehow summoned a smile.

He turned and walked to the door, then turned to face her. "I'd feel more at ease if someone were here with you. Are you certain there isn't anyone I can call?"

"Honestly, no, it's quite unnecessary. I would rather be alone."

He looked troubled and hesitated before answering. "Very well, but promise that you will ring me if you need something. My activities today do not involve anything that can't be interrupted."

"I promise."

"Until later, then."

Mary nodded and managed a stifled thank you.

As Coyle stepped out of her bedroom, her hands clenched. She rested her head back against her pillow and thought of Peter and the future that could no longer be. She lay motionless, feeling sick, frightened beyond any fear she had ever known. What she had chosen to ignore about their relationship had at last been affirmed. And with it came the realization that the love and happiness she had yearned for, still yearned for, had been lost forever. Praying for a miracle she no longer believed in, she closed her eyes, battling the waves of nausea.

It was now past noon, and the telephone had been ringing incessantly throughout the entire morning. Fearing
it might be Peter on the line, Mary had refrained from
picking up the receiver, allowing the answering machine
to take over. She did not want to speak to him. Yet there
were so many unanswered questions. Foremost in her mind
was how she could have been so misguided about him. The
evidence must have been there all along. Rachel and Coyle
had spotted it and had tried to warn her. But she had been
too blind and deaf to acknowledge it.

At exactly one o'clock the telephone rang again.
Remembering that Coyle had said he would check in on her
then, she picked it up. "Hello?"

"How are you, Mary?" came his voice at the other end
of the line.

"I'm much better, thank you."

"Are you up?"

"No." Actually, she had lingered in bed, hoping to sleep,
for it was the only way to dull her senses.

"Is there anything I can do for you?" he asked.

"No. But thank you for offering."

"Mary, about our meeting Monday morning, we can
defer it to another day."

"No, there's no need."

"Are you sure?"

"Yes."

"Well, in that case, let's meet at ten, ten fifteen."

"That sounds fine."

Coyle paused briefly before he spoke again, his voice earnest and sincere. "But only if you feel up to it."

"I'll be fine. And thank you for calling," she replied and hung up.

Almost immediately, the phone rang again. Thinking it was Coyle with an afterthought, she picked up the receiver.

"Mary, it's Peter."

She was too drained to respond.

"Mary, don't hang up. Please!"

"Peter, I've nothing to say to you."

"Mary, I must speak to you and won't give up until I've seen you." When she failed to answer, he said, "Please!"

She was not ready to confront him in her present condition, yet she knew it was inevitable and relented. "Very well." She hung up without saying anything more.

As carefully as she could, she tossed aside the blanket and got out of bed—the effort making her slightly dizzy. Once on her feet, she stood for a moment, waiting for the dizziness to pass. She then wrapped herself in her housecoat, walked to the living room, and waited for him to arrive.

Half an hour later there was a knock at her door, and she opened it. Seeing Peter brought forward last night's scene, carrying with it the reverberating pain.

When she did not move, he asked, "May I come in?"

She stepped aside, her movement mechanical, and slowly headed toward the living room.

Peter closed the door behind him and followed her. Before he could say anything, she turned to face him, her face drained. When he had called, she had felt only grief. But now, a stronger force moved her—an obscure desire to know, to understand. She murmured, "All this time, you were working against me. Coyle suspected you from the very beginning, but I refused to believe it. Why would you do such a thing, Peter?"

He gazed at the floor, mute, in obvious discomfort.

"Why?" she repeated, barely audible.

"He promised me a…" Peter lowered his voice, visibly embarrassed by his own words, "…a partnership if I helped him."

Though his confession had not been unexpected, Mary felt the wind go out of her, as though she'd been punched.

"He wanted to see what was in your briefcase and demanded I get it for him," he continued.

"He?"

"Beasley."

"What did Beasley expect to find in my briefcase?"

"Papers that could incriminate you." Peter paused, and then added, "When he first approached me, I honestly didn't consider my actions all that reprehensible. My job was simply to get as much information as possible, which, along with corroborating evidence, would either inculpate you or set you free. Knowing you were incapable of doing anything illegal, I consented, albeit reluctantly."

"When did he ask you to do this?"

"At my parents' reception."

The memory of Beasley and Peter coming out of Mr.

Burbidge's library came bursting through. "And you took my briefcase from where?"

"I found it lying beside your hallway table after I drove you home."

Once again, Mary felt as if she had been slapped. She leaned on the arm of the sofa. "It was you. You did that?" she cried in a feeble voice, still hoping he might refute it. Her voice began to quiver. "I can't believe this, Peter. Tell me it isn't true."

"Mary, even with my mother and father's contacts, I wasn't able to draw enough clients to the firm. He warned me that if I didn't help him in this, I could say goodbye to any aspiration I might have of ever becoming a partner. I did what I had to do to protect my job…our future."

"Being a partner was so enticing that you would do this? Did I mean so little to you?"

"It would've made me a partner for you to be proud of."

"I was already proud of you."

"How could you be? I had nothing to offer you."

"I had your love. Or at least I thought I did."

"One cannot survive on love alone, Mary. I'm afraid I don't view poverty as ennobling as you do."

"I don't perceive poverty ennobling, nor do I consider it degrading. It's just another state of being with different choices to make." Their conversation was weakening her. She shook her head to clear her mind, and then said, "Peter, attaining a partnership with power and status has always been your mother's dream for you, not mine. I was content with commitment and esteem for each other."

"What's wrong with having power and position?"

Unnerved by his lack of understanding and on the verge of tears, she said, "Nothing, essentially. It's how you use it that is important. For your mother, power means manipulating people for her own self-interest. For me, power means getting up every morning and dealing with the difficulties I face without giving in to corruption and broken values."

"There was no alternative. I had to do what Beasley demanded or lose my job."

Mary stared at him, unbelieving. It was as if she were seeing him for the first time, without the irrational eyes of one smitten by love. Finally, she managed to say, "On that point, at least, you're absolutely correct. Any time you've been given a choice, you never had one because you repeatedly went for the easiest way out. Deep down, I…I recognized this. Only, I refused to believe it. I couldn't reconcile myself to the notion that you could be that disloyal. Did what we share ever mean anything to you?"

"Mary, you have to know that I love you. For me, there could never be anybody else. But you may as well face it— nobody in today's world gets anywhere on merit alone. In case you haven't heard, honesty and integrity are no longer prerequisites for success. Just look at you, you're going to lose this case, regardless that you're innocent."

"Just because most people have embraced that concept doesn't mean we need to submit to it," she replied sourly. "I still feel I can make a difference on my own terms. I refuse to live by the diminished values of others."

"You're so naïve. You fail to see life for what it is. What you don't recognize is that you're living in constant denial."

"That may be so, but I prefer to call it optimism. Despite everything else, it provides me with the courage to move on or at least be hopeful about the future. It's better than burying myself in self-pity and deceit."

"Mary, they'll destroy you if you persist on that route."

"True. But at least I'll go down fighting."

Peter gave her a pained look. "It was never meant to end this way."

"Oh? How exactly was it meant to end?"

"It all started so innocently." Peter grimaced as he met her gaze. "All Beasley wanted was for me to persuade you not to fight them. I didn't see any harm in that and complied with his request. I knew you didn't have a chance against him. He's too able and influential for you."

Mary recalled their conversation after they'd left his parents' dinner party with Beasley, when Peter noted that she never discussed her impending trial with him. At the time it had sounded like well-meaning concern.

"Beasley was convinced that you didn't have the necessary courage to fight them," said Peter. "Even now, it escapes me why you continue to oppose Beasley and the Crown attorney. It just doesn't make sense. You have nothing to gain by going against them."

"Nothing but my self-esteem," she replied.

The remark was ignored. "Unfortunately, once committed, the die was cast and there was no turning back for me."

"Why didn't you confide in me? I would've understood, and we could have worked it out together."

"It was already too late. But I'm willing to come clean now."

She looked at him, sadly. "Like you said, it's already too late."

"Can't you see I did this for you, for us?"

Mary shot him a disgusted look. "You didn't do it for me. You talked yourself into believing that when, in actual fact, you were focusing on your own ambitions. You sabotaged what we had together for a partnership in the firm."

"Okay, maybe I did. I was going to lose everything that I had worked for. Can't you see? I did what anybody would do to get ahead. I did what I had to do."

"You honestly believe that, don't you?"

"Yes, I do."

"In that case, there can never be anything between us, Peter, for a loving relationship is all about meeting each other's needs, not just your own."

The words were quietly voiced, but the effect was as devastating as if she had slapped him across the face. "Why did you have to go against them all?" he asked, his words barely audible. Louder, he moaned, "There was no way in which you could win."

"Unlike you, I had a choice. And I chose to honour my promise to Mr. Kerr."

"They all predicted you would give in. And the only reason I went along with them was because I had hoped my actions would hasten it…giving in, I mean."

This revelation was so startling that Mary was uncertain how to respond. Yet it all became clear. Recalling Peter's past behaviour, she could see that it was inevitable that he would be involved, and the weight of it all was crushing her. Depleted, she let herself fall on the sofa. Then she remembered the scene with Mr. Beasley and his parents. "That evening in your father's library, what did Beasley demand of you?"

He stared at her with a stunned expression.

"I was in the garden and happened to overhear the last part of your conversation," she elaborated.

"Oh, Mary, I was so ashamed of the role I had been forced to play against you that I alerted Beasley that afternoon of my intention to reveal everything to you. Unbeknownst to me, he called my mother to seek her help. She knew nothing about my removing the briefcase from your apartment, but he convinced her that I couldn't plausibly side with you on this case if I wished to remain with the firm. As a result, she instigated the dinner party."

"And after that, you did everything you could to dissuade me from going on with the trial." Mary's words were spoken barely above a whisper.

"It was a vile thing to do, and I regret it immensely. I can see now it was what brought me beyond the point of no return."

Mary swallowed, seeking to still the pain swelling inside her. Speechless, she covered her face with her hands.

As though weakened by his own words, Peter sat on the couch beside her. "Mary, what we have together is the best thing that has ever happened to me, and I'm asking you to give me a second chance." He lowered his voice. "I don't deserve it, but I'm asking for it regardless. If you do, I promise I will make it up to you, even if it takes the rest of my life."

"How can you ask for a second chance when everything we've shared in the last months was founded on nothing but lies and deceit? Even those rare moments when you demonstrated concern for me, I realize now, were ploys to access my papers, so you could turn them over to Beasley."

"Mary, I was desperate. I didn't know what I was doing."

"You had to know. How could you have been so faithless?" she replied in a strangled voice.

"Mary, I love you. If you believe nothing else, at least believe that."

"Then how do you explain Courtney's presence in your apartment?"

"It didn't mean anything. I was upset at you over our argument the previous evening and not thinking properly. She was a mere diversion."

"*A mere diversion?*" Mary was stunned. It was not only a fickle answer, but also crude and demeaning, filling her with revulsion and indignation. How could she have fallen for such a man? Obviously, the relationship they had developed could never have been what she had aspired to. Yes, at the beginning, when there were just the two of them, it had been glorious. Wooed by his charming personality, the flowers, the love notes, and the magic of romantic love, she had not heeded the whispers of warning and had remained oblivious to the aberrations that marked their relationship. With things as they were, she recognized that her love for Peter had been built solely on infatuation, a product of dreams and imagination. Now that real life had set in, the fascination had faded away and the euphoria that had initially bonded them no longer existed.

"What we have together is special." Peter's words hung in the air, cold and sharp as a blade.

Mary shook her head. "What makes a relationship special is how one partner helps the other in arduous times. I knew you didn't approve of what I was doing, but I certainly didn't expect you to side with your mother, Courtney, and Beasley in their fight against me," she said bitterly. "You can tell your mother that she need not concern herself about me anymore. And as for Courtney, you may as well return to her, since it's entertainment you seek. It's obvious you deserve each other."

"I don't want to lose you," was his feeble reply.

"You should have thought about that before plotting against me."

"Mary! I—"

"Please leave. You and I have nothing further to say to each other." She removed the diamond ring from her finger and set it on the coffee table in front of Peter.

"You can't mean that!"

Mary found she could no longer speak. There was no more fight left in her.

He reached out to touch her arm, but she recoiled from his hand. "You've had your say. Now leave," she ordered. The finality in her voice struck cold even to her own ears.

"Oh, Mary! Tell me this is not happening," he implored.

"Leave me, please," she repeated. The emotions she was holding back were pressing deeply, and tears were threatening to come. Needing to put distance between herself and Peter, she went to the window and stared blankly through the glass. She stood immobile, listening to Peter's footsteps as he walked to the front door. She heard the door creak open then close quietly. She leaned her head against the cold glass and closed her eyes, wishing she could shut off her memories. She had loved him. She had trusted him. And all the time, he had been plotting against her. She wondered if she had really known him at all.

When she opened her eyes again, she saw Peter step out of the building, and a panic threatened to grab her. She wanted to cry out for him to come back, but she remained frozen. Feebly she watched him get into his car and drive away. She dragged herself from the window and staggered toward the kitchen as if in a trance. There, she collapsed into a chair. Already she could feel a gnawing loneliness seep inside her. Try as she could, she found it impossible to let go of a painful yearning that marred her whole being. She once more buried her face in her hands and wept like she had never wept before.

Tears continued to flow as Mary made her way to her room and lay down on her bed, staring blankly at a vacuous space in front of her. "He's gone. He's gone," she repeated to herself. As much as she tried, her mind failed to steer away from his deception. There was no relief for her.

It was raining again, and the heavy air in her apartment hung over her like a cold, suffocating blanket. She closed her eyes and tried to conjure a more pleasant memory, anything. But she found nothing. Only bleakness. It descended on her so completely that she barely noticed the day turning into evening. When finally she could tolerate it no longer, she rose from her bed, went to the phone, and dialed Rachel's number.

There was a long wait. Then, in the distance, she heard the voice of the friend who had been her constant champion.

"Hello?" repeated the voice.

"Rachel, it's Mary. Is this a bad time to call?"

"Oh, hello, Mary! No! I was in my office, hidden in my books. It simply took me a while to resurface. What's up?"

"Rachel, are you free to come over?"

"What is it, Mary?"

"I just need to speak to you, that's all," she replied, unable to keep the vulnerability out of her voice.

There was a brief silence, where Mary could almost feel the weight of the bewilderment at the end of the line. Then came Rachel's voice, "I'm on my way."

Twenty minutes later, she appeared at Mary's door. Rachel was silent—a rare occurrence for her—as she sat on the couch sipping the tea Mary had insisted on preparing. She waited, her gaze fixed on her friend's contorted features and red eyes. When it became apparent Mary could not or would not address the issue at hand, she said uneasily, "Mary, what is it that's troubling you?"

Struggling to keep her emotions from running away with her, Mary blurted out everything, including her discovery of Courtney at Peter's place. "Oh, Rachel, I never thought anything could destroy what we had." She paused, trying desperately to contain herself. "I'm so disillusioned, I doubt that I will ever be able to trust again."

"Mary, don't allow yourself to be brought down by a man who cares about nothing but his own gratification and is willing to pursue it at any cost—even at the risk of harming the people who love him."

Rachel's voice was soothing, sympathetic, but Mary was beyond consoling and made no attempt to answer.

"With time, you'll get over this," Rachel insisted with the full force of her conviction. "That may sound cliché, but it has proven accurate time after time."

"What's wrong with me, anyway?" Mary asked, more to herself than to Rachel.

"What makes you ask such a question?"

"You were able to see through Peter, why couldn't I?" Mary sighed. "What a fool I was."

"We all have the capacity to fool ourselves," Rachel replied. "When we desire something fervently enough, our brain can't distinguish reality from fantasy. You've been on your own most of your life. You've coped well enough, Mary, but all the same, you unconsciously yearn to be part of a family. And Peter represented that for you."

It amazed Mary how her friend had been able to intuit her deepest desire. Because her parents had been unable to love her, it was an emotion she had neither expected nor understood—until she met Peter. Despite her miserable childhood, her dream of a happy family had remained.

"I'm convinced it was never Peter's intention to harm me," Mary insisted.

"That may be so, but in the end, everything he did was of his own volition. It's not as if he were ignorant of what was acceptable and what was not."

"I hear what you're saying. But deep down, I know he's a good person."

"Frankly, Mary, I've always considered you too trusting."

"Is that a fault? Does it make me weak?"

"No, it makes you an easy target for anyone without scruples."

"If I appear to be too trusting, Rachel, it's because I need to believe in people."

Mary's anguish obviously touched a sensitive chord. Rachel said, "Forgive me. We all have our own survival skills, and yours are not any worse than mine. Remember, however, that when you live in a fantasy world, reality gets blurred."

Her eyes welling, Mary murmured, "Before today, I was swayed by Peter's attention to me. Now all I can think is, did he ever love me? It's hard to think rationally about him, to know what he really felt."

"It's impossible to know everything about a person—even someone you love dearly," Rachel replied.

"Oh, Rachel! I feel humiliated, demeaned. Rationally or not, I feel lacking."

"Mary, don't let him do this to you. Don't you dare let him define you!"

"As the saying goes, that is easier said than done." Mary blinked rapidly, refusing to let herself cry. "I just don't know what to do anymore."

"You pick up the pieces and deal with them."

"Which is also easier said than done," Mary acknowledged with a rueful smile. She paused to recover the little confidence that remained and then posed the question that had occupied her mind but been left unspoken. "Rachel, you once confided in me about your ex-husband, Daryl… how hurt you were. Did he ever want to come back to you?"

"Why do you ask?"

"Peter is totally devastated by the way he has treated me and has begged me to forgive him. But I can't. Yet when you love someone, truly love them, you should be able to forgive them anything." This last part was spoken more as a reflection than a statement.

"You might have been able to forgive him one deception, but not two. It was too much, too early in your relationship," Rachel replied. "And as for him being repentant, that does not make what he did any less reprehensible. Trust me, you're well out of it. He never deserved you."

"You haven't answered my question."

"It's yes. Daryl did ask me to forgive and forget." Rachel released a tortured smile. "Strange about relationships.

When he proposed marriage, he told me that he had felt a connection the moment our eyes met. He swore eternal devotion. Yet his last words before leaving me were, 'The passion in our lives is gone, I don't love you anymore.' He moved on to another woman, named Jennifer. As it turned out, it didn't take him long to discover that Jennifer did not hold the secret for passion either. And he begged me to take him back, proclaiming that leaving me was the greatest mistake he had ever made."

"Why didn't you?"

"I couldn't do it. Living with him hadn't been easy in the first place. It would have required too much energy, and I was tired of the effort."

"With what you know today, would you have accepted him back into your life?"

"It's feasible, but it would never have worked. That is one thing these past years have reinforced for me. To have a future together, we both would've had to change. And before one can bring that about, one has to recognize the need for it. He, regrettably, refused to acknowledge he had a problem. Whatever was troubling him, it was easier to blame it on me and our marriage."

"Do you believe that someday you will meet someone special who will love you genuinely?"

Rachel seemed to sag under the weight of the question. At length she answered, "In this world of personal gratification above everything else, I've grown to not expect much genuine love from any man." She paused then added, "For that, you could call me a pessimist."

"I never perceived you as a pessimist. A trifle out of

the ordinary, perhaps. But definitely not a pessimist." Mary chuckled.

Rachel gave her an amused look. "It's encouraging to see you've regained your sense of humour."

Before Rachel could say more, Mary spoke in a more serious tone. "You know, before all this, I believed that if you loved someone truly and unconditionally, that same love would be returned. How idiotic!"

"Not everybody is as insensitive as Peter," Rachel replied. "Despite everything I've said, deep down in the depth of my soul, I still want to believe there are a few noble men out there who value a caring and nurturing relationship. Unfortunately, I haven't met one, or one who is not already committed."

"Oh, Rachel, will I ever be able to trust again?"

Her friend nodded. "I know what you're going through, I experienced it too. But with time I learned, as you will, that life continues." Reverting to her old self, Rachel managed a sly smile, obviously meant to cheer her. "And don't be so melodramatic. People make erroneous choices all the time. It shouldn't mean the end of the world. Early in a love affair most people appear loving and caring, until they're forced to reveal their dark side. There's no way of predicting whether the person you love is honourable. Just be grateful you found out about Peter's true nature before you were married and not after."

Mary smiled bleakly. There was wisdom in Rachel's counsel, which reinforced her conclusion that Peter was not the admirable person she had envisaged. Having acknowledged the inevitable, her thoughts drifted, and a touch of misgiving crossed her face.

"What is it?" Rachel asked.

"I was thinking about Coyle," she replied. "He had no way of foreseeing this court case would come to this, and he must now be regretting his decision to help me."

"You're mistaken there, kid."

"How do you mean?"

"Nothing happens to Coyle without everyone in the legal system knowing. There's been a great deal of gossip about him doing the rounds since he was fired. And the buzz is that McLeod pleaded with him to return to the firm, said his threat to fire him was a most unfortunate outburst and that he had had no intention of following through with it. He even implied that if he returned, he could write his own agenda. McLeod went so far as offering to add Coyle's name to the firm's. But he rejected the offer, saying that he knew the threat was not serious and, for that reason, did not see it as punitive. He was not angry or upset with him, only more determined to map out his own future."

"You're kidding me!"

"No."

"How did you learn all this?"

"Someone in your old office listened in on McLeod's telephone conversation on an extension. It ended with something like: 'Damn it, Patrick. You can't do this to me.' Apparently, Coyle's answer was: 'Sorry, Henry. It can't be helped.'"

"I wonder what Coyle has in mind for his future then?"

"That's the question everyone's asking," Rachel was quick to say.

When Mary walked into Coyle's office Monday morning, he was at his working table, documents and papers spread all over the surface. He looked up and acknowledged her warmly. He had called earlier in the morning to see how she was and had suggested deferring their meeting to another day if she did not feel up to it. She did not and had been tempted to say so, but she knew their time before the trial was limited, and they could not afford any delay.

"How are you holding up?' he asked after she had seated herself beside him at the table.

"I'm getting there," she assured him, determined to remain strong.

"I'm pleased to hear that," he replied. "But if you feel even the slightest distress, I want you to call an end to this meeting. Is that understood?"

"Yes." She waited a moment to steady her voice then said, "Before we proceed, however, I feel impelled to apologize to you."

"I can't imagine why."

"For refusing to believe you when you suggested that Peter might be complicit in my case."

"Yours was the only reaction acceptable at the time."

"No. After all, I am a lawyer. If it was evident to you, it should have been to me too."

"It's not easy to be objective when you're in love." His tone was kind, sympathetic.

"That's no excuse," she murmured.

"I wouldn't worry about it, if I were you," he insisted.

She attempted a smile. "I promise to be more accommodating in the future."

"Good. We have a lot to cover, so why don't we get started."

"Very well."

After working for several hours, Coyle asked without preamble, "What are you up to this weekend? Any Thanksgiving plans on your agenda?"

She had none but was fearful that admitting it would evoke pity. So she replied, "Right now, they're uncertain."

"Any relatives in the area?"

"No."

Running his hand through his hair, he frowned. "I had hoped to get a lot more done today. There's still so much to do, and I don't see how we can get it all in before your trial next month."

Coyle's concern was also hers, but there seemed to be no resolution to their quandary.

"Since you have yet to decide about the weekend, might it be too presumptuous of me to suggest you join my mother and me at our family residence in Pakenham?" he asked. "It would allow some valuable time to work on your file."

"You're inviting me to your mother's home?" she asked, incredulously.

His gaze rested on her with an almost imperceptible smile. "Yes, I believe that's what I suggested."

"It's very good of you, but I couldn't possibly impose on your mother like—"

"I know she would be eminently pleased to have you join us," Coyle interrupted. "Since Dad passed away four years ago, she's often mentioned that the house feels uncomfortably empty."

"Your mother must have read about me in the paper. What will she think?"

"My mother is an instinctively shrewd person and a good judge of character. Meeting you, she will undoubtedly think you're a woman with integrity and intelligence." He stated the last part with a touch of humour.

Still, Mary was tempted to decline. They had been working together for some time now, but in so many ways, they remained strangers. And spending a weekend with him and his mother would most definitely prove awkward. Yet she replied, "In that case, I accept with pleasure."

"Great. I'll pick you up Saturday afternoon…say one o'clock? That will give me sufficient time to give you a tour of the village on the way."

Nodding graciously, she said, "I look forward to it." Yet she remained skeptical. Although she suspected Coyle's mother was all that he described, in every loving mother there is that protective instinct that makes it virtually impossible for them to circumvent certain negative feelings toward their children's companions. Mary also wondered whether his mother might assume there was something more than a professional relationship between them.

At 12:45 on Saturday afternoon, Rachel appeared at Mary's apartment. "Sorry turning up like this without ringing, but I was on my way to the ByWard Market and hoped you might join me."

"Thank you for thinking of me, but Coyle has invited me to his mother's home in Pakenham for Thanksgiving, and I expect him any minute now."

Rachel's eyebrows shot up. "Might he be falling for you?"

Mary allowed a small laugh to escape her lips. "I'm nothing but a client to him."

"So, he gives up a partnership with a law firm most lawyers would give up an arm and a leg for and now invites you to meet his mother. It would seem that his behaviour is more dictated by infatuation than anything else."

"Don't be absurd. He just happens to be a man of integrity, who took up my cause because he disapproved of the way I was being treated. And as for this weekend, we'll be reviewing my file." Feeling quietly guilty, Mary added, "Right now I regret bringing this on him."

"Why should you feel guilty?"

"He's given up so much for me."

"Uh!" was Rachel's response.

"Rachel, you don't appear to care. Don't you have any sympathy for him?"

"No."

"Why not? You're continually fighting for the under-privileged and the people that are put down."

"Don't be fooled. Once this trial is over, he'll have half the law firms in Ottawa inviting him to join them. That will certainly not be the case for you, even if you are acquitted. In my opinion, the only underprivileged in our society are women, children, and animals." She shook her head. "Women, at least, can speak for themselves and are not totally defenceless. Children and animals, however, are subject to their parents' or owners' whims, good or bad."

Mary could not help smiling. Rachel was a hard-working and tirelessly energetic lawyer—with an all-or-nothing, push-to-the-limit mentality—who fought fiercely for her clients, most of whom were women. But one never felt her true wrath until they had mistreated a child or animal. "I see you were quoted in last week's *Ottawa Citizen* again," she said.

"Yeah, someone has to stir this complacent public," Rachel replied.

"Well, at the risk of sounding rude, would you mind leav-ing?" Mary pleaded. "I'm expecting Coyle any minute now, and I don't want you around making wild insinuations."

"I hear you and get the message. But I expect a complete rundown upon your return. Did he say what time he was bringing you back?"

"He mentioned that Thanksgiving dinner would be on Sunday, so probably late Monday afternoon. Why do you ask?"

"Well, I expect to be away all day Monday, and I was hoping you would come in to feed Bear, if it's not too much trouble. Normally, I would ask Angela—Bear loves to play with little Jesse, they've become best buddies—but she and Jesse are away right now, visiting her parents in Almonte." Bear was a lovable Newfoundland dog that Rachel had rescued from a shelter.

"No trouble at all. Do you still keep your dog food in the fridge?"

"Yes, of course. Now remember, there are two varieties. Whatever you do, don't mix them. Otherwise, he won't eat. And make sure you heat it up. He takes exception to cold food."

"Should I set a place for him at the table too?" Mary asked.

"No, he most definitely would take exception to that type of formality."

At this point Mary couldn't tell whether Rachel was being facetious so decided to quit while she was ahead. "Rachel, you're the only person I know who heats up her dog's food and serves it in separate courses."

"Bear enjoys his food just as much as I do. Why should I treat him differently?"

"Whatever makes you and Bear happy," Mary replied with a shrug. "Now, please leave?"

"Okay! Okay!" Making her way to the door, Rachel looked back over her shoulder with a teasing grin. "Do you think Coyle might let me join you if you were to ask politely? I could alter my plans for this weekend, and I'm certain Bear would love to get away from the city."

"Get out of here!" Mary retorted with the slightest of smiles.

Mary was waiting in the lobby when Coyle pulled up to the curb in front of her building. When he stepped out of the car, she noted his wool trousers and well-tailored tweed jacket with leather elbow patches—completely different from the three-piece suit and courtroom attire she was accustomed to seeing on him. In no time, he was at her side, reaching for her bag and ushering her to his car. "The meteorologists are predicting exceptionally warm weather for the weekend," he announced, placing her bag in the back seat.

Mary lifted her face to the warm rays of the autumnal sun. It was the most splendid day one could hope for at this time of year. "Yes, I can already feel it in the air," she replied.

He opened the car door for her, and she climbed in. He settled into the driver's seat, and they pulled away from the curb and threaded their way out of Ottawa.

Once on the Queensway, Mary stole several glances at Coyle, wondering whether to start a conversation. But the traffic was especially heavy, so she focused instead on the scenery. The city dropped away, and she enjoyed the rolling hills, the rich landscape of the Ottawa Valley, and the colours of the trees along the route as they approached Highway 17. The countryside was resplendent with grass that was still green and fields already prepared for next year's crop.

At one point Coyle's gaze briefly met hers before he returned his attention to the road. "Have you ever been to Pakenham?"

"I have, numerous times, for downhill skiing."

"Really!"

"While the hills themselves aren't particularly challenging, their proximity to Ottawa makes them easily accessible." She paused, suddenly grave, as she remembered her visit to the ski hill on her most recent birthday.

———

After several hours on the hill, she and Peter made their way toward the lodge, his arm around her. The early January evening had been cold with a hard wind, and, exhausted, they were looking forward to a few moments of rest in front of the open fireplace before their ride back to Ottawa.

She was delighted to find they had the entire place to themselves. Ridding herself of her ski jacket, she lounged deep in the huge sofa facing the fire. Peter joined her. He seemed to be wrestling with himself mentally, so she sat quietly, giving him time to articulate what he wanted to say.

Without a word, he gathered her into his arms and kissed her. She pressed into his side, enjoying the feel of his arms around her. When finally he disengaged himself from their embrace, he said, "I've been yearning to do this all evening." Mary felt a shiver travel through her, as his warm hands cupped her face. She waited, expecting him to kiss her again. Instead, he reached inside the pocket of his jacket and produced a small, delicate velvet box. Mary guessed what was inside, and her heart filled her chest.

Displaying a beautiful diamond ring, he smiled at her, his endearing eyes pleading. "Marry me?" he whispered, his voice thickened with emotion.

At once she was back in his arms. She breathed his familiar scent and felt the shuddering of her body against his. Truth was, she had been expecting it. All evening, he had treated her with such special love and reverence that it had been impossible not to foresee he had a specific purpose in mind. Still, she was genuinely touched by his emotional proposal.

⸺

"What other outdoor activities do you take pleasure in?" asked Coyle, interrupting her reverie.

Mary recovered instantly and answered, "Most sports, as well as hiking, camping, canoeing—mostly at Algonquin Park. Have you ever been, Mr. Coyle?"

"Not as often as I would like," he replied. "No justification, I'm afraid, since it's so close. Too busy with other things, alas." He paused, and then added, "You know, Mary, you can call me Patrick. No need for formality. We're just having an enjoyable conversation."

Mary still felt slightly uneasy about calling him by his first name. She could not understand why it should feel so foreign to her. Perhaps because he was so notable, so out of reach.

A short distance away from the town of Arnprior, they exited the highway and moved onto Route 29, heading toward Pakenham. Ten minutes later, Mary sighted a cluster of homes lining the route.

His face brightened. "We're almost there."

As they drove on, Mary spotted the majestic Mississippi

River gliding gently on the left side of the road, relentlessly pursuing its journey to the Ottawa River, just east of Arnprior. Neither she nor Coyle spoke, the silence both calming and comfortable, like the smooth, cascading water of the river.

When they arrived at the village, Coyle slowed down and pointed left. "That bridge was built at the turn of the century. There isn't another one like it in all of North America."

Mary noted the unique five-span stone bridge. On the other side of it was a stone mill. They formed a very picturesque scene and brought her back to the day when she and Peter had stopped to admire it.

Veering away from the bridge, Coyle continued onto the main road and resumed his commentary. "On your right is Saint Peter Celestine Catholic Church."

The imposing church stood on the bluff dominating the village. "Most impressive," she remarked.

"Quite so. It was built in the classic style of southern Europe. We're fortunate that it has been preserved in its original state."

Mary admitted, "That a church as magnificent as a cathedral should exist in such a small, isolated village has always been a source of bewilderment to me."

Coyle nodded. "It was built the way people from the old country remembered, a legacy from their past. Apparently, it took years for the priest to raise enough funds to build it. Every family was asked to pledge a special donation each year—what they could afford. Some were pitifully meagre, a couple of dollars a year. There's a story about two young men who went to the lumber camp and laboured all winter for seventy-five dollars each. Upon their return from the lumber camp in the spring, they donated their entire winter's earnings to the church fund."

"One has to admire such dedication," Mary uttered solemnly.

"The village may be small, but in it reside good, hard-working people," acknowledged Coyle. "It's also a village with a lot of history. The Pakenham General Store that you see on your left is the only general store in Canada that has been continually open, in the same location, for over 130 years. It has also maintained its original form with wooden floors and the original wooden counters."

"I've been a frequent visitor, but I never learned the history of the village," admitted Mary. "What is the major industry here?"

"At one time it was a lumbering community, but farming is now the principle occupation of the area," he replied as their route took them out of the community and onto a secondary road.

They drove in silence for several miles, then Coyle pointed to a farm deep in the valley. "That house is my mother's home."

This announcement sent a ripple of anxiety through her. She closed her eyes and suddenly felt cold as she thought of the encounter to come. *Why did I accept his invitation?* Suppressing her trepidation, she opened her eyes and focused on the house. It was a beautiful, white, three-storey building with a symmetrical façade and gable roof, typical of the English colonial style. Situated back from the road and nestled against a backdrop of trees, the house looked majestic with pillars accentuating the entrance and well-tended flower gardens. As they moved closer, she noticed a walking trail that cut across the field. It led to a barn and, beyond it, a wooded slope in one direction and the shoreline of the Mississippi River in the other.

Coyle pulled into a circular drive that enclosed a bed of late-blooming daisies and chrysanthemums. He stopped the car, and as they stepped out, a tall woman with white hair appeared at the door. She was in her late sixties, Mary assumed, and was still trim and erect—a handsome woman in an understated way. And whatever doubt had remained about her reception was quickly dispelled when Coyle's mother walked up to her and extended her hand. "Hello, you must be Mary. I'm Sara, Patrick's mother. Welcome to our home."

"I'm delighted to make your acquaintance, Mrs. Coyle. Thank you for having me."

"My pleasure entirely," Mrs. Coyle replied. She then reached up to her son, hugged him affectionately and stepped back to get a better look. "Patrick, you've lost weight."

"You say that at every visit, Mother."

"I say it because it's true. You really need to take care of yourself." Addressing Mary, she apologized. "Forgive me for voicing my concern this way, but it's hard for a mother to give up caring for her child, even when he's grown up and living away from home. To me, he'll always be my little boy."

Mary had not missed the note of pride in Mrs. Coyle's voice. She smiled, and said, "Totally understandable."

Mrs. Coyle beamed. "Do come in, Mary, and make yourself comfortable while Patrick parks the car in the barn."

"Mother, don't be in such a rush to get rid of me," he admonished in a tone of feigned annoyance. "I've just arrived."

Just as fervently, she replied, "Face it, Patrick, it's not every day you bring home an attractive young lady. So allow me to get to know her."

An amused boyish expression settled on Coyle's face as he looked at Mary. "My mother is the one who gives the orders around here, so you'll have to forgive me for abandoning you." Before getting back in the car, he surveyed the grounds, taking in the pleasant view, and then turned to address Mary one more time. "I forgot to mention that my mother is not only a great cook but a hard-working and highly inspired gardener."

This accolade caused Mrs. Coyle to appear a little self-conscious. "Patrick tends to exaggerate about my cooking skills, but I do admit the grounds are a source of pride, and I tend to devote considerable time and care toward their upkeep."

Mary gazed about at the manicured grass, the mature trees, and the profusion of flowerbeds with the fall colours of yellow, gold, and purple spread out throughout the lawn. Joe-pye weed and mums added an attractive touch to the barn, which stood at the edge of the yard, bringing to mind days gone by. Completing the landscape was a sprawling vegetable and herb garden, where cabbage, turnips, carrots, and squash fought for attention among the bright flowers interspersed among them. And along the perimeter of the garden, Coyle's mother had planted Russian sage with its wispy wands of lavender, providing a spectacular backdrop.

"It's beautiful," Mary acknowledged.

"You've outdone yourself this year, Mother," Coyle murmured sincerely.

Mrs. Coyle gave him another long embrace. "It's wonderful to have you home again." Then, pushing him away gently, she said, "Now, get along with you."

Coyle slipped behind the wheel and said to Mary, "Don't worry about your suitcase. I'll bring it in." Waving, he drove away.

Mary gave his mother a tentative glance. "It's exceedingly gracious of you to accept a stranger into your home like this, especially one tainted with so much controversy."

Mrs. Coyle's eyes softened as she gave her a long, concentrated appraisal. "My dear, no such thought ever crossed my mind." Then after a moment of reflection, she added. "To be honest, I was looking forward to meeting you."

And no doubt curious to learn why your son would risk his whole career for me, mused Mary.

Mrs. Coyle continued to study her thoughtfully and then broke into a smile. "Do come in, Mary."

Mary followed her into a wide foyer with a high ceiling, typical of old homes, and an elegantly carved mahogany staircase. As she stepped into the living room, she was struck by how beautifully put together it was. It was a room that made her feel immediately at home—large, with an elegant fireplace dominating the focal wall. On one side of the fireplace was a sofa, on the other, two matching chairs, all of them covered in a soft, flowery chintz in a delicate design of an artful garden. On the south side of the room were two large windows and between them a wide sliding door that allowed access to a beautiful deck overlooking the gardens and the river. The windows were open to a gentle breeze. It had the effect of warmth and freshness. "How lovely!" Mary remarked.

With a modest nod, Mrs. Coyle shared, "Patrick's great-grandfather built this house. Though it has undergone several renovations over time, we've managed to preserve the integrity of the original structure." She paused, then continued, "It is destined to be Patrick's, and I hold onto the hope that one day he will choose to make it his permanent home. Being not far from Ottawa, he can easily commute."

Mary noted several picture frames on the mantel and walked over to examine them. One featured a young man in a skiing outfit, displaying a medal around his neck. "Your son has a striking resemblance to you," she observed, smiling.

"Yes, so I'm told. Fortunately, he has inherited his father's judiciousness and fortitude, which makes me exceptionally proud of him."

In the picture young Coyle was smiling confidently at the camera. Mary could see evidence of the man he would become.

Before she could say anything more, Coyle appeared at the door. "Mother boasting about me again?"

"I only do because you won't," his mother countered. She turned to Mary. "You and Patrick most likely have work to do, so I'll leave you. He will show you to your room."

Mary watched as Mrs. Coyle withdrew. When she looked at Coyle again, she saw that he was holding her suitcase in one hand. With the other, he motioned to the staircase. "Why don't we head upstairs and get ourselves situated."

When they reached the second floor, he led her to the end of the corridor on the right, then stood aside to let her enter a large room. The walls were pale blue, and a king-size bed with a single bedside table and reading lamp dominated the room. There was a dresser against one wall with a good number of books on the shelves above it. The other two walls featured large windows, which made the room sunlit and airy. The uncluttered look appealed to her.

Coyle went over to the window facing the wooded slope and set her luggage down. "I asked Mother to give you my room because it has the nicest view." He cleared his throat and added, "It's also isolated from the other rooms for more privacy."

Mary's eyes softened as she surveyed the room. "You are exceptionally thoughtful."

"My mother is very attentive to her guests' needs, but if the room should be lacking, please let me know."

"Thank you. I can't imagine anything more perfect."

"I'll leave you to unpack and freshen up. If you are agreeable, we can meet in the library whenever you're ready. We've a few hours remaining this afternoon, and we may as well make the most of it. Just turn left at the foot of the stairs and you'll find me."

"I won't be long," she replied.

After he had closed the door behind him, Mary again surveyed the room. She discovered an adjoining, spacious bathroom stocked with towels and toiletries, even a new toothbrush—everything necessary for a comfortable stay. Next to the separate tub and shower, the closet lay empty of Coyle's clothes, apparently to make room for her to hang her things.

She went to the window with a view to the east. In the distance stood the picturesque Mount Pakenham, now free of snow, and once more she was reminded of Peter. Would she ever be able to see those ski hills without thinking of him? She had known so much loss in her life—her parents, her uncle, Dr. Cowen, and Mr. Kerr. But she had never imagined she could miss anyone as acutely as she did Peter, the thought of his duplicity compounding her pain. Grief-stricken, she tried to wrench him out of her mind. Obliterate him from her memory. But the deceptive thing about memory is its refusal to fade. The more you push a memory away, the more it lodges itself into your subconscious, ready to be retrieved, thereby making it unforgettable.

When Mary stepped into the library fifteen minutes later, Coyle was already seated behind a huge mahogany desk, a file spread out in front of him. He rose as she entered the room. "This is my office when I'm home," he said by way of greeting and then motioned to a chair beside him. "I think you will find this chair comfortable."

She joined him, scanning the room with curiosity. Like the rest of the house, it was put together with taste and care—an oriental carpet on the floor, the desk strategically placed near the window to take full advantage of natural light and the beauty of the outdoors, and most of the walls lined with books. The tall ceiling was painted a dark brown, bringing it closer. Overall, the room carried a traditional colonial style with warm earthy tones, giving her a welcome sense of tranquility and stability.

They immersed themselves in her file, as well as Mr. Kerr's, methodically going through every paper. Courtney and Richard were most likely in this for the money, and Coyle wanted to examine all aspects of their father's finances.

After several hours, he looked up and consulted his watch. "I had no idea it was so late. Maybe we should call it a day."

Mary sighed, trying not to appear disheartened. "There's still so much to do."

"Yes. But it can wait."

Mary needed to voice her concern, though she knew it was pointless at this time. "We've conferred on a great deal of material, but we've yet to discuss the strategy you intend to take."

Coyle confirmed what she already knew. "It would be unwise and perhaps even futile to set up a strategy before we know what the prosecution has in mind. It's best to be prudent and wait until after pretrial discovery is completed. After we've seen the documentation and I've interviewed the witnesses under oath, we'll have a better idea of Baxter's strategy."

"Can you foresee what it might be?"

"Baxter will undoubtedly try to build a wall of evidence against you, and I'll do everything I can to demolish it."

"And then what?"

"After that, we'll take another look at the facts and build on what we know, rather than what we assume."

It was not what she had hoped to hear, but she had to be content with his answer. At least it showed that he felt more confident about the case than she did. It also provided a rare glimpse into the drive that lurked behind his cool exterior.

Coyle closed the file. "I suggested to Mother that we go out for dinner tonight. I trust that meets with your approval?"

"Fully."

"There's a popular inn in Calabogie—the village is not far from here. The restaurant there is small, but its excellent cuisine and the view of the lake make it one of the most desirable dining spots in the area."

Mary nodded her gratitude. "I've been to Calabogie on weekends to ski but never managed to make it to the restaurant, so that would be lovely."

He flashed Mary a smile, totally disarming. "Good. I'll make a reservation for seven. Let's meet in the living room for a drink at six."

As she stood to leave, Coyle's smile vanished, and concern took its place. "Baxter is calling a Miss Cowen... Dorothy Cowen, I believe it is, as a witness. Can you think of any reason why he would call on her?"

Mary immediately thought of Dr. Cowen, prompting a slight discomfort. Could this woman be his daughter? Still, she replied, "None whatsoever."

"Yet I distinctly noticed that your features stiffened when I mentioned her name," said Coyle.

"The name is familiar, and I was trying to remember who she could possibly be."

Coyle brunched his brows in consternation. "Baxter wouldn't summon her unless he was convinced she could bring something germane to the case. Care to speculate?"

"I can't think of anything." Mary looked away as she spoke the half-truth. She regretted lying to Coyle. But the alternative—admitting certain things about her past— was inconceivable.

He shook his head in obvious bewilderment. "When preparing for trial, it's paramount to anticipate what your adversary is planning. In this case, I have no idea what's on Baxter's mind or where he's going. It's most disconcerting."

Mary remained silent, for she, too, felt not only a pang of unease, but alarm as well. Had Dr. Cowen, her benefactor, perhaps related to his daughter what she had revealed to him in confidence?

ary was in her room getting ready for dinner. As the time grew nearer, she became increasingly anxious. She had been comfortable working with Coyle, but meeting him on a social level over dinner was entirely different. What would she say to him? How would he react? Though it was not in his character to intimidate people, he was so formidably intelligent that he remained an unnerving man, especially at times when his warm hazel eyes searched hers in a way that could utterly disarm and thrill her at the same time.

He had suggested she dress casually for their outing, and she was curious what *casual* meant to him. She had taken a bath and tried to decide what she should wear. She had packed two sets of clothing, not knowing what to expect. Modelling both in front of the mirror, she felt all the indecision of a teenager trying to decide what to wear for a first date. She settled on something simple but flattering—a tan cashmere sweater and a dark brown skirt, which fitted her exquisitely. To dress it up, she added a tastefully understated, light-brown scarf that complimented the colour of her hair.

She left her room and quietly made her way down to the main landing. A brief look at her watch showed she still had fifteen minutes before their agreed meeting time. She contemplated going outside to view the property but decided against it and instead chose to go to the living room. The lights were on, and the fireplace was lit, the smell of pine creating a peaceful, soothing atmosphere.

Once more, Mary was drawn to the pictures on the mantel. She picked one up, that of an older gentleman whose eyes peered straight at her with an unobtrusive, earnest expression. But the power of his concentrated gaze and the serenity of his face confirmed an active mind. At the sound of footsteps, she swung around and saw Coyle entering the room. The picture still in her hand, she confessed awkwardly, "I always enjoy looking at family photographs."

"Why?" he asked. "These can't be all that exciting for you."

"But they are. They give us insight into lives that no longer exist."

He looked at her, his expression suggesting a quiet fascination. He then approached to look down at the photo and nodded. "That picture of my father was taken shortly before he died."

Mary examined it more closely. When she glanced back at Coyle, he said, "Unfortunately, Mother will not be joining us for dinner tonight. A neighbour called to say she required her input on some local project they're managing, so I'm afraid it's just you and me."

Mary regarded him, taking in his poised and assured manner. Never had she expected that one day she would be dining with him. And despite her uneasiness, the prospect of being alone with him was a welcome one. Still doubtful about her attire, she drew his attention to it and asked, "Will it do?"

"Very nicely, I'd say," he replied, smiling. He then walked over to a cabinet against the wall and asked, "Would you care to join me for an aperitif?"

"With pleasure."

"Any preference?"

Mary spotted a bottle of sherry on the surface of the cabinet. "I'll have a glass of that sherry, if you don't mind."

She replaced the photograph and sat down on the sofa.

Coyle poured her drink and handed it to her. He then poured himself a Scotch and sank comfortably on the sofa beside her. Neither spoke as the fire hissed and crackled.

Mary shifted in her seat, his proximity unsettling.

Coyle seemed completely unaware, deep in thought. He merely regarded her without speaking, his sombre gaze alluring. That was something Mary had noted about him— he was averse to fill every silence as some people do.

Finally, having endured all the silent scrutiny she could abide, she pointed toward the mantel. "I gather from one of the pictures that you're a skier."

"Yes. I practically grew up on Mount Pakenham. As well as the ski hill, we have lovely trails. Tomorrow morning, we can take a quick hike up the mountain, if you wish. It shouldn't take too much time away from preparing for your trial."

"That would be a most welcome outing."

An hour later, Coyle and Mary were walking up to the Calabogie Inn. When they reached the front entrance, he held open the door for her. Inside, the maître d' greeted them warmly. "Home for the weekend, Patrick?"

"Yes, arrived this afternoon."

"Welcome home then."

"It feels great to be back," Coyle replied. He then turned to Mary, smiling beside him and added, "Allow me to introduce you to a colleague, Mary Clark. Mary, this is Mark Thomas, the owner of this fine establishment."

"Delighted to meet you," said Mark, returning her smile. The subtle hint of surprise that briefly flickered across his face made Mary wonder whether having a lady accompanying Coyle for dinner was an unusual occurrence.

Picking up two menus, Mark motioned for them to follow him. The restaurant was full, but a small, quaint table in the corner near a window overlooking the lake had been set aside for them. Mark handed them their menus and smiled. "Martha will be along presently to take your order. Enjoy your meal."

They had been sitting at the table only a few minutes when a short, trim young woman came over to their table. "Good evening, Mr. Coyle. It's so nice to see you again," she said with great enthusiasm.

"Good evening, Martha. It's always a pleasure to see you, too."

Martha glowed with pleasure at the compliment.

"What's good on the menu tonight?" he asked.

"You know that we strive for excellence in everything we serve, Mr. Coyle. But you might prefer the haddock over the beef."

"Haddock it is, then."

Coyle turned to Mary and tilted his head in inquiry.

"I'll have the same, thank you."

"As for wine, have you a preference?" he asked.

"White, thank you."

Addressing Martha, Coyle smiled. "Then I suggest a bottle of your Sauvignon Blanc."

"Very well," she replied and retreated to the kitchen.

"You're apparently well-known here," Mary observed, spreading the linen napkin on her lap.

"I was born in the area." He didn't say anything else, just studied her.

Self-conscious, Mary let her gaze drift appreciatively over the pleasant decor. It was a large dining room running the whole length of the inn, with windows overlooking the water and an enormous fieldstone fireplace on the adjacent wall, its fire radiating a delightful warmth into the room. The tables were covered with white linen and were spaced so that people could speak freely at their table without fear of being overheard.

Martha returned with some water, followed shortly thereafter by wine. Minutes later she reappeared with a platter and two plates. She placed them on the table, the platter revealing succulent stuffed portobello mushrooms topped with melted cheese and garnished with slices of lemon and fresh thyme. "When I announced in the kitchen that you were here, Mrs. Burns was in the process of preparing these and insisted on sending some out to you. She remembered that they were among your favourite appetizers."

Coyle smiled, delighted and honoured by the gesture. "They are indeed. Please convey my sincere thanks to Mrs.

Burns. And tell her nobody makes crab-stuffed portobello mushrooms like she does. She's the best."

"Oh, we all know that, but knowing that you still think so will make her very happy," Martha acknowledged warmly, then discreetly withdrew.

Coyle forked two mushrooms onto a plate and handed it to Mary. "Enjoy," he said.

Mary waited for him to serve himself before taking a bite. "Mmm, they're delicious," she said.

"Yes. As I said to Martha, nobody makes crab-stuffed portobello mushrooms like Mrs. Burns does. She has to be the best."

"You must miss this place when you're away."

"Yes, I do." He emitted a small sigh. "After your trial is over, I've decided to leave Ottawa and open an office in Pakenham."

Mary was momentarily lost for words.

Coyle continued speaking, slowly, calmly. "My father was a lawyer in Pakenham for thirty years, right up until the day he died. He was a remarkable person. He stood for things that were decent and honest. He loved the people here and devoted his whole life to them. They are deferential to me, but I recognize that it's out of gratitude for him. My father has left me a legacy, and it's time I lived up to it. It's time I, too, start giving and earn the respect these people have given me."

Coyle's gaze wandered over her face. "You appear somewhat perplexed."

There was tightness in her throat as she spoke. "It's odd how one's life can change so dramatically. Six months ago,

I was on top of the world and thought life couldn't be more sound. Now my world is upside down and things couldn't be worse. And you were an aspiring partner with one of the most prestigious law firms in Ottawa, and today you're compelled to rent a two-room office in the Chambers Building."

He smiled. "A loss need not be the end of the world. It can frequently lead to greater things. Like my decision to open an office here in Pakenham. I'm now convinced that subconsciously this is what I've always longed to do. Only I was caught up with the excitement Ottawa offered and momentarily forgot what was meaningful to me. I'm glad it happened…being fired from the firm, I mean. It prompted me to re-examine the life I had chosen."

A shiver rippled through Mary's entire body as she wondered what positive things could conceivably come out of her present crisis.

Coyle did not pursue their conversation. And in the silence that ensued, it was Mary's turn to study him. His features were masculine and strong. His looks were hardly classic Hollywood, but there was something about his manner that superseded all that. He had the gift of making her feel so very special whenever he spoke to her, and she found herself enjoying his company, despite her earlier apprehension.

Martha returned with their main course, and the two of them settled comfortably in their seats, appreciating the meal and a more casual conversation. When they finished eating, Martha resurfaced with the dessert menu. Without scrutinizing it, Coyle stated, "I'll have your dessert specialty, poached pears in port. Is it still available?"

"I regret having to disappoint you, Mr. Coyle, but we're

completely out." Nodding discreetly toward a couple at the other extremity of the room, she added apologetically, "Mr. and Mrs. MacDonald had the last servings."

"No poached pears in port? How unfortunate! In that case, what would you recommend, Martha?"

"The plum tarts are excellent."

"Plum tart it is then."

Martha turned to Mary. "Would you care for a dessert, Miss?"

"I'll have the same. Thank you, Martha."

After they had finished their dessert and tea, Coyle said, "I hope you've enjoyed your meal."

"Thank you for a wonderful evening," Mary replied. Indeed, the entire evening had been delightful in every sense: the meal, the ambiance, especially Coyle's company. She did not know if it was the drink or Coyle's relaxed approach, but she suddenly felt free of the pressure and suffocating tension that had dominated her entire being these past months—the relief immense.

As far as Mary was concerned, the evening had passed too swiftly. When they arrived back at the house, Coyle proposed they take a few minutes to review a file they would be working on the next day. Reviewing it would give them a chance to ponder the information overnight and help them formulate a plan of action. When she agreed, he offered to make her a cup of tea. While he was in the kitchen, Mary made herself comfortable in the library and reflected on the night. At the office, Coyle had remained an enigma to most employees, but he was no longer an enigma to her. During that evening, she had seen him with a boyish grin, teasing eyes, and the deferential charm of a gentleman. He was the most captivating person she had ever met.

She smiled as he entered the room with tray in hand. He placed it on the desk and handed her a cup of tea. Her smile widened when she saw that he had added milk.

"I noted that you took milk in your tea," he said, grinning.

"Thank you," she replied and then waited for him to serve himself.

He set his cup on a side table, sat down beside her, and opened his file. He regarded her for a moment and seemed to hesitate before saying, "Mary, I need to speak frankly to you about Peter and revisit the information you've given me regarding the contents in your briefcase. No room for wounded feelings. Would you be agreeable to that?"

It was the first time he had brought up Peter's name since that dreadful evening, and Mary understood that he had to. She picked up her pen and scribbled a note to herself on a legal pad sitting on the desk. It had nothing to do with his question. It merely allowed her time to control her emotions. Having regained her voice, she managed to say, "I understand that we need to discuss Peter's involvement in this case. As for the briefcase, I can't remember everything that was in it other than the signed note I requested from Mr. Kerr, the appraisal sheet, Danielle's letter, and my reply to her. Otherwise, it contained mainly personal papers."

Coyle took a deep breath and said, "I've no idea how much Peter has contributed to their case. It could amount to nothing. But then it could be momentous." He paused and then continued slowly in a matter-of-fact manner. "So far, Baxter has charged you with fraud and undue influence. You can be sure Courtney and/or Richard will be there to testify against you. At the end, it will be your word against theirs, and right now I suspect the jury is more disposed to lean their way. We have to find a way of disqualifying their testimony or proving yours. I'm afraid that's unlikely to happen unless…" There, he stopped.

"Unless what?" she asked.

"Mary, I don't mean to alarm you, but this case is not progressing as anticipated. Therefore, I need to subpoena Peter. With him on the stand and exposing Beasley's deception, you'd have a greater chance of gaining the judge and jury's sympathy."

"No! I can't allow it."

"What do you mean, no?"

"There has to be another way," she replied mechanically.

"At the moment, it's the sole defence we have." Coyle was not a man who openly displayed his emotions, but Mary sensed his disappointment. When she failed to respond, he spoke in a more conciliatory voice. "Mary, I know this is a trying time for you. Please don't make it more trying by refusing to accept the facts. Forgive the indelicacy of my saying it, but Peter wasn't concerned about your welfare when he switched to the other camp. And I can assure you that whatever documents Baxter has obtained from Beasley as a result of Peter's actions, he will deploy them to their full advantage. You can't deny this and expect a happy ending."

He was stating the obvious, but Mary still answered, "I can't do what you ask. Please, don't press the matter."

"I assure you, I'm not enjoying this, for it's obvious that you're hurting. Yet, for your sake, I must insist." Getting no response, he said in a questioning tone, "It simply escapes me how you can make so light of what he's done."

"I'm not making light of it. I'm fully aware of what he's done."

"And yet you continue to defend him?"

"Defend is hardly the word I would use."

"Shield him, then," he corrected and then added, "You most definitely have a subtle mind, but you're young and perhaps a little too trusting."

Although he looked much younger, Mary had estimated Coyle to be ten or twelve years her senior, which would explain his comment. But it did not impede her from replying, "That may be so, but I'd rather be trusting and gullible than cynical and distrustful of everyone."

Her words brought a smile to his lips. He looked up at her and nodded. "Despite Peter's deceit, you wish to believe in him. That may be honourable, but it will not deter Baxter from exploiting any material Peter provided through Beasley. No matter how trivial, Baxter will find a way of using it against you."

"Forgive me if I appear disobliging," she replied, meeting his gaze. "Your advice is sound, but..." She could not finish the sentence.

"Mary, is it that you're still in love with Peter?"

Mary felt her throat begin to constrict, inhibiting her from speaking her mind. If she could, she'd say: *It's strange how you can love a person so intensely when you're infatuated with him, only to discover later that you don't love him nearly as much as you thought.*

"I recognize it's an intrusive question," Coyle said, "but I need to know."

It was a moment before she could respond. And when she did, it was with a shake of her head. "I don't know."

He looked at her with his hypnotic eyes, studying her.

"No," she admitted finally.

"Then what is it?"

"Peter..." Mary began, and then stopped. What was the point? How could she come up with a plausible explanation when she had none? Inhaling deeply, drawing strength from the air, she slowly let out a sigh. "I'm unable to explain my feelings for him."

"I suggest you try," he said in a quiet but resolute tone.

"To me, love is more than a feeling; it's a choice. I'm…I'm no longer in love with Peter. Whatever love we had, along with any romantic illusions I might have had about love, was blighted the night I found him and Courtney together. But I don't hate him…at least not enough to give me reason to hurt him as some people might justify. Why, you may ask? I'm afraid there's no answer for you there, either. Maybe it's because I still believe there's goodness in him. I've witnessed it. On those occasions, I've seen him vulnerable and loving. I also witnessed how manipulative his mother can be, so I view all of that as some sort of mitigating circumstance."

"Nothing can justify him hurting you the way he did."

"Nevertheless, I can't bring myself to do what you ask. I'm not completely convinced it would advance my case all that much…only make life more miserable for him."

"You're not exactly objective about this, are you?" he remarked.

She started to argue the point, then realized she had no defence. Coyle was spot on. Where Peter was concerned, she could hardly be objective.

"I have a hard time comprehending this leniency," Coyle continued. "Why don't you want Peter to take the stand? Are you afraid of what he may say?"

"No."

"Mary, it occurs to me I know next to nothing about you—only that you graduated from Ottawa University with honours and have been employed by Woodbury & McLeod five years and, of course, that bit about your association with the Kerr family. But I know nothing about your personal life. Even that meeting in your home revealed nil about you and your family. I saw no photographs of your parents, no memorabilia of your childhood." This last part was spoken reluctantly.

Again, Mary marvelled at how little escaped his attention. "What more can I tell you?" she asked.

"Everything—your family, your education, what moves you." When she failed to respond, he pressed on. "Mary, I dislike having to burden you with these invasive questions, but if I'm to defend you properly, there can be no secrets between us."

"There is nothing I can say that I haven't already told you…my studies, my work, my relationship with Peter, and my mother and father who were killed in that tragic accident."

"What you've communicated to me so far is rudimentary. I need to know more about your private life, what moves you and…" Coyle must have perceived the signs of heightened distress in her deportment, for he shifted in his chair and stopped midsentence. After a moment of silence, he patiently closed his file and pushed it aside. "Let's declare détente for the time being at least. We'll discuss it further later."

"I've in fact no defence, have I?" she lamented.

He regarded her in that quiet way of his and replied, "No case is ever entirely lost until the end, or if you give up on it. And you can rest assured I will continue to defend you. That much, at least, I can promise you." Coyle allowed several moments to elapse and then added, "I admire your loyalty to the people who make up your life, even those who are undeserving. While I don't believe in revenge, I do believe people should take responsibility for their actions. As such, Peter should be held accountable for what he's done."

She was simply too worn out to argue.

The tortured look in her eyes must have moved him, for he added, "As you wish then," and fell silent.

Finally, she murmured, "You've given up so much for me. And right now, I feel unworthy. Please understand that despite my lack of co-operation, I'm most eternally grateful to you."

He looked at her, his gaze intent and pensive. He nodded and said, "Let's hope you don't come to regret your decision."

Mary lay awake in her bed that night. She kept thinking about Coyle and his disappointment that she had opposed his proposal to put Peter on the stand. She had admitted she was no longer in love with Peter, so why was she protecting him? If she had been able to read deep into her own soul, the answer would have come to her that the greatest calamity in life was never to have been loved. With the support of someone's love, one could face any tragedy. Peter had loved her, and she had so cherished that love that she found it almost impossible to accept that it was gone. Never in her life had she felt so utterly alone.

Coyle had not promised a positive outcome. As a lawyer, such a promise was unlikely. Courts were unpredictable. There were too many variables. And confronted with the stark reality of the impeding evidence against her, he would be compelled to acknowledge that unless factual information supporting her story came up, her prospects of acquittal were most improbable. Her whole case screamed of deceit and treachery.

Mary had prided herself on her coping skills, on managing her life without the destructive emotions that had dominated her youth. Now there was nothing left for her but despair, that combination of nausea and numbness that continued to threaten her. She squeezed her eyes shut, striving to bring some calm to her nerves. She needed to anchor herself—to dispel the feeling of hopelessness that was threatening to overtake her. She pushed aside her blanket and sprang out of bed. Wrapping her dressing gown around her, she left her room and quietly edged her way downstairs for a glass of water. Nightlights had been strategically placed along the way, making it easier to see. As she approached the kitchen, she detected a sliver of light seeping underneath the slightly open door. She leaned against it and saw Coyle with his head buried in his arms folded on the table, which was littered with notes, documents, and books. Shoved to the side were an empty plate and a half-full glass of milk.

She was about to retreat when his head shot up, a startled expression on his face. "I must have dozed off," he murmured, shaking his head slightly.

"Sorry." She smiled. "I didn't mean to disturb you."

Again, he shook his head, dismissive. "Don't be. I had no intention of napping." He then arched his eyebrows. "May I fetch something for you…to eat perhaps?"

"No, thank you. I couldn't sleep and happened to see the light in the kitchen." She had forgotten about her thirst.

As he put order to his books, she felt instant remorse. Never had she seen him looking so drawn and overworked. She had brought this on him. She shuddered at the thought.

"I was just going over some of my legal books," he said. He paused for a moment to study her. Then, as if gaining resolution, he added, "Mary, I'm worried about you. The trial is six weeks away, and you've been through so much lately that, emotionally, I don't think you're ready."

"I'm fine," she replied stoically.

He stood slowly and stared into her eyes. "Are you, truly?"

The intensity of his scrutiny caught her off guard and she turned away. She found herself fighting to mask the raw emotions raging inside her. "I'm fine," she repeated and turned to walk away.

Coyle moved close and placed a hand on her shoulder, his touch both steady and reassuring. "Mary, please tell me what is bothering you. You have an astonishing way of guarding your feelings, but I sense that you're troubled."

"I'm facing a criminal trial; what else do you expect?"

Undeterred, he turned her gently, forcing her to face him. "No, it goes deeper than that. I suspect it goes back to your past—how far back, I don't know. And about your story, there's something specious about it."

"What do you mean by specious?"

"There's an inconsistency…something you're not telling me. But I can't figure out what it is."

His perception was dead on, and her first instinct was to tell him everything—to open her heart to him—but she felt her throat begin to constrict.

"What is it, Mary? What is it you're holding back? You know that whatever you say will remain between you and me. Let me help you," he urged.

A chill passed through her. His sympathetic tone was too much for her to bear. She opened her mouth to tell him about her past, but the feelings that surfaced rendered her speechless. How could she tell him her world was spinning out of control? Since meeting Peter, she had been clinging to the only love she had ever known. But now, that love had been pulled away and there was nothing left for her to hold on to. Nothing but a boundless void. Overcome by despair, she started to cry. Before she knew what she was doing, she had buried her head into his shoulder and was sobbing disconsolately.

Coyle's arms encircled her firmly, drawing her closer. She could feel the warmth of his body pressed lightly against hers. "Everything will be fine," he whispered into her ear, his lips grazing her temple as he did so. "Everything will be fine," he repeated.

For several moments, she clutched at him. Then her mind cleared and she instinctively broke free. Embarrassed by her own weakness, she fought to regain her composure. She quickly moved away from him, wiping her tears with the back of her hand, and walked to the door. With her hand on the knob, she stood silent for a moment, and then turned to face him. "You needn't concern yourself about me. I can handle anything they throw at me. As for my emotions, I can handle them, too."

Coyle nodded, but his troubled eyes indicated that he did not agree.

Back in bed, Mary leaned against her pillow and reflected on that fleeting moment in Coyle's arms. Never had she felt so secure. Yet she had pulled away from him. At the time she had viewed her reaction as a defence against showing vulnerability. But she now knew differently. It was because she had failed to be perfectly honest with him. She also knew that he was aware of this failure and had needed to let her know, for it was not in his nature to be anything less than totally forthcoming with her.

When Mary entered the kitchen the following morning, Coyle had already helped himself to a cup of coffee.

He smiled, lifting up his cup, the scent enticing. "Care for some?"

"Yes, please."

"How do you take it?"

"Just cream, thank you."

Casually, he walked over to the coffee pot brewing on the stove. His hair was still damp, and he wore well-fitted corduroy trousers and a lightweight sweater over a sport shirt. Seeing him dressed in casual outdoor clothes, she could detect the graceful body of an athlete.

"Did you have a good sleep?" he asked, handing over her coffee.

An honest reply would have been, "Not really, no," for she had tossed and turned most of the night. But she didn't want to sound ungracious, so she uttered, "The best in a long while."

He acknowledged her answer with another smile. "I told Mother I would get breakfast this morning, so why don't you sit back and relax while I prepare my favourite French toast recipe." He raised his eyebrow. "I hope you do like French toast."

"Yes. As a matter of fact, I do."

He returned to the stove and went about his chore, while she gazed in awe at how comfortable and relaxed he appeared in that domestic role. In less than twenty minutes, he yielded an excellent breakfast: French toast topped with fresh fruit and whipped cream and served with maple syrup.

After they had finished eating, the two of them lingered at the kitchen table with a second cup of coffee.

"So, will we do that hike, as you proposed earlier?" she asked.

"Yes, let's. We can hit the books after lunch," he replied.

"Sounds like a splendid idea." In fact, Mary had worn her woolen slacks and a long-sleeved pullover with that in mind. She hadn't brought her hiking boots but had a suitable pair of walking shoes.

"It gets windy up in the mountain, so you'll need a jacket," he suggested.

Mary picked up her plate. "Let me help you with the dishes first."

"No need. I'll stack them in the dishwasher while you fetch your jacket."

"I won't be long."

When she returned a few minutes later, Mrs. Coyle was sitting at the table. "How was your meal last night?" she asked.

"It was exceptional."

"I regretted having to cancel," Mrs. Coyle said ruefully. "But I trust you enjoyed your evening."

"Yes. Very much, thank you."

Streams of sunlight were pouring in through the window. "It's going to be another flawless day," Mrs. Coyle remarked.

"Mary has consented to join me for a hike up the mountain," Coyle informed her.

"Splendid! The colours at this time of year are spectacular."

The air outside was cool, the sun bright, the sky a resplendent blue. Mary tipped her face upward and drew a deep, invigorating breath. "My, it's refreshing to be in the country."

Coyle nodded with equal delight. "An ideal day for a hike."

They headed toward the river and followed the edge to an entry into the woods. There they paused to admire the view. The leaves of the maple trees were glowing red, yellow, and gold—a most wonderful palette of colours, which shielded the branches like a warm cloak.

"How beautiful!" Mary exclaimed.

"The hardwood forest of this section of the valley makes this one of the most colourful areas in the province," Coyle said, then walked on decisively. Deep into the woods, he pointed out an abandoned cabin. "As a boy, I used to help my grandfather collect sap from the sugar maples in early spring and make it into syrup here over a wood fire."

"Was this a business for your grandfather?"

"No, just something he did on the side for family and friends," Coyle replied.

As they moved along, the forest became hilly, with an upward slope. Ferns carpeted the ground. Following in Coyle's footsteps, Mary sighted a squirrel scurrying to bury nuts in the forest litter, and she could hear a bird singing. She stopped to listen, her lips parted.

Coyle turned to face her. "That's a northern mockingbird. They sing in the fall, to claim their feeding territory."

"I often wondered why we call them mockingbirds."

"It's because they imitate other birds' songs."

"If that's the case, how can you be certain it's actually a mockingbird we heard and not some other bird?"

A sheepish smile tugged at his lips. "It happens that I saw one flying around and recognized it."

"Oh!"

His smile broadened. "If you watch carefully, you might be able to spot one. They have white tail feathers and white wing patches, which flash when they're in flight."

Farther up the slope, the path became narrower and the terrain more arduous. In some spots, the soil was spongy and moist from the last rain and made it awkward for her to manoeuvre. It did not, however, detract from the surrounding beauty. Stimulated by the freshness of the mountain air and the warmth of the mid-morning sun filtering through the trees, she continued to climb, following Coyle. It felt good to be out of the city.

When finally he reached an opening at the top of the escarpment, he leaned over and reached out to her. "Watch it," he cautioned. "It's a bit tricky here."

"Thank you," she replied, accepting his hand.

His grip, firm yet not overpowering, steadied her as he assisted her into a clearing.

Mary stepped up beside him and gazed at the luminous blue sky. There were no clouds in sight, and the rays of the morning sun were warm against her skin. They were on a ridge overlooking the depth of the Ottawa Valley. Awed by the winding path of the embankment, the trees, the river, and the October wildflowers opening wide to embrace the new day, she murmured, "It's a veritable paradise."

Coyle pointed to a drop-off. "As youngsters, my friends and I challenged each other to climb that cliff face."

"That must have been extremely dangerous!"

"Yes, it was. But it never struck us at the time." He shook his head. "Bizarre what young people will do. We felt invincible." He stared at the drop-off for several seconds and then turned to her. "Not many people come here…too rugged a trek. I hope I haven't pushed you too hard."

"On the contrary," Mary affirmed, taking in the beauty of the setting. "I appreciate you bringing me. How fortunate you are to have this in your own backyard."

"Yes, I am. I love climbing the mountain. But, even more, I love peering down into the valley." Pointing to a log on the ground beside him, he said, "Join me."

After they had settled comfortably on the log, their eyes met, his grave, apologetic. "I regret our quarrel last night. I momentarily disregarded how special Peter was to you… highly insensitive of me."

Pulling her jacket securely about her, she replied, "What makes an individual special is how one acts when the critical moment comes." Mary's tone became quiet, reflective. "It's easy to be loving when things are easy and carefree. But it's in a crisis that people's true personality comes through. Before now, I had taken Peter's love for granted. How incredibly naïve of me." The last two sentences were murmured more to herself than to Coyle. Embarrassment overtook her. She had not intended to reveal her innermost feelings. Coyle had caught her at a vulnerable moment. "Forgive me," she mumbled, "I don't normally burden other people with my personal life."

"Would you care to talk about Peter?" Mary made no reply, so he went on. "It sometimes helps to voice what is troubling you."

Mary knew she could rely on his total discretion, but pulling at her jacket again, she shook her head. "No. I would prefer not to, if you don't mind."

Coyle rose, took off his jacket, and draped it over her shoulders.

"Please, don't," she pleaded. "You'll catch cold."

He waved off her concern then sat down beside her, this time a little closer. "Your life may appear chaotic right now, but things do have a way of working out."

Not trusting her voice, she simply nodded.

The silence that followed became strained. Mary thought it prudent to change the subject. "I heard you were engaged," she said, then realized that her comment was inappropriate.

Ever the gentleman, Coyle reacted only by raising his eyebrow. "Yes. She was…a lawyer, now living in Toronto. Her name is Melanie. She left me for someone else."

Mary was completely nonplussed. "My question was indiscreet. Please know that it was without intent."

"No need for concern. We were ill-suited for one another."

Mary was taken aback by his direct answer. Coyle was the most private person she had ever met. Private confidences were not natural to him. Not that people considered him reserved and unapproachable. He was easy to be with, relaxed and self-assured. Nevertheless, it had both surprised and flattered her to hear him speak with such openness, for she knew he would not have been so candid unless he had an absolute certainty of her discretion.

"We must go," he said, getting to his feet hastily. He extended his hand, and his firm grip helped her from the log. As she rose, his jacket started to slide off her shoulders, and she struggled to keep it from falling to the ground. She would have lost her balance had he not encircled her waist. He drew her closer and then gently released her.

Unbidden, the thought of how it would feel to be kissed by Coyle flew into her mind. But as it moved through her consciousness, she deliberately freed herself from it, returned his jacket, and walked away from him.

***

Back at the house, they sat down to a delicious lunch prepared by his mother—seafood quiche, green salad, and crème caramel. They then retired to his study, where they spent the rest of the afternoon wrestling over the intricacies of the case until his mother announced that the Thanksgiving dinner would soon be served.

The meal with Coyle and his mother was like nothing Mary had ever experienced. The ambiance was warm, and Mrs. Coyle served her family's traditional turkey dinner with such grace and courtesy that Mary felt her cup over-flowing. She even allowed herself to indulge in the fantasy that things could work out for her, as Coyle had hinted at earlier that day.

More than anything, she was intrigued by Coyle—how one minute he could be grave and aloof, the next animated and witty. It was obvious he was devoted to his mother. There was so much love and warmth around the table that for a brief moment at least, it rendered her vulnerable to the hollow emptiness she felt inside—that part of her life that was missing. She could not remember ever having shared anything together with her parents.

"Is everything all right, Mary?" Coyle asked gently.

"Yes. Why do you ask?"

"You seemed distant."

"Everything is fine," she assured him with a smile. "It's been a long time since I've spent Thanksgiving in such joyful company, and I'm a bit overwhelmed." *And I don't want it to end*, she thought to herself.

He reached out and touched her hand. It was a deferential gesture, obviously without thought, for, looking embarrassed, he quickly withdrew his hand and said, "Well then, we'll have to do it again, won't we?"

Mary looked away but not before becoming acutely aware of Mrs. Coyle's intelligent eyes staring at her with an expression of curiosity, as though contemplating the role Mary played in her son's life. Mary, in turn, found herself pondering the same thing.

The following morning, after another delicious breakfast prepared by Coyle for Mary and his mother, Mary and Coyle spent the rest of the day in the library going over court business specific to her case and what to expect from Baxter, stopping only for lunch. For hours, Coyle threw questions at her, preparing her for what she could and could not say. It was a useful exercise, for she knew Baxter was going to ask her some pretty pointed questions, and she needed to be prepared. The prospect of facing him, however, terrified her. She wished she had a better idea of the extent of what he knew or had deduced.

At four o'clock, Coyle consulted his watch and sighed. "I promised Mother we would have tea with her before leaving. So maybe we should call it a day." He closed his file, and then said, "One other thing. Baxter has listed a Dr. Benjamin Shapiro, whom he will be calling in as an expert witness. Have you ever had an opportunity to meet him? He's a professor at Carleton University; he teaches abnormal behaviour."

Mary nodded. "Yes. As a matter of fact, I attended one of his lectures not that long ago."

"Oh?" Coyle seemed impressed.

"I accompanied a friend whose child has a developmental disorder, Asperger's syndrome, and she was hoping to get some insight into his condition."

"And did she?"

"In abnormal psychology, there are few hard and fast answers, but Dr. Shapiro did give an excellent presentation."

Coyle reached for another file. He found the document he was seeking and studied it, his expression contemplative. "Dr. Shapiro has been asked to issue a statement on depression. I checked into this man's credentials. From what I've learned, he's well-known in his field and highly respected. An acquaintance of mine who works at Carleton said Shapiro is a nationally recognized psychiatrist. His credentials, expertise, and published papers have brought much recognition to their institution."

Mary's thoughts raced. "The attack made on Mr. Kerr's will, in addition to the allegation of undue influence, also raise the question of mental competency. I suspect Baxter plans to move on to lack of testamentary capacity and claim that Mr. Kerr suffered from senile dementia."

"My feelings, precisely," Coyle replied. He paused once more to study the document in front of him and added, "I can understand why Baxter would be calling on Dr. Shapiro, but I'm still at a loss why he would be bringing in Dorothy Cowen."

There was a discreet knock on the door, and Mrs. Coyle stepped into the library. "I have some refreshments set out in the sun porch. Won't you join me?"

"With pleasure, Mother." Coyle gathered his papers and fitted them into his briefcase. "We're finished here."

They followed her through the kitchen and walked into an enclosed sun porch, extending the full length of the back of the house and overlooking a garden. It was a pleasant day and the sun streamed in through the glass. In one corner, a table covered with a white linen cloth had been set up with a tray of sandwiches, Petit Beurres, and tea, ready to be served.

Mary was grateful for the effort Mrs. Coyle had put in to creating a lovely setting but was unable to fully appreciate it. She was struggling with the idea of Dorothy Cowen as a witness. Like Coyle, she was curious why Baxter would be calling her, and not having been able to address it with Coyle, she was left with certain misgivings.

"Mary, Patrick didn't tell me what part of New Brunswick you're from. Do you still have family there?"

Hit by a wave of grief and pain, Mary glanced anxiously at her hands, and then back at Mrs. Coyle. Her query had been innocent enough, but its suddenness rendered Mary powerless to answer without faltering.

Coyle said, "Mother, Mary's parents are both deceased."

Mrs. Coyle covered her mouth. "Oh, I'm so sorry. I didn't know."

"How could you?" Mary assured her.

"Still, I shouldn't have asked without knowing more about you. My inquiry has no doubt revived sensitive memories."

"Please don't worry; I'm fine," Mary assured her, though in truth she felt a sudden discomfort.

Mrs. Coyle placed a consoling hand on Mary's arm. "Please accept my apologies and my deepest condolences for your loss."

"Thank you. And there's no need for you to apologize. You've been nothing but kind all weekend."

"I do hope you've enjoyed your visit."

"Immensely," Mary replied, perhaps too hastily, as the

pins-and-needles sensation in her body threatened to overcome her—a telltale sign of a panic attack.

Mrs. Coyle offered her another sandwich, but she declined, not wanting her to see the tremor in her hand. Mary was now beginning to feel disoriented and needed to leave the room but hesitated. A hasty exit could only bring attention to her malaise, which would unnecessarily distress Coyle's mother. But with each moment that passed her panic loomed larger until she could feel the perspiration on her forehead. Finally, when she could stand it no longer, she rose from her chair and said, "Will you excuse me, please; I still have some packing to do before we leave."

Mrs. Coyle smiled, indulgent, a little pensive. "By all means."

Without further explanation, Mary hurried away, but not without noticing Coyle's apprehensive look as she left the room.

A man of discretion, Coyle had not questioned her departure. He did, however, tap on her bedroom door a short while later. "Mary, is there something wrong?" Hearing the apprehension in his voice sent a wave of anxiety down her spine. The walls buckled and swayed around her. She closed her eyes, fighting the feeling of nausea that gripped her trembling body.

"I'm fine. I just needed to pack a few more things before leaving," she managed to say without slashing the words too badly.

"Are you certain?"

"Yes. Please know, however, that I appreciate your concern," she said as another wave of anxiety gripped her.

There was a pause. Then Coyle announced, "I'll be downstairs, whenever you're ready."

She was breathing with difficulty now, her mind thrashing. Mrs. Coyle's inquiry about her family normally would not have treaded on delicate ground, but in the light of all that had happened in recent months, recalling her past brought excessive emotions to the surface, even panic attacks. In the last years, they had come less often. But when they did surface, they struck without warning.

She leaned against the door and drew huge drafts of air into her lungs until gradually the anxiety subsided. It was evident Coyle was worried about her, and she could not put off going downstairs any longer; so she went to the washroom, rinsed a facecloth in cold water, and held it against her face, letting the cool fabric revive her. Once she had sufficiently recovered, she straightened herself and studied her reflection in the mirror. She looked pale and weary. Repelled, she again closed her eyes, her thoughts racing, including grave misgivings about the outcome of the trial. Her thoughts plagued her, because she had not been completely honest with Coyle. Yet his genuine feelings had touched her like nothing else, and she once more found herself wanting to confide in him, to tell him everything. But she knew that part of her would forever remain hidden. Would she ever be freed from the torment that pressed over her? Probably never.

Fifteen minutes later, Mary closed the door on the room and descended the stairs, carrying her luggage. She placed it on the floor and walked to the porch. It was empty. While deciding what to do next, she heard subdued voices coming from the kitchen. Moving closer to the door, she overheard Coyle's mother say, "Do you see a defence here?"

"Until we get in court, it's hard to say."

"She appears harmless." Mrs. Coyle's voice was sympathetic. "But then that's not an enduring factor where truth is concerned, is it?"

"No, some of our worst criminals have the most innocuous appearance."

"Do you think she's telling the truth?"

"Yes," came his reply. "It was pretty small-minded of McLeod to fire her, considering her obvious dedication to the firm. But what boggles my mind is that he should consider her guilty. She's far too ethical and smart for that. Even in our office, where only the overachievers are recruited, she stood out from the crowd. Had her intentions been fraudulent, she would've concealed her actions more efficiently. For that reason alone, I assume she's innocent of the crime. That's a precarious assumption for any lawyer to make, but I'm already committed."

Mary felt she had eavesdropped long enough. She waited a few moments and then pushed the door open. Coyle and his mother were standing at the kitchen sink, Mrs. Coyle washing the teacups and Coyle drying them.

Managing an apologetic smile, Mary said. "How inconsiderate of me, I should be helping."

"Not at all. Mother and I were just tidying up and making conversation." Coyle studied her guardedly, probably wondering whether she had overheard them.

There was silence. It was momentary, although it seemed

like an eternity. Finally, Mrs. Coyle turned to her son. "Let me see you and Mary to your car."

Together they walked to the front entrance, where the car was waiting outside. Coyle placed their luggage in the back seat then opened the passenger door for Mary. Before climbing inside, she extended her hand to his mother. "You've no idea, truly, how much this weekend has meant to me, Mrs. Coyle. I will never forget your generosity."

"I'm glad you came. It was a pleasure meeting you. Do come again, soon."

On impulse, Mary leaned forward and embraced her. "That would be lovely, indeed." She had whispered those words ruefully for, inside, she doubted she would be making a return visit. She was strangely saddened by the thought, for she had felt more secure in these last three days than any other time in recent memory.

———

The chill of a grey afternoon descended upon them as Mary and Coyle approached Ottawa. As they were making their way back to the city, Mary had asked Coyle what it was like growing up in a small community. He had spoken about his youth—the friends he made, the schools he attended, and the teachers who influenced his life. He talked especially about a classmate who had contracted polio and how it had brought out the best among them. Though partially paralyzed by the disease, his friend had at all times been included in their games. During the winter hockey season, he would be the goalie, and in summer they made him the catcher whenever they played softball.

It made Mary feel so special that Coyle had opened up to her, and she did not want the trip to end. But a glance at her watch told her it was late, nearly dinnertime.

"Anything on your agenda this evening?" Coyle asked.

"No, not really."

"I was thinking if you don't have any plans, you might like to have dinner with me at Chez Henri."

Mary was flattered. Not only did she like being in Coyle's company, but being invited to the famous restaurant in Hull, Quebec—just across the Ottawa River from the city—was a pleasant surprise. "Sounds delightful," she uttered quietly. Then she remembered Rachel's request and added, "I promised a friend I would drop in for a minute to feed her dog. Would you mind?"

"Not in the slightest."

When they arrived at Rachel's home, they found her snacking on a bag of chips and Bear sitting on the couch, his eyes pinned on the television set. The movie *Old Yeller* was on.

"Rachel, have you met Mr. Coyle?"

"How do you do, Mr. Coyle?' Rachel greeted him. "I've had the pleasure of observing you in the courtroom."

"Likewise," he replied, shaking hands with her—a warm acknowledgement between two colleagues who openly respected one another.

Bear clambered down from his perch and trotted to where they were standing. His tail wagging, he inspected them as dogs do.

"No, Bear, don't sniff there, please," Rachel called out. "It's bad manners."

The dog reluctantly obeyed, his head seemingly hanging in shame.

Mary squatted to pet him. She laughed as he gave her a sloppily joyful lick on the face. Looking up at Rachel, she said, "I expected you to be away."

"Unfortunately, the client I was meeting with fell ill, so we had to cancel."

Mary pointed to the chips. "Is that your dinner?"

"Yeah. For the time being, at least."

"You know that stuff will kill you."

Rachel gave her one of her *no kidding* smiles. She then reached to remove the protective covering on the sofa where Bear had been lying, and gestured to them. "Do have a seat."

"Thank you, but Patrick has invited me out for dinner. We just came by to feed Bear."

Rachel's eyebrows rose at the sound of Coyle's Christian name.

"Would you care to join us?" he offered politely.

Rachel appeared ready to accept, but then she smiled and said, "I'm afraid you'll have to manage without my irresistible presence."

Mary smiled. "That's what I like about you, Rachel, your genuine modesty."

"Face it, Mary," her friend replied, "you'd be lost without me."

"Yes, but there are moments when I sure would like to try."

"Well, in that case, you both better leave before I change

my mind about my plans for this evening and decide to join you," Rachel threatened, pushing them out the door.

As they walked toward Coyle's car, he remarked, "I envy the camaraderie between you and Rachel. Is she always that unrestrained in expressing her mind?"

"Actually, this is one of her tamer moments. I've seen her far more voluble."

A smile tugged at his lips. "She's what you call *peerless.*"

"Yes, she is. Sometimes it can be an asset. But most times, she aggravates me insufferably. Yet I don't know what I would do without her."

"How fortunate you are to share such a true friendship," he acknowledged earnestly.

Mary felt that no truer words had been spoken.

The weekend before Mary's trial, which had been scheduled for Monday, Rachel picked her up for a drive to Gatineau Park—a favourite jaunt and a welcome change from the chaos and despondency the lawsuit had instilled in Mary. Bear had been left behind to play with little Jesse.

As they drove along quietly, Mary remembered her last visit to Rachel's apartment. Jesse's mother had needed to attend an important meeting, and Rachel was looking after him, something she often did to offer her neighbour a brief reprieve from her demanding schedule. On that visit, Mary had observed how the dog's gentle, passive disposition had endeared him to the child. She had also marvelled at how well they played together. With his abbreviated arms, Jesse hung on to Bear's neck, while the dog lugged him around the apartment. The child's shouts of glee had warmed Mary's heart.

"How are you?" Rachel asked, interrupting Mary's thoughts.

"Fine," Mary replied, forcing a smile. "In the past six months, my client and dear friend passed away, I lost my job, I broke my engagement, and I'm presently being sued for fraud. Other than that, I'm fine. And thank you for asking."

"God knows you've taken quite a beating, haven't you—more than one should have to."

"Forgive me for sounding facetious, Rachel. It's just that things are happening so fast in my life that I'm at a total loss what to do."

"How does it feel working with Coyle?" Rachel asked.

"Fine. It's working out well enough."

Mary had tried to downplay his role in an attempt to discourage her friend from further inquiries, but unfailingly Rachel would have the last word. "And?"

"And what?"

"Is he romantic?" Rachel asked impatiently.

"Don't be absurd. Coyle couldn't conceivably have any romantic thoughts about me. For him, it's purely a professional relationship. If anything, he's well displeased with me at the moment."

"Oh?"

"He wants to put Peter on the stand to expose Beasley's treachery, and I won't allow it."

"Jesus, Mary," exclaimed Rachel. "Which side are you on, anyway? Why are you protecting that imbecile?"

"I'm not protecting him. I...I'm only..." Mary could not conjure any words of defence.

"Mary, any caring person will tell you that the worst transgression against a relationship is deceit, especially deceit against those who hold you in trust."

Heaving a sigh, Mary asked, "And what about Peter?"

"What do you mean, what about Peter?"

"Wouldn't it be my deceit against him, if I allowed Coyle to put him on the stand?"

"That's different."

"How is it different? Peter may never have challenged

himself to have a greater conscience, but that doesn't mean I have to follow suit. Can't you see that going against him like that is more repulsive to me than his vile behaviour? It goes against everything I feel. He was, after all, my fiancé, and some of the feelings I held for him are still haunting me." Stirred up by deep emotion, she blurted, "In this world of corruption and lies, there has to be something for me to believe in. Presently I stand behind my conscience to choose what is right or wrong. To you and others that may appear inconsequential, but it's all I have. If I go against that, I lose all meaning." She faltered, and then added weakly, "In my heart I know I can't do this to Peter. Considering his upbringing, he's as much a victim as I am."

"I admire you for standing by your values. Regarding Peter, however, you may believe you're standing up for a sacred principle, but that's not going to help you in court. Mary, you're sacrificing yourself for, what, a man who values himself over everybody else?"

"That may be so, but I refuse to measure my actions by his conduct."

"Mary, you speak about your commitment to Peter's memory—what you shared together. What about Peter's commitment to you? I don't pretend to have all the answers and certainly don't want to appear as though I'm delivering sermons on what's appropriate and what's not; nonetheless, I'm convinced you're allowing your feelings for Peter to distract you from making the proper decision here. You've been a lawyer long enough to appreciate the subtleties of our courts. If nothing else, putting him on the stand would buy you some sympathy with the jurors."

"I agree about the jurors, but I…" Mary was unable to finish her sentence. Technically, she had no argument.

Rachel's grip tightened on the steering wheel. "Whenever I see him at the office, I think of what he's done to you. It's appalling. It almost makes homicide justifiable." When Mary didn't reply, Rachel's expression turned grave. "I'm loath to tell you this, but I hear Baxter has a strong case against you."

"Where did you hear that?"

"From Eleanor Reid. I met her at the market the other day. Apparently, there's been a lot of action between McLeod and Beasley…numerous phone calls back and forth between the two offices. She quite happily rattled on, telling me all about it."

"How do you know Eleanor?"

"It's difficult not to know Eleanor—she's such a great source of information."

"I can't understand why McLeod himself would be involved with Beasley," Mary said, shaking her head.

"Let's face it, Mary. In a civil lawsuit, McLeod and his firm may be held jointly responsible for your presumed malfeasance. You were their employee. He's afraid of a lawsuit against his firm and is bending over backward to endear himself to Courtney and Richard. The obnoxious bastard is out to save his own skin."

Mary remained pensive. It never ceased to amaze her how far people would lower themselves to safeguard their own interest.

Rachel looked at her and then back at the road. "If I were you, I would let Coyle put Peter on the stand. You can't afford not to."

"Please, Rachel, let's not discuss it any further. Please."

"Listen, it's your life, and I can't tell you what to do. But I can tell you this. Peter definitely did not have your welfare in mind when he turned over your briefcase to Beasley. And however admirable your intentions, Baxter will have no compunction in employing all the ammunition he has to convict you, including anything the conspiring Beasley may have given him."

Mary held her breath as her friend manoeuvred a sharp corner. She hated driving with Rachel. She drove as if the devil were hot on her heels. They had driven a short distance out of the city, and already Mary's knuckles were white from hanging on to her seat. Finally, when she could stand it no longer, she grumbled, "For God's sake, Rachel, slow down. I know my life isn't worth a damn right now, but I still care to hang on to it."

"Oh! Am I driving too fast?"

"You're only doing sixty in a thirty-miles-an-hour zone. Why not give the gas pedal a break?"

"It's just that I'm so angry."

"Why are you angry?"

"Because you're not," Rachel retorted. "When will you ever start showing your true feelings?"

"What makes you think I'm not?"

"When people are victimized, it's normal to feel indignant. What Peter has done to you is so despicable that it's beyond my understanding. In your shoes, I would be outraged. How is it possible that you're not?"

"Tell me, Rachel. What would venting my anger accomplish? What would I gain by it? Would it bring back everything I've lost?"

"No, but you'd at least have the satisfaction of seeing that shameless contriver squirm, while you put him in his place."

Mary let Rachel's comment go unanswered.

"Mary, you perpetually look toward the good side of people, defending their actions and looking out for their feelings, even when it means ignoring your own. Such self-abnegation is unhealthy. For once in your life, why don't you look after your own interest?"

"I'm sick and tired of people who care only for themselves," Mary replied irritably. "Can't you see that the reason my life is in chaos today is because of these people's selfish, self-serving nature? Everyone clinging to the accepted notion that the self is more important than everything else. And I mean everything else, including relationships, friends, even family…" By this time, Mary was inflamed and actually shouting.

Astounded by Mary's impassioned outburst, Rachel slowed down and pulled to the side of the road. "Mary, please forgive me. I'm so utterly incensed, I…" Rachel stopped, leaving space for Mary to elaborate.

Mary explained, "Before this unfortunate affair regarding the Kerr estate, Peter was the only person who ever demonstrated any genuine love for me. Despite his deception, I have to believe that at least part of our relationship was true."

A mixture of curiosity and compassion crossed Rachel's face. "You say Peter was the only one who ever loved you. Your mother must have loved you. And I love you."

Mary smiled apologetically. "I did not mean to undermine our friendship. It means far too much to me." She slumped back in her seat. "What I'm talking about is the love that goes beyond friendship, the love of a lover or future spouse—the most intimate emotion two people can share. And the love of a mother, father…" Her voice faltered, and she wiped a hand across her eyes.

"What about your mother and father?"

Mary hesitated then said, slowly, "My mother wasn't a wicked person. Her only shortcoming was that she was so focused on pleasing my father that she had nothing left for me. To tell you the truth, I don't remember ever being cuddled by her. Most of the time, she ignored me. I called it benign neglect. Now I wonder how benign it was."

"What about your father? How was he with you?"

"I'd rather not talk about it right now." Mary felt the insufferable longing ignite inside her chest, felt it grow, so strong that she feared it might engulf her. What she wanted to tell her friend but stifled was that never having been loved by your parents was to live life with some essential part of you missing, a hole in your heart that could never be filled. She shivered as she thought about her interminable drive to make herself whole, about the endless yearning.

Rachel's insistence could sometimes be overpowering, but she was astute and seemed to recognize that there was more to Mary's past than she was prepared to reveal. She restarted the car and pulled away from the side of the road. She stayed quiet for all of five minutes, then said, wistfully, "Regardless of your feelings for Peter, you need to let Coyle put him on the stand. From what I've observed, he can use the most negligible evidence and turn it into a court-room feat."

Mary did not respond. Instead, she gripped the armrest

and braced herself as the car shot down the narrow country road. Desperately trying to pay no heed to the speedometer, she peered out the window at the lush rolling landscape, but that did not provide the desired relief. She glanced at her friend, who had grown uncharacteristically mute, and it struck her that Rachel's silence bothered her more than her stormy driving. When she could tolerate it no longer, Mary blurted, "Okay, what is it?"

"I can't help it, Mary. When I think of what Peter has done, I could just scream. He's nothing but a vain and arrogant cheat who deems himself more important than anybody else around him. One day, someone will have to teach him a lesson that will shake his—"

"Only, that someone will not be me," Mary interrupted.

"That's what tortures me. I hate to see you being taken advantage of like this."

"Don't worry. I'm not the pushover I once was."

"As far as I'm concerned, you're still too trusting. Anybody else would've seen Peter for what he was." Rachel eyed Mary for a moment then said, "But I presume each of us has to travel our own journey."

Rachel had always been outspoken about her dislike for Peter, but Mary still had difficulty acknowledging that things had been less than ideal for him and herself before the Kerr affair. Or had they? It made no difference. It was too late, she realized, to make a difference now.

"Mary! Did you hear me?"

"Forgive me, Rachel. What did you say?"

"I asked what it felt like being with Coyle all that time."

"You mean besides the infinite hours of drilling and work?"

Rachel breathed out a sigh. "Now, there's a guy you should be falling for…more suited to your character, and you to his."

"Hardly. His sole interest in me is that I present a challenge for him in the courtroom."

"I find that hard to believe," replied Rachel with a devilish grin. "He's quite the hunk, the kind that radiates sex and allure. And even more important, he's one of a rare breed, a man you can trust."

On that score, Mary agreed but remained silent.

"Has he ever attempted to flirt with you?"

"Forget it, Rachel."

Which of course, her friend ignored. "I'm curious, that's all."

"Can you not get it into your head that Coyle is just not the flirtatious type?"

"You mean to say, he hasn't touched you even once during all the time you've been working together?"

Mary didn't answer. She thought of those two fleeting moments on the Thanksgiving weekend when he had held her close. She had tried to rid them from her mind but acknowledged they had had more of an impact on her than she wished to admit.

"I read recently that the word 'flirt' comes from a French word, *fleureter*, which means 'to touch lightly,'" Rachel said.

"How interesting," mumbled Mary.

"According to this book, the touch is used to

communicate to the other person that they are appreciated. It can also be a way of finding out how the other person responds."

Mary tried to remember how she had responded that evening when Coyle had encircled her in his arms. What message had she sent? It could not have been a positive one. She had felt so conflicted that trying to compensate for it had made it impossible for her to be her natural self. As for Coyle, his gesture had been an instinctive impulse of reassurance, nothing more.

Rachel interrupted her thoughts. "How can a man and a woman be together all that time and not know whether they're sexually attracted or not?"

Mary threw her an exasperated look. "Oh, Rachel, whatever shall I do with you?"

"Well, tell me!"

"I'm not the least bit interested," insisted Mary.

Rachel was obviously not buying it. "Yeah, right."

Mary was not convinced herself.

The sun was shining on the Carleton County Courthouse in the middle of downtown Ottawa, but Mary was oblivious to it. She and Coyle had agreed to meet there half an hour ago, and still no sign of him. She was concerned—punctuality was one of his strongest traits. Subduing the tremble in her legs, she walked toward the front door of the magnificent structure. In her torment, the courthouse's powerful columns and wrought iron fence struck her as alarming, almost threatening. Even more ominous was the walled Georgian building connected to it by a tunnel—the Carleton County Jail.

With only ten minutes to spare before her ten o'clock trial, Coyle appeared, handsome in his pinstripe suit and with his lawyer's garb draped over his arm. "Good morning, Mary. My apologies. There was an accident on the Queensway, and I was held back by the traffic."

Suppressing the growing despondency that threatened to overwhelm her, she feigned a laugh. "It always happens when you least need it."

"You look lovely," he said in a manner that was more matter-of-fact than flirtatious.

"Thank you." Mary had dressed with care for the occasion. In the course of her work, she had learned that dressing to impress the jury was essential. For this occasion, she had worn a light brown business suit, elegantly projecting the professional that she was.

Coyle led her upstairs to the courtroom assigned to their case. He paused in front of the closed door and grinned. "So, this is it."

Mary's voice would not function, so she simply nodded.

"Ready to face them?"

She briefly closed her eyes to collect herself before replying, "I'm not sure that I am."

"You'll do fine."

Before she could respond, he pushed through the door, and she was staring at the inside of the courtroom. Court 14 had been opened to the public half an hour ago and was already full, packed with reporters and inquisitive onlookers, drawn by all the publicity.

Mary surveyed the courtroom and focused on the jury sitting in judgment of her. The day of their selection there had been challenges for cause, peremptory challenges, and both prosecution and defence had spent a good deal of their case vetting potential jury members. Her mind racing, Mary wondered, *Will they find me guilty?*

Determined not to let her nervousness show, she confidently walked to the defence table and slipped into her seat. She steeled her nerves and turned to look at the opposing counsel. Sitting at the table beside them were Baxter and his associate going over some documents. In the bench directly behind them sat Mr. Beasley, Richard, and his attractive wife.

Mary felt painfully outnumbered, and a ridiculous urge to flee gripped her. Again, she closed her eyes, hoping the room would be less threatening when she opened them. The effort only filled her with an overwhelming terror of what was to come. She could not believe this was happening. Until six months ago, she had regarded the courthouse as a workplace, a milieu where she felt comfortable and confident. She knew how intimidating the court system could be for a client, but nothing had prepared her for this. As an accused, everything around her was threatening, leaving her with a disquieting sense of unreality.

She wondered if Peter was in attendance and, once more, gazed at the crowded room, seeing but not aware of the people. Then her eyes registered him sitting at the back, his face a mask of regret. He was by himself, no doubt wishing to keep a discreet presence. Mary immediately looked away but had to admit she was grateful he was there.

Everyone waited silently for the judge to arrive. It seemed to Mary that they'd been waiting for hours, but it was only a few minutes, for at precisely ten o'clock the clerk of the court walked in to herald the arrival of the magistrate. "All rise. Court is in session. The Honourable Justice Frank Stark presiding in the case of the Crown versus Mary Clark."

Mary had entered the room feeling fragile and vulnerable, but upon hearing her name read out loud, all she felt was a deep-seated resentment at the injustice of this case against her. *They think they can fight me on this*, she caught herself thinking, *but we'll show them*. With a new-found determination and the dignity that had always made her distinctive among her colleagues, she stood erect, her head high, ready to face her oppressors.

Justice Stark entered the room in his red-sashed robe,

exuding the confidence of one who has been through this procedure multitudinous times. He had a handsome face and presented an imposing figure. Briefly surveying the crowded courtroom, he took the high desk underneath a photograph of Queen Elizabeth II then motioned for everyone to be seated.

Hugh Baxter opened the prosecution's case. Never short on self-assurance, he denounced Mary as the worst kind of offender, who used her position of trust and friendship to prey upon the old and the innocent. He finished his preliminary address by saying, "And so, ladies and gentlemen of the jury, I can assure you, the Crown will prove beyond a reasonable doubt that Mary Clark not only lied to her client, Mr. Robert Kerr, but stole from him as well—a music box worth three million dollars. I will also prove beyond a shadow of a doubt that she did this intentionally and maliciously. And I'm convinced that once you have heard the evidence, you will have no trouble finding her guilty of mismanagement and fraud."

As Baxter spoke the jurors' eyes were fixed on her, grave and condemning. Her heart thundering, Mary turned to Coyle, seeking some form of encouragement from him.

He turned her way, his expression formal but reassuring. He reached out and touched her hands, grasped firmly in her lap. "Don't worry," he whispered. "I, too, will have an opportunity to speak."

Justice Stark then invited the lawyer for the defence to make his opening statement. Coyle rose to face the jury. His deportment was calm and solemn as he took a moment to look at each juror. Then slowly and in a perfectly modulated and controlled voice, he said, "Ladies and gentlemen of the jury, I commend my opposing counsel on his usual eloquence. He has a formidable ability to speak and has amply demonstrated that to you in his opening address. In assessing his words, however, you have to recognize that my learned friend's objective is a conviction against my client, and he will say whatever is required to make you believe him. I also need to warn you that though he speaks eloquently, he doesn't always take the time required to get to the bottom line of a situation, to relate the whole story, which is something I intend to prove to you in this trial."

Coyle paused, ensuring he had the jury's attention. "One fact among many that he has failed to acknowledge is that my client was offered an opportunity to circumvent these proceedings. All she had to do was what many of my learned colleagues would've done—go back on her promise and put her own welfare ahead of the dying wishes of her friend and client, Mr. Robert Kerr. Doing so would inevitably have facilitated things for her. But her integrity would not allow her to take that offer. She couldn't because at the end of his life, Mr. Kerr had entrusted to her the most important document he possessed, his last will and testament. To my client, that written testimony is more than just a set of papers to be repudiated or discarded for greed, self-interest, or convenience. It is a sacred trust."

Mary glanced at the jury to see how they were taking his words. Until then they had listened with impassive faces. They now seemed alert.

In his mellifluous voice, Coyle proceeded. "When selecting a lawyer to manage his estate, Mr. Kerr had the choice of the top seasoned professionals in the city of Ottawa. Yet he assigned Miss Clark, a young woman just five years out of law school. At the time, like most of my colleagues who knew Mr. Kerr, the reasoning behind his decision had elicited certain questions on my part. It wasn't that I doubted Miss Clark's expertise. We worked for the same law firm, and, from what I observed, she was perfectly competent. But foremost upon my mind was, why Miss Clark over the more experienced attorneys at his disposal?

"Today, in view of all that has transpired following the disclosure of his will, Mr. Kerr's sound and shrewd judgment is obvious to me. In selecting an estate lawyer to assist in preparing his will and an executor or, in this case, an executrix for his estate, Mr. Kerr wanted more than a competent attorney. He suspected his last will and testament would be challenged, and he wanted someone he could trust, a lawyer he knew would fight for him at all costs. He chose Miss Clark because he saw in her a woman of integrity, resolve, and courage, a woman who values honour above all other considerations." Coyle paused and turned to look at Mary. His face softened as he added, "For that same reason, I have elected to defend her against the false charges she finds herself facing." He hesitated a moment then addressed the jury distinctly and forcefully with these final words: "Ladies and gentleman, at the conclusion of this trial, you will know for yourself this prosecution is not only an error, but a grave injustice to my client."

When Coyle sat down, there was no mistaking that his opening speech for the defence had touched the majority in attendance, the jurors pre-eminently.

Mary, too, had been moved but could not help wondering if his description of her had been heartfelt, or had he simply praised her for the benefit of the jurors? As a lawyer, Coyle, like Baxter, would say whatever he deemed appropriate to bring about a not-guilty verdict. Yet was it possible that he had meant every word?

After Coyle's opening statement, the first witness was called. She made her way to the stand, where she was sworn in. After the preliminaries were taken care of, the judge addressed her. "You may be seated."

The prosecutor stood and walked toward the witness. "State you name and address please, for the record."

"Caroline Sully. I live at 194 Rideau Street, Ottawa."

"Miss Sully, what do you do for a living?"

"I'm a real estate broker."

"How long have you been working in the field of real estate?"

"I worked as a salesperson for various firms in and around the city of Ottawa for ten years before obtaining my broker's license three years ago and then starting my own firm, City Real Estate."

"What essentially are your duties?"

"Well, I sell houses for people, or I find houses for them, all aspects of the buying and selling of houses."

"Does that entail the disposal of estates?"

"Yes, I regularly work with individuals and sometimes trustees or law firms who wish to dispose of a property to settle an estate."

"Have you ever had business dealings with a Miss Mary Clark?"

"Yes."

"Do you recognize that same Mary Clark in the courtroom here today?"

"Yes."

"Could you point her out to the court?"

"Yes, she is sitting over there in the light brown business suit."

Instinctively, Mary sat up straighter in her chair, shoulders back, as everyone in the room turned to stare at her.

Baxter turned to face the judge. "If it pleases, the court will acknowledge the witness is pointing to the accused, Miss Mary Clark."

"The court so recognizes," the judge replied.

Baxter redirected his attention once more to the witness. "Could you enlighten the court as to the business dealings you had with the accused?"

"Well, she came to our office in April and requested we do an appraisal of Mr. Kerr's home."

"And did you?"

"Yes. But I later found out that she was having two other real estate companies do appraisals as well."

"Would that be a standard practice in your industry?"

"Yes, but she was rather secretive about it…and her later conversations with me were peculiar."

"What exactly did you find peculiar about her conversations with you?"

Coyle stood up. "Objection, Your Honour. This is all very interesting, but I don't see what it has to do with the trial."

"What does counsel wish to ascertain from this question?" asked Justice Stark.

"It's a relevant question, Your Honour. I'm establishing that Miss Clark was motivated to dispose of Mr. Kerr's property in a manner that did not represent his true testamentary intention."

Justice Stark pondered Baxter's words for a moment, and then nodded. "Objection overruled. You may proceed."

"Thank you, Your Honour," Baxter replied. Facing Miss Sully, he repeated his question. "What exactly did you find peculiar about her conversations with you?"

"It sounded as if she intended to buy the house for herself."

There was a loud murmur in the room.

"Objection!" Coyle was on his feet. "This is strictly an opinion."

"Sustained."

Seemingly unperturbed, Baxter resumed his interrogation. "Miss Sully, what did Miss Clark say to give you that impression?"

"When I quoted a price for the house, she seemed astonished. I remember her saying, 'Are you sure? It's not in the price range I had predicted.' And I said, 'Well, what price range had you in mind?' And her answer was 'Frankly, I expected it to be much less.'"

Mary remembered Miss Sully well, mostly for her unprofessionalism. She had come to her business meeting with Mary totally unprepared. And the quote she had proffered for the sale of the house was incommensurate with those received from the two other real estate professionals, who had taken into account all the repairs that would be required on the property to justify a higher price. Both had provided her with detailed information packages. One realtor had even gone through the trouble of furnishing her with the names of potential contractors who could reliably do the work.

"Anything else?" asked Baxter.

"Well, when I inspected the house with her, her inquiries were more those of a buyer than a seller. They were subtle. But in my business, one gets an instinct for these nuances."

Again, Coyle demurred, and His Lordship agreed.

Baxter went on, unfazed. "Could you give us an example of some of the questions she asked?"

"Well, throughout the inspection of the house, she drew my attention to all the repairs that would be required and kept asking me how it would affect the sale of the house."

"Really?"

"Yes. It sounded as if she expected me to quote her a lower price. So I inquired if she had a buyer in mind. She didn't answer me, but she had this odd look in her eyes that made me think she had other intentions about the disposal of Mr. Kerr's property."

"Miss Sully, did Miss Clark choose your company to sell Mr. Kerr's home?"

"No, she went to a competitor. I can't understand why because we had quoted her a higher price for the house, and we have an excellent reputation for selling."

"How did you know the other quotes were lower?"

"Because I asked her. But, even there, she was hesitant about giving them to me."

"Thank you, Miss Sully." Hugh Baxter returned to his table.

Before Coyle could stand to cross-examine, Mary reached for his pen and writing pad sitting on the table in front of him and wrote: *Woman grossly inefficient.*

Coyle nodded, acknowledging her message, and then stood to address the witness. "Miss Sully, did Mary Clark actually say she wanted to buy Mr. Kerr's home?"

"No, but it certainly sounded that way."

"But she never said it?"

"No."

"You stated that Miss Clark went to a competitor. Do you know what real estate company it was?"

"Yes…Caldwell International."

"In your opinion, would you say they were a reputable company?"

"Yes," she acknowledged after a slight hesitation.

Coyle turned to the jurors. "Indeed, Caldwell International Inc. is one of the most prestigious real estate companies in Ottawa, who last year won an Excellence Award for the most sales of the year. One could scarcely fault my client for that." Then turning to the witness, he smiled faintly. "Thank you, Miss Sully. That will be all."

Next, Baxter called Dr. Arthur Stevens to the stand.

A tall, lean man of around forty with thinning black hair and dressed in a fashionable dark suit was ushered into the courtroom. He walked assuredly up to the witness stand on the elevated platform and took the oath. Once the witness was settled comfortably in his seat, the Crown attorney approached him. "Dr. Stevens, please state your profession and where you are employed."

"I'm a general surgeon at the Ottawa Civic Hospital."

"Dr. Stevens, would you describe your relationship to Mr. Robert Kerr?"

"Mr. Kerr was my patient."

"How long had you known Mr. Robert Kerr before he passed away?"

"About two months. I was working emergency and was required to operate on Mr. Kerr, who had developed an infection as a result of his condition."

"So you saw a lot of Mr. Kerr before he died?"

"Yes. I saw him regularly over that period of time and got to know him fairly well."

"What was his state of mind then?"

"He knew his illness was fatal."

"Dr. Stevens, do you feel Mr. Kerr was in full use of his mental capacity during that period of his illness?"

Coyle stood up. "I object, Your Honour. Dr. Stevens has already stated he is a surgeon, not a psychiatrist or psychologist, and as such lacks the expertise to comment on Mr. Kerr's mental capacity."

Mr. Baxter interjected. "Your Honour, I'm asking Dr. Stevens in his capacity as a medical doctor treating his patient for two months. I believe he is entitled to a professional medical opinion. The court can weigh its significance."

The judge allowed the question.

Dr. Stevens considered it for a moment and then said, "Although Mr. Kerr put on a valiant front, it was undoubtedly a challenging time for him. And from what I observed, he wasn't in the best emotional health."

"Dr. Stevens, did Mr. Kerr ever talk about his children?"

"Yes. He seemed extremely fond of them."

"During that period, did he ever mention anything about the Robert Kerr Palliative Care Trust?"

"No."

"Are you certain about that?"

"I'm sure I would remember if he had."

Baxter thanked Dr. Stevens then directed his attention toward the bench. "I have no further questions at this time, Your Honour."

Justice Stark turned to Coyle. "Your witness."

Again, Mary reached for his pen and writing pad and wrote: *Never saw this doctor in Mr. Kerr's room in any of my visits.*

Coyle rose to his feet. Slowly, he made his way to the witness stand, seemingly pondering. Finally, he addressed the witness. "Dr. Stevens, as a surgeon, I would imagine your work is exceptionally demanding."

"We're on call almost twenty hours a day."

"I assume then that you have very little time for yourself?"

"Yes, my work schedule can be exhausting. I frequently have to operate on five patients a day."

"And you have to pay a visit to all these patients while they are in the hospital?"

"Yes, until they are discharged."

"Dr. Stevens, I consulted with the nurse in charge of the ward Mr. Kerr was in, and she informed me that most of your visits with your patients are indeed brief."

"Yes, but I allow them whatever time they need." This was pointed out in a righteously indignant tone.

"Then you would scarcely have time to discuss at length any of their personal business, would you?"

From his expression, it was obvious that this last remark had caught Dr. Stevens off guard. "Well, no, but I…" His voice trailed off as he turned to look at the jury.

"Thank you, Dr. Stevens. You may step down."

Dr. Stevens left the stand deflated and even more indignant. Indeed, Coyle had managed to show that the doctor's statement, under Baxter's interrogation, afforded little importance.

Mary glanced at the Crown attorney. If his expression were any indication, it was obvious he had not attained the results he had hoped for with Dr. Stevens's testimony.

Despite Coyle's success, Mary was uneasy. She wondered why Caroline Sully had consented to appear as a witness against her. What had her statement accomplished? Though a biased witness, nothing she had revealed was sufficient to warrant a conviction against Mary, since there had been nothing unusual or illegal about their meeting. Yet Mary knew that Baxter did nothing without a purpose.

As it was close to noon, the trial was adjourned for lunch.

Upon stepping out of the courthouse, Mary and Coyle were joined by Rachel. "I would like to treat both of you to lunch at Chez François," she offered.

"How very kind of you, Miss Vogue. Unfortunately, I must decline," Coyle replied with genuine regret. He then turned to Mary and added, "Mary, this morning's session brought up certain questions that demand my return to the office. I hope you don't mind?"

Mary had hoped to discuss her concerns about the last witness but forced a smile and said, "Of course not. Please go ahead. I'll meet you in the lobby before the trial resumes."

During the afternoon of the first day, Baxter brought in several other witnesses, friends and business associates of Mr. Kerr, all supporting the prosecutor's line of questioning: that Mr. Kerr was too much of a family and business man to surrender his life savings to people he hardly knew; that he had shown signs of depression—most notably in the last months of his life; and that they were all utterly taken aback by the will he had left behind.

The afternoon could not have gone more badly, and Mary was hoping Justice Stark would call it a day when she spotted one of Baxter's associates walk up to his superior and whisper something into his ear. Smiling, Baxter stood and, addressing the judge, said, "I call Miss Dorothy Cowen as my next witness."

Coyle stood up. "May I move we continue with Miss Cowen tomorrow morning? I would—"

Baxter interrupted. "Your Honour, this is a reluctant witness. Since she drove all the way from Toronto to testify on our behalf, it would be inappropriate for us to delay it, especially when a delay is not entirely necessary."

"In that case, I will allow you to go ahead," Justice Stark replied. "Please bring in the witness."

The court clerk went out to fetch her, while everyone sat back, staring at the door.

After a moment, an attractive woman in her mid-thirties entered the room, her head held high. She wore a luxurious, haute couture, blue ensemble that might have come straight from a Paris design house, and she radiated calm and self-confidence. There was also an aura of innocence about her as she settled into the witness box. Yet Mary feared the outcome of her testimony.

Coyle was looking at Mary. "What is it?"

Suppressing the dread she felt inside, she just shook her head helplessly.

Before Coyle could say more, Baxter spoke. "Please state your name and place of residence, for the record."

"My name is Dorothy Cowen and I live at 1041 Brayer Street in Toronto."

"Miss Cowen, are you the daughter of the late Dr. Marshall Cowen, a prominent surgeon who practiced at the Sunnyside Hospital in Toronto?"

"Yes."

"Would you please tell the court how you became acquainted with the accused, Mary Clark?"

Dorothy Cowen turned her attention across the room to where Mary was sitting. "Miss Clark and I have never met."

"Oh," replied Baxter, apparently bemused. "But wasn't Miss Clark a beneficiary in your father's will?"

"Yes, I was made aware of my father's bequest to Miss Clark, but we never met."

"Explain to us then, how did she come to be a beneficiary in your father's will? According to the records, your father bequeathed fifty thousand dollars to Miss Clark, a significant sum by any standards."

Mary glanced discreetly at Coyle to see if Baxter's words had incited any reaction. There was none visible.

"Miss Clark and my father met when he was a patient at the Élisabeth Bruyère Hospital, here in Ottawa. His lawyer informed me she was a young, struggling law student, and my father, moved by her situation, wanted to help her."

"Ottawa?"

"Yes, Ottawa was his original home, and he chose to retire here."

"I see. And you say he met her at Élisabeth Bruyère Hospital."

"Yes."

"In what capacity?"

"I believe she was a volunteer on his ward."

"I see. And you knew nothing else about her?"

"Very little, except that my father enjoyed hearing her play the piano. He let it be known in the codicil to his will that she had brought immense comfort to the final days of his life."

"How did you feel about him leaving such a substantial bequest to a complete stranger?"

"Obviously, she was not a stranger to my father. And I thought this rather sweet of him."

"Miss Cowen, did you not consider it peculiar that your father would bequeath money to someone he met briefly in a hospital?"

Coyle spoke up. "Objection. The witness has already answered that question."

"Sustained."

Baxter continued. "Understandably, your father was

vulnerable at that time. Did you not think perhaps she might have abused their friendship to promote that sort of generosity?"

Coyle was on his feet. "Your Honour, I strongly object."

Justice Stark shot Baxter a look of admonition. "That's enough, Mr. Baxter. You are taking too many liberties."

His face stolid, Baxter resumed his interrogation. "According to the records, your father also willed a huge portion of his estate to the Élisabeth Bruyère Hospital Foundation."

"Yes."

"Had your father ever mentioned anything about this to you?"

"No."

"Did you suspect anything illegitimate at the time?"

"No."

"You mean you didn't find any of this unusual?"

"Well, I questioned it then. It had come up rather suddenly, without explanation."

"And you didn't contest it?"

"My father had already willed me a substantial amount of money, more than I will ever need, and according to his lawyer, it was his wish that the remainder of his estate go to a good cause. If you had known my father, you would understand. He was an exceptionally generous man." She paused, contemplative, and then went on. "Contesting his will was something I never considered. As far as I was concerned, it was his money to do with as he pleased."

"What if I were to tell you this foundation was operated

by an acquaintance of Miss Clark? Would it make you regard the matter differently?" asked Baxter.

"I don't see what difference that would make."

"Well, don't you find it odd that this same woman who was involved with your father, who subsequently left an ample portion of his estate to a foundation run by a friend of hers, is the same person who today is suspected by my clients of having influenced their father to leave most of his estate to a charity, which she alone can manage?"

Coyle stood. "Your Honour, this is outrageous. Counsel is leading the witness. Nowhere in the evidence does it show Miss Clark influencing Mr. Kerr or Dr. Cowen one way or another."

"Sustained!" cried the judge.

Before Baxter could say anything else, Justice Stark addressed the jurors. "There will be a ten-minute recess." Then turning to Baxter and Coyle, he commanded in a stern voice, "I want to see both of you in my chambers."

While Mary sat waiting for them to return, she could well envisage what was happening in the adjoining room. Without a doubt, Baxter was being admonished for his overt transgressions of court rules.

When they re-entered the room ten minutes later, Justice Stark addressed the jurors. "The jury will please disregard the prosecutor's last comment." He then instructed the recording clerk to strike it from the record. Finally, he looked at Baxter. "Do you have any further questions?"

"No, Your Honour," he replied in a subdued voice, a departure from his customary tone.

In the brief silence that followed, Justice Stark redirected his attention to Coyle. "Do you wish to cross-examine the witness?"

All eyes were now on Dr. Cowen's daughter, none more than Coyle. He stood, walked to the witness stand, and fixed her with a serious gaze. "Miss Cowen, you claim that, until today, you had never met Mary Clark. Were you aware of her presence in your father's life while he was in the hospital?"

She returned his gaze, her demeanour proud yet sensitive. Hers was a fine, dignified face, reminding Mary of dear Dr. Cowen. "Yes, my father had mentioned her name several times in his letters to me."

"How did you feel about her?"

Dorothy Cowen appeared saddened by his question. Then giving Mary a diffident glance, she said, "Unfortunately, I…I wasn't able to be with my father during his stay at the hospital or in the Extended Care Unit. He had insisted I finish my studies in Paris. So, I…I suppose I was thankful there was someone there for him…someone who would make the last days of his life happier than they would otherwise have been."

"During your father's illness, how would you describe his mental condition?"

"What do you mean?"

"Was he coherent?"

"My father may have been physically incapacitated, but I assure you he was in full control of his mental capacity right up to his last breath." She was clearly miffed.

"Thank you, Miss Cowen. I've no further questions."

Before she could leave the witness stand, Baxter was on his feet. "A question on re-direct, Your Honour?"

"Very well."

Entitled to re-examine on a point requiring clarification, Baxter approached the witness. "One more question, Miss Cowen, if you don't mind. I realize how difficult this must be for you." He tried to appear sympathetic as he spoke, but coming from him, the words sounded unnatural.

She nodded in acknowledgement and waited.

"Miss Cowen, you've just told the defence counsel that you were unable to be with your father during his illness, that you were in fact living in Paris. Did you have a chance to discuss his will with him after it was written?"

"No."

"Thank you, Miss Cowen. That will be all." His point had been made with the jury.

Mary stared at Justice Stark, who was studying the witness. Like her, he must have noticed the tortured look in her eyes, most likely incurred by the memory of her father facing death alone, for in a soothing voice, he said, "You're free to leave now, Miss Cowen. Thank you for coming."

Again, all eyes were on her as she slowly stood and stepped down from the witness stand. When she approached Mary's table, she hesitated and smiled awkwardly at her, as if she wanted to say something, a timorous moment during which Mary sensed what she must have been thinking—that both had shared the love of a singly special person. Then Dr. Cowen's daughter straightened herself and exited the room, closing the door behind her.

Mary felt Coyle's gaze on her, its intensity unnerving.

But she could not will herself to face him. She remained frozen in her seat, her eyes fixed ahead, her hands clenched on her lap. Even once the court was recessed, she avoided looking at him and worked to remain free of any emotions as he steered her away from the journalists outside the courtroom.

It was pouring when they stepped out of the building—a complete transformation in weather since that morning when she had chosen to walk to court—so she accepted a ride home. Together they crossed the parking lot to his car, where he opened the door for her. Once behind the wheel, he suggested they stop at his office to review the results of the day's trial, but she declined. "If you don't mind, I would like to go home."

It was four thirty and already the traffic was heavy with government employees leaving work. As Coyle drove through the city, Mary could feel the leaden silence between them. When finally he pulled up to the curb in front of her apartment, she could abide it no longer. "I didn't tell you about Dr. Cowen because I didn't think it was pertinent to this case."

"Mary, surely you don't expect me to believe that. From someone else who has never dealt with the law and does not understand the legal system and how it functions, maybe. But not you! Especially when I questioned you about Miss Cowen. You must have—"

"Everything I've done or said has been twisted and altered to make me appear scheming and insidious," she cut in, giving him a sharp look. "Even this business about the sale of the house. Why did he bring that up? In my mind, it has no specific purpose."

"It's Baxter's way of operating. He throws everything in the book at you in the hope of misleading the jurors."

Mary wrapped her arms around herself, suddenly feeling cold to the bone. "This whole trial has become a nightmare, a ghastly, horrible nightmare."

Coyle did not reply, but Mary saw his grip tighten on the steering wheel.

Wearied, she struggled to explain. "About Dr. Cowen, he was just one more acquaintance in my life. A very noble person, mind you. There's hardly a day goes by that I'm not reminded of him in some way or another." Trying not to sound defensive, she reiterated, "I never imagined my association with him would be relevant to this case."

"And this money he willed to you?"

No answer.

Coyle was markedly distraught, yet in a controlled voice he said, "Would you mind telling me what you did with the fifty thousand dollars Dr. Cowen bequeathed to you?"

"I used it to pay various expenses, and the remainder, I invested."

"What expenses?"

"I can't tell you that."

His face muscles tightened. "You mean you won't."

"I mean I can't, as it's personal. But you need to believe me, I've done nothing to be ashamed of."

"Mary, I trusted you when nobody else would. Isn't it time you learned to trust me?"

Mary's cheeks flushed red. Indeed, he was right on that count, but she could not bring herself to unveil that part of her past, even to him.

"You know that what you say to me will be held in strict confidence," he assured her. She could hear the sincerity in his voice.

She shook her head. She then moved closer to the door and reached for the handle. Before opening it, she murmured feebly, "You no longer believe me." Though it was spoken as a statement not a question, she waited should a reply be forthcoming. When he didn't reply, she insisted, "All this evidence against me is pure speculation."

"Most possibly, but it's the kind of speculation juries love. What's more, I don't think your case can afford any more surprises like the one this afternoon."

Mary started to say something, but Coyle silenced her with a severe look. "Is there anything else that might come up to deleteriously affect the proceedings? If so, tell me now."

Bracing herself against the emotional torment that flooded her whole being, she answered firmly, "No." She was, again, deceiving him and felt remorse but not enough to deflect her. Some things were too personal to disclose.

"Then there is nothing more to discuss, is there?" His tone was impassive, but his eyes made Mary painfully aware of his displeasure.

Mary was unwilling to leave him thinking of her so adversely but knew that anything she chose to say at this point would be the wrong thing. Still, she felt compelled to say, "You've heard some damaging arguments against me, but you need to trust me on this. Things are not what they appear." Before he could respond, she stepped out and quietly closed the door, but not before the tears started to glisten in her eyes.

Alone in her bedroom that evening, Mary tried to brush aside the hopelessness and vulnerability that engulfed her. Concentration eluded her as she grappled with her thoughts. What awaited her? Her world had transformed into a dreaded horror with no end in sight.

She knew she had to rest, so she undressed and went to bed. But she was afraid to close her eyes, afraid of what sleep would bring. For some time, she had been freed from her nightmares. But lately they had revisited her with a vengeance. After staring for sleepless hours at the emptiness in front of her, she drifted into a blistering slumber, an alternate world over which she had no control.

She is awake, alone in the void and silence of a darkened space. She does not recognize the room, only that it is unsafe. In the ominous stillness, she hears footsteps approaching. The door opens and, in the dim light of the moon from her window, she sees a shadow coming toward her but not a face. She is frightened now. Not only frightened but petrified—certain of the outcome. Caught in this engulfing terror, with no escape, no one to call to, no place to go, she waits, trembling.

Mary woke up gasping, oblivious to her surroundings. All she could remember were agonizing flashes from her recurring nightmare and the raw memories it brought. Filled with dread, she burrowed her head deeper into the pillow and drew a long breath, and then a second, trying to control her breathing. Her head began to clear, and she realized she was in her own apartment, that she was safe. With the waking came the process of recalling the past, rendering her despondent. The guilt was the worst. *What did I do wrong?* She closed her eyes, willed herself to forget, but her subconscious would not allow her that reprieve.

She switched on the lamp on her bedside table. It was one o'clock, only two hours since she had fallen asleep. She tossed her head from side to side. Tumultuous emotions competed with one another—blame, rage, despair. Unable to sleep, she lay in the dark, the nightmare repeating itself in her mind. Going over it all horrified her. It recalled parts of her life that she had managed to erode. But they would always be with her. Mary forced herself to imagine a different world and was reminded of Coyle. The hardest part of the previous day had been not telling him the truth, he who had believed in her. Did he still? He must know she was lying. She considered calling him. To confide in him. If he reworked his defence now, while there was time…

But there was no time left. It was already too late.

Besides, it was a part of her life too private to reveal—a part of her past that she wanted to expunge from her memory. How she wished things could be different.

She wondered what future remained for her. She did not dare contemplate what awaited her if found guilty. It was all too frightening. There seemed to be no escape, neither in her dreams nor in the real world.

In an effort to dispel the lingering sense of foreboding, Mary employed the relaxation technique she had been introduced to when things had become too arduous, a means of dealing with her destructive feelings. She used it whenever these moments overtook her. She breathed deeply and slowly, sensing the air flowing in and out of her body.

She tried to evoke pleasant thoughts, something soothing and cathartic. Unconsciously, she once more found herself thinking of Coyle and their weekend together at Thanksgiving. That time in his mother's home would forever be engraved in her mind. What was it about him that was so relaxing? His warm eyes and manners, perhaps? Or was it the way he radiated self-confidence and security? Whatever it was, it comforted her.

The following morning, the day Courtney and Dr. Shapiro were to testify, Mary parked close to the Lord Elgin Hotel and made her way to Coyle's office. The sun was shining, the light November breeze refreshing. For a few moments, Mary allowed her mind a respite from what the day had in store for her.

Before entering his building, she paused and hugged herself against a sudden chill. Would Coyle still be angry with her? What would she say to him? Whatever it was, she would face it. She walked inside, her poise expressing both dignity and reserve.

Kate greeted her warmly as she entered the waiting room. "Good morning, Miss Clark. Mr. Coyle is expecting you."

"Thank you," Mary replied, and gently pushed open his door. As expected, she found him hunched at his desk, labouring over his working papers. He glanced up when she greeted him. "Oh, good morning, Mary."

She handed him a copy of the *Ottawa Citizen*. "Our trial is still on page one, right next to another quote by Charlotte Whitton," Mary said, referring to the first female mayor of the City of Ottawa, who was no longer in office. Ms. Whitton was an inspiration to most women, a relentless crusader and a driving force behind various social issues, especially child welfare. But she would be best remembered for saying,

"Whatever women do, they must do twice as well as men to be thought half as good. Luckily, this is not difficult."

Coyle took the newspaper and tossed it across the desk. "I've already read it," he said, favouring her with the warm grin she liked so much. Then he pointed to a side table and added, "There's coffee in the thermos. Help yourself."

Relieved that all seemed to be well between them, she smiled. "I'm fine, thank you. I just finished breakfast and had my quota."

She drew up her customary chair beside him and noted a stack of transcripts and law briefs neatly piled at the corner of his desk. He handed her a document, saying, "You may want to read this."

It was a transcript of Miss Cowen's testimony.

"What am I looking for?" she asked.

"Anything…anything that doesn't fit."

Mary nodded knowingly. Coyle's expedient and sometimes unconventional mind was one of the reasons she enjoyed working with him.

While Mary read, Coyle took out his pipe from his pocket. "Do you mind?"

"No, not if it helps you think." She couldn't help asking, "What are you thinking?"

"Well, this morning should prove interesting," Coyle replied with calm assurance. "I'm especially eager to hear what Courtney has to say. And then there's Dr. Shapiro's testimony. I don't know what to expect from him. Even in discovery, I failed to learn what exactly his role was. I must admit that he, too, seemed rather vague about it."

Mary returned to the transcript. After reading through it, she set it down. "Nothing useful here, I'm afraid."

He handed her several other papers, notes to himself. "Would you mind glancing through these? I would appreciate your thoughts, observations—anything that might assist me in my line of interrogation."

They were a comprehensive personal history of Courtney and Richard from the time they were born to the present. On each page, Coyle had inserted his observations. There were also notes about Dr. Shapiro.

He took a quick swallow of his coffee and leaned back in his chair, giving Mary time to read. When she finished, he raised his eyebrows, prompting.

"You've pretty much covered everything. Yet about Dr. Shapiro, I'm puzzled, a little concerned even."

"Oh?"

"Well, I find it odd that Baxter would call on him, an expert in abnormal psychology, to issue a statement on depression when we have in Ottawa a renowned psychiatrist in that field, Dr. Proulx. No doubt you've heard of him. He's been called in as an expert witness numerous times to express his opinion about depression. So wouldn't you think he would be the preferable choice to broach that subject instead of Dr. Shapiro?"

"You have a point there," said Coyle, scratching his head meditatively with his pencil. "Any suggestions?"

"No. It occurred to me that it's somewhat odd, that's all."

Coyle did not answer, just looked thoughtful.

"It makes me feel that Baxter may have an ulterior motive," she continued.

"I'm inclined to agree with you and shall definitely give it more thought," he replied. "Right now, however, we're running out of time, and I need to question you further about Courtney before we leave for the courthouse."

She nodded. "Yes, of course."

"About Courtney, is there anything else about her you can tell me? Her weaknesses? Her strengths?"

"There's not much to say, really. Her strength would most definitely be her beauty…but then I suspect that's also her weakness." Reflecting on what she knew of Courtney's past, Mary added, "As I told you, she moved to New York after graduating from Elmwood, aspiring to establish herself as a high fashion model. There, she met a fashion designer, married him, and her career became her whole identity. She attended parties hosted by famous designers, met all the important people, and was even featured in a few magazines. But she never made it to the top—few models do. She was one among many, and the competition simply proved too immense for her. Her marriage also failed, and after a fiery divorce—according to what her father told me—she returned to Canada. So, her greatest fear right now, or weakness if you will, has to be losing her looks. At her age, they're already beginning to fade, which is fatal in modelling. But having fallen heavily for the excitement and illusion of glamour, it's doubtful she's willing to do anything else."

"What about current friends? Does she have any?"

"On that question I'm rather vague. I was her only friend at school. I don't know why. She was popular enough and was always invited to parties. But she never really extended herself. And in her present line of work, you don't have much time to develop any true friendships, from what I gather. As I mentioned, it's all very competitive."

Coyle checked his watch and rose from his chair. "Well, let's see what happens."

They made their way to his car and drove to the courthouse. Once inside, Mary stopped abruptly and heaved a sigh. "Somehow, I have a bad feeling about today."

"You'll be fine," he reassured her.

As she walked to the defence table, she discreetly surveyed the room, more from instinct than general curiosity. Richard was seated in the spectators' section. Rachel and Francis, who came to support Mary whenever they could, were seated there too. Behind them sat Peter. Mary looked at him and saw—or thought she saw—a trace of concern in his eyes.

Why had he even bothered to come? Her question was promptly dispelled when she noticed Beasley sitting beside him. He merely stared at her, his eyes devoid of expression. Mustering all the courage she had, she faced them calmly, with a confidence she did not feel.

Before taking a seat in the chair Coyle had pulled out for her, Mary's attention was briefly drawn to a middle-aged woman staring at her from the back of the room. Mary sensed a nervous tension about her, the slightly shifty air of a person who wanted to be anywhere but in this room. That was not the only thing that intrigued Mary. As she sat, she struggled to remember why this woman looked familiar and who she might be.

From the front, Mary heard, "All rise." She rose from her seat and watched Justice Stark enter and settle into his chair.

"Good morning," he greeted them. Opening the file he

had carried with him to the bench, he addressed Baxter and Coyle. "Counsels, are you ready to proceed?"

"Yes, Your Honour," they both replied.

Turning to the Crown prosecutor, Justice Stark said, "You may call in your first witness."

In a precise and assured voice, Baxter called out Courtney's name.

With the poise of a professional model, she walked up the aisle to the witness stand. Instead of her typical high fashion, Courtney was dressed in a modest black suit and a simple pearl necklace. She was the model of a grieving daughter. It was clear why Baxter had asked her to testify instead of Richard. Juries are more easily swayed by beautiful females who look innocent and mournful than by male businessmen.

After Courtney was sworn in and had introduced herself, Baxter stood before her, visibly pleased with her grand entrance. "Miss Kerr, do you know Mary Clark?" he asked.

"Yes. We were roommates at Elmwood School, here in Ottawa."

"How would you describe your relationship?"

"When we first met, I found her pleasant, and we immediately became close friends. At school, we spent a lot of time together, on holidays especially, when I invited her to my home."

"Did she not have a family of her own to go to?"

"Yes, but she gave me to understand that she and her parents didn't get along, and she preferred to stay away."

Mary had avoided speaking to Coyle about her parents and wondered what he was thinking.

Baxter carried on. "Did you ever question her about it?"

"Yes. But when I did, she became anxious and abnormally angry, so I would move on to a different topic."

"Did Miss Clark often show signs of anxiety?"

"I...I find it difficult to explain. The thing is, I never knew what to expect from her. I did enjoy her company greatly, but there were moments when she responded to situations in maladaptive ways. That is what eventually destroyed our friendship."

"Maladaptive in what way?"

"Well, she was unusually prone to find hidden meanings in people's actions and frequently responded in an erratic, almost unstable manner."

Baxter waited a moment, no doubt to ensure that Courtney's words had sunk in. Then in a slow and deliberate voice he asked, "Can you describe for us how she displayed this erratic and unstable behaviour?"

When she didn't answer, Baxter pushed her. "I know that speaking against a former friend can be painful, but the court needs to hear how this maladaptive behaviour manifested itself."

Giving Mary the most unsettling look, the look of one compelled to say something unpleasant about someone for whom she cared, Courtney carried on, "Well, with my father and stepmother, for instance, she became abnormally possessive of their affection, almost to the point of competing with my brother, Richard, and me...especially regarding my father. She idolized him. She once stated he was the father she never had. I'm convinced she wanted my father to believe she cared more about him than we did and spared no effort to ingratiate herself, not only with him, but with our stepmother." Again, she hesitated before adding, "That was particularly wounding to me and my brother."

Mary recoiled from her words.

"How did your father respond to her attention?"

"He was flattered, of course. He was moved by her affection for him and seemed unmindful of the other side of her." She then hastily qualified, "Mary was fun to be with—it's just that she had these moments where her personality changed drastically."

"Miss Kerr, please describe the other side of Miss Clark you talked about."

Courtney stared at Mary, and then her expression turned apologetic. With apparent effort, she said, "Apart from being possessive of my father and stepmother, she sometimes had periods of depression and became distraught at the smallest provocation."

"Yet you remained friends?"

"Mary could be sweet and amenable when she wanted to be. And despite her faults, we still enjoyed being with her. And there was my father, who insisted we invite her to our home at every opportunity."

"And you did?"

"As I mentioned, she could be all those things, and it was much later in our relationship that I perceived a pervasive alteration in her character. By then, we had graduated and gone our separate ways." Courtney's voice dropped to a near whisper. "It wasn't until my father's illness that we met again."

"How would you describe your relationship with her now?"

"Not good…especially during that week before my father passed away. It was marred by an abusive outburst on her part, and our meeting ended quite angrily."

Courtney's words spun in Mary's head. She closed her eyes, and her last memory of Mr. Kerr came rushing through. His doctor had told him that he had little time left, and in a last attempt to bond with his children, he had called Courtney and Richard to his bedside. He had also asked Mary to be present. In those last moments of his life, Mr. Kerr had hoped to bring up with them things he had failed to say in the past. To her chagrin, they had acted as if his illness was nonexistent. They had come with implausible statements such as, "You look great today, Dad" and "You've improved since our last visit." They had declared this even when it was obvious that he was at his weakest. Because Mary knew then that Mr. Kerr had come to accept his death and wanted a more meaningful conversation, she had taken Courtney and Richard aside to speak to them. It was not that she was being censorious. She knew that not everyone was comfortable with people's terminal illnesses, and it was conceivable Courtney and Richard were unable to cope. By bringing up the issue, she had hoped to let them know their father had worked through the emotional stress of his imminent death and desired only to bond and communicate with them. Needless to say, her conversation with Courtney and Richard had been futile. Instead of promoting an acceptance of what their father was going through, it had ended in an acrimonious exchange—with them accusing her of meddling in their personal lives.

Emerging from this disquieting memory, she heard Baxter say, "What was the subject of your conversation?"

Courtney took a small lace handkerchief out of her purse and carefully applied it to her eyes. "She accused us of not showing concern for our father. That, of course, was totally false. My brother and I cared for him. He was our whole life." With that, Courtney began to cry. Baxter stood silently, waiting for her to recover. But Mary was not fooled. He knew the value of a dramatic pause, and this charade had obviously been orchestrated to influence the jurors' sympathy. She glanced their way. It had succeeded.

After Courtney had dried her eyes, Baxter regarded her with apparent sympathy and understanding. "Miss Kerr, I recognize how disturbing this is for you, but I must ask you to tell the court about the events that transpired prior to your father's death."

She did not answer beyond a nod of her head.

"Did your father ever discuss the Robert Kerr Palliative Care Trust with you or your brother?"

"No! Never."

"Did your father, at any time, indicate to you or your brother that you weren't the sole beneficiaries of his will?"

"Again, no, never!"

"Miss Kerr, do you believe Miss Clark falsified your father's will?"

"Objection!" Coyle was on his feet. "He's calling for a conclusion from the witness."

"Sustained."

"Let me rephrase the question," Baxter said. "Do you believe this is the will your father intended to leave?"

"No. At all times, he assured us we were his sole beneficiaries. That's why we can't believe he would do this. We were all he had in this life, and he meant the world to us." She turned to the jury with a most pitiful gaze. "It's not only the will that is deeply distressing to us; it's the thought that Father was so physically and mentally feeble that he would allow himself to be manipulated in this manner. He was always such a strong man, mentally." With that, she once more burst into tears.

The courtroom was hushed, sympathetic.

Justice Stark maintained a neutral expression. Allowing time for her to compose herself, he finally asked, "Are you able to continue?"

Putting on a brave face, Courtney straightened up and squared her shoulders. "I'm fine," she answered quietly. But the irrefutable poignancy in her eyes told everyone differently.

Baxter looked at Courtney with a well practiced benevolence. "Would you describe your father to us, Miss Kerr?"

"He was like a rock. The one person we could endlessly count on. The one person who had never failed us. He was our protector. But after he became ill, he changed completely."

"How, precisely, did this change manifest itself?"

Courtney allowed a pause, then said, "Well, he became temperamental and sulky. Considering what he was going through, Richard and I understood. Naturally, it was depressing for him to be in the hospital. Toward the end of his illness, however, he became uncharacteristically indifferent to us, showing no interest, concern, or feeling, as if we were of no consequence or importance. It then occurred to us that these weird behaviours were most evident after Mary had visited with him."

"You mean Miss Clark?"

"Yes."

"What did you do?"

"There wasn't anything we could do but try to be patient and caring."

"At the end, did his emotional condition improve?"

"No. He became more depressed, almost to the point of despair."

"That's not true," Mary whispered to Coyle.

"I'm sure all this must have been inordinately conflicting for you," Baxter remarked.

"Yes," Courtney replied, barely audible.

"Miss Kerr, how did you feel when you learned about your father's last will?"

"At the time, my brother and I were too devastated by our father's death to appreciate what was happening." Pausing to look at the jury, she added in her most bereaved voice, "We were still grieving for him. But after our minds had cleared a little, we recognized that we needed independent counsel, so we set up an appointment with Mr. Ralph Beasley."

"Is this the law firm of Beasley, Grant & Skelton?"

"Yes."

"Did you suspect anything then?"

"No, except that it was apparent we needed to speak

to someone other than the firm for which Mary worked." Seemingly distressed, Courtney gave Mary a curt glance. "It wasn't until we learned about the music box that we became aware of certain discrepancies."

"Clarify that for me, please?"

"Mary had never revealed anything to us about the music box, let alone its value."

Mary remembered the arrogance—the disdainful attitude with which they had scorned Eugenie's trunk and the music box—and how it had inflamed her at the time.

"Everything we learned after that pointed to fraudulent actions on Mary's part," Courtney continued with a frown that spoke of unendurable deception.

Mary stifled a smile. *Fraudulent actions* was hardly a phrase Courtney would use. It was obvious she had been well briefed. Throughout her questioning, her responses had been instant and, to Mary's ears, plainly rehearsed.

His voice measured and toneless, Baxter said, "One final question. How do you feel about Miss Clark now?"

"I find it inconceivable that Mary would do anything like this, when you think of all the things we did for her." Here, her eyes, positively desolate, settled on the jury. "Nothing is more heartbreaking than being betrayed by a friend. It's all been too much for us."

Baxter nodded in obvious agreement. "Thank you. That will be all, Miss Kerr. Please accept my deepest sympathy for your loss."

The judge looked at Coyle. "Your witness."

Coyle remained in his seat, studying Courtney. She was wiping tears from her eyes.

If Courtney fails to be a model, she could be a first-class actress, Mary thought to herself. She wondered what judgment Coyle held. Until now, he had heard her story only and had seemed convinced she was innocent. But Courtney's testimony had taken Mary by surprise. She had predicted it would be more malicious, more condemning. Instead, her apparent dismay over Mary's behaviour had come out as sincere and genuine—so credible that Mary felt Coyle too had to question his previous impression of her culpability. She studied Courtney, patiently waiting to be cross-examined, her face a portrait of grief and vulnerability—the perfect victim.

Mary wondered how Coyle would proceed. Courtney had to be discredited. Yet Mary knew they did not have enough evidence against her to provoke contradictory testimony. Therefore, nothing could be accomplished by cross-examining her right then. It would only exacerbate Mary's situation, possibly offend the jury and consequently lose their empathy, if they had any toward her. In the midst of these ruminations, she heard Coyle say, "No questions, Your Honour."

Justice Stark dismissed Courtney. Then turning his attention to the Crown attorney, he said, "Mr. Baxter?"

Baxter rose and approached the bench. "I now wish to call Dr. Benjamin Shapiro to the stand."

Mary had read Dr. Shapiro's statement. He had been invited to speak on the topic of depression; undoubtedly Baxter was trying to establish that Mr. Kerr was depressed. To help speed up the procedure of the trial, Coyle had already acknowledged the doctor's expertise as a witness.

Mary watched as a distinguished looking man, one of Ottawa's most imminent psychiatrists, walked into the courtroom. He was a bald, undersized man with black-rimmed glasses, but his entire bearing conveyed a confident professional reserve.

In his usual curt manner, Baxter disposed of the preliminaries and started with a pressing question. "Dr. Shapiro, when a person is dying, what are the emotions he is most likely to feel?"

"Shock, disbelief, anxiety, fear, guilt, and sadness about the impending death would be among the emotions felt. Really, there are many, and they would vary with each patient."

"What about depression and despair? Would they also be among the emotions felt?"

"Yes, the process of dying can most definitely bring on feelings of depression and despair for some people."

"Dr. Shapiro, would you define the word *depression* for us please."

"Depression is a general term used to explain one's mood. Everyone has suffered from general depression at one time or another. But then there is clinical depression, whereby depression has advanced to the point of being disruptive to an individual's social functioning and/or activities of daily living."

"Can you give us an example of some of the symptoms depressed people are more likely to experience?"

"The behaviour of depressed people is generally marked by great sadness and apprehension, feelings of worthlessness and guilt, withdrawal from others, loss of sleep, appetite, and sexual desire, or loss of interest and pleasure in common activities."

"You mentioned clinical depression. Would you simplify for the benefit of the court what that term means?"

"Clinical depression is not something you can just 'snap out of.' It's provoked by an imbalance of brain chemicals, along with other factors. Like any serious medical condition, it needs to be treated."

"By clinical depression, you mean disorders such as schizophrenia, manic depressive, or borderline personality disorder?"

"Yes, depression can be present in these other disorders."

"Many of us already have an idea what schizophrenia and manic-depressive mean; would you define borderline personality disorder for the benefit of the court?"

"Borderline personality disorder, also known as emotionally unstable personality disorder, is a mental illness characterized by a long-term pattern of unstable relationships, a distorted sense of self, and extreme mood swings. For some clinicians, the term implies that the patient is on the borderline between neurosis and psychosis. Different mental health professionals have varying perspectives on the disorder and its classification."

Mr. Baxter remained pensive for a moment and then said, "Despite the controversy surrounding the diagnosis of borderline personality disorder, surely there must be some consensus among clinicians about its symptoms and treatment. Would you agree?"

"Yes."

"Could you mention some of the symptoms for us, please?"

"An actual personality disorder is usually defined by the extremes of several traits." Adjusting his glasses, he added, "And for someone to be diagnosed as BPD, as we call it, there would have to be several of the traits of emotional instability present. In addition, the patient would have to show signs of emotional upheaval."

"You mean difficulty controlling their emotions?" asked Baxter.

"Yes, difficulty controlling emotions, and the behaviour would have to be characteristic of many of the criteria of several personality disorders."

Mary was eager to learn where Baxter was leading; in her mind, his questions were not pertinent to Mr. Kerr's situation. She looked at Coyle. There was no expression on his face, a professional trait of a well-trained lawyer.

Baxter seemed intent on continuing the same line of questioning. "You've stated that this actual disorder is defined by the extremes of several personality traits?"

"Yes."

"Could anger, dependency, and inability to maintain relationships be some of those traits?"

"Yes. Emotions are unpredictable and can shift abruptly. These individuals have not developed a clear and stable self-image and have a penchant for ambivalence about their values and loyalties and sense of self. They are also subject to chronic feelings of depression and inappropriate and intense anger."

Baxter turned to Mary and his features tightened. Without directly looking at him, she could feel his gaze burning into her and wondered why he had turned to look at her so purposely. She forced herself to stare hard into his eyes and thought there had to be more behind his apparently relaxed interrogation.

He turned back to face the witness stand. "Dr. Shapiro, what do you understand to be the causes of borderline personality disorder?"

"There is still very little known about what causes it. According to the prevailing view, however, the preponderance of those diagnosed with this disorder appear to have been individuals abused or traumatized during childhood."

Mary was overcome by the disquieting feeling she had felt before entering the courtroom.

"Do men suffer from borderline personality disorder?" Baxter asked. His voice was casual, but Mary thought she detected an underlying excitement.

"Yes, but it's known to be more common in women."

"Is there a cure?"

"Lithium is used to control some of their symptoms, but therapeutic outcomes are generally poor."

"During our brief exchange, you also mentioned having met the accused, Mary Clark."

A sudden, viselike grip of fear assaulted Mary's whole being. *That's what you were leading to. It's I you intend to discredit, not Mr. Kerr.* She had come prepared for many scenarios, but this was so beyond anything imagined that it numbed her mind.

In the turmoil that overwhelmed her, Mary heard the witness reply, "Yes, she attended one of my lectures in May of this year."

"What was the topic of your lecture?"

"Abnormal psychology. It was directed more to the general public, not just my students."

"Still, after all this time, you remember her?"

"It was a small audience, and we had an opportunity to introduce ourselves after the lecture. I found her immensely knowledgeable."

"Do you remember what you spoke about?"

"Just things in general, the uncontrollable nature of psychopathology and the importance of clinical findings."

Baxter fell silent, allowing the jury to absorb what they had heard. Mary could still not comprehend what he hoped to accomplish by calling in this witness, but the triumph was unmistakable in his eyes as he said, "Thank you, Dr. Shapiro. No further questions."

Justice Stark turned to Coyle. "Your witness."

Mary glanced at Coyle. What was he thinking? His face remained impassive, but she was not fooled. Like her, he must know where Baxter was leading with his line of interrogation. Though Mary knew Coyle had been prepared for his cross-examination of Dr. Shapiro—after having carefully vetted the testimony Dr. Shapiro would be providing through discovery—it did not surprise her when he shook his head. "None at the moment, Your Honour. But I would like to have your permission to question Dr. Shapiro later this afternoon." It was clear to her that Coyle was biding his time, waiting for the right moment to strike back.

"I am amenable to grant you permission to cross-examine the witness later this afternoon but will need to hear your reasoning as to why you are not ready to proceed now," replied Justice Stark.

"A word, Your Honour?"

"Counsel may approach the bench."

Mary watched as Coyle walked over to the bench and briefly conferred with the judge. The reason he gave must have been satisfactory, for the judge looked up and announced, "Permission granted." He then glanced at his watch. "Since it's getting close to lunchtime, I suggest a recess to the court's proceedings until two o'clock."

As the courtroom buzzed with activity during the recess, Mary reflected on the intricacies of the legal dance unfolding before her. The questions about her encounter with Dr. Shapiro lingered, casting doubt on her own understanding of the situation. She felt like a pawn in a game she did not fully comprehend, manipulated by forces beyond her control.

Mary was still grappling with the proceedings when Coyle proposed that she join him for lunch. Knowing he was the one person who could help her make sense of things, she gratefully accepted. As they exited the courthouse, they saw Courtney talking animatedly with the press. All seemed enamoured by her.

Evading them, Coyle guided Mary to his car and together they drove to the ByWard Market. He parked and led her to a restaurant she had never noticed before. As they waited to be escorted to a table, the maître d' arrived, greeting them both with a broad smile. "Good afternoon, Mr. Coyle. It's always a pleasure to see you. Your usual table?"

"Yes, please."

They were led to a secluded corner table. "I come here regularly, though usually for dinner, not lunch," Coyle informed her. "They have an excellent menu, and it's easier than cooking for myself. I sit at this table because it's away from the stream of traffic. That way, I can bring work with me."

All the tables were occupied, and they were enjoying as much privacy as one could in a public place. After they had ordered, Coyle sat back in his chair and said, "By the way, you were dead on about Dr. Shapiro. I apologize for overlooking it. I should have foreseen it."

Mary dismissed the idea with a toss of her head. "The whole thing was so subtle, it was easy to overlook."

"Yet you sensed it," he insisted.

"Call it woman's intuition," replied Mary, and suddenly laughed, shaking off her gloom.

He smiled. "Obviously, Baxter intends to discredit you. But you needn't worry. I'm prepared for him now."

"If he hopes to discredit me, as you suggest, should we perhaps revisit our decision for me to testify?" she asked tentatively. From the beginning, she had expressed her reluctance to do so. Putting her on the stand would allow the Crown attorney to cross-examine her, a daunting prospect.

"There's always a potential danger there," he acknowledged, "but as far as I'm concerned, you're my greatest asset. I intend to show you as a woman of integrity—bold, courageous, and prepared to fight for her client at any cost."

Mary chuckled. "I wish I were as confident as you are."

He fixed his gaze on her. "Why aren't you? Is there anything in your past that I need to know?"

Mary hesitated for a fraction of a second, then said, "Everyone has their share of experiences, don't they? That's life. But I can assure you that my commitment to this case is unwavering."

"I value your assurance, Mary," Coyle responded, his tone calm but probing, "however, I can't shake the feeling that there might be more to your story. Is there any additional information you're withholding? If so, I urge you to share it with me now. It could make a significant difference in my approach to the case."

"I appreciate your concern, but I've told you everything that could possibly be relevant," she asserted, meeting his eyes.

"Then you needn't worry," he assured her. "Everything will work out fine."

Mary wondered how many times she had heard that maxim, how many times it had failed her.

"So what did you think of Courtney as a witness?" Coyle asked.

Mary hesitated, disappointed by what she thought was an abrupt change of subject. She wanted to resume their previous conversation but realized there was nothing else to discuss. She replied, "Her entire testimony was a lie. Still, I must admit that she's not the mindless person she sometimes portrays herself to be. As a matter of fact, I thought she put on an excellent performance, had everyone eating out of her hand."

"Yes, definitely an affable prosecution witness type. But with people who lie, memory often becomes a hindrance. Inevitably, it fails them, and they trip up."

In Mary's profession, she had learned to discern a lie. Yet Courtney's testimony had been persuasive. Was she lying, or had she spoken the truth as she believed it to be? "All the things she said, I have no way of disproving them. But that's not what bothers me the most. In court, she seemed to begrudge having to testify against me, yet, with a soft brush, painted me as a totally dysfunctional person. The truth is I never suspected she felt such ill will toward me. I knew we had grown apart, but it appears that—in her eyes at least—I've become her archrival, her nemesis. I can't imagine why. There was nothing between us to warrant such hatred."

A slow smile spread across Coyle's face. "Unlike you, I

can understand why. You're a standing rebuke to her. Every time she sees you, she is reminded of the person she could never be."

"Still, her words spoken aloud like that in court held a certain authority, reality even," Mary replied.

"It's reasonable that you should feel that way, Mary. Those vindictive words were designed to unsettle you and mask the facts. But you shouldn't attach too much importance to them. Words spoken like that in court can easily be dispelled by later arguments."

"You're right, of course, but it doesn't alter the fact that her words were like salt on a raw wound."

Before they could get any further, they were interrupted by the waiter, who had come to take their order.

Coyle looked at Mary with a questioning expression. "Are you in the mood for a bite right now, or are you okay to wait briefly?"

"Really, I'm not hungry. I would prefer to wait," she replied.

With Coyle's instructions to delay the delivery by forty-five minutes, they continued to share thoughts about the morning's events. Their food arrived as directed, and, for a brief while, they forgot the trial and enjoyed their meal. When they had finished their lunch, Coyle sat back in his chair and looked up at Mary, studying her. "How do you feel about your testimony this afternoon?"

"Nervous. I can't wait for it to be over." Mary heard the note of desperation, almost of fear, in her own voice.

"I would be alarmed if you weren't." Coyle paused then asked, "Are you ready for Baxter?"

"I think so. I have to be. But can one ever be ready for him?"

Coyle nodded, suddenly grave. "It's hard to foresee exactly what he will do; he consistently does the unexpected. This morning, for instance, he had me at a complete loss. For a while at least. I now realize it's you he intends to discredit, not Mr. Kerr. Even so, he and I are indisputably not on the same wavelength. Have you any opinion about where his questions may be leading?"

Mary did not answer straightaway. She was struggling with her own reflections, then was dissuaded from speaking by the appearance of a beautiful woman approaching the table. The woman reached her hand out to Coyle. "Patrick, darling, how delightful to meet you like this. I haven't seen you in ages. I would swear you were avoiding us on purpose."

Smiling, he rose to greet her. "Nothing could be further from the truth, Francesca. How are you?"

"Fine. You didn't make it to my little fête last week. Everybody was asking about you, especially Barbara."

Mary was intrigued. The tone of Francesca's voice implied intimacy between Coyle and Barbara.

"Sorry I had to miss it. I did leave a message saying I wouldn't be available."

"So I was told, but you know how I like having you at my parties."

In reply, Coyle said, "Francesca, I would like you to meet a colleague of mine, Mary Clark. Francesca Booth."

Up until then, Francesca had fully disregarded Mary. Now that Coyle had drawn attention to her, Francesca eyed her with intense scrutiny. "How do you do?" she greeted her finally.

Mary met her gaze and nodded. "I'm pleased to meet you."

Francesca seemed unsure how to respond. Then, exhibiting a gracious smile, she turned to Coyle. "I'm having a small gathering at the house this evening. I hope you will be able to join us."

"How kind of you, Francesca, but I will have to decline. I'm tied up with a major case at the moment."

"Yes, I know." Shifting her attention to Mary, she remarked, "You can't go anywhere in Ottawa without tripping over the news. It's all over the city. You've become quite the notorious woman, Miss Clark."

When Mary failed to respond, Francesca looked marginally embarrassed. "What I mean is…" She laughed weakly, and then left the sentence hanging. As though the thought was better left unspoken, she bestowed upon Coyle another feline smile. "Now, Patrick, you mustn't forget your friends." Then, with a brief side glance toward Mary, she sauntered off to greet an acquaintance at another table.

Coyle's expression was sympathetic as he seated himself. "Please give no consideration to her words. She's not a bad sort, really, once you get to know her. Her only fault is that she's never mastered the art of thinking before speaking."

Still, Mary felt uneasy. It had never entered her mind that his involvement with her could disrupt his social life. How did his friends perceive her? "I regret keeping you away from your friends. Is Barbara someone special in your life?" The question had come unsolicited, as if surfacing from the subconscious.

"No…just an acquaintance. Francesca tends to exaggerate things."

"It's truly unnerving," she murmured.

"What is?"

"Six months ago, we barely knew each other. And now, I rely on you so completely that it frightens me."

An unexpected tenderness, guarded yet visible, showed in his eyes. He opened his mouth as though to say something but instead made a show of checking his watch. Warmth still fixed to his features, he announced, "Sorry, Mary, I'm afraid we're running out of time. We have to leave." He motioned for the bill and then said, "But before we go, I need to caution you against Baxter. Remember, in the first part of his questioning, he will try to get you off guard by asking you extraneous questions. Once he feels he has you sufficiently comfortable and complacent, he will hit you with his full arsenal. Try to remain calm. Answer his questions as briefly as you can, just like we practiced. Whatever you do, don't let him get you unravelled."

"You forget that I'm a lawyer. And you have prepared me well."

He smiled. "Right. But it doesn't hurt to be reminded."

The court convened, and Coyle stood up to open the case for Mary's defence. First, he brought in Elaine Travis, head of the recovery room unit at the hospital, and then Mr. Kerr's physician, Dr. Hereford, who both confirmed the patient's emotional well-being. After they had finished testifying, Coyle introduced his one remaining witness, Mary.

With the same indomitability she had exhibited in Mr. McLeod's office, she rose from her chair and walked to the stand—evading all the stares that followed her. As she was being sworn in, she glanced across at Coyle.

He responded with a broad, easy smile. Moments after she introduced herself, he stood, thoughtfully facing her. Mary, of course, was ready for his first question. "Miss Clark, would you explain to the court your connection with Mr. Kerr?"

"I was appointed by the law firm Woodbury & McLeod, here in Ottawa, to assist Mr. Kerr in preparing his will."

Coyle had vigilantly planned his defence on Baxter's assault and, by all appearance, was determined to exploit every angle opened to him. His next question to Mary would allow her to describe how she had dealt with the prevailing sex discrimination in the law profession. "As a woman lawyer in a male-dominated profession, you must have encountered many barriers being appointed to prepare Mr. Kerr's will?"

Baxter was immediately on his feet. "Objection, Your Honour. Whether the law profession is inclusive or exclusive to women is not relevant to the evidence against Miss Clark. Mr. Coyle is deliberately seeking to shift the court's attention to a sensitive topic that will only serve to blur the issues."

Coyle refuted, "My query is relevant because I believe this criminal case is based solely on prejudices and discrimination against my client. I earnestly doubt it would have taken place had Miss Clark been a man and less principled."

Justice Stark nodded, acknowledging the incontrovertible fact that the topic was a sensitive one. He looked down at Mary as she sat, waiting for his pronouncement. "I will permit this," he said finally to Coyle, "but I will terminate this line of interrogation if I see you are merely developing accusations against the system to mislead the jury."

"Thank you, Your Honour." Then turning to Mary, Coyle repeated his question.

The court was silent as Mary spoke of the complexities and disillusionment at work and the interminable struggle to establish herself into an almost impenetrable institution.

When queried about her position with the firm Woodbury & McLeod and the reason for her dismissal, Mary replied, "After Mr. Kerr's last will was read and his children found out their father had willed most of his assets to the Robert Kerr Palliative Care Trust, they immediately announced they would contest the will and threatened to sue the firm unless it submitted to their demands. I, personally, could not comply. Though I was employed by Woodbury & McLeod, as executrix of Mr. Kerr's will, I naturally assumed my primary obligation was to my client. In my opinion, even a potentially legally enforceable request by his children would have meant going against his wishes. Despite my dismissal from the firm and present court case, I still believe I acted ethically."

"Would you please tell the court all that took place between you and Mr. Kerr between the time you were assigned to him and the day he passed away?"

Knowing what needed to be revealed, Mary guardedly and calmly told the court her full story, starting with her first rendezvous with Mr. Kerr in the Civic Hospital right up until the day he died. As the jurors leaned on her every word, she gave a detailed account of how she had learned the value of the music box after meeting with Courtney and Richard at the house, making it clear she had indeed informed Mr. Kerr about its true value the following morning. In simple terms, she stated Mr. Kerr's directions to her, which were to return the trunk to Eugenie's family, including the music box.

After she had finished, Coyle asked, "Miss Clark, as the estate lawyer and executrix of Mr. Kerr's estate, you must have seen a great deal of him?"

"Yes," Mary answered. "I visited him at the hospital numerous times every week for about two months before he passed away. In the final week, I made an effort to be with him daily."

Coyle's eyebrows furrowed. "Was his estate so complex that it necessitated daily visits?"

"No. The work on his will was finalized well before he died. Only, by then…" She hesitated, painstakingly choosing her words. "He was lonely in the last days of his illness and welcomed my company. My being there seemed to mean a lot to him."

"What about his children? Did they not visit him?"

"Unfortunately, their other commitments did not allow them many visits."

"During Mr. Kerr's stay in the hospital, would you say he was overly depressed?"

Baxter looked up from his notes. Mary thought he was about to object, but he didn't. Instead, he appeared keen to hear what she had to say.

"I think every person facing death goes through some phase of depression. And I'm convinced he must have felt it when he was initially diagnosed. But when I visited him in the late stage of his illness, depression was definitely not what he conveyed. Neither was despair. By then he had come to grips with the threat of his illness and wanted to use whatever time remained to settle his estate. If anything, he was annoyed, angry even, at the decline of his physical health."

"Angry?"'

"Yes. Mainly because he was used to being in control, and it was hard for him to acknowledge that there were certain things that even he had no power over."

"Indeed, it must have been a trying time for Mr. Kerr, having been in a position of power most of his life," Coyle replied knowingly. He then asked, "Was that all he felt, anger?"

"No. There were other strong feelings he had…feelings of failure, sadness, and regret."

"Regret for what?"

"For having perhaps invested too much energy in his business and not enough in people. Up until his illness, Mr. Kerr had put tremendous value on material things and success."

"How was he able to deal with these strong feelings you mentioned?"

"At the end, his preoccupation shifted to something else entirely."

"How do you mean?"

"Working through his affairs was his way of dealing with his imminent death. By reorganizing his will, he was creating some structure of control over his situation—a form of compensation, if you wish."

"In your meetings with Mr. Kerr, did he share any personal information about his family?"

"Yes."

"In what context?"

"He wrestled over memories of his past or, more accurately, the lack of them. All the things he hadn't done with his children—not having had more quality time with them, not being as close a father as he might have been. All these things elicited deep disappointment, which was heightened by the fact that they seldom visited him."

Coyle was silent, a listening, expectant silence.

She went on. "This is not intended as criticism of Courtney and Richard Kerr. As family, they were no doubt overwhelmed by their father's imminent death."

Although Coyle failed to show it, Mary intuited his displeasure with her last statement. But without those conciliatory words about his children, Mr. Kerr would have come across a failure as a father. Her esteem for him would not allow this.

Coyle moved on but not before conveying to her through his eyes that she was not promoting her cause. "Was Mr. Kerr depressed by the fact that he was alone and dying?"

"His emotional balance had changed, perhaps, but by no means was he mentally less acute."

"Still, all those feelings of frustration, sadness, and regret you mentioned must have created a depressing time for him?"

"Yes, he was burdened by those feelings, but at no time did they overpower him. In everything, Mr. Kerr was a businessman. Having reached the end of his life, he took inventory of what he had accumulated over his lifetime. He had provided for his children and had excelled at his job. I presume that with the threat of death, however, he took on a fundamentally different set of values. The role of providing for his children wasn't as pressing as guiding and teaching them the more important values in life, values he himself had rebuffed. Being a man of action, he was determined to bring about what he had overlooked in the past. That is when he decided to create the Robert Kerr Palliative Care Trust. His wish may seem incongruous, but never was it meant to reflect negative feelings toward his children. He saw it as a means of providing Courtney and Richard with an opportunity to grow on their own merits. It was a difficult decision, but Mr. Kerr cared enough about them to make it."

"Then how would you explain the fact that he never clarified these feelings to his own children?"

"I think he had hoped to, initially, but they were not around long enough for him to discuss his intentions with them."

"Did Mr. Kerr leave any instructions with you that might have enlightened them?"

"Yes. When writing his last will, he asked me to convey his love and concern for them. I tried, but they were too incensed by their father's will to listen."

Coyle nodded thoughtfully. "Then let us move on. In your statement, you reported Mr. Kerr directed you to return the trunk, including the music box, to Eugenie's family. Is that correct?"

"Yes."

"Why did Mr. Kerr want the music box sent to Eugenie's family when he knew it was worth millions of dollars?"

"When I asked him that question, he resolutely answered, 'We should never have had it in the first place. That music box had been intended for Eugenie alone, a special gift that had great significance to her family.'"

"How did he justify that?"

Mary smiled faintly at the question. "Anyone who ever worked with Mr. Kerr would know he didn't lose time and energy justifying his reasoning behind a personal decision. He never volunteered that information, and I never asked."

"Indeed, I tend to agree with you, Miss Clark. But

during all that period with him, surely Mr. Kerr must have said something that would justify his motive?"

"He did reminisce a great deal in the last days of his illness. He remembered those who had made a lasting positive impression on him. Eugenie, his second wife, was one of those people, and he regretted having neglected her. When he directed me to return the trunk, including the music box, to Eugenie's family, I saw his actions as an act of contrition, if you will…a belated request for forgiveness."

"I'm afraid I'm left somewhat bewildered here," Coyle confessed. "If Eugenie had made an enduring impression on him, as you say, why then had he neglected her?"

"As I mentioned, with the end of his life in sight, his values changed. While in the hospital, he recognized he had placed too much emphasis on material gains," she replied and, hearing how the jury might infer criticism or judgment, she quickly added, "I'm not implying materialism is intrinsically wrong. Only, when it encompasses your whole being as it did for Mr. Kerr earlier in his career, it's easy to lose sight of what is essentially important in life."

"At the end, what was important for Mr. Kerr?"

"He seemed to value human contacts and interrelationships above everything else."

"Interrelationships with whom?" Coyle asked.

"With everyone around him," Mary replied.

Coyle nodded, solemn and thoughtful. Then he said, "At any time during his illness, did Mr. Kerr exhibit signs of incompetence?"

"No, never. His illness was a period of huge adjustment, but in no way did it affect his ability to make decisions. In his life, before the illness, he had been a courageous, hard-working person who ruled with knowledge and boldness. He died as he lived, maintaining his self-confidence to the very end."

Coyle's features acknowledged his satisfaction as he dismissed her. By all appearances, her entire testimony had gone splendidly, and Mary sensed it had won her, for the time being at least, the sympathy of the entire jury.

As Coyle returned to his seat, Justice Stark said, "Your witness, Mr. Baxter.

Picking up a document, Baxter stared at Mary with an inquiring expression. "Miss Clark, please explain to the court how you came to be the estate planning lawyer for Mr. Kerr's affairs."

"How do you mean?"

"Why did he choose you, let's say, over somebody more experienced?"

Mary knew his intention was to intimidate her, but it only incited her to fight him. "Knowledge of estate cases and governing laws were prerequisite in my law studies, and this one was well within my capabilities."

"Indeed, I've examined your papers relating to the Kerr estate and must admit being impressed with your work."

It was stated as a compliment, but Mary was not deceived. She anticipated there was more to come.

He went on. "As a matter of fact, you kept a meticulously detailed record of every transaction involving the estate assets." He paused, fractionally, but still too long. "With one exception, a music box worth three million dollars. Not only did you not record it, you kept it in your possession."

This revelation created a surprised reaction in the room.

Again, Baxter waited a moment, obviously to let the

information settle in. "Could you explain to me why you chose not to report the music box and its value, although you knew what it was worth?"

"I acted according to Mr. Kerr's specific instructions to me. He requested that his deceased wife's trunk be sent to her family in France, along with the music box; and he equally requested that its value not be revealed to anyone, including his children. He instructed me to excise all evidence of the music box from the file. I explained to him at the time that I would carry out his wishes as to the disposition of the trunk contents, including the music box, but I would have to document his intentions to both safeguard that it was his true intent and to protect me and my firm against precisely what is now occurring. He agreed and signed the document. As for the trunk and the music box, I had them in my apartment, the music box securely placed in a safety deposit box purchased for that purpose, because I hadn't decided how I was going to get it to Mrs. Kerr's sister, living in Brittany. Since it was extremely valuable, I had even contemplated delivering it personally."

"And where is this signed document that you requested from Mr. Kerr."

"It disappeared with my briefcase, which I believe was stolen."

"How very convenient," he sneered with an unmistakable note of skepticism. Baxter then turned to address Justice Stark. "Your Honour, I have here a memo written by Miss Clark. It's shown as Exhibit 10 on the admissions of facts." He handed Mary the paper. "Is this the letter that was to accompany the trunk?"

Mary's pulse quickened as she examined it. It was the letter she had written to Eugenie's sister Danielle the night she had discovered the value of the music box.

Baxter became impatient. "Well, Miss Clark, is it or is it not the letter you wrote to Mrs. Kerr's sister Danielle LeBreton on May twentieth of this year?"

"Initially, yes."

"Would you read it for us, please?"

Despite the pounding in her chest, she maintained a measure of control in her voice as she read aloud what she had written.

Dear Madam,

My client, Mr. Robert D. Kerr, has invited me to contact you.

We are in the process of selling his home, and it is the family's wish that Eugenie's trunk and its contents be forwarded to her sisters. I trust it has arrived safely.

Mr. Kerr has requested that I convey to you his regrets for not writing to you personally. Unfortunately, he is ill and incapable of handling this matter himself.

Should you require further information, please do not hesitate to contact me.

Yours respectfully,
Mary Clark, B.A., LL.B.
Woodbury & McLeod
Barristers & Solicitors

After she had finished, Baxter took the letter from her and offered it to the court clerk. Then, addressing Mary, he said, "Miss Clark, you argue that your intention was to return the music box to Eugenie's family."

"Yes."

"Yet nowhere in the letter do you mention the music box. How do you justify that?" This was delivered with such insistence that even to Mary, the intended allegation felt justified.

"When writing to Eugenie's sister, I didn't itemize the contents of the trunk because everything would be self-evident when the trunk arrived."

For a moment, Baxter relented, but only briefly. "You stated earlier that Mr. Kerr directed you not to tell anyone about the value of the music box. Is that so?

"Yes."

"Let us assume, for one moment, that this is what actually took place. Please explain to me why Mr. Kerr chose not to inform his children about it?"

"He feared that knowing about the value of the music box would make them feel cheated out of their inheritance, and he didn't want to hurt them unnecessarily."

"Indeed, Miss Clark, I think we can all agree on that point! Or is it that you didn't tell anyone because you had every intention of keeping it for yourself?"

Immediately, Coyle spoke up. "Your Honour, I strongly object to Mr. Baxter's ignoble remark."

"Sustained," replied Justice Stark. He then looked at Baxter and added, "In the future, I expect you to keep any speculation to yourself."

Seemingly unperturbed, Baxter plowed on. "According to Mr. Kerr's children, their father didn't know these people, so why would he give them a music box worth three million dollars?"

Mary took a moment before responding. "It's hard to say…an act of love for his wife, perhaps. When a person is dying, values change and money no longer holds the same significance." She paused. "Also, it's important to understand that the music box has a unique history. It was a gift to Eugenie from her family and had been in their possession for some time."

The prosecutor's look was supercilious, as if to say Mary should be able to come up with something more relevant than that. "I need to ask what engendered this sudden change," he said stiffly.

"He didn't say."

"You mean, just out of the blue like that, he gave up his entire life savings to complete strangers?" His smile was sardonic as he half-turned toward the jury.

"I carried out his wishes as he expressed them," she defended as she braced herself for the next question.

"You'll forgive me, but I feel quite sure you're—how shall I put it—not being entirely forthcoming with your information." Baxter shifted seamlessly to another seemingly unrelated question. "Tell me, Miss Clark, what is your yearly salary?"

Coyle was on his feet. "Objection! I don't see—"

"Your Honor," interrupted the prosecutor, "a previous witness stated that Miss Clark's behaviour had indicated interest in buying Mr. Kerr's residence for herself. I'm trying to ascertain whether she was financially capable of buying it."

"It's an appropriate question. The witness may answer."

Mary remembered Coyle's warning. Wondering what Baxter had in store for her, she replied, "Ten thousand dollars a year."

Mr. Baxter raised an eyebrow, a flicker of surprise crossing his face. "Ten thousand a year? That's a rather meagre sum for someone in your profession."

"Indeed, Mr. Baxter, it reflects the unfortunate reality for women in the legal profession. However, my dedication to my work goes beyond monetary considerations."

Mary's straightforward acknowledgement of the wage disparity seemed to catch Baxter off guard. With an impatient, dismissive gesture, he said, "Miss Clark, there's one more grey area in your handling of Mr. Kerr's estate. That's the sale of his house."

Noting his hostile stare, Mary waited for him to proceed.

"We learned earlier you approached three companies to do an appraisal of Mr. Kerr's home on..." Baxter consulted his notepad, as if searching for the name, which he would have known perfectly well. "...Ridge Road. Is that correct?"

"Yes."

"Would you name them please?"

"Founders Realties, Caldwell International Inc., and City Real Estate."

"Yet nowhere in your papers do you mention City Real Estate." His eyes narrowed "Why is that?"

"Probably because I didn't think it noteworthy."

"You don't strike me as one who would overlook recording any transaction of business, no matter how insignificant," he counteracted, a note of sarcasm in his voice. "Anything else you may have omitted?"

"I—" Mary started to answer but stopped when she saw the prosecutor was actually walking away from her.

She watched in fraught silence as he picked up a document from his desk and returned, eyeing her malignantly, his face muscles flaccid, his eyes lifeless. He smiled, but Mary was not fooled. As a novice lawyer, she had noted how he used that artificial smile just when he was about to pounce on his witness. Standing close to her, he appeared to relish what he was about to do. Mary tried to appear poised but did not feel she was entirely successful.

Baxter leaned a little closer and asked, "Miss Clark, have you ever received psychotherapy?"

A chill enveloped her. For a moment, her world ceased. The courtroom went silent—the murmurs of the jury and members of the public, even the shuffling of papers. Then, as if from a distance, she heard Coyle's voice. "Objection, Your Honour. I—"

Again, Baxter cut in. "Your Honour, I assure you this question is relevant to this case. It has to do with Miss Clark's credibility as a witness."

Justice Stark pondered the matter briefly. Then looking at Coyle, he nodded. "Whether one had a previous psychological condition is an acceptable topic for counsel to address, and I will allow the question." Then addressing Mary, he said, "The witness will please answer."

Mary remained wordless. In her mind, no answer was required since Baxter already had it. It was a well-known axiom of the practice of law that a lawyer should never ask a question to which they did not already know the answer and that they must ask the question that would result in what they wanted the court to hear. Worse still, she knew where he was leading, and her response could only discredit her. Mary became acutely uncomfortable. No matter how she replied, it would further the bias against her. Torn by Baxter's question and numbed by the sudden precipitation into her painful past, she stared blankly at him. *Oh God, please let there be an end to this*, she prayed silently.

But there was to be no mercy for her, and Baxter's words, cold and gruelling, leached into her consciousness. "Miss Clark, I repeat. Have you, at any point in your life, received psychotherapy?"

Mary's trembling lips moved, but no sound emerged. She was acutely aware of the jurors' eyes upon her, and the room charged with anticipation had suddenly become claustrophobic. Dispirited, she unwittingly glanced at the judge, as if for support.

Justice Stark's voice, kind but definite, seemed to come out of nowhere. "The court needs you to answer."

Not trusting her voice to co-operate and forgetting the rules of the court, she nodded.

"Miss Clark, would you state your answer for the court, please," demanded Baxter.

Mary could hear the belligerence, could feel his eyes boring into hers.

She sat frozen in her seat, working hard to hold back the panic that threatened to overtake her. "Yes," she said finally.

"And what were you being treated for?"

She murmured something barely audible.

"I'm sorry, Miss Clark, but I must ask you to speak up."

This time, she spoke louder, but there remained a tremor in her voice. "Sexual abuse as a child by my father."

A gasp went up from the audience, and people started murmuring.

Justice Stark slammed down his gavel. "Order! Order!"

Mary faintly heard Baxter ask, "How old were you when the abuse started?"

He was trying to break her, to weaken her defence, which made her all the more determined to fight him. "Eleven years old," she replied, her voice resolute.

Most people would have been touched emotionally by such an admission. But Baxter was one of those lawyers who was at his best when he had his victims defenceless and vulnerable. "When did you begin treatment?" he asked.

That date was so embedded in her brain that the words came out instantly. "In July 1960."

"Miss Clark, according to my records, you are twenty-seven years old, born in 1939. That would make it approximately ten years between the time you were abused and the time you actually sought professional help. Is that correct?"

Mary could scarcely think or hear what Baxter said to her, but it no longer mattered. She answered, "Yes."

She knew where he was leading, and there was no way out of it without making things worse for her. She looked up at Coyle, expecting to see pity or perhaps scorn for not disclosing this information to him. But his face betrayed neither. Instead, he appeared to be pained.

"How would you describe your emotional condition during that period?" Baxter's demeanour remained outwardly calm, but there was no mistaking the intensity beneath the surface.

"I was distraught."

"Yet you sought no counselling?"

"No."

"Can you explain why?"

"I could not afford it until then."

"What ultimately changed in your life that you were suddenly able to afford it?"

"Dr. Cowen's bequest to me." She paused briefly, and then clarified, "It was more than I needed for treatment, but it made it possible. Until that time, I thought I could handle it on my own."

"Are you saying that, after all that time, life had become intolerable for you?"

Every muscle in her body tensed. He was asking a series of questions to show a potentially tenuous state of mind in an attempt to explain the existing professional aberration—the fraud. And there was no way she could curb him. "It's a trauma from which no one totally recovers, but I…I needed to sort out my emotional state," she replied. Her voice had become raspy and faint. She realized she was trembling.

"How long were you in treatment?"

"Three years."

"During those three years, how frequently did you see your therapist?"

"Once a week."

"How long," Baxter asked crisply, "were these sessions?" He had a rhythm now.

"One hour each."

"So you were in therapy one hour, once a week, for three years. Isn't that an atypically short period for someone suffering such a trauma?"

"It was long enough."

"And did you sort out your emotional state as you implied?"

"Yes."

Baxter waited, obviously allowing her to expand on her *yes*. When she didn't, he queried, "How could you tell?"

"By then, my nightmares had ceased and my life had returned to normal."

Baxter gave her a dubious look. "What does normal mean, Miss Clark?"

"It's difficult to describe the word *normal* because it means different things to different people."

"Evidently. But please describe to me what normal means to you."

Mary bowed her head momentarily and felt a burst of panic but quickly suppressed it. *I refuse to be intimidated by you. You will not break me.* She struggled not to give in to the tears that were close to the surface, for she knew what Baxter could do with a frightened or panicked witness, the evidence he could manipulate out of them. Striving to keep her face impassive, she slowed her breathing, not yet able to channel her new-found resolve. Then slowly, quietly, she said, "The emotional and behavioural effect of an uncaring mother and sexual abuse by a father can be devastating. I was no exception. The lack of love and trust from my childhood were having an adverse effect on me. Fortunately, I had an uncle and other compassionate people in my life who recognized my distress and were able to teach me to love rather than hate. And later, I was again fortunate to have an efficient therapist who taught me to deal with the crushing feeling of guilt that was paralyzing me. It didn't happen overnight. It was part of a long healing process. Under therapy, I was able to explore those experiences and emotions. During that period of introspection, I gained a clearer insight into my parents' weaknesses and was able to forgive them. That freed me from the oppressive feelings of hopelessness and helplessness that had prevented me from moving on."

In the silence that followed, Mary felt certain she could hear the sound of her own heart. She threw the Crown attorney an ice-cold look. "So, Mr. Baxter, to me, normal means no recurring nightmares; it means no longer feeling rejected, lonely, or unloved; it means having overcome my irrational guilt; it means having worked through the rage I felt; and—"

"Thank you, Miss Clark. I get the picture," Baxter cut in firmly.

Mary leaned forward, her stare riveted on him. "Forgive me, Mr. Baxter. You asked me to describe what normal means to me. So allow me to finish." Before he could object, she continued, her voice growing stronger. "Along with the things I've just mentioned, normal means awareness; it means being able to get in touch with my inner self and learning to cope with negative feelings and depression; it means no longer being handicapped by a past filled with pain and suffering; it means learning to be grateful for other things in my life, other people in my world who genuinely care for me; it means forgiving, dispelling wrenching memories because the only alternative is a terrible, all-consuming anger…and pain. And at the end of all this, it means I finally realized it was I who was the victim."

Mary's reply was most definitely not what Baxter had expected—a classic example of what might result if you didn't know the answer to a question you asked—and he seemed thrown off slightly, but not for long. Again, he smiled his cynical smile. "In your opinion, Miss Clark, is treatment a sure path to complete recovery?"

Mary's expression became guarded as she fought the tears that had welled in her eyes. There was no safe answer to that question. If she answered yes, it would show her as a person with an unrealistic view of therapy. Yet a no response would support Baxter's effort to expose her as an unstable person, capable of transgressions. Either answer would ultimately give him what he wanted, so she replied, "In life, one can seldom be certain about anything."

"Exactly," Baxter confirmed and then added, "At any time, were you diagnosed with borderline personality disorder?"

"No."

"Are you certain about that?"

"Yes."

"Yet according to Dr. Shapiro, child abuse, anger, depression, and inability to maintain relationships all rank amongst the criteria of borderline personality disorder, and to quote your own words, Miss Clark, in life, one can seldom be certain about anything." With that, he turned his back to her and again walked away. "No further questions."

Mary made no attempt to move. She was powerless, depleted of all resistance. In painting her as a dysfunctional person, the prosecutor had finally found a way to fit her past into his guilty scenario and had ingeniously delivered a debilitating blow to her case.

To herself, she all but admitted defeat. Not even Coyle could help her now. Unable to face him and overwhelmed in a fog of emotions, she focused instead on her hands trembling on her lap, oblivious to the curious stares of everyone in the room. Then from a distance, as though from a tunnel, she heard Justice Stark say, "Mr. Coyle, do you wish to redirect the witness?"

Immediately, Coyle stood and started making his way to the witness stand. Mary knew he was about to accept the judge's offer, for this was his chance to mitigate the damage that had come from Baxter's cross-examination. She also knew that she was incapable of answering any further questions. Completely spent and on the verge of total collapse, she whispered for his ears only, "Please, please don't make me do this."

Her words made him hesitate, and she could see that Coyle was torn; he needed to defend her against Baxter's vile insinuations. This was the first time she had ever seen him waver in court. For a moment he looked as if he were about to ignore her plea, but her eyes continued to beg him not to proceed. Finally, he said, "No, Your Honour."

Justice Stark turned to look at Mary. With genuine sympathy on his face, he nodded. "Thank you, Miss Clark. You are released."

With all her defences down, Mary was surprised she was capable of walking to her table without faltering. Coyle held out her chair for her then resumed his own seat. In the distance, she heard Justice Stark say, "Your next witness, please, Mr. Coyle."

A piercing feeling of having failed Coyle swept through her whole being as she waited for him to respond. He had heard the worst of what could be revealed about her. What must he be thinking? What valid argument could she provide for concealing her past, for putting him in this compromising situation? Had she been more honest with him, he would now be better prepared for his next line of defence.

Mary was exhausted. She felt empty. She wanted an end to this case—anything that would extricate her from this room. Struggling with the feeling of defeat and disappointment, she watched Coyle stand, seemingly immersed in thought. What was he thinking? She knew that he must be annoyed, more still, disillusioned with her.

But, to her amazement, he reached down and tenderly, reassuringly, put his hand over hers. He then smiled, a smile so full of empathy and compassion, it told her all she needed to know. She watched as he straightened and turned toward the judge. "I call Dr. Benjamin Shapiro to the witness stand," he announced in his usual confident manner.

An uncomfortable stillness ensued as Dr. Shapiro once

more made his way to the chair awaiting him and took a seat.

Justice Stark addressed him. "I remind you that you are still under oath, Dr. Shapiro."

Slowly, Coyle approached the witness, his shoulders straight and still—almost too still.

Mary imagined what he must be deliberating, what he was already rehearsing in his mind. *Be prudent. Only ask the essential questions, but make sure you cover all the bases.*

With his propensity for going right to the core of a subject, Coyle began, "Dr. Shapiro, when describing some of the emotions patients are most likely to feel when faced with their imminent death, you stated that emotions varied with different people. Would you explain what you meant by that, please?"

"What I meant was that the emotions dying patients develop are subject to one's priorities."

Coyle waited a long moment before saying, "In other words, the impact of an illness on patients depends principally on what is meaningful to them?"

"Yes. For example, if you are a pianist, and your entire life was centred on playing the piano, in that case some form of paralysis to your hands would definitely be viewed as a tragedy. Conversely, if you're a businessman and can continue to manage your business, the impact of paralysis to your hands would be less tragic and more manageable."

Unknowingly, Dr. Shapiro had given Coyle precisely the answer he had hoped to elicit, but Mary doubted he had anticipated it so soon in his cross-examination.

Coyle advanced to his next question. "Dr. Shapiro, in

your previous statement, you described borderline personality disorder as a long-term disturbance. Am I correct?"

"Yes."

"You also stated that the most consistent finding in the search for causation is a history of a childhood trauma."

"Yes."

"Including sexual abuse?"

"Yes."

Coyle paused, obviously struck by another thought. "Is the diagnosis of borderline personality disorder a common one?"

"No. It's extremely rare. Much rarer than films or novels would have you believe."

"How frequently, would you say, is it made?'

"The incidence has been calculated as two percent of the population."

"Two percent of the population," echoed Coyle. "That is indubitably not a wide prevalence, when one considers all the children that have been abused in our society. If the cause were childhood trauma, wouldn't you expect a greater occurrence of borderline personality disorder?"

The witness shifted in his chair. "As I stated earlier, there is still very little known about what causes it. As a result, much controversy surrounds the diagnosis of BPD. There are those who attribute it to childhood trauma, some researchers have suggested a genetic predisposition, and others have highlighted some abnormalities in the serotonin metabolism."

Mary fought to restrain the mournful cry that threatened her inside.

"Then let us move on," said Coyle. "In your opinion, Dr. Shapiro, do all individuals who have been traumatized as children develop a long-term personality disorder?"

"Oh, no. It's especially important to be aware that a good many are survivors, and those who do survive grow to be strong individuals who have learned from their experience." Pausing, he looked at the jury. With unambiguous sympathy, he continued. "Yes, it's true that a serious trauma in childhood can have a profound effect on an individual's long-term development, but it need not be deleterious. Many learn to come to terms with the tumult of their inner lives, emerging as compassionate adults. It isn't easy, but with counselling, they manage. The psychological condition of the victim is more often related to the overall quality of life in the years that follow."

Coyle paused again, allowing the jury to absorb this. Then he went on, "One more question, please, Dr. Shapiro. Is it not true that we all possess certain characteristics of personality disorders?"

Dr. Shapiro cocked a brow. "I'm not sure I follow you."

"Well, I have various acquaintances. Some are overly depressed and dependent, others abusive and aggressive. Would all individuals showing these characteristics be diagnosed as having a borderline personality disorder?"

"No. Indeed, many of us show symptoms such as you describe. Only, most have developed over the years some apparently persistent means of dealing with life challenges. For these characteristics to be diagnosed as a personality disorder, they'd have to be extreme, recurring, and dysfunctional."

"With that in mind, would you describe Miss Clark here as having a personality disorder?"

"I was asked to speak on the subject of depression only. I've not interviewed Miss Clark and therefore am unqualified to issue a judgment on her personality or behaviour."

"Yes, I appreciate that. Nonetheless, you've had an opportunity to speak to her. In your opinion, would you say Miss Clark demonstrated any signs of borderline personality disorder?"

"No, but again I—"

Coyle smiled. "Thank you, Dr. Shapiro. That will be all."

M ary would not have made it out of the courtroom had it not been for Coyle. In court, she had defended herself bravely, but now, sensitive to the people's stares of pity and, in her mind, repugnance, her bravado had disappeared. Still vulnerable, she allowed him to lead her away, like the wounded child she once was.

Outside the courtroom she came face to face with Courtney and Richard. A rush of anxiety blindsided her. Physically, she was on the verge of collapsing, but she would not allow them that satisfaction. Standing tall, she forced herself to meet their eyes and resolutely walked on, surprised that her legs could carry her.

Rachel suddenly appeared at her side. "That deplorable man," Rachel seethed, furious. "Baxter is a monster, utterly devoid of a conscience. If anyone needs a psychiatric evaluation here, it's he."

But Mary was beyond consolation. Her only wish was to leave the court without breaking down, but by then she could hardly move.

"Here, Mary, lean on me."

Mary was so lost in despair that it took a moment for Coyle's words to register. "Please, just get me out of here," she murmured.

He took the arm she extended to him and, placing it firmly into his, he guided her to the main floor, Rachel following in their footsteps. At the foot of the stairs, Mary halted. "I'm fine now," she said. She was not, but all she wanted was to be alone.

"Let us assist you to your car," Coyle implored.

"No," she replied, her voice shaking. "I'd rather you didn't."

"Then allow me accompany you," Rachel offered.

"Thank you…no, Rachel. More than anything, I need to be alone."

When they failed to move, she pleaded, "Please!"

"Mary there's most likely a scrum of reporters waiting for you outside. There's no way I'm going to allow you to face them alone," Coyle insisted. When she did not reply, he went on, "Let us at least help you get past them."

Emotions raged inside her as she glanced at the exit, her thoughts racing in different directions. Finally, she nodded submissively.

Cushioned securely between Coyle and Rachel, Mary left through the front entrance, weaving through the reporters, ignoring the questions shouted at her. Coyle and Rachel fought off the photographers desperately trying to get a picture of her and led her away from the building and the mass of people.

When they had managed to move a fair distance away, Mary heard herself say, "I'll be all right now."

Clearly reluctant, her friends stepped aside, and Mary made her way aimlessly down Elgin Street, stumbling past people, her pace trancelike. It was four o'clock, and a grey afternoon chill had descended upon Ottawa. She shivered and wrapped her arms around herself.

Minutes later—she could not say how many—she

found herself, pulse thudding, on a bench in Confederation Park, across the street from the Lord Elgin Hotel. For her, as for many, this park held a particular appeal. It was peaceful and secluded, and she habitually came here to think, to find refuge and solace—a place where she retreated whenever life became unbearable and she needed to be alone with her thoughts. Right now, however, she wanted only to forget. Yet despite her efforts, those horrible moments in court kept stomping into every corner of her brain. What had she hoped for from this legal procedure? Justice for Mr. Kerr and herself? A final clarification of what had really happened? The questions eddied insistently in her mind only to remind her that, at the end, she had come out of the experience looking incompetent and deceitful. She shivered again, more against the turmoil of her reflections than against the cold.

Drawing her coat round her, she stared at the fountain, longing for the days when it had provided a sense of peace, a peace that now eluded her.

"Mary?" whispered a voice above her.

Mary looked up to find Peter staring down at her, his eyes pleading. The sight of him proved too much for her, and she covered her eyes with her hands and cried in agony, "Leave me. Please!"

Then Coyle and Rachel approached, and Peter drew back, astonished.

"Haven't you done enough to hurt her?" Coyle exclaimed. Through her sobs, Mary could hear the irritation in his voice.

"I'm here to offer my help," Peter replied.

"Your help!" cried Rachel. "It was your help that brought this on her, you deceiving—" She broke off, fighting to control her temper.

"Do you think I don't know what I've done?" Peter cried. "Believe me, there will not be a single day in my life that I won't be haunted by it." The misery in his voice was unmistakable.

He turned to Mary. "You must believe me, Mary, when I say that I never dreamed it would come to this," he pleaded. "To be honest, I don't know what I expected—but definitely not this."

When Mary failed to answer, Rachel spoke up again. "That's bullshit. You may be an insidious weakling, but you can't be totally dense. When you backed Beasley, you must have known that the evidence you provided would be used against her, and there could be only one outcome. You only refused to acknowledge it, that's all."

"Mary." Peter's voice was pleading, full of anguish. "God help me, I didn't know what I was doing. I had no idea it—"

Mary cut him off. "Please don't say any more, Peter. Please don't."

"Mary, God forgive me, I deceived you, but..." He stopped, letting the rest of the sentence disappear. Then he picked it up again. "In every deceit, there are extenuating circumstances. My actions were inevitable. To succeed, one has to compromise, sometimes push ethical boundaries. The end justifies the means. All those things were taught to me from an early age."

"What other life instructions have you received from your mother?" Rachel retorted. "That you are fundamentally different from other people? That you are the cream of society and born to rule? That it is your right, and you have to reach that position at any cost, even if it means destroying the people who love and trust you?"

"What new angle have you come to scheme now for Beasley and his lot?" Coyle asked reprovingly.

"No angle, believe me," Peter replied. "What Baxter is doing to Mary is pure torture to me. I can't bear it any longer."

"Spare us the melodrama," Rachel said. "You'd have us believe you were the victim here instead of complicit."

"I made a wrong decision."

"Yes. And Mary will end up paying for it," Coyle retorted stiffly.

"How was I to foresee it would come to this?"

Rachel shook her head. "You're something else, Peter. You're the only person I know who makes all the wrong decisions and still hopes for positive results at the end."

"If she hadn't fought so hard, the charges would have been dropped. How was I to know that she would fight them to the end, even at the risk of being imprisoned?"

"No, I imagine someone like you wouldn't understand that, because to do so would require a conscience. And you, Peter, have no sense of responsibility toward anything or anyone."

Ignoring Rachel's remark, Peter once more turned to Mary. "Tell me what to do. I'll do…" He did not finish. He did not need to. Witnessing the crushed person before him, he could see it was already too late. Nothing could undo what he had initiated. "Forgive me, Mary. Please forgive me," he murmured.

Mary could feel the anguish in his voice but was too shattered to care.

In the silence that followed, Peter seemed to want to say something but then relented and slowly departed.

Mary struggled to her feet. Coyle and Rachel attempted to assist her, but she averted her eyes from them and waved her hand in a dismissive gesture. She could not bear to let them see how defeated she was. "Please leave me," she pleaded. "I'm all right, really. I just need to be alone."

She saw them hesitate. "Please," she implored.

And so they parted, and Mary walked dejectedly to her car—endeavouring to focus on a reality less severe, less malevolent.

It was dark when Mary finally let herself into her apartment—the only sanctum available to her. Completely spent, she collapsed onto her bed. For a long time, she lay rigid and awake, unable to sleep, sorting through the events of the week and reliving the day's tragedy. How angry, no, disappointed Coyle must feel at her failure to trust him with that critical information about her past. He had asked her to tell him about her family, but she had been unable to cut through the painstakingly constructed fortress she had erected around herself.

Talking about her dysfunctional parents would have breached the gates to a flood of wounding memories, a part of herself that she had abandoned as a way of coping. And on top of that, how does one tell someone like Coyle that your father sexually abused you, and your mother knew but did nothing to end it?

Lying in bed, staring into the empty darkness, Mary's mind drifted to the world of her childhood.

It was evening, and her father came to her room to say good night, a routine he had recently adopted with increasing frequency. Considering he had not previously been so attentive, this new routine brought her immense joy, and she eagerly anticipated his visits. Occasionally, he would read her favourite stories, and on other occasions engage in playful games. She was ticklish, and he would constrain her on her bed and tickle her until she could stand it no longer. That night, however, his hands moved to the intimate parts of her body. He treated it as another game. In her child's mind, it was impossible for her to conceive that his fondling, stroking, and caressing was not normal behaviour between father and daughter. He claimed she was special, and this was his way of loving her. Desperate for love, she went along with it. Yet visceral feelings of aversion were developing inside her.

As she grew older, her aversion to his "playing" became stronger. As much as she craved her father's love and attention, her instinct warned her there was something unnatural about what he was doing.

One day she resisted, telling him she no longer wanted to play that game. For a brief period after that, his offensive behaviour ceased. Then one evening, when Mary's mother was away visiting relatives, he came to her room and forced himself on her. She was eleven years old.

Reacting to the physical pain, as well as the shame, she started to cry. Her father did his utmost to console her, saying he loved her deeply. But that was little comfort. She now felt contaminated and miserable.

Her father told her that if she ever disclosed what he had done, they would take him away to prison, and she would be sent to an orphanage. Fearful, she remained silent, hoping he would leave her alone. But he only became more aggressive. When it became unbearable, she went to her mother with an appeal for help. Her mother refused to acknowledge that her husband was capable of such an abominable act. To Mary's horror, her mother accused her of making it all up. The fact that Mary woke up screaming at night failed to make her think differently.

In the years that followed, life for Mary became a living hell. Her mother's refusal to acknowledge the incest not only empowered her father to continue abusing her, but also underscored for Mary that there was no escape. She scorned her mother for that. Yet she dreaded her mother leaving the house for any reason.

Victimized and rejected, Mary took on a self-defeating mindset, accepting the blame for what her father was doing to her, feeling inadequate and turning against everyone, men in particular. The cycle persisted for four years. Mary never told anyone, even her maternal grandfather, who was her sole refuge. Wretched and defeated, she doubted anyone would believe her. So it remained a secret, one whose weight pressed so heavily on her that she lost all hope of ever being free of her father's crushing abuse.

Then, late in the summer before she was to start high school, while her father was on his annual fishing trip, her uncle Morton, who lived in Toronto, came to visit. A bachelor and a parole officer, he was attending a conference in Fredericton and had driven to Bathurst to spend a couple of days with his only sibling, Mary's mother, who was much younger than he. He was a big man in his early fifties and at the cusp of retirement. He was not the most voluble person but must have sensed something was amiss, for he asked her privately, "Is something troubling you, Mary?"

She wanted to tell him about the sexual abuse but said nothing, despite her torment. He was a man, and she had come to distrust all men. Yet, in the end, it was he who helped her find meaning in a life that up until then had been meaningless. He was her saviour.

The last night of his visit, Mary had gone to bed early and had fallen asleep but awoke sometime later to a conversation coming through the heating vent in the floor. She couldn't make out what was being discussed but heard her name mentioned. She slipped out of bed to stand closer to the vent.

"I heard her scream last night," came her uncle's voice.

"She has nightmares."

"What about?"

"She refuses to talk about them."

"Have you sought help for her?"

"No."

"Why in God's name haven't you?"

"Mary can be demanding, and I suspect it's her way of getting attention."

Out of the blue, he asked, "Has Mary ever spoken to you about any type of abuse?"

"What makes you ask that question?"

"I've worked with a lot of troubled kids. I know children her age don't simply withdraw from life for no reason. It appears to me that she's exhibiting symptoms of abuse."

"There's nothing wrong with her," her mother insisted. "She's a teenager. What do you expect?"

"What disturbs me right now is your obvious lack of concern for her."

"I'm not concerned because, I repeat, there's nothing wrong with her. It's all in your head. What's more, why should you care? She's not your daughter."

"I'm her uncle, and it's perfectly natural for me to be

interested in her welfare. Mary is not exhibiting normal behaviour for a girl her age, and I want to find out what is causing it."

Her mother chuckled. "Morton, you've been working so long with dysfunctional people that you're now beginning to read their symptoms in everybody you see."

"Don't be ridiculous."

"You're the one being ridiculous," she retorted.

"Listen to me, Joyce," he replied, his voice severe. "Mary is exhibiting signs of distress. Since you're not prepared to help her, tomorrow, before I leave, I plan to visit the local Children's Aid Society and see if they can't find a counsellor for her—someone she can talk to."

A fracas ensued, her mother accusing him of meddling in their affairs. In a reproachful tone, she said, "Mary is a problematic child who makes up stories about people. Right now, she wants to go to a boarding school and will say anything to get her way."

"What stories? Why a boarding school?" he demanded.

"It's none of your business. So drop it, will you?"

The conversation ended there, but Mary was to learn that her uncle was not one to surrender.

The following morning, he addressed her. "Your mother tells me you want to go to a boarding school."

She nodded in reply but was skeptical.

"What about your mother and father? Wouldn't you miss them if you were to leave home?"

Mary did not answer. She had asked to go to a boarding school because it would provide an escape from her father. But her insistent urging had failed to move her mother.

"The school is not that far away," she said, evading the question. "They could visit on weekends."

"Mary, I sense something is troubling you. Won't you tell me what it is? I may be able to help you."

Again, Mary resisted. Having lived in a home where there was no one to rely on, she had grown to mistrust everyone. But her uncle was a patient and kind-hearted man, and she eventually unburdened herself, revealing the intolerable humiliation that visited her at night—a cycle of horrendous abuse while her mother looked away.

Repulsed by what he heard, Morton once more confronted his sister. This time Mary was present. When her mother refused to listen, he threatened to go to the authorities. Only then did her mother agree to allow Mary to go to a boarding school.

She left that day in the company of her uncle. At the beginning of the school year, he escorted her to the Elmwood Campus. He had a friend who was a professor there and felt confident she would be well cared for.

Having finally escaped from her father and mother, Mary had no desire to return home, and she would find reasons to stay at school on long weekends, holidays, and summer breaks whenever she was not going to be at the Kerrs'. Otherwise, when she left the school it was to be with her uncle in Toronto. After so many years of abuse, his home, like the Kerrs', was a refuge.

On one such visit near the end of her second year at Elmwood, while the pair sat contemplating his backyard filled with flowering trees and shrubs, Mary became aware that he was struggling with his thoughts. Finally, he announced, "I've been diagnosed with pancreatic cancer. I'm told I have less than a month to live."

"Uncle Morton," she whispered, her voice catching in her throat. "This can't be true. We'll find the best treatments, get second opinions. You can't leave. I won't accept it."

"I've had a good life, Mary. I could go on a bit longer with aggressive treatment but decided against it. Before I go, however, I need to secure your future. Whatever money I have will be yours and will carry you through your years at Elmwood. After that, unfortunately, you'll be on your own."

"You needn't worry about me, Uncle Morton."

"But I do worry about you. You've come to mean everything to me." He paused, as though debating with his thoughts. "Mary, when you entered Elmwood, you begged me not to disclose your home situation. You expressed fear that people would judge you if they knew. I respected your wishes. But I realize now that it was a grave error on my part. You should be in therapy."

"We can't afford it."

"You can't afford to be without it," he retorted. A fresh anxiety surfaced in his voice. "Mary, we all have demons in the dark recesses of our minds, and the only way we can get rid of them is to bring them out into the light. Nobody, to my knowledge, has ever overcome what you've gone through without the support of a competent and experienced counsellor."

"That was in the past," she replied. "The time since then has diminished my memory."

He smiled, his sensitive brown eyes conveying that he doubted it. He was not a handsome man, but Mary loved to see how his features softened when he smiled. They radiated intelligence, integrity, and, pre-eminently, compassion.

She suddenly felt overwhelmed with grief at the thought of losing him and fought to hold back tears. Directing her gaze to the sprawling rock garden and the remarkable flower beds that were a source of pride for him, she found solace in their beauty.

Her uncle put his arm around her shoulders and, drawing her toward his broad chest, said, "You need help. But first, you need to go home and face your parents. You suffered terribly while you were with them, but now is the time for healing and forgiving."

Those were among his last words to her before he died.

There was no funeral. He wanted it that way. He wanted his family and friends to remember him healthy and alive.

She did return home—once. Her parents were attentive but guarded. When she left, her father accompanied her to the station. As the train was pulling away, he called out, "I love you." Mary could not bring herself to say she loved him too. To have violated the responsibility and care of a child entrusted to him in such an abominable manner, he could never have loved her. And that is what tormented her.

Three years after her uncle's death, news came of her parents' fatal car accident. She was in her second year of law at Ottawa University and was preparing for a mid-term. After rescheduling the date of her exam, she flew to Moncton, rented a car at the airport, and then drove to Bathurst to attend the funeral.

As she stood at her parents' gravesite, with their friends and neighbours beside her, she remained tearless while listening quietly to the priest describing her father and mother as warm and loving people whose lives could well serve as a model to the rest of the community.

Mary was saddened by the irony of those words. Outward appearance had been foremost to her parents, and to that end they had devoted their entire energy. They had succeeded. *But at what cost?* she asked herself. They say that children are resilient, but that's not entirely true. They accommodate, transform. Because they cannot handle the abuse, they sublimate the knowledge of what has happened. It's called *displacement*. From a book she had read, Mary learned that a big part of healing for people who had been violated as children was being able to confront those who had harmed them, to make the aggressors aware of the gravity of their actions. It would have meant so much for Mary to hear her parents say, "We're sorry" or "We didn't mean to harm you." They had denied her even that. When she had confronted them in her one visit after having moved away, they had shown no interest in acknowledging the harm and pain they had inflicted on her. Their parting had been without apology or apparent regret. And now they were gone, and she would continue to live with the legacy they had left her.

As she stood at the gravesite, gazing down at the closed caskets, Mary convinced herself it did not matter. She had long stopped hoping for her parents to give her the love she never received as a child. Yet the injury persisted. Having disassociated herself from her parents for so long, the fact they were now departed filled her with a different kind of guilt and gloom. She knew the guilt was irrational and tried to put it out of her mind. Nevertheless, the nightmares returned, and her life seemed to be falling apart again. By all definitions, she remained a marred child.

Then, miraculously, she met Dr. Cowen, her new-found confidant and mentor. He too urged her to seek aid from a professional counsellor, someone he knew. He even offered to pay for her therapy. She declined. But shortly after his death she learned of his bequest. There were no conditions attached to his gift, but out of a feeling of obligation to him and deep regard for his memory, she used the money to rehabilitate herself. In an effort to penetrate the last residue of the protective barrier she had created for herself and overcome the emotional stagnation it had elicited, she entered a period of psychotherapy that was indispensable for her rehabilitation.

Recollecting her past sent an intolerable fear into Mary's heart. Almost as strong was the feeling of worthlessness that had settled over her. Notwithstanding Dr. Shapiro's testimony, Mary had learned that most people—especially those uninitiated in the field of psychology—assumed that all victims of incest were mentally tarnished, that part of their mind was distorted by the experience, their persona irrevocably altered.

She tossed and turned until, finally, sleep enveloped her. Still, there was no respite. She dreamed about her trial, her subconscious conjuring up scenes of the likely aftermath— her facing the jury, the foreman's condemnatory voice pronouncing the word *guilty*, the gradual realization of her fate, and the disbelieving look on Rachel's, Francis's, and Coyle's faces as she was escorted from the courtroom.

When Mary stepped outside her apartment building shortly after dawn the following morning,
she had reconciled herself to her fate. She was
on the precipice of being found guilty and was powerless to
do anything about it. What would become of her, she could
not even begin to contemplate.

Despite the gloom of the day, it was good to be out in the
fresh air. Pulling up her collar against the bracing autumnal
breeze, she took several deep breaths, dug her hands deep
into her coat pockets, and started to walk toward Coyle's
office. It was a long distance away, but she needed that time
to think things through. As she moved along, the events of
the past week flooded her mind. Most people would feel
apprehensive about the outcome she could expect in court
today. But surprisingly, she felt relief, respite. She had kept
her secret of abuse inside her for so many years that it now
felt as if a heavy cape had been lifted from her shoulders.
Her body felt light, rejuvenated, ready for anything the
court had in store for her—even a guilty verdict.

Now that she had embraced her inevitable fate, her
thoughts shifted to Coyle and, as so often in recent days,
her regret at having failed him. She had failed at many
things over the past few months but failing him was beyond
bearing. All his efforts and sacrifices had been in vain.

Coyle had called her earlier that morning and suggested

they meet before going on to the courthouse. He had sounded revived, but she dreaded the meeting. She was convinced her case was lost, and there was no one to blame but herself. Steeling herself against the guilty verdict that was bound to follow, she approached the front door of the Chambers Building. Just as she reached for the doorknob, the door opened, and a woman stepped out.

For a moment, they merely studied each other, and then the woman excused herself and briskly walked away.

There was something familiar about her, and Mary tried to remember where they might have met.

Perplexed, Mary entered the building and made her way to the third floor. When she entered Coyle's waiting room, she noticed a lone white envelope on the floor. It had apparently been slipped underneath the door. She picked it up and saw that it was addressed to Coyle and marked "Urgent." Kate was not at her desk, which was surprising.

Mary heard movement in Coyle's office. She moved closer to the door and was about to enter when she heard, "I watched you in court yesterday." The voice belonged to Coyle's mother.

"Oh! I didn't see you there," Coyle responded.

"I was late arriving and took a seat in the back row."

"And what brings you here so early this morning, Mother?"

"I stayed the night with my friend Clara. I knew you would already be at work, so I thought I would drop in before the trial."

Mary was uncomfortable eavesdropping on their conversation but lingered at the door, not wanting to interrupt.

There was a long pause, then Mrs. Coyle said, "You look exhausted."

"I haven't had much sleep lately."

"You fear for Mary?"

"Yes."

"Do you still believe she's telling the truth?"

Mary anxiously awaited his reply, but it did not come.

"She does have a troubled background, and that could explain some of her actions," continued Mrs. Coyle.

"For God's sake, Mother, she was sexually abused by her father. Must she be interminably stigmatized because of it?" There was no disrespect in his voice, only melancholy.

"Patrick, I hold Mary in high regard and never intended any offence. But right now, my concern is for you."

"Forgive me, Mother, for sounding off the way I did. It was unwarranted."

There was a long silence.

"You didn't answer my question, Patrick. Do you still believe she's telling the truth?"

"In my job, whether I believe her or not is irrelevant. Foremost in my duty is to convince the jury that the Crown attorney failed to make out its case against my client beyond reasonable doubt."

"I will never understand why creating substantial doubt around a case is more important than proving someone's innocence," replied Mrs. Coyle. Her voice dropped lower. "Tell me, Patrick. What is so compelling about Mary that would make you risk your career for her?"

Mary felt guilty about listening in but needed to hear his response.

"She radiates an honesty unlike any I've ever seen." After a pause, he said, "Why this sudden interest in Mary, Mother?"

"For some time now, I've been worried about you, Patrick. I've been feeling that your obsession with work was something you carried almost to extreme. Hardly any social life." There was a pause, as though she was waiting for a reply. When none came, she went on. "Do you realize that Mary is the only woman you've invited to the farm since your breakup with Melanie? And that was a long time ago."

"When I took on this case, I assumed it was because of my resentment toward McLeod for bullying a member of the staff. You know how I abhor unfairness. But that was only partly true. In a world where most people look after their own interest, Mary dared to be different. She stood up for a client when just about every lawyer would've given in. It took courage and bravery to fight the system, and I admire her for that. It incited me to examine my own life, and I realized I had lost touch with my own optimism and faith for a better world. I needed to get back to that."

"In the face of such self-abasement, words fail me, Patrick. Have your years with the firm not been happy?"

"Happy is a relative term, Mother. It all depends on your perspective."

"You know very well what I mean."

"To answer your question, I've been neither happy nor unhappy, only vaguely dissatisfied. I know what most people think. They see me as a successful lawyer. I make big money and am well acknowledged within my profession.

But if I were to sum up my life, it would add up to merely existing. I'm—"

"That's an unfair assessment," his mother interrupted. "You've done outstanding work. There's nothing that says one has to be poor and struggling to be able to accomplish meaningful things in life. Over the years, I've watched you excel in your profession, and I'm so proud of you as a person—your values, your integrity."

"I'm glad you think so, Mother, but McLeod didn't hire me because I adhered to high moral principles or professional standards. It was because I won cases for his clients, and that brought in new business. Much to my chagrin, I've found over the years that it has become easier for me to overlook certain discrepancies rather than confront him and his lot. Mary's situation forced me to revisit those decisions."

"Patrick, I won't stand for you being critical of yourself like this," Mrs. Coyle interjected. "You haven't changed all that much. In these last few years, you may have become a bit cynical, but that comes from sometimes having to work with the worst kind of people, a professional hazard, if you like. Despite all, you remain your own person, fighting for the things you believe in. You've tirelessly done what you knew in your heart was right. That has been your strength, and nobody can take that away from you."

"I wish you had been there, Mother, the day Mary confronted McLeod," Coyle said, his voice warming up. "She reminded me of all the ideals I had set aside in order to reach my position and status in the firm. And I felt so deficient."

Mary was shaken to hear Coyle sound so vulnerable, he

who always appeared so poised, the self-assured lawyer who, at all times, knew what to do.

"Patrick, my dear. In all your life, you have never acted irresponsibly. Whatever it is that is troubling you, I'm confident you'll be able to resolve it. As for Mary, I'm convinced you'll find a way to help her, too."

There was silence, and then the movement of chairs, followed by footsteps.

Before either one of them could come through the door, Mary knocked and entered the room.

Surprise flitted over Coyle's face. "Mary!"

She greeted them with a stoic smile. "Good morning. Am I intruding?"

"No…of course not. I just wasn't expecting you so early. But do come in. Mother, we have a few things to review before we head to court. Will you forgive us, please?"

"Of course, Patrick." Mrs. Coyle turned to Mary, and enfolding her in a warm, maternal embrace she whispered, "Good luck this morning, Mary. I'll be rooting for you." She then stepped out of the room, closing the door gently behind her.

Almost as soon as she had exited, Mary stammered, "I…I feel I owe you an enormous apology."

"Mary, you—"

She held up her hand. "No, please. I need to say this."

Reluctantly, he nodded.

"From the very beginning, my refusal to disclose any personal information about my past has been a source of difficulty for you. Yet you bore it without reproach or judgment." A sudden flood of tears filled her eyes. Gathering strength, she continued. "I wish I had been more honest with you."

"Why didn't you tell me about the abuse?"

"I was ashamed. I thought you might think less of me."

"Oh, Mary. How could you think that?"

When she didn't answer, he continued. "You have no reason to feel ashamed. As you so well stated in court, you were the victim."

"I know, but despite what I said, there's always that small vestige…that trace of guilt that remains. Probably always will. It bears down on you and leaves an indelible imprint on your mind. You can never get rid of it, not entirely. No matter how hard you try."

Coyle looked pained. "You've been pitifully preyed upon and have had much to forgive. No one should feel guilty for having experienced more hardships than one should ever need to endure."

"What you say is perfectly rational, but I don't know that it's possible to go through what I have and remain totally unaffected, emotionally—even with therapy. But that never stopped me from taking ownership and control of my life. Little by little, I learned to trust myself in most things. And one never knows. With time, I may well be able to totally rid myself of the negative emotions that persist." She paused. "In any event, all this does not alter the fact that if I had been more honest with you, the outcome that I face in court today would be different."

"Mary, this trial is not over—I've yet to give them my closing statement. Fortunately for us, Baxter has an infinitely active ego. Blinded by hubris, he failed to recognize that bringing up your child abuse and psychotherapy could risk alienating the jurors and provoke sympathy for you. I intend to profit from that good fortune."

"Forgive me. I've no doubt that your closing statement will be brilliant, but I'm trying to be realistic. Every time you get ahead, new evidence surfaces to undermine your work. I can't help wondering what new evidence will come out today."

For a moment he looked bemused. Then humour lit up his face. "Why? Would you, by any chance, be withholding further information from me about your past?"

"No, you pretty much have my entire life history," she replied, returning his grin.

"In that case, there's nothing to worry about, so why don't we get to work. I'd like to go over my closing statement with you before we head to court."

"Of course." Remembering the envelope, Mary handed it over to him. "I found this on the floor in the front room. Someone must have slipped it under the door. Since Kate was not at her desk, I thought I should bring it in to you. Is she ill?"

"No, she must've stepped out for a moment."

He opened it, pulled out a sheet of paper, and read it quickly. His expression went slack with obvious disbelief then lit up with pleasure. "Did you see who put it there?"

"No." Then she remembered her encounter with the lady at the front door. Could it have been she?

Before she could say anything else, Coyle gently drew her toward a chair. "Please be seated while I make a telephone call."

"What is it?" she asked.

"There's been a new development."

"That letter?

"Yes."

"What does it say?"

"I don't have time to explain, but whoever delivered this, a certain Miss Doris Martin, may be in a position to help us."

The name sounded familiar, and Mary struggled to recall who this Miss Martin might be.

Already Coyle was at his desk and dialing the number. "Something tells me that we're going to win this case." His voice was neutral, but there was a promising glint in his eyes.

Mary held her breath. What new development could possibly have come up? Definitely nothing that could prove her innocent, since there was no such evidence. None she was aware of, anyway. Yet the excitement in Coyle's eyes and the assurance in his voice conveyed that she would come out of this triumphant. Her confidence restored, she waited for him to complete his call.

At exactly ten o'clock, Justice Stark came through the side door and walked to the bench. As he did so, a voice called out, "All rise. Court is in session. The Honourable Justice Frank Stark presiding in the case of the Crown versus Mary Clark." Justice Stark seated himself and addressed Coyle and Baxter. "Counsels, are you ready to proceed?"

Coyle stepped forward. "Your Honour, new evidence has come to light, and I would like to bring in a new witness, Miss Doris Martin, who is an employee at the Ottawa Civic Hospital. Therefore, I ask for a brief postponement, so that both I and the counsel for the Crown may have an opportunity to question Miss Martin under oath."

Baxter's reaction was quick. "Your Honour, Miss Martin has not been listed as a potential witness in this proceeding. It's entirely inappropriate for counsel to present this witness without allowing prosecution the courtesy of proper notice and procedure of—"

Coyle interrupted. "Your Honour, I acquired this evidence only this morning, and there was no time to inform you or my learned friend here until now."

The Crown attorney persisted. "This is highly irregular, Your Honour. All the arguments have been given, and it's too late to introduce a new witness."

Coyle remained calm. "Your Honour, this witness is

crucial to the defence of my client. It's imperative that she be heard."

Looking pensive, Justice Stark said, "I must admit that this is a deviation from trial protocol."

"I agree, but if Miss Martin isn't allowed to testify now, there will most definitely be an appeal and another trial, should my client be found guilty."

Justice Stark turned to Baxter. "I could call a brief adjournment to allow you to prepare for the witness. Are you in agreement?"

"Your Honour, this is not in accordance with the accepted standards of—"

"I know, I know," Justice Stark broke in. "But if this will avoid a mistrial, for the sake of expediency and in the interest of justice, are you in agreement, yes or no?"

When Baxter didn't answer, the judge grew impatient. "Mr. Baxter?"

Grudgingly, Baxter nodded. "Yes, Your Honour. For the sake of expediency and in the interest of justice."

"Thank you, Mr. Baxter. The trial is therefore adjourned until one o'clock this afternoon. This should allow you and defence counsel enough time to discern what evidence this witness may have."

—

At exactly one o'clock, Justice Stark entered the courtroom, walked to his bench, and seated himself. He briefly surveyed the room, then addressed Coyle. "Please call in your witness."

"I call Miss Doris Martin to the stand."

After a brief delay, a woman entered the courtroom. She appeared to be in her early fifties, thin, with a kind face and demeanour.

Mary watched anxiously as the woman timidly took the oath. She and Coyle had already met with her, and amid the tension Mary felt, there was a glimmer of relief. Finally, this pivotal moment had arrived. The weight of the trial and the uncertainty of the outcome had been bearing down on her. Now, with the witness taking the stand, there was a chance for the truth to be revealed.

Coyle smiled at the witness reassuringly and said, "Please state your name and place of employment, for the record."

"My name is Doris Martin. I am an employee of the Ottawa Civic Hospital."

"How long have you been working there?"

"Twenty-eight years."

"Would you state your occupation, Miss Martin?"

"I'm a Certified Nursing Assistant."

"What does that position entail?"

"We provide basic nursing care like answering patients' call bell, serving meals, making beds, and helping patients dress and bathe."

"As a nursing assistant, were you ever in contact with Mr. Robert Kerr?"

"Oh yes. I was working in the palliative care unit at the Civic Hospital when Mr. Kerr was a patient there."

Pointing to Mary, he asked, "Are you familiar with the defendant, Miss Clark?"

She smiled at Mary. "Yes. Miss Clark was a frequent visitor while Mr. Kerr was in the palliative care unit."

Coyle walked over to his table, picked up a sheet of paper, and returning to the witness stand, handed it to Miss Martin. "Do you recognize this?"

The witness checked the document briefly before looking up at him. "Yes, it's a letter that I delivered to your office this morning."

"Would you read it aloud for the court, please."

"Now?"

"Yes, please."

Doris's gaze drifted over the room before slowly resting on her letter. Then in an edgy voice, she read:

November 23, 1966
To whom it may concern,

My name is Doris Martin, and I am writing this letter in defence of Miss Mary Clark.

I am an employee of the Ottawa Civic Hospital and was working in Mr. Kerr's ward while he was a patient there. During that period, I overheard a conversation between Miss Clark and Mr. Kerr that might well prove her innocence.

Yours sincerely,
Doris Martin

Justice Stark looked down inquiringly at the witness. "Miss Martin, would you explain to the court why you didn't come forward earlier with this information?"

"I've been in Nova Scotia nursing my mother who was ill. I only got back a few days ago and did not know what was happening in the trial."

Justice Stark turned to Coyle. "Counsel may proceed."

"Thank you, Your Honour." Addressing the witness, Coyle said, "Miss Martin, have you ever met Mr. Kerr's daughter, Courtney Kerr?"

"Yes. Shortly before he died, she and her brother came to visit him at the hospital."

"Please tell the court everything you remember about that day."

"I was putting in my last shift when…" She faltered and looked around the court apprehensively.

"Just what you remember, in your own words," Coyle urged in his calm, pleasant voice.

"Well, I was working in Mr. Kerr's room when he asked me to place some papers in his briefcase. My hands were wet at the time, so I told him I would do it as soon as I was finished cleaning. He agreed and set them, the papers I mean, on his bedside table. Only, when I finished my chores, he was asleep. So, as quietly as I could, I took the papers and put them into his briefcase. This is when his daughter and son walked in."

"How did you know they were Mr. Kerr's children?"

"Because the lady yelled at me, 'What are you doing rummaging through our father's briefcase?' I explained about their father's request, but they didn't believe me. Furious, she, the daughter, ordered me out of the room and threatened to report me to my superior if I ever dared touch anything else that belonged to her father."

"What did you do then?"

"I left."

"So that was the last time you saw them?"

"Yes."

"Did Miss Clark visit Mr. Kerr that day?"

"Yes, she was with him when I returned to the room that afternoon."

"So later you actually went back to Mr. Kerr's room?"

"Yes. That afternoon I noticed that my schedule sheet was missing. I knew I must have left it in his room. So I went back to get it. When I got there, he was asleep, so I quietly tiptoed into the room. When I couldn't find it, I went into the washroom to check there. It was on the vanity table. But as I was ready to come out, I heard a female voice. I thought it might be the daughter and was scared stiff. The last thing I wanted was for her to catch me in her father's room."

"So what did you do?" asked Coyle.

"Because her previous visits had always been very brief—she and her brother usually just popped in and out—I decided to wait for her to leave and remained in the washroom. Shortly after, however, I realized it was Miss Clark and not his daughter who was with Mr. Kerr. Still, I remained in the room. I didn't mean to spy on them. Only, by then, I had already heard more than I should have, so I waited for Miss Clark to leave. As for Mr. Kerr, I wasn't concerned because he kept falling in and out of sleep."

"Did you hear any of the conversation that took place between Miss Clark and Mr. Kerr?"

"Yes, all of it. The door was partially opened, and their voices carried into the washroom."

"What was it they were discussing?"

"A letter about a music box. I heard Miss Clark say that the music box was in a trunk. She hadn't received the appraisal sheet yet, but it was believed to be worth three million dollars."

"What did Mr. Kerr say?"

"He asked her where the music box and trunk were. She replied that the trunk was in her apartment along with the music box, which was secured in a safety deposit box. She asked him what she should do next." Doris shifted nervously in her seat and looked at the jurors, who were intent on her every word. "By then I was really scared…if they had caught me, they would've known that I'd been eavesdropping."

"Did Mr. Kerr finally say what he wanted Miss Clark to do with the music box?"

"Oh yes! He took his time, mind you. But when he did, he instructed her to return the trunk, including the music box, to Eugenie's family. I had no idea who Eugenie was. Only, I recall her name because he spoke it with a French accent, and it sounded so pretty."

"Did Mr. Kerr say anything else about the trunk?"

"No, but he told Miss Clark not to include the appraisal sheet in the file. He didn't want his children to learn about the value of the music box. 'No need to distress them further,' was what he said."

"Did Mr. Kerr or Miss Clark mention anything about a will?"

"Yes, Miss Clark did. She asked Mr. Kerr if he had discussed his last will with them."

"You mean his children?"

"Yes, sir. Miss Clark mentioned them by name, Courtney and Richard."

"What was his reply?"

"He replied, 'I've tried to, but I can't communicate with them. God damn it, Mary, what else can I expect? I've made them what they are.'" Here Miss Martin blushed, somewhat ill at ease. "Those were his precise words."

"Please continue, Miss Martin."

"Well…then in a low, dispirited voice, he said, 'Courtney, Richard, and I were never able to communicate before my illness. Why would I expect it to be different now?'"

"What did Miss Clark say?"

"She asked him if he wanted her to speak to them on his behalf."

"And what was his answer?"

"He answered that she could, but he doubted it would do any good."

"Did Miss Clark say anything else?"

"She warned him that his will would most likely cause ill feelings."

"What did he respond to that?"

With the facial expression of one desperately trying to remember, Miss Martin replied, "He said, 'I suspect they will contest it. Promise me, Mary, that you will not give in to their demands.' He then begged Miss Clark to forgive him for leaving her alone to face his children's foreseeable anger and possible ill will. Only he was tired and didn't have the stamina to fight them anymore. He finished by saying that he still loved them dearly and hoped that one day they would understand."

"What followed after that?"

"Miss Clark assured him that they would."

Mary recalled that moment. Her words were meant to

comfort Mr. Kerr, but in her heart, she had known them to be untrue.

"Was there anything else?"

"She told him not to worry, that she would see to it that his wishes were carried out precisely as he had dictated them. Those, too, were her precise words."

"Is that all you heard that afternoon?"

"Yes, sir. Miss Clark stayed with him until he fell asleep and then left."

"Miss Martin, when I spoke with you this morning, you mentioned you had attended our last court session."

"Yes."

"Is that when you decided to reach out to me?"

"Yes, I had no idea what evidence had been brought in against Miss Clark but felt that what I had overheard might be important to you."

"Yes, indeed, Miss Martin. And I thank you most sincerely for the great assistance you've rendered not only to my client, but to the integrity of this court."

After Miss Martin's testimony, Mr. Baxter was called to cross-examine the witness. An able Crown attorney, he used every possible means to cast doubt on her story. But she remained firm, never once deviating from it.

Still, in his closing argument, Baxter reminded the jurors that though Mr. Kerr had given Miss Clark instructions to return the trunk, including the music box, to Eugenie's family, she had not complied. Instead, she had kept it in her possession in her apartment, which clearly indicated her intention to keep the music box for herself. Along with pointing out the many incongruities in her behaviour as executrix of Mr. Kerr's estate, he reminded the jury of the letter Mary had written to Danielle. In it, she had failed to mention the existence of a music box, once more indicating that she had every intention of keeping it for herself. His summation was so convincing that, when he finished, Mary could not help thinking that her next two years were already destined. *What will become of me when I'm released from prison? Where will I go?* She tried to imagine her future, but it all seemed too surreal.

As promised, Coyle came through for her—his closing statement so powerful that she could hardly take her eyes off him. For half an hour he spoke about the positive accomplishments in her life, despite the adversities that had marred her youth. He spoke about the dreams she had made for herself. Dreams of longing and hope for a better, happier world. Condemning Baxter's insensitivity for having tried to turn Mary's tragic past into an admission of guilt, he reminded the jury that it was precisely that tragic past and her unrelenting struggle to cope with it that had made her the very special and remarkable person she had become. A person of character, resolve, and courage. At this point he stared at her with the same measured calm she had come to admire so much and added, "A person who would risk going to prison rather than ignore the dying wishes of her friend and client, Mr. Kerr."

Finally, at three o'clock, it was left for the jury to decide, and they retired to consider their verdict.

While Mary and Coyle waited in an antechamber, she looked up at him and attempted a brave smile. "It seems unbelievable that it's almost all over," she said.

He nodded, his expression displaying confidence at the outcome.

Mary had suffered so much emotional upheaval in her life that she could not share his self-assurance. But she was more grateful to him at that moment than she had ever been.

Most times, it is impossible to estimate how long it will take for a jury to reach a verdict, but in this case, it was unconventionally brief. At four forty-five, everyone was called to the courtroom, where the court clerk announced that the jury was ready to present its verdict.

Justice Stark addressed Mary. "Will the accused please rise and face the jury."

Slowly, Mary rose from her seat, Coyle beside her.

"On the first charge of mismanagement, how do you find the accused?" the judge asked.

"We, the jurors, find the accused, Mary Clark, not guilty," replied the spokesperson.

A sudden collective sigh of relief was heard throughout the court.

In the surging tumult of relief, Mary barely heard Justice Stark's next question. "On the second charge of fraud, how do you rule?"

"Not guilty."

The liberation Mary felt was so immense that the tears she had been holding far too long began to fall, everything becoming a blur.

In the background, the words of Justice Stark addressing the jury were muffled, "Members of the jury, it only remains for me to thank you for your careful deliberations. You leave with our gratitude. The jury is dismissed."

Then turning to Mary, he pronounced, "Miss Clark, you are free to go."

Overwhelmed, Mary shifted her attention to Coyle, who was beaming at her. She held his gaze and suddenly felt an irresistible impulse to throw herself into his arms. Yet all she managed was to say, "Thank you."

Exuberantly, Coyle wrapped his arms around her. He held her for a moment and kissed her lightly on the lips. She felt her cheeks warm up, but before she could react, he gently released her, looking self-conscious. As if to restore propriety, he said, "It was the only plausible outcome."

Mary felt a surge of affection for him. She turned for fear of giving herself away. She caught sight of Peter looking at her from the back of the courtroom. She detected soft-ness in his eyes, which she took to be a wordless apology. She nodded and smiled.

Not one to take pleasure out of seeing an opponent defeated, Coyle extended a conciliatory handshake to Baxter, who quietly accepted it, his feistiness gone, and bearing a look of trampled resignation.

Coyle then turned to face Mary again and touched her arm gently. "Ready to go home?"

"Please," she replied, suddenly exhausted.

As they were getting ready to leave, Mary caught sight of Courtney and Richard, still seated. She observed them as they looked at each other, incredulous. Defiant, they stood and turned to leave the room. Mary was reminded of a time when their presence in her life had meant so much to her, but now they only evoked pangs of melancholy, reflections of a time that could never be recaptured.

Two weeks later, Mary was carefully securing each of the contents inside Eugenie's trunk, including the music box, which had been insured. The trunk was to be couriered to Eugenie's family in France.

Coyle was there to assist her. Since the trial they had become very close, and she had come to depend on him greatly. They stopped to rest, and he settled comfortably into her sofa, she beside him.

"When are they picking up the trunk?" he asked.

"Tomorrow."

"Will you require any further assistance from me?"

"No. I can manage, thank you," Mary replied without thinking. Instantly, she felt regret. Why had she declined his offer when, deep down, she desired his company more than anything else and could use his help? In the silence that followed, she studied him. There was a great deal she wanted to tell him—how much he had come to mean to her, more than she ever thought possible, and how much she valued his support. He had been her champion, her knight in shining armour, never once veering from his dedication. All this she was tempted to say to him. But something compelled her to repress her true feelings. She knew she was resisting becoming involved with him because she feared being hurt again. And she was aware he knew it too, for he was allowing her time—never mentioning love to her. There was no need to. His actions spoke louder than any words of love he could have spoken.

Their hands sought each other across the sofa. Their fingers intertwined. It felt lovely and safe to sit there together in the silence that enveloped the room.

He looked at her with unconcealed affection. "Does Danielle know the trunk includes the music box?"

"Yes."

"All this should make you very happy."

"Very," she replied.

"Yet you look pained."

She nodded. "When I found Eugenie's trunk, I found it hard to believe this small chest represented the sum of her existence. I was even troubled by it."

"Why?"

"Well, it seemed so trifling. All she had ever owned of any lasting value could be found in this one trunk, abandoned in the attic of an unoccupied house." Mary paused to collect her thoughts. "Her whole life was one of serving. Yet had it not been for the music box, nobody would've known about her. She would have remained a person of no significance."

"Is it so essential that we should have known about her?" Coyle asked.

"At the end of a lifetime, isn't it what everyone wants… to be remembered for something worthwhile that we've accomplished or left behind?"

"Not necessarily. There are two types of people in this world—those who perform to be acknowledged, and those like Eugenie, a woman of basic goodness, who live to serve.

From all you've told me, it sounds like she was happy, ful-filled, leading a purposeful life. The rest of the world may not have known that, but she would have known."

"There's also the matter of the music box," Mary said contemplatively.

"What about the music box?"

"If only she had known about it, that it would be sent to her family. Can you imagine what joy that knowledge would have given her?"

Coyle reflected for a moment. When he spoke again, his voice was low and ruminative. "I never met Eugenie, but from what you've told me and what I've heard about her, I've grown to respect her. She was a person who represented what's good in humanity and epitomized everything most people strive for in life, but few accomplish. That's what makes me believe that the most noteworthy thing for her wouldn't have been the valuables she left behind but what she took with her—her experiences, her memories of a loving family and friends in France, her sense of having lived a meaningful life, her knowledge of having helped where and when she could, her own conviction that she had done the best with what she'd been given. Those silent lega-cies are far more rewarding than any charitable bequeathing of personal assets through wills and estate plans."

Mary thought of her parents. What memories and expe-riences would they have taken with them? As she mused over this, an overpowering emptiness washed over her. She desperately wanted to believe some virtue had existed in them, that their lives were not completely wasted.

"Actually," Coyle said, "everything I've heard leads me to

believe that Eugenie left behind a great deal. In her quiet, unassuming way, she was able to touch the hearts of most people who got to know her."

"I guess you're right. Even after she died, she remained a beacon to people like Mr. Kerr. He was perhaps late recognizing her strengths and his weaknesses, but when he did, he endeavoured to make amends. That's something in his favour."

"It's unfortunate Eugenie wasn't able to touch his children as well," Coyle remarked.

"Well, they were dominated by their father, who clearly affixed too much importance to money. That was all they could identify with."

Coyle nodded. "Hopefully, with time, Courtney and Richard will come to question their distorted beliefs, just as their father did." His tone became quiet, reflective. "According to the prevailing psychology books, challenges are an excellent opportunity for growth. When you overcome them, you develop emotional and mental strength. Their father's last will and testament has definitely challenged them. I'm curious to see if it will help them grow."

As they resumed packing, Mary thought about that first meeting with Mr. Kerr in the hospital and marvelled at the chain of events that had transpired since then. She smiled to herself as she recalled what he'd said to her that day—something about wanting to use his final moments to set things right.

When she picked up the last book to store it in the trunk, she admired how beautifully bound it was. It looked well used. Curious, she opened it to the bookmarked page.

It was a poem by Ralph Waldo Emerson, several passages
carefully underlined. It read:

> To laugh often
> and love much;
>
> to win the respect
> of intelligent persons
> and the affection
> of children;
>
> to earn the approbation
> of honest citizens and
> endure the betrayal
> of false friends;
>
> to leave the world a bit
> better, whether by a healthy
> child, a garden patch, or a
> redeemed social condition;
>
> to have played and laughed
> with enthusiasm and
> sung with exultation;
>
> to know even one life
> has breathed easier
> because you have lived…
> this is to have succeeded.

Seven months later, on June 24, 1967, Mary Clark and Patrick Coyle were married in the lovely church in Pakenham. It was a simple ceremony with close friends and relatives.

In the months prior to the wedding, Mary and Danielle had developed a deep bond through their correspondence. In one heartfelt letter, Danielle shared her and her sisters' plan to visit Ottawa, intending to lay flowers on Eugenie's resting place. Given their close ties to Canada, it felt fitting to undertake this journey in the country's centennial year. They also planned a special pilgrimage to Sainte-Anne-du-Bocage in New Brunswick, the place where their ancestors had briefly found refuge during the Expulsion of the Acadians.

Upon receiving this news, Mary promptly invited Danielle and other family members to her wedding. Danielle responded with enthusiasm, and she and her sisters travelled all the way from France for the occasion. From the moment she first laid eyes on Danielle, Mary was struck by her resemblance to Eugenie. As Mr. Kerr had once remarked, they could be mistaken for twins. Throughout their visit, Mary observed Pauline's husband, Claude, whose ebullient nature and skillful manoeuvring of his wheelchair made her think he must have been a formidable adversary before the Gestapo crippled him. Eugenie's other sister,

Françoise, was unaccompanied. After her husband, Jacques, was interned in the German concentration camp, he was never heard from again.

At the wedding, Francis MacDonald gave her away, and Rachel was matron of honour. After the ceremony, Mary observed with delight as Rachel and Francis, who had connected during the trial, engaged in a harmonious debate on politics and gender equality. It was evident they had forged a friendship, as Rachel seemed impressed with him, and he appeared equally smitten.

At the wedding reception in the hall of the Calabogie Inn, Coyle's mother embraced Mary with warmth. She then turned to her son and, taking his face in her hands, kissed him on both cheeks and whispered, "How I wish your father were here today. He would be so proud."

She turned back to Mary and smiled. "From the first moment we met, I saw a special kinship between you and Patrick. It reminded me of the wonderful relationship his father and I shared. Patrick is so much like him. So today is a joyful day for me. In my heart I know that you will bring as much happiness to your relationship as he will."

As Mary listened to her words, she could not help reflecting that it was only a year ago that she had been planning an entirely different marriage, with Peter. She could think of him now without the pain in her chest. Had she loved him? Yes, for a brief period, at least. She had loved him and had wanted to be his partner in marriage. She started to re-examine what had moved her so about him but quickly dispelled it. A relationship of that kind, based on lies and deception, could never have succeeded.

Mary was suddenly reminded of the common expression "every cloud has a silver lining." Fate had indeed been kind to her. If it had not been for Courtney and Richard's accusations brought against her, followed by Peter's devastating deceit, there would not have been a need for Coyle to defend her. The chaos in her life had marked the beginning of a close relationship between them, which merged their lives in a way neither of them could have imagined. Paradoxically, she realized that without the chaos, she would never have known what love truly was.

Following the trial, local papers covered Mary's exoneration, and the limelight shifted away from Courtney and Richard. Rarely did Mary and Coyle speak about them. Like her proposed wedding with Peter, they were part of her past, and it was best that they remain there. But since then, Mary had often thought how promptly a dream could curdle into a nightmare.

Before the wedding, Coyle and Mary had moved to Pakenham, where Coyle had established a law practice with Mary as a partner. To their good fortune, Kate had moved to Arnprior, a short distance away, and would carry on as their secretary. She had, of course, been invited to the wedding.

Once all their guests were seated for the meal specially prepared for the wedding, Coyle stood. "Ladies and gentlemen, if I may indulge your attention for a moment," he began, raising his glass. Once the room had quieted, he turned to Mary, his eyes reflecting admiration and affection. "Mary, my love, today is not just a celebration of our union but a triumph of your unwavering spirit. In the courtroom, where justice is sought, you stood resilient against false accusations, and the truth prevailed. You emerged not only exonerated but with grace that captivated the hearts of everyone present."

Coyle's words prompted a warm round of applause. When it died off, he continued. "This journey we've embarked on is a testament to the transformative power of love and the unforeseen paths life may lead us down. Fate has woven our stories together, and I am grateful for the twists and turns that brought us here."

Raising his glass higher, he toasted, "To Mary—my partner in law, love, and life. May our days be filled with joy, understanding, and an enduring love that grows with each passing moment. Here's to us, to the pasts that have shaped us, the present that unites us, and the future that awaits with boundless promise."

Acknowledgements

First and foremost, I want to express my profound gratitude to my editor, Marianne Ward, a realist, mentor, and friend. Her unwavering encouragement and understanding have been my pillars of strength, empowering me to overcome challenges and pursue my dream.

A special acknowledgement goes to my dear friend Alexander (Sandy) MacKinnon for his invaluable legal guidance in the creation of this novel. Any errors are solely the result of my own misinterpretation.

I am deeply grateful for the exceptional work of proof-reader Paula Sarson and of designer David Edelstein.

Lastly, I want to convey heartfelt thanks to everyone who supported me along the way, helping me reach the finish line. They know who they are.

Yvette Ward MacDonald

Yvette attended Maillet College, a private girls' school, and earned a B.A. in Psychology from Carleton University. Dedicated to learning, engagement, and community service, she forged a career grounded in the spirit of altruism and leadership. Yvette co-founded Cornwall Youth Residence, offering refuge to teenagers from dysfunctional families, and served as president of the Arnprior & District Memorial Hospital Auxiliary. She also co-founded the Ottawa Valley Music Festival, a summer-long celebration of classical music that spanned the Ottawa Valley for over twenty-five years. She served as a board member for the Victoria Order of Nurses, her local District Memorial Hospital, and performing art series.

Yvette embodies the belief that learning, active participation, and community service are the pillars of a fulfilling and successful life. Her commitment to growth and achievement extends to fourteen years of piano study. Writing is an additional journey, enabling her to delve into her life and uncover its inner meanings. *Honour Above All* is her debut publication.

Read more at www.yvettewardmacdonald.ca.